WESLYNDE

THE WESLYNDE CHRONICLES

RON TERBUSH

PRAGMATOPIA

CONTENTS

WESLYNDE

Copyright 2025 by Ron Terbush

Published by Pragmatopia Press LLC

Bethesda, Maryland USA

Print ISBN 978-1-7359923-3-4

eBook ISBN 978-1-7359923-4-1

Editor: Laura Josephsen

Cover design: Tom Semmes

Cover illustration: Bilal Haider

Map of Weslynde: Ron Terbush

The Weslynde Chronicles

Book 1: Weslynde

Book 2: Dax (publish date 2026)

Book 3: The High Wizard (publish date TBD)

 Formatted with Vellum

For Evelyn and Eleanor

MAP OF WESLYNDE

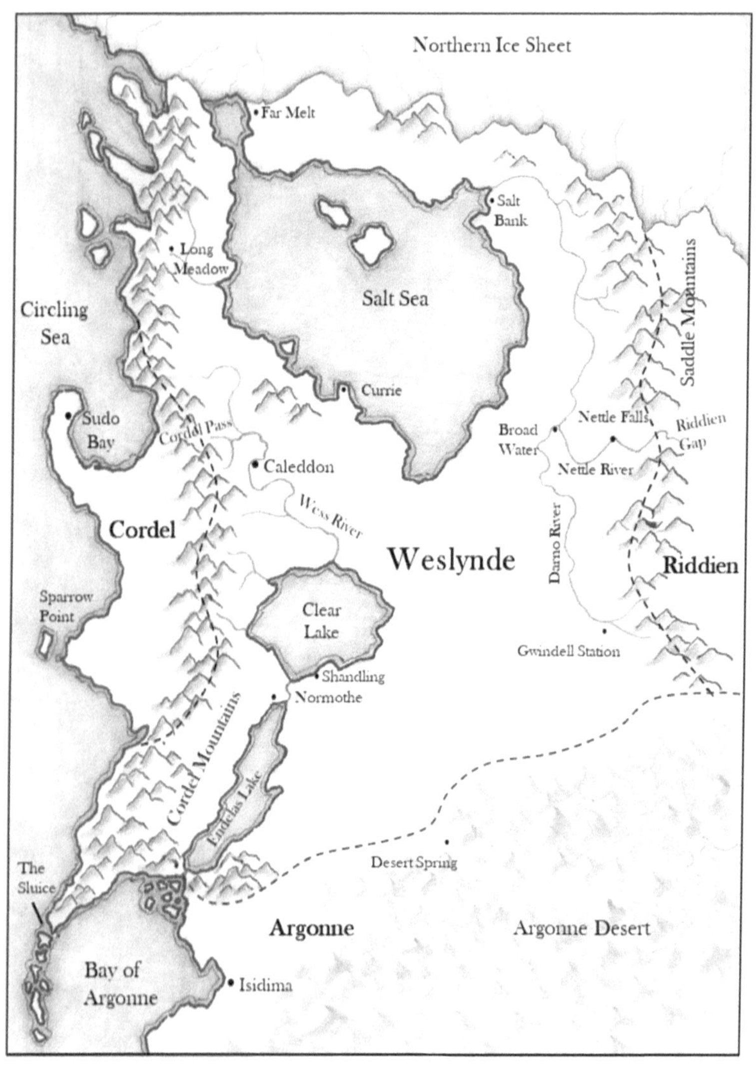

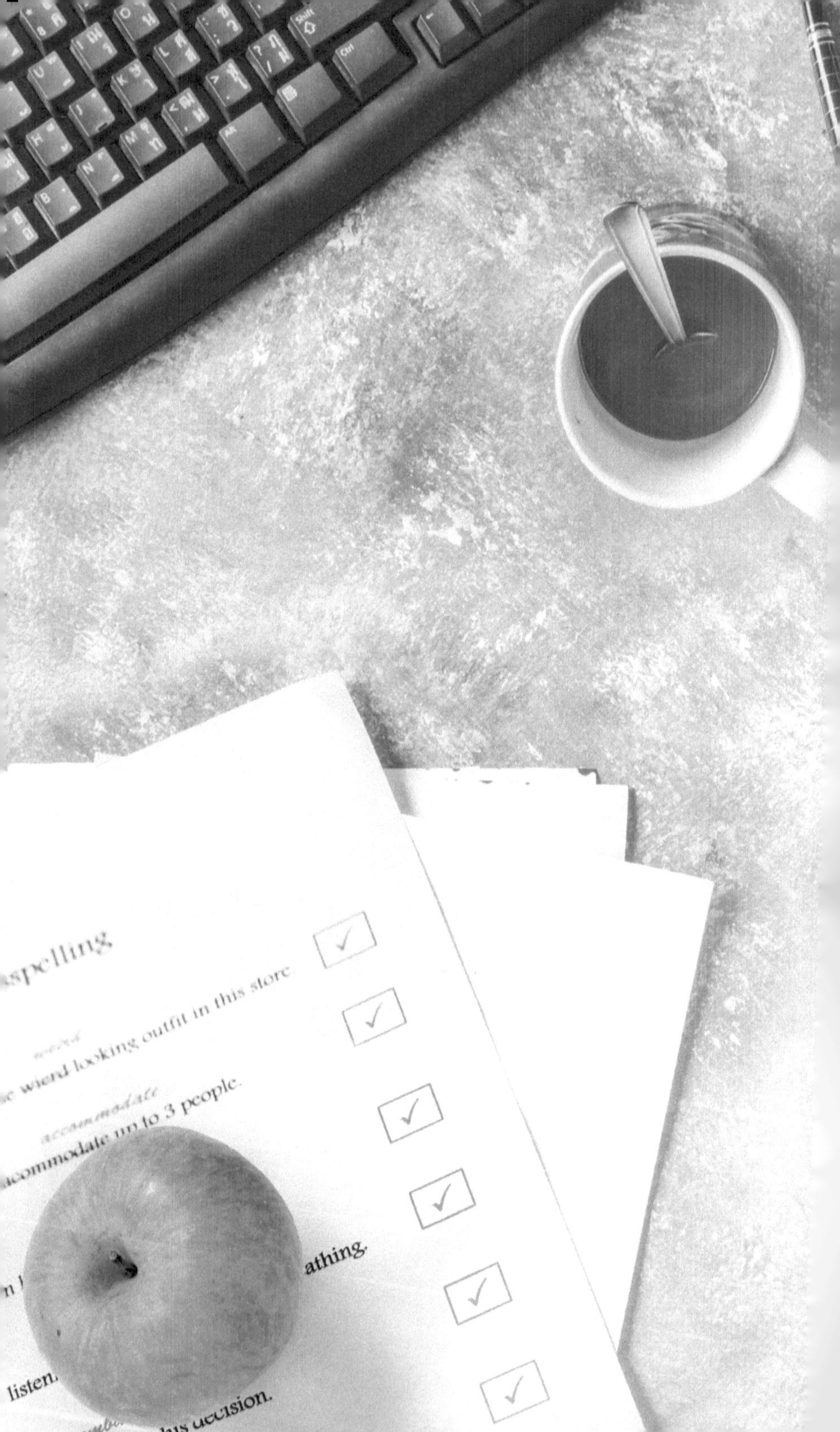
spelling
word
wierd looking outfit in this store
accommodate
accommodate up to 3 people.
athing.
listen
his decision.

Chapter Two

STELLA

"WHOEVER DECIDED ANNOTATED BIBLIOGRAPHIES should be a thing deserves a very long and painful death," I groan as I drop my head on my laptop's keyboard. "Seriously, I think Professor O'Connor is a masochist". I look up to see Rory just staring at me.

"You mean sadist?" I see the corner of his mouth turn up.

"Yeah, whatever. My bad that I am not well-versed in the world of BDSM. Point still stands."

Rory and I have become friends pretty recently, and he's a really fun person to be around. He's quiet. Not in an awkward way. But in a comforting way. He's in my Feminist Literature class, possibly one of five guys. From what he's told me, ignoring the fact that he is genuinely a feminist, if his mother found out he was doing an English degree and didn't take this class, she'd go ballistic. I told him I like the sound of her. He knows exactly what he's doing with his degree.

We became friends after the first assignment when we

were the only two people to get above 70%. I wasn't kidding when I said O'Connor was a masochist, or sadist, I guess. Once I saw Ror's blue hair a few rows down, it was hard to deny the inevitability of a friendship.

He takes his AirPods out. "You know this assignment would probably be easier if you actually, you know, worked". Now it's my turn to just stare at him. He smiles before putting his AirPods back in, looking back at his computer.

"I'm hurt, Rory. What happened to the nice guy from class who kept his mouth shut?" I shoot him a look, amused.

"My thoughts haven't changed; you just weren't lucky enough to hear them before." I roll my eyes before looking back at my computer. I would never tell him that I do feel lucky to be his friend now. I don't want to scare him off.

Looking back at my computer, I switch tabs to look at the classes I have this week. My degree individually is seemingly useless, mainly being filled with electives, but I'm hoping it'll give me better directions. When I saw I could get credits in a Feminist Literature class, it was a no-brainer for me. I thought we'd only be analysing revolutionary texts. Instead, I'm stuck writing about the limitations and values of using a source for a theoretical paper I'm not even going to write. If I hear one more lecture about academic integrity, I might fulfill my jokes about dropping out of university.

Honestly, one of the main reasons I'm still here is that the university itself is on this beautiful old campus that feels like it's right out of Scotland. Every building has that Gothic design with a slightly scary-looking statue on the peak of every edge. There are around five or six different parks on campus. During spring and summer, they are covered with wildflowers. There really isn't a better place to go to journal, read, or just think. And despite O'Connor being a pain in my ass, the faculty overall is good, and my advisor is an angel for putting up with me.

Not to mention if I dropped out, Keets would stalk me down with a chainsaw. All the sunshine and rainbows are really a facade for the psychotic killer underneath. Deciding I've done enough work to deserve a study break, I pull out my headphones and phone. Not missing the stare from Rory as I do so. I'm highly aware that we've only been here for less than an hour, but it truly was grueling work. Not to mention the black hoodie I'm wearing feels like a blanket, so it feels wrong to do anything but relax when wearing it. It doesn't take long for me to pull up TikTok and start the notorious death scrolling, stopping when a video comes up on my feed I can't help but rewatch. My break is interrupted by the sound of a laugh coming from Rory. I look up only to see a phone in my face filming me. There is a split second of confusion until I realise I started tearing up at the video I was watching. A fact Rory seems to find extremely funny.

"Sue me, I'm emotional, okay." I turn the phone towards him to show the video I was watching, trying to coax him into a similar reaction. "Look, they are so in love. You'd have to have no heart to not cry." No reaction, just more smiles as I turn it back towards myself and watch it again, tearing up more. Naturally, Rory's laughter gets louder.

I'm about to tell him to shut up, but I'm cut off.

"What's so funny, Wrenford?" My head whips around at its own accord to see Luke Astor standing behind me. I kind of hate the fact that I know his name without having ever interacted with him, but most people do. He's one of the bartenders at the best student bar in town, the Black

Lantern. Luke is that type of guy who everyone loves because he makes you feel like he's your best friend from the moment you meet. I've known those types of guys, and they are never as nice as they seem.

He looks down at my face, something like concern twisting his face as he notices the tears in my eyes. I kind of hate that.

"You okay?"

"Allergies," I say quickly, ignoring the pristinely clean library we are currently in. I don't think a speck of dust exists anywhere in the vicinity. His eyes fall to the desk, probably noting my second cup of peppermint tea sitting on the desk. I drink at least one a day. I'm trying to avoid caffeine, and people say it's the best natural alternative.

Luke nods and turns back to Rory. "What were you laughing at?"

I glare at Rory, mentally trying to send daggers his way. Hoping that I've somehow developed some Jedi mind powers. Ror doesn't blink.

"This is Stella. She was watching an edit of a Disney movie and started crying. Kind of hard not to laugh at that." He smiles at me sweetly. I'm going to kill him.

"I can get behind some Disney." He goes back to looking at me. "Can I see it?"

I swallow the shock that comes from that statement. Something about his sleeve of tattoos doesn't scream Disney fan. I unlock my phone, showing him the video.

He stares at me for a second before I hear the laughter leave his mouth, low and warm. Rory joins in almost instantly, although at least he has the decency to try and cover it in a cough.

"You're crying to an edit of Tangled? An edit of the big

romance scene? That's happy. Literally, the opposite feeling that comes with tears."

I look back at Rory, and he stops laughing pretty quickly when he sees my face. I don't know why it irks me so much when he says that, but it does. There might be nothing worse in the world than when someone makes fun of you for something you love or the feelings you feel. He did both. In one minute. I hate how it brings back memories of someone I'd rather forget.

I take a slow breath, trying to swallow the snarky retort that comes up, but inevitably choose not to. Straightening up, I plaster on a saccharine smile. "Kind of sad that you've never experienced enough happiness to have happy tears. Might want to get on that one."

"Are you offering your services? You seem like a ray of sunshine." His grin widens, clearly unbothered and enjoying this interaction. That makes one of us.

"Yup, I'm exactly like the sun. I'll burn you if you get too close." I watch as he moves closer to me, his face still.

"What if I like the heat?" There was a pause, his words hanging between us. I didn't blink, didn't flinch. He laughs softly, straightening. "Then again, you are crying to a Tangled edit, so I think I'll take my chances."

I roll my eyes and fully turn back, opening my laptop. Somehow, I'd rather be doing my annotated bibliography than continuing this conversation.

"What's up, man? Did you need something?" Rory asks.

"Yeah, I just wanted to let you know I won't be at my shift tonight. They have asked me to a last-minute absolutely unskippable dinner."

In the reflection of my computer screen, I can see his face fall slightly. His smile was getting just that much smaller. It's not a massive change, but for someone who is known for always being the 'happy' guy, it's hard to ignore.

"No problem, I'll find someone to cover you. Let me know if you need a lift or something." Rory's voice carries more weight than it did moments ago. It's clear I'm missing something here.

"You sure?" He asks, his voice wavering. Rory nods immediately, his face certain. "Thank you, genuinely." I see him start to walk away, but before he's out of earshot, he turns around, grinning.

"Bye, Goldie."

And with that, he walks out of the library.

Goldie?

All I can think to say as I turn back to Rory is "What the hell does that mean?"

Chapter Three

LUKE

THERE ARE A LOT OF FUCKING PLACES I'D RATHER be than driving to my parents' house right now. I used to like being inside that house. When they found out I got into Brookstone, they were genuinely proud. Dad saw the business degree and thought I was going to start some Fortune 500 company and "make the family proud" or whatever. Mum thought I'd get there and immediately meet the next Mrs. Lucas Astor and start a family by 20. They both saw the pieces of their puzzle coming together.

I knew back then they were proud of me – not just for who I was, but for starting the future they had envisioned, but it didn't matter. It was better than getting ignored or receiving lectures in Dad's fucking office. And honestly, the part that made me happiest was that for one night I existed and my brother, Leon, didn't. It felt like it was my turn.

Inevitably, when I started sharing my plans with them and talking about what I was doing at university, the joy fell pretty quickly. And once Leon met his girlfriend and then got into UNSW for law, it was pretty clear that I was put back on the back burner. So now this drive brings me nothing but dread.

My parents live in a small town two hours away from my university. They have absolutely no qualms about asking me to drive the two hours at the drop of a hat. Their steel gate opens as I drive up their obnoxiously long driveway. The house looms over the rest in the neighbourhood, with a fountain and bushes in the middle of the driveway that are meant to make it feel welcoming. The thought makes me release a dry laugh.

I park my car around the side but don't move.

It's just dinner, I remind myself.

In two hours, I'll be back on the road going home, and I won't have to hear from them for at least another month. I don't know why they called me here tonight, but the whole situation makes me nervous. I don't hear from Dad unless they have a serious reason for needing me.

Rory and Beck know a bit of it. They know I have overbearing parents, and they know me and my brother don't get along. They have absolutely no idea how deep it runs. How long has it been going on? They always tell me I could tell them, and they would run to my side and be there. But no matter how much they repeat themselves, I just don't believe them. I can't. Every time I open my mouth to try and tell someone what it's like, the words get caught in my throat. A familiar emptiness settles inside of me, realising that they might never care how I need them, too.

I'm pulled out of my thoughts by a buzz on my phone.

> Leon: Are you here? Or are you running
> late again?

I open his texts.

Me: Yup, I'm here, coming.

I pull myself out of the car and straighten my jacket. There's a wrinkle on the sleeve, and I feel my heart speed up a little bit. I'm not in the mood to be berated right now. Taking a deep breath, I try to smooth it as I walk into the house. I can hear the sound of my Dad's laugh in the living room, causing me to turn towards them.

Anyone walking into my house would think it should be a museum. Mum decided to make it her mission when she married my dad to raise us in a proper household, meaning every piece of furniture had to look like it came from Marie Antoinette's bedroom itself. Leon is sitting on the couch with his long-term girlfriend Camilla. He's holding onto her left hand tightly, and she's looking at him as if he's the stars to her moon. She's actually really nice. They've been dating since his first year of high school. Inseparable.

"Luke. How nice of you to finally join us." My dad turns to look at me, shaking his head and empty glass, the sound of the ice hitting the side of the crystal echoing.

I struggle to speak, opting to sit on the couch opposite Leon instead. My mum walks over and presses a kiss on the top of my head. It's one of the few affections she gives me, and I like to pretend it's a silent message that she cares. Even if she won't say it.

"Hey darling, Leon was just about to tell us something."

He stands up, holding onto Camilla – pulling her up with him. His other hand starts to shake as he stands up. I see him ball it in a fist, taking a deep breath.

"Mother, father, Luke." My name is sharp on his tongue.

It wasn't his idea for me to be here. "We have some exciting news. Over the weekend, I proposed to Camilla, and she accepted." He looks down at her, smiling. I hear my mum gasp and run to hug Camilla. My father walks over to Leon, patting him on the shoulder.

"Good work, son. I'm proud of you."

You know those moments in life when it feels like someone has plunged a dagger straight into your gut with reckless abandon? Every time I hear those words, it's like repeated stabbing until I can't breathe. Dad goes over to where Camilla and my mum are standing, where they are already fawning over the wedding details. I take a breath and walk up to my brother.

"Congratulations," I say, putting my hand out for a handshake. He stares at my hand for a moment before deciding to shake it.

"Thanks." he pulls me closer. "Thought one of us should carry on the family legacy." He pushes me back, causing me to stumble. I catch myself quick enough to meet his eye. There's a hint of sadness or something behind it. I shake it off – it's not my job to make sure he's fine. It hasn't been for years.

"Okay, okay. No tears!" Mum swipes at her eyes. "Leon and Camilla head into the dining room for food. We just have to have a quick chat with Luke."

Mum ushers them towards the dining room and shuts the door the second they're out. It's almost comical how fast she's able to wipe those tears from her eyes and straighten up.

"Have a seat, darling." And here's the real reason I'm here. "As you know, the Astor family reunion is happening in Byron this year."

Yes, the stupid reunions my family feels the need to do

every year. It's basically a massive pissing contest. A chance for each member to show off who really has the biggest dick. I avoid it.

"I know you feel the need not to come to these events." My dad pipes up behind me. "And frankly, we've never complained – It's easier to overlook certain changes when you're in a different city."

Stab.
Stab.
Stab.

"Yes, but this year we will be announcing Leon's engagement. We need to present a strong family front. So, you will be coming." They must have already known he was proposing. Mum grabs my shoulder, patting it lightly. She's always the nicest to me when she needs something. I know I could say no, I'm 22. Free will and all. But they're my parents.

"Okay."

Mum claps her hands together. "Fantastic. So, we will see you and your plus one in Byron!" My eyebrows furrow. Plus one? Is my coming not enough for them? She stands up and walks to the dining room, closing the door once more behind her. Dad walks around the couch and stands in front of me. He likes having people look up to him.

"You will bring a suitable girl and will not embarrass us. You wouldn't want to lose the possibility of your bar, would you? Do you understand, son?" The word son sounds like poison on his tongue. That's how they control me.

"Understood."

He nods and gestures towards the dining room. I get up

and follow behind him. I feel like a sheep. Herded by them until my use is up.

It's two hours later when I'm finally sent out the door with my jacket and a box of chocolates. We usually do coffee and dessert there, but tonight they were discussing wedding details. I wasn't needed, as my mum so eloquently put it. I get into my car and pull my phone out to text the group chat I'm in with my two roommates.

> Me: I feel like I'm going to vomit blood if I don't get some tequila in me. Down?

It's not long before I get a response from both Beck and Rory.

> Beck: Tequila, Vodka, Fireball. Always down.

> Rory: I'll be home in 20. See you then.

I like both their messages and started driving. Tonight was weird. Not my parents, nothing about them is ever different. But with Leon. I kept noticing him staring at me, his eyes completely blank. His mouth kept twitching as if he was trying to hold back something. And as I walked out the door and turned around to say goodbye, he was staring at me again, his eyes glazed over. It's the same face he'd make when we were kids, right before he'd burst into tears. I brush off the worry that's rising. He has a fiancée now. She'll look after him.

I pull into our house. We have a small garden out back and a one-car driveway. Since my parents bought this place, I get parking rights. There are three bedrooms, three bathrooms, a kitchen, study, and living room. It's perfect for Ror, Beck, and me.

When I walk in, I see they are already sitting at the kitchen island waiting for me.

"Hey guys." I put my keys and shit on the entryway table. Without a word, Beck hands me a shot glass that I take immediately.

"You want to talk about it?" Rory asks as I sit down next to him.

"Nope." I downed the shot. The burn as it flows down my throat cuts through the fear and doubt I feel rising. No matter how many times they ask, I know they don't really mean it. No one wants to hear about someone's issues that much.

"It might help."

I sigh lightly, trying to figure out how to articulate my thoughts without making them truly aware. "It's just a stupid family reunion."

"Ah, yes, the infamous who has the biggest dick contest." Beck chimes in as he's pouring another shot for us. I fight the urge to laugh as he voices my exact thought from just a few hours ago.

"Yeah. I have to go this year. Non-negotiable." They both stare at me, that look of pity slowly creeping up. The second they start pitying me, start questioning why they are friends with me, that's when I lose what I have left. "It's fine, seriously. They just want me to bring a date. But I don't want to lead a girl on by bringing her to meet the family, you know?" I down another shot. "I just don't know what to do."

Rory pats my shoulder. I know he's thinking that I should be done with them. But we've gone down that road too many times for him to bring it up anymore.

"Oooh, wait, I have an idea." Beck pauses to take a shot, and likely for dramatic effect. "Just like, pay someone to go with you. Tell them exactly what they need to do, and bam! Plus, if you hire the right person, you'll get laid, too." He wiggles his eyebrows.

"Beck, this is why you get a drink thrown in your face daily," Rory says, taking the bottle of tequila from him.

"I may get a drink thrown in my face, but I always manage to turn it around. Everyone loves Beck."

I roll my eyes. I admire how confident he is in himself. He doesn't need to prove anything to anyone. He just is.

"Okay, changing the topic." I stand up to grab and pour myself a drink, mixing a Redbull with the shots Beck is pouring. The drink numbs the memories of tonight swirling around my brain. Stella wanders into my mind, replacing the space my family was just taking up. There was something different about her. There is no denying that she is gorgeous. The way her hair was just perfectly messed up from her studying, and Jesus, her eyes were insane. But it's not that; something else made me want to keep talking to her. I'm not sure why I'm still thinking about her, but I haven't been able to stop contemplating the way she immediately bit my head off.

"Do you think that girl Stella is actually mad at me after the library interaction today?" I ask lightly.

Rory turns and looks at me, confused. "I have no idea. Why do you care?"

"I don't."

I do. I upset her.

And now I have this overwhelming urge to make sure she's okay and doesn't hate me. Plus, something about her is stuck in my head. I want to know her. But saying that sounds crazy.

Rory raises his eyebrows, clearly not believing me.

"Umm, Stella? Library? Are you guys hanging out without me?" Beck moans, causing both me and Rory to groan. "Guys, trios only work if we are all honest and love each other equally. C'mon, Powerpuff girls or nothing."

I shake my head, choosing not to respond. Rory fills him in on what happened, and every so often Beck interrupts with some inappropriate joke about how I'm finally going to get some. I disagree each time, not sharing where my mind wanders to thinking about her and the way she looked at the library.

Eventually, Beck shifts the conversation to his latest hookups, offering far more detail than anyone asked for. I drink just to drown out the mental images he's so generously provided.

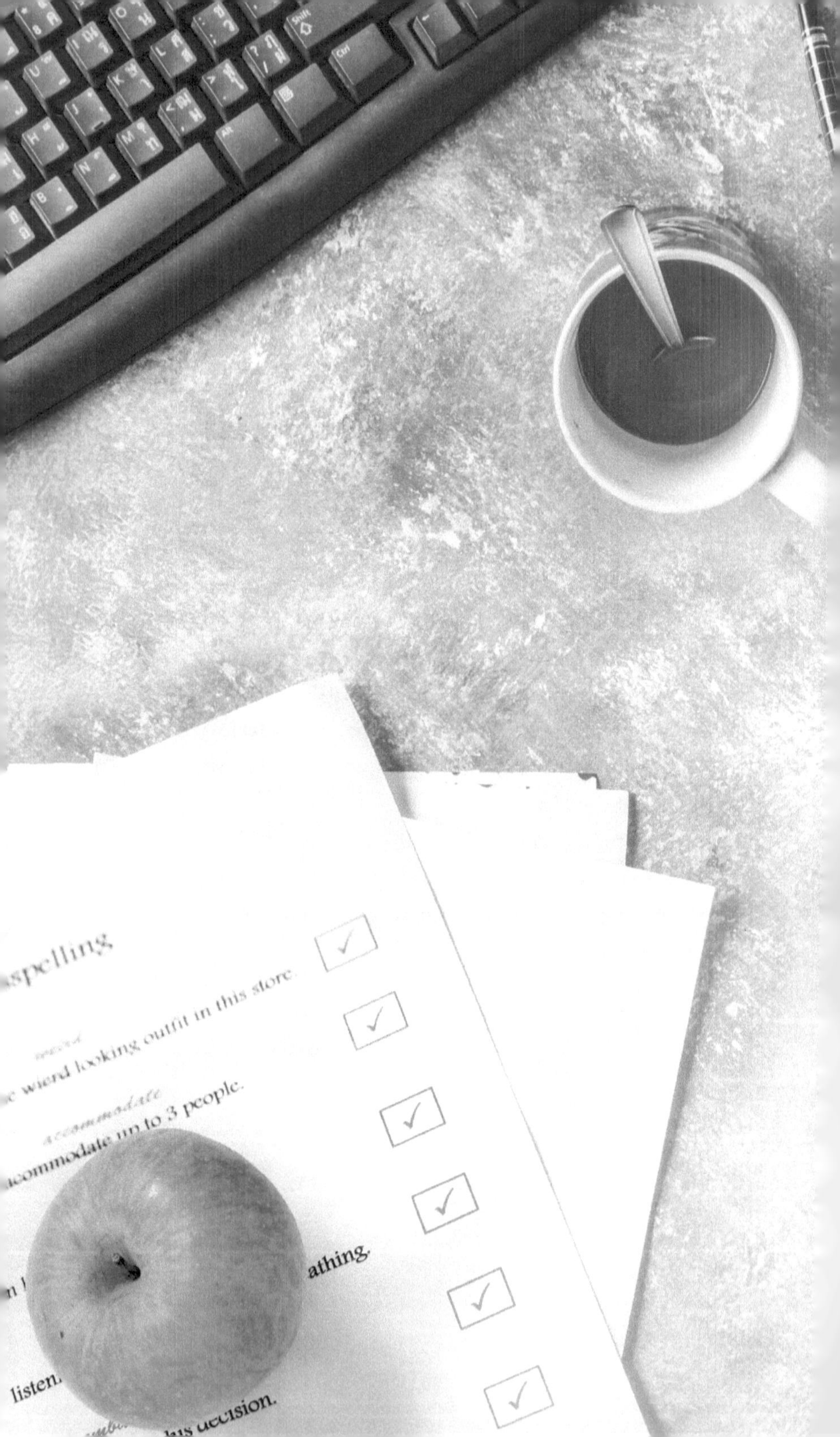
spelling
e wierd looking outfit in this store
ccommodate up to 3 people.
athing.
listen.
decision.

Chapter Four

STELLA

KEETS AND I GOT REALLY LUCKY AND GOT AN apartment in Abernathy Hall, accommodation that's usually reserved for third and fourth years. Abernathy Hall is a ten-minute walk from our favourite library if you cut through one of the parks I love, and about fifteen minutes from the Black Lantern. In third year, studying and getting drunk is basically all we do, so it works out perfectly. The building itself is one of the only dorms left that still have the original exterior. There are carvings all over the side, Latin words that we've drunkenly tried to translate numerous times over the years. The only downside of living here is the lack of an elevator. We are on the fifth floor, so climbing these stairs every day feels like modern-day torture.

The apartment itself is two bedrooms coming off a main living area. We've covered it pretty much floor to ceiling with posters of everything we've ever liked. Keets also dictated in the first year when we were roommates that real plants were non-negotiable. I agreed, making it clear I'd never kept a plant alive before. That didn't deter her from making our living room and her bedroom look more like a jungle than a university accommodation. There's a small kitchen that has all the necessities, and it works because neither Keets nor I is a fantastic chef.

My phone buzzes as I walk into our apartment, so I drop my bag on the couch and check the text.

> Keets: Hey, Julie invited us to go out with her and her mates from the theatre. You down?

I groan, knowing I'd rather be anywhere else than a bar tonight. I text her back.

> Me: nope :)

> Me: counteroffer. I make us dinner, and we watch some trashy reality show we find on Netflix.

It's less than a minute before I get her reply.

> Keets: Be home in 20

This is one of the many things I love about Keets. We've always had a sort of telepathic understanding with each other. Despite what it sounds like, we do have the ability to lead separate lives. I can't remember the last time we weren't in sync.

I open my phone and press shuffle on my Taylor Swift playlist, heading to the kitchen. While I may not be a world-renowned cook, my pesto pasta is a meal to be reckoned with. It's about twenty minutes later when I hear Keets open the door. I can tell it's her immediately because she starts singing along to the music as she makes her way towards the kitchen. She puts down her stuff and ties her long blonde hair into what could only be described as a nest on top of her head.

"Hiya!" She walks towards me and kisses me on the head, grabbing a bottle of water from the fridge.

"Hi, my love." I pick the pan up off the stove top to show her the meal. Feeling pretty proud of myself with this batch.

"Oooo yum. Pesto. See, this is why I'm single - who needs a boyfriend when I've got a best friend who looks after me so well."

I laugh as she pushes herself up to sit on the counter next to me. I start plating up the meal.

"Okay, so you'll never fucking believe who I spoke to today."

"Who?" She puts her bottle down on the counter, her voice laced with curiosity.

"Lucas Astor."

She looks at me, her face contorted.

"The bartender at Black Lantern?"

Realisation flashes across her face. "Oh yeah! Sorry, I thought his name was Luke. Wait, why'd he come up to you? Did he see your dazzling looks and was just unable to look away?" She smiles. Both Keets and I love romcoms and romance books; it was probably the thing that made us click so well.

"Ha ha," I drawled. "No, he came over because he had to talk to Rory about something to do with the bar."

"Okay, and we are now freaking out because he looks like a modern-day James Dean or..."

"No, we are freaking out over the fact that he is a condescending asshole."

She hops off the counter and spins me around to face her. "Okay, wait, what? He's, like, notoriously nice – what happened?"

I tell her the whole story about what happened in the library. Down to the way his hair fell in front of his face as he looked me down, waiting for me to respond to each comment he made.

"How dare he?!! Insult you, a grown woman, for crying at a children's movie!" She clasps her hand to her chest and gasps. Her eyes are comically wide, and her mouth is dropped open. She's really putting on a show.

"You're not taking me seriously."

"Mhm." She pulls a piece of paper out and scribbles something down quickly.

"What are you doing?" She laughs and shakes her head. "Keets!"

"I'm sorry, Stel, but it sounds like the guy was just chatting you up. Which, by the way, I don't blame him when you've got all of this," she uses her hands to gesture to my body, "going on."

I laugh. Keets never fails to put me in a good mood.

"Okay, no, but it was the way he said it. It was so dismissive. And the look on his face…"

"Was gorgeous?"

I pick up the wooden spoon that's been resting on the half-empty pan and flick the pesto in her direction.

"Hey! You're the one who told me about the way his hair fell and the way his big brown eyes looked at you. Both details that are not important to the story of his so-called assholery actions."

Logically, I know she's right. However, something about him just rubs me the wrong way.

Keets looks at me earnestly. "Are you sure this has nothing to do with..."

"No," I cut her off before she gets the chance to say his name.

She takes a breath, nodding, clearly getting the signal. "Look, I love you, so if you hate him, I hate him too. Solidarity, sister."

I think for a second before responding quietly. "Well, hate is very extreme."

She jumps up and screams, "I knew it!" Before she gracefully falls on her face. Coordination has never been her strong suit.

My hands are clawing at an invisible apparition in front of me. I can't make out a face or any defining details, but my body knows to be scared. There's a faint red light clouding my eyesight, blocking me from seeing anything. My eyes are moving around the room, quickly, trying to adjust to the darkness.

They won't adjust.

My room. Look around, Stella. Figure out where you are.

Damn it, why can't I see anything?

Where's Keets? Where's anyone? I can't see anything.

But I can tell there is something here.

I can feel the stare.

I can feel the hands digging into my flesh. Every time I scream, it falls on deaf ears. The red light disappears, and my hands drop. I stop fighting, going limp. It's still black. Dark.

My eyes open, and I shoot up, gasping. The back of my neck is wet, and my clothes are sticking to my body. I wipe the tears streaming down my face as I try to catch my breath.

My chest is tight, and I can feel my heart pumping to its full capacity. I quickly shoot my head around my room searching for him. But all I can see is my blanket tossed on the floor.

It was just a nightmare. No one is here.

I'm only up for a second when I hear the door open, the light from the hallway illuminating a silhouette. Keets is standing there in her pajamas, her face twisted in concern. She says nothing as she walks into the room and climbs into bed next to me. She wraps her arms around me and brushes my hair through her fingers, each touch steadying me. I don't need to say anything; she just knows. Keets lies there next to me until I fall asleep, knowing she'll be there when I wake up.

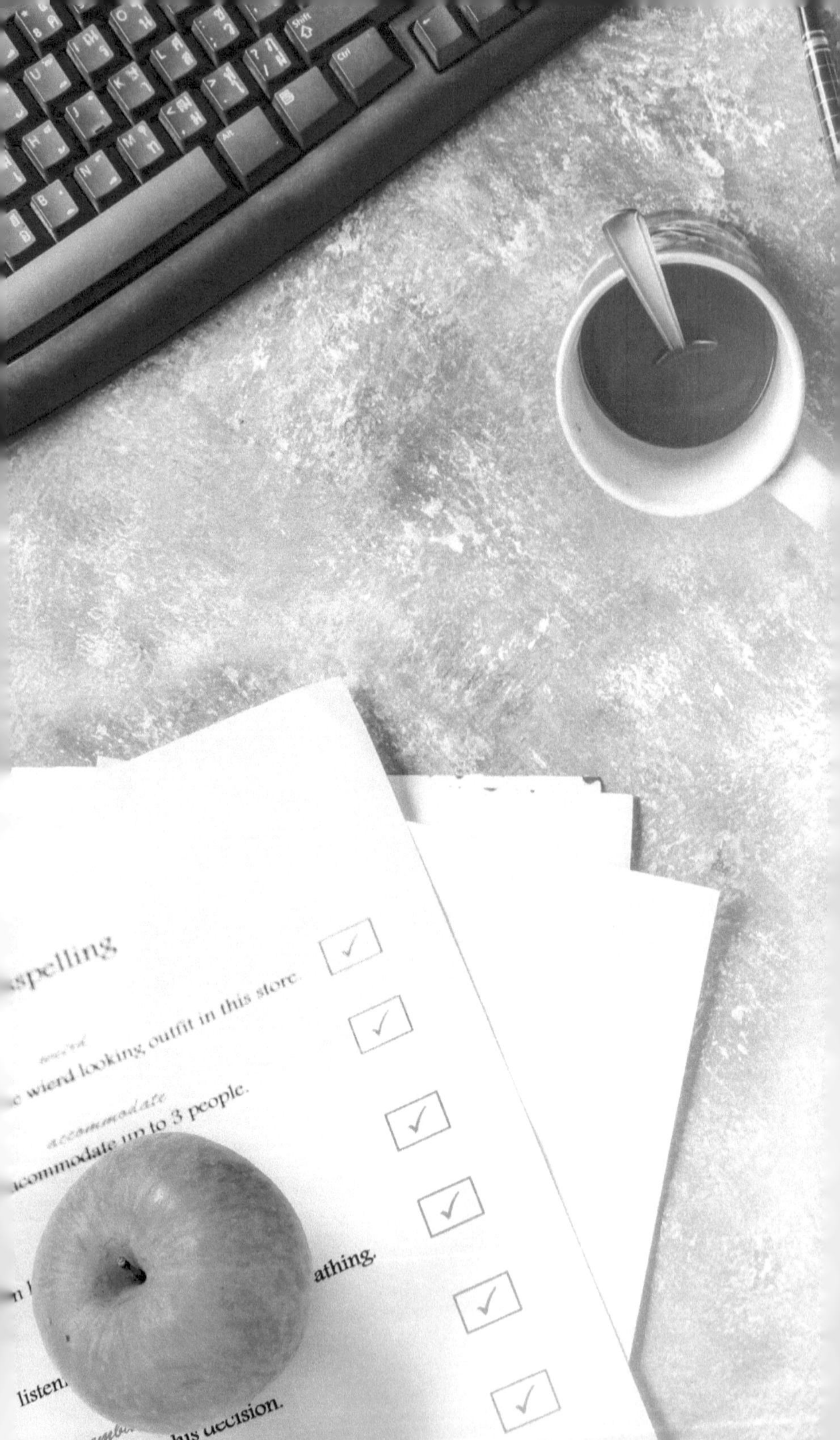
spelling
weird
e wierd looking outfit in this store.
accommodate
commodate up to 3 people.
athing.
listen
his decision.

Chapter Five

STELLA

"DO YOU WANT TO TALK ABOUT WHAT HAPPENED the other night?"

Keets' question pulls me out of my thoughts. It's been nearly a week since she came into my room to help me sleep. It's not an unusual occurrence for me to have nightmares. And while it's less frequent, she knows about it; that still happens.

"Nope. It happened. I woke up. I'm good."

She looks at me hesitantly, her head tilting slightly.

"I'm okay, I promise. Plus, any snuggle time with you is never a bad thing." I throw the stuffie that's sitting next to me on the couch, and she laughs, looking back at her book, dropping it.

It's not that she wouldn't understand or be there for me. I just don't like to dwell on the past. Thinking about it and talking about it won't help. It'll just take me back to that dark place, and I don't want to go back.

"Do you wanna go to the Lantern tonight? I'm feeling a night out."

Keets looks up from her book, her eyes slowly finding mine. I stare at her for a beat, raising my brow in disbelief. Keets always likes a night out, but usually she prefers going to one of the proper clubs that are closer to the big city. A blush starts to creep up her neck. "Okay, and I think Rory's working tonight."

"Your crush is becoming just a tad obvious."

She scrambles to her feet. "Not to him though, right?"

I close my laptop, laughing as I stand up and walk towards my room. "No, babes, just to the person who's lived with you for two years." I open my door. "Leave in an hour?"

"Yeah, sounds good." I hear behind me, along with her heavy breathing.

The Black Lantern is always full, no matter the day. It's the closest bar to all of the accommodation and has the cheapest prices. I think part of its popularity comes from the vibe of the place. When you walk in, you are immediately greeted by a long bar with a brick wall behind it. Vintage arcade games line one of the walls, games where people usually get a tad too aggressive once they've had a drink or two. Shelves are covering the walls, filled with the most random memorabilia you can think of. There's an old TV that is stuck playing Charlie Chaplin movies and a coffee machine sitting on one of the shelves where the pot has a fake aquarium. And my personal favourite, the ceramic frog playing a banjo - he has a top hat.

The Lantern isn't big by any standards, but it still manages to fit everyone every night. It's impossible to go without hearing at least one conversation about that test

PROLOGUE

Five hundred years ago, during the reign of Queen Astride, a catastrophe occurred that very nearly destroyed all of Weslynde. The ancient caldera that had lain dormant beneath Weslynde Province for centuries came to life and the ground split open, sinking a large part of Weslynde's fertile valley into the immense chasm underneath. The great northern ice sheet that separated Weslynde from the ocean collapsed and its waters poured in, creating an inland sea that submerged most of Weslynde's arable farmlands. Countless lives were lost, and decades of famine followed. Two days before the terrible tragedy, Queen Astride of Weslynde had given birth to twins.

The catastrophe came to be considered an act of divine retribution. The church decreed that the queen giving birth to twins had insulted the gods; they considered it an act of human arrogance.

From that day on, in order to appease the gods and prevent further disasters, whenever twins were born to a royal family, one was left to die. The practice spread throughout the province, and soon after, a healing woman attended every birth in Weslynde to prevent any mother's temptation to defy the gods and hide her twins.

Since the disaster, there have been no recorded instances of twins in Weslynde, and its people have prospered.

PART I

THE LADY OF ARGONNE

CHAPTER 1

The great chameli sidestepped unexpectedly, forcing Tregan to grab the railing to keep from sliding off the riding platform. Her escort, Rence, sitting next to her, gave a little "oof" of surprise.

"Sorry, my lady," the chameli's handler apologized. He shouted a harsh command to the huge animal from his perch on the beast's neck. The chameli flicked its tongue in response, and its cheek spots changed from blue to red.

"He doesn't like those spiny bushes," thirteen-year-old Dax offered from the bench behind them.

"Did the beast tell you that?" Rence asked dryly, his silver beard bristling. "Do the lizards talk to you now?"

"He's a chameli, not a lizard," Dax muttered under his breath.

Tregan suppressed a smile. She was glad Dax was with them; he had brightened the long trip north. He was an easy target for Rence's sardonic wit, but she knew Rence was fond of him.

The handler twisted around to talk to Tregan. "The chameli don't like those gorse bushes that grow here in the north—it irritates their hide. I'll keep an eye out."

Tregan could practically feel Dax's smug smile.

Today I am twenty-three, she thought as they neared the capital city of Caleddon. *There are a thousand different ways I would rather spend this day, but instead, I will present myself to the king of Weslynde, a man I have never met.* What kind of man was he? Would he even like her? She had contemplated turning around and returning to Argonne many times during the trip north, but so many people back home were counting on her, most of all her father. She sighed and tamped down the anxiety growing in her chest.

Tregan and her companions had been traveling north for weeks now, following along the Wess River as it snaked its way through Weslynde, a valley filled with vineyards, crystal lakes, and breathtaking geysers. It was magnificent and overwhelming all at once. This was Tregan's first time away from the desert province of Argonne, and everything about Weslynde was unfamiliar: the people, the weather, even the thorn bushes.

The city of Caleddon was very different from Isidima, the city of her birth. She missed Isidima very much: the market square with its noises and smells, the views of the bay from her villa's terrace, the soft ocean breezes rippling through the hanging gardens, not to mention her father and her friends.

Isidima, the capital of Argonne, rose up out of the sand, its many businesses and residences carved into the sides of an extinct volcano. It was pressed into narrow strip of land between the ocean and the vast Argonne Desert and was a landmark sailors could see from miles away. The city of Caleddon, on the other hand, sprawled out before her like a carelessly thrown blanket. Caleddon's white plaster buildings with their terracotta roofs were scattered about randomly, interspersed with winding streets, open plazas, and manicured parklands. Caleddon's dazzling gold-domed palace stretched in unrestrained splendor across the entire top of a hill overlooking the Wess River. Everything about it seemed extravagant and excessive, like it was dressed for a ball.

Groups of onlookers began to gather along the side of the road. They waved as Tregan and her entourage passed by, and some even cheered and shouted her name. Tregan was convinced that most of them only wanted to catch a glimpse of the great chameli, an animal not often seen this far north. The handler steered the beast up the center of the main boulevard, and the gold dome of the palace slowly rose up to meet them. *My new home,* she thought, her anxiety creeping in again. She smiled and nodded to the people lining the road, masking her nervousness, wondering what they thought of her arrangement with the king; it wasn't as if he would marry her. She sought out something familiar, anything she could anchor herself on. That was when she noticed that no one waving looked like her. They were all Weslynders, shorter than she was, sturdily built, most with a dusting of freckles across their pale faces.

"Why are no Argonnians here?" Tregan whispered to Rence. "Caleddon is supposed to be the center of the commonwealth."

Rence, a Weslynder himself (who seemed to know everything about Caleddon), shrugged and scratched his close-cropped beard.

"The citizens do look rather pale, don't they," he quipped. Then he brightened. "Ah! Tregan, over there. Argonnians."

Three tall slender men with dark brown faces stood next to a fountain, their braided black hair cascading down their backs. They towered over the Weslynders next to them. She noticed they were the only ones in the crowd not smiling or waving. She nodded to them when they drew close, and the three raised their palms outward in a sign of respect.

"Only three of my brothers in this whole crowd? We have our work cut out for us, Rence."

"That's why you are here, my lady." Rence smiled. "To bring Argonnian grace and beauty back to Caleddon."

His easy banter helped relax her. "You blend in, at any rate," she teased. "Some sun would help. You look like a cave lizard. I don't think you stepped outside the whole time you were in Argonne."

Dax squeezed in between them, green eyes sparkling with excitement. "Is that the king?" He pointed up the road in front of them.

"You've got good eyes, lad," Rence said. "It appears they've come out to meet us."

Tregan's heart jumped. The broad-shouldered man she assumed had to be King Franklin was jogging down the middle of the boulevard straight toward them. Two guards trotted next to him, trying to keep up. Behind them ran a handful of well-dressed men and women and two gangly boys pushing and shoving each other. Several barking dogs bounced around them, adding to the circus atmosphere. Tregan realized the two boys must be the king's bastard sons. She hadn't considered the fact that they might be with him.

King Franklin was a solidly built man with a square face, smooth brown hair pulled back in a knot, and a neatly trimmed beard that was starting to gray. He looked like he was dressed for gardening rather than receiving important guests. His ragged brown tunic was stained, and his large boots were muddy, very different from how she had imagined he would dress to meet her, given the elegant trappings of the palace behind him. Had he forgotten she was coming?

The handler brought their carrier beast to an abrupt stop as the king approached, cursing and waving away the people who had encroached on the great chameli get a better view.

"Happy birthday to me," Tregan whispered. She squeezed Rence's hand for reassurance. He winked at her and squeezed back. She sat up straight and smoothed her gown.

The king ran forward to help Tregan down from the carrier beast and took her hand as she stepped off the ladder. The crowd shouted hurrahs, and the king cheerfully waved back at them. He ushered her forward, and she gave the crowd a practiced wave. Now that she was standing next to the king, Tregan saw she was a good six inches taller than he was. He squeezed her hand, and she noticed how her smooth dark brown skin contrasted with his pale complexion. His freckled arms were sunburnt and mud smeared. He even had dirt under his nails. She felt overdressed. The white linen gown she had chosen for this occasion rippled gracefully about her ankles in the breeze, and the gold bands she wore on her wrists and around her neck gleamed in the sunshine. Her beaded braids were piled high on her head, making her appear even taller. The king tilted his head up at her, and his blue eyes sparkled.

"I needed someone to look up to." Grinning, he raised her hand up and presented her to the crowd. "Behold! Our desert princess, Lady Tregan Anthelia."

The crowd cheered again, and she broke out in a genuine smile, won over by the warm welcome.

Tregan was somewhat charmed that the king continued to hold her by the hand as he led her and her entourage through the palace gates and into the courtyard in front of the great hall, dogs barking, and his boys, Barton and Lowden, darting in and out as the crowds continued to cheer.

Once inside the gates and out of view of the crowds, the king abruptly let go of her hand. "I must leave you now," he said. "The staff will show you to your rooms."

"Oh," Tregan said in surprise. "I thought we would be together."

"We will meet later. Goodbye, Lady Tregan." The king gave her no more notice and began shouting orders at a harried staffer, something about horse stables and drainage. Suddenly and awkwardly alone, she glanced around for Rence.

"This way, my lady." A severe-looking woman was staring at her, hands clasped at her waist. She beckoned Tregan to follow and disappeared into the palace. Tregan picked up her skirts and rushed up the steps after her, wondering if the mercurial shift of focus she had just witnessed was typical of the king.

The brusque woman quickly ushered Tregan into the rooms that were to be hers, swinging wide the double doors on a chamber that was spacious, bright, and well appointed. Glass doors on the other side of the room led out to a terrace overlooking the river and mountains beyond. A soft breeze lifted the sheer curtains framing the terrace door.

"Everything is so elegant, my lady!" Merta gasped. Tregan's indispensable attendant had come in behind her carrying some of their belongings. She dropped the bags and ran her hand across a polished side table.

Tregan had to agree. Everything was lustrous and refined. There was even a tray of fresh fruit and a pitcher of wine set out. *I am the desert princess*, she thought, smiling to herself.

Merta was a tiny Cordelian woman with the olive skin and straight black hair typical of her people. Her parents had emigrated from Cordel to Argonne before Merta was born. They had worked for Tregan's father, Senator Tregor Anthelia, for many years. After her parents had died, Merta had stayed on to serve as Tregan's attendant. They'd grown up together, and Tregan considered her part of her family.

Merta tied up her long black hair into a bun and started unpacking.

Rence breezed through the door, bushy eyebrows creased in a frown, and began issuing orders to the palace staffers bringing in more boxes. He demanded they provide him a separate office next to Tregan's bedchamber.

"It is not my problem the room next door is occupied," he barked. "See that the ambassador is moved somewhere else immediately!"

The staff scrambled to do his bidding. She could hear him continuing to berate them as he followed them out the door and down the corridor.

Rence must hold a higher position than I imagined, Tregan thought. *I must keep him on my side.*

Rence was a member of King Franklin's personal staff. The king had assigned him to serve Tregan as liaison. Tregan had grown fond of him on their journey north from Argonne. He had proved to be an unexpected gift, filling her in on the politics and protocols of life in the palace. His witty observations and warnings about some of the more notorious palace staffers had made her laugh and kept the lessons palatable.

After he left, Tregan grabbed Merta by the hand, and they took a few moments to explore. They were especially delighted by the indoor bathing room that adjoined her bedchamber; it featured a cunning spout that poured hot water directly out of the ceiling onto the bather.

"How do they keep the water hot?" Merta asked, astonished. "Is someone tending a stove up there?"

Dax burst through the door and dropped his boxes with a loud thump. "Please, my lady," he said, green eyes beseeching her. "I wish to go with the animal handlers. They are taking our carrier beast to the hot caves. I've never seen a hot cave."

Dax had a special bond with the great chameli. His talent with the animals was one reason he had been recommended to an apprenticeship at the University of Magic. He stood there, practically dancing on his toes. Tregan nodded, and he ran out the door, his dark braid flying behind him.

A final staffer plumped up a pillow and stepped out of the room, closing the double doors quietly behind him. Tregan gave Merta's hand a squeeze. Merta poured the two of them some wine, and they sank onto the divan together, giggling like little girls. Up to this minute, the whole arrangement had seemed forced and unpleasant. Maybe things would turn out better than Tregan hoped.

⚜

A formal search had been conducted across the commonwealth to find a mate for King Franklin, one who would bear his child, the heir to the throne. Although young, Tregan was already an influential figure in Argonnian politics. She was a member of the great house of Anthelia, and her father, Tregor Anthelia, was a famous senator. Her lineage and her connections made her the best candidate to join with the king and strengthen ties between the two provinces.

There had long been complaints among many Argonnians that Weslynde continued to disregard Argonne's contributions to the commonwealth. A small but growing group of voices was calling for secession, a split from Weslynde. This concerned Tregan and her father, Senator Anthelia, greatly. They both believed Argonne benefited from being part of the Western Commonwealth, a united alliance made up of three provinces, Weslynde, Argonne, and Riddien. A royal baby with family ties to Argonne would strengthen that alliance.

Tregan had negotiated a trial period into her arrangement with the king. She needed time to evaluate King Franklin before she signed the contract and committed to having his child. So, with that goal in mind, over the next few weeks, she met with the king at least once a day—sometimes attending lavish formal gatherings, other times sitting with him by the fire in his private hall, served by a quiet staff who brought refreshments and played music. His two boys were a constant presence, terrorizing the staff and calling Tregan the desert princess. She protested whenever they did this, but it secretly pleased her.

King Franklin himself proved to be a mixture of bombast

and charm, and he was subject to sudden mood swings. One evening he called for her, and when she arrived, he handed her a glass of wine and bade her sit next to him by the fire.

"You light up this room like a desert sun wipes away the winter," he said. "Tell me about Isidima and your people, everything you know." He sat at her feet in front of the fire and listened to her stories with rapt attention and asked all kinds of questions about her family and Argonne. She relished his attention and began to open up. She started to tell him a marvelous tale of a famous desert raid her ancestor had led when he interrupted her mid-sentence.

"This very day, a flax farmer came to the hall complaining about taxes. Can you believe it? A flax farmer! He had nothing to complain about. Their harvest was unmatched this year." He proceeded to rant on and on about loyalty and sacrifice for the common good, and any threads of their prior conversation were lost. She discreetly took her leave when he went to the door and began shouting for a scribe to come take down his latest thoughts on tithing.

Franklin was funny and profane and prone to fits of anger. She went with him to look at a well that had gone dry, a serious matter putting a farmer in danger of losing his grapes. A magician from the university was able to locate a new underground seam in the rock and redirect the water, but Franklin flew into a rage when muddy water burst from the new vent and came cascading down, dowsing Tregan and Franklin with sludge. The poor farmer, blessed with good fortune, tried not to seem overly happy as the king cursed and threw clods of muddy dirt at the horrified magician, threatening to banish him from Caleddon forever.

Once Franklin calmed down, he wiped the mud from his eyes and started to laugh. He stood on tiptoes and whispered to Tregan, gesturing toward the magician, who had prostrated himself on the grimy soil in fear.

"Magicians always look better from that angle, don't you think?" he quipped.

Tregan covered her mouth to hide her smile.

The weeks flew past, and the time came when she had to make a decision: have the king's child and endure all the intrusions that came with it or decline the arrangement and return to her life in Argonne. The opportunity presented itself when they were walking together by the river. Barton and Lowden splashed in the shallows nearby.

"Franklin," Tregan began, "I've been thinking about our contract."

"You have? Good." Before she could say more, the king heaved a heavy sigh and said, "If you must know, Tregan, I find the whole contract thing off-putting. It's like dog breeding." He casually tossed the colored rock he had been admiring into the river; it skipped across the water's surface, three, four, five times.

"Dog breeding!" Tregan was shocked and a little insulted. "Is that what you think this is?" Her cheeks grew hot.

Before he could answer, they were interrupted by Lowden's loud screams, and the boys came running toward them.

"Lowden threw a rock at a wasp's nest," Barton yelled as he ran.

"You dared me!" Lowden howled, waving his hands in the air, his face marked with red welts.

"The gods curse you both!" Franklin yelled. "You've not a brain between you." He grabbed Lowden roughly and sat him down on a rock. "Sit still," he barked. "Stop screaming!" Lowden clapped his hands over his mouth. "Barton, get my knife out of my pack." Barton scrambled to obey.

Tregan dampened a cloth in the river and winced as the king pulled the stingers out of Lowden's face.

"You can't breed common sense," Franklin muttered as he worked on his son.

"What do you mean?" Tregan asked.

"Dog breeding! You can breed a dog that is pretty to look at and will win all the ribbons, but what good is a pretty dog if he can't catch a rabbit?"

Tregan realized he cared about more than the politics of their union. He wanted an heir he could be proud of, someone to continue his legacy.

Franklin wiped away Lowden's tears and held the boy's chin up and smiled with his eyes. "You're not going to win any prizes by making wasps angry, Lowden. Now go and catch a rabbit." He gave Lowden a shove and chuckled as he ran off to join his brother.

"Breeding and bloodlines really don't matter, do they, Tregan?" he said, taking her hand and letting her pull him to his feet. "It's all about how you raise 'em up. Gotta make sure they're useful."

Tregan imagined what he would be like as the father of her child. Rough, yes, intimidating no doubt, demanding in every way, but caring underneath. A child could thrive under such guidance. Tregan watched him toss a ball to Barton, whooping his approval when the boy caught it. He loved his boys. Her choice was made.

⚜

Once Tregan returned to the palace, she went immediately to Rence, who was writing in his office. "I'm ready to sign the contract." She sipped the tea Rence had offered, tamping down her nervous excitement.

Rence put down his pen and clapped his hands together in satisfaction. "That's good! That's very good. It's been quite a journey from the time the search was convened until now."

"It has. My father pushed me hard from the very beginning to choose this." A map of the Western Commonwealth hung on

Rence's wall, and her gaze lingered on each province: Weslynde, Riddien, and her beloved Argonne. "King Franklin shares my hopes for the commonwealth alliance. This union will strengthen the ties between Argonne and Weslynde. Tamp down some of the unrest at least. This will be good for my people—to have an Argonnian on the throne." She paused and said a little doubtfully, "And I could get used to life in Weslynde."

"Signing the contract doesn't mean you have to give up your life and move here permanently." Rence tapped the table with his finger. "You are Lady Tregan of the great house of Anthelia. You are an influential advocate for your people, and your future in the Argonne senate is secure."

"I know, I know," Tregan said. "But I couldn't imagine having a child and then leaving the baby behind. I want to stay here and raise my child my way."

"You don't have to decide that right now."

"That's good, because I can't." A little part of her still questioned if the child would truly be hers or if she would be sidelined once the baby was born, just another caregiver, grooming the heir to replace King Franklin as sovereign. She pushed her nagging doubts aside. "All right, then. It's decided."

"The king needs to be informed immediately of your decision. Do you want me to send a message to Franklin?"

"No, I'd like to tell him myself." She set down her teacup with a click and filled two glasses from the pitcher of wine on Rence's desk. She handed one to Rence and held hers aloft. "To Argonne and the alliance." She drained it in a single gulp.

⚜

The very next day, in a sparsely attended ceremony, Franklin né Rosin, King of Weslynde, and Lady Tregan Anthelia of Argonne signed the contract naming her royal mate. A child stemming from their union would be Franklin's heir, first in line to the throne of Weslynde and leader of the Western Commonwealth, placed before any other child previously sired by the king. The document was witnessed by a senator from each of the three provinces, and it was stamped with the king's crest. When the king pressed his signet ring into the wax, Tregan thought it had all the romantic appeal of signing a loan.

A tattoo identifying her as royal mate was inked onto her forearm, cementing her status in Franklin's household. Shortly after, she reluctantly bid farewell to most of her entourage, stoically watching as they loaded up the carrier beast and started the long journey back home to Argonne. Merta and Dax remained with her. Merta continued on as her personal attendant, and Dax had petitioned to remain in Caleddon and study. His request had been granted, and he would resume his training to be a magician at the university, focusing on animal charms. She realized with some regret that she had sent every Argonnian who had come north with her back to Isidima; Merta was Cordelian, and Dax was from the far north. He had the smooth fair skin, green eyes, and dark shiny hair of the people who lived near the great ice sheet.

Tregan felt isolated. Very few Argonnians lived in the city, and even fewer worked inside the palace, and her hopes of blending in with a diverse population were dashed. The Argonnian senator who lived in the palace was a grumpy old man who liked to keep things formal and rebuffed her attempts to be friendly. She was treated with respect everywhere she went, but it was like she was on display; she was a head taller than everyone she met, and her dark skin and braided hair made her stand out. There was nothing to be done about this, of course; she had signed the contract and had sent a message back to the Prime Minister of Argonne stating such, so she pushed her loneliness aside and mentally prepared herself to focus on the business at hand: creating a child for the king.

The first time Tregan lay with the king, it was as quiet an affair as could be arranged under the circumstances. She thought Franklin was very kind and respectful and even a touch romantic. He took her to a small inn that he had cleared of other guests in advance. There they enjoyed a light supper served by the innkeeper and his wife, which included some strong wine that made the fire brighter and the jokes funnier. Tregan relaxed. She took Franklin by the hand and led him to the room that had been prepared for them.

After that first night, things got much more clinical. Every day she had to meet with the palace physician (a sour man with breath that smelled like onions), who took her temperature, examined her intrusively, and asked very personal questions. When her monthly flow commenced, the physician huffed and crossed his arms.

"Are you certain you know how babies are conceived?' he asked condescendingly, insinuating she must be doing it wrong somehow. He gave her a journal to write in and a calendar upon which dates were marked with times and temperatures. Tregan pushed down the unflattering names for him that formed in her mouth and managed a docile expression.

Her itinerary was updated so that she was available at optimum times to accommodate the king. One evening she was attending a dinner party in her honor hosted by the Riddien senator at his nearby residence. She had just been seated for the meal when there was a commotion at the door. The senator excused himself, and when he returned, he hurried over, red-faced, and whispered, "The king is here. He only has a few minutes."

A server pulled back her chair, and Tregan excused herself, extremely self-conscious. The others at the table stared down at their plates or up at the paintings on the wall. She was escorted into a nearby study where Franklin was waiting for her. Their coupling was brief and perfunctory, leaving her cross and a little sore. After he left, she readjusted her clothing as best she could and made her excuses to the senator's wife, who was very understanding and helped her escape through the scullery. She vowed to triple-check the king's calendar before she ventured forth again.

Tregan attended more patronizing sessions with the palace physician where he explained, with drawings and hand motions, which positions were best to facilitate conception. He even gave her a list of foods she was to consume or avoid. After the second month without results, any feelings of desire she may have once had for Franklin were gone. She was nothing more than a broodmare. To work off some of her frustration, she invited Franklin's bastard sons, Barton and Lowden, to spend time with her. She had become quite fond of the boys. They had Franklin's charm and wit but fewer of his more volatile traits (Lowden more so than Barton). Neither seemed to care that if she had Franklin's child, they were no longer first in line for the throne. Barton wanted to be general of the army, and Lowden dreamed of going on a quest in search of the mythical winged chameli.

Tregan changed into an Argonnian leather fighting vest and leggings and met them on the palace training grounds. The boys tumbled into the arena, happy to see her, and grew very excited when she tossed them each a long stave, her favorite weapon.

"Today I am going to teach you to spar," she said, moving immediately into a fighting stance. The boys sprang to attention and held their staves up defensively. Tregan was a trained fighter and an expert with the weapon. She disarmed both of them in three short moves.

"Again!" Barton shouted, sounding very like his father. "You caught us off guard." He pounced and thrust the end of his stave at her.

She easily parried his thrust and whacked him on his buttocks as he charged past, sending him sprawling. Lowden burst into peals of laughter. Barton threw down his stave and jumped on his brother. Once Tregan got them separated, she showed them a few classic moves. The boys were quick learners and had no qualms at all about tackling her and wrestling her to the ground when they managed to best her. The palace physician caught them rolling around in the dirt and, horror-struck, beat the boys off of her with a stick, swearing until flecks of spit flew from his mouth. Tregan rolled on the ground with the boys, laughing until her sides ached.

The weeks marched on, and Tregan kept herself distracted as best she could—she even volunteered to help in the palace kitchen. One afternoon she was alone in her sitting room, reading a book, when the king's voice began raging in the corridor outside her door.

"If you don't move this blasted thing out of my way, I'll throw you from the rampart!"

She opened the door in time to catch Franklin upending a food cart that was blocking his way, cursing at a very unhappy staffer who cowered submissively in a corner. He stormed into her room and slammed the door behind him, collapsing on the divan. She perched next to him and put her hand on his arm.

"Franklin, what has happened?"

"These sodding physicians, they won't leave me alone!" he cursed.

"What do you mean?"

"The physical intrusions I have to endure, just to produce a child! Something the lowest animals can accomplish while farting and eating hay."

Tregan kept herself from laughing at his misery. *He has no idea*, she thought. "Tell me."

"I don't know if you want to hear this, Tregan."

"Go on," she encouraged. "I can handle it."

"The first thing they tried to do was measure my balls, which was bad enough, but then they told me they needed a sample, gods curse them."

"A sample? I don't understand. A sample of what?"

"You know. My, uh, er, uh...my seed." Frankin's cheeks flushed red.

"Oh, I see," Tregan said, enjoying his discomfort. She patted his hand reassuringly. "You need some wine." She filled two mugs as the king continued.

"They gave me this little cup to catch the sample. I asked them, you want me to"—the king made a rude hand gesture—"into this? They said yes, and then, Tregan, then they stood there like they were going to watch me!"

"Oh, no! Then what happened?" She handed him his wine and put her hand over her mouth, trying to suppress her giggles.

"What do you think happened? I threw them out. But they came back—and told me I couldn't go to the baths anymore, that I had to start washing my privates with a cloth."

"Why?" Tregan was openly giggling now, trying hard not to spill her wine.

"They said I needed to ensure the royal sperm were not cooked before they could be put into service."

Tregan burst into laughter, sloshing her wine on the divan. She grabbed a hand towel and started blotting it up, still laughing. The king started laughing along with her. She loved this side of Franklin.

"Today was the last straw, Tregan," he said, suddenly

straight-faced. "Today they came in and told me to stop pleasuring myself—said I was thinning the herd too much, letting the best boys out of the gate too soon!"

They broke into gales of laughter.

"The—best—boys." Tregan wiped the tears from her eyes.

"So I said ox balls! You medics won't stop until you know the color of my shit!"

"Stop it, Franklin." Tregan hugged herself. "I can't breathe."

"So I threw them all out and came here."

"Oh my, oh my." Tregan leaned back and put her head on his chest, taking deep breaths, bringing herself back under control.

"I thought you would know what to do." Franklin put his arms around her and pulled her close.

His heart beat against her cheek. "I do know what to do," she whispered into his neck, brushing her lips softly against his skin.

That night the heir to the throne of Weslynde was conceived.

⚜

When Tregan missed her next cycle, a healing woman named Gwyn was dispatched from the Ministry of Medicine to confirm if she was pregnant. Tregan was fully aware that healing women tended every pregnancy in Weslynde. Rence had informed her that a healing woman assigned to attend the mother of the heir was charged with ensuring the health and well-being of the royal baby over that of the mother, and, even more disturbingly, in the extremely unlikely event of twins, determining which child was the fittest and would survive. She shuddered at the thought of it.

"You are most definitely with child," Gwyn said matter-of-factly, holding up a vial that had turned from clear to bright blue. The square-jawed healer seemed all business at first, but then her face lit up and she crinkled her freckled nose. "Congratulations, my dear. The citizens of Weslynde thank you. You need not worry about anything from now on. I will attend you until the baby is born and stay with you and the baby until weaning is done." She squeezed Tregan's hand warmly. "Which room is mine?"

"You're staying here?" Tregan asked, caught off guard by this take-charge woman and unfamiliar with this new protocol. She was exhausted by the constant scrutiny and had hoped for peace and quiet now that she was pregnant.

"Yes, my lady, I am under King Franklin's orders to never leave your side."

"Oh, I see," Tregan said, knitting her brow. "No one told me—"

A voice behind them interrupted them. "You won't be staying here." The house chaplain, Bishop Rutter, a round man with sagging jowls, had entered the room unannounced and had overheard the last part of their conversation. Behind him, Caleddon's house mage, Gerard Mort, stood in the doorway. Gerard Mort was a thin sallow man with long snow-white hair pulled back at his neck. He wore the formal black robes of his station. His dark eyes darted around the room, examining everything. It put Tregan on edge. The mage stepped aside, and two staffers entered the room, pushing empty carts.

"What is this?" Tregan demanded, affronted that they had entered unannounced. "What is it you want?"

"You are to be sequestered at the abbey, my lady," Bishop Rutter explained, mopping his forehead. "The king has determined the abbey is the safest place for you to carry the heir to term. Once you are behind the abbey walls, we can protect you from unwanted visitors who might carry disease. Don't worry; the abbey has comfortable rooms suitable for someone of your station. Healer Gwyn, go and gather your belongings and meet us at the abbey."

Gwyn bowed and hurried out.

The abbey! Tregan thought in dismay. *Ugh. That place is a dungeon, cold and dark.* "I feel perfectly safe here in the palace."

"The king feels differently," Gerard Mort hissed, dismissively.

"Are there rooms in the abbey for my personal court?" she asked, thinking of Rence, Merta, and Dax.

"Church novices serve the guests of the abbey," Bishop Rutter said. "Your people are free to return to their homes."

Tregan was now genuinely alarmed. "No, that won't work at all. They must stay with me."

"But, my lady, there is no need for them any longer," the bishop said as if speaking to a child. "They should be sent away."

Tregan had heard enough. She rose from her chair and stood at her full Argonnian height. "My people stay with me," she said firmly, locking her eyes with Bishop Rutter. "I do not need to feel alone and exposed at the time I am most vulnerable. That is not what the king would want, no matter what you say."

Bishop Rutter glanced furtively at the house mage, who nodded slightly. "Of course, my lady," he acquiesced, bowing his head. "I meant no offense."

Gerard Mort motioned to the attendants. "Gather Lady Tregan's things and bring them, as well as those of her personal court."

The attendants moved into the room with their carts.

"Step aside," Tregan ordered, glaring at the mage as she moved to the door. "I must speak to Rence." She forged ahead, and Gerard Mort was forced to step out of her way.

Tregan hurried down the corridor to Rence's office. Something felt ... different. Suddenly she was no longer the center of everyone's attention, the one they called the desert princess. Instead, she had become this vessel, this incubator, needing to be locked up and put away for safekeeping. And she didn't like the look of the house mage; he was clearly behind this new arrangement. Bishop Rutter was obviously his lackey. She rapped loudly on Rence's chamber door.

"Enter."

Tregan rushed in, closing the door hard behind her. Rence glanced up from his paperwork and rose when he saw her face.

"What is it?"

"We are being moved to the abbey now that I am officially pregnant. I am to be sequestered." The thought of being locked up inside that cold dark edifice was unbearable. She had to tell Franklin; he would sort it out.

"That was not mentioned in your contract," Rence mused. "Congratulations, by the way. Who gave you this order?"

"The house chaplain, but the house mage is behind it."

"Gerard Mort." Rence shook his head. "Bless his dark soul."

"He tried to have you sent away. Merta and Dax as well."

"Mages always get a little power drunk over time. Moving all those objects with their minds makes them think they are special. We will need to keep an eye on him." He took her hand and spoke soothingly. "Don't worry; I work for the king, not the house mage. I am here to serve you by his command, and here I will stay."

Tregan felt a little better. "I must tell Franklin I carry our child, although I am sure he already knows; these walls have ears. And I am sure that when I tell him I wish to stay here in the palace, he will see it done. But, Rence, they are already moving my things. Will you make sure nothing gets lost or ruined? And will you tell Merta and Dax what is happening?"

"Of course, leave everything to me." He winked and added, "I will have Dax put a protection spell on your undergarments; he's doing well at magic school."

Tregan smiled in spite of herself and headed out the door, grabbing a young page that was running past. "Go quickly and announce me to the king, then come back and escort me there."

The boy looked up at her with saucer eyes. "Yes, my lady, I go at once!" He broke into a big-toothed grin and dashed off.

I'm still the desert princess to some, she thought grimly, striding down the hall toward the king's private wing of the palace.

⚜

When Tregan arrived at the king's office, the guards bowed and opened the double doors for her. The page had done his job. She winked and mouthed a "thank you" to the boy. He grinned and dashed off to tell his mates, she was sure. She straightened her shoulders and entered the room, confident that Franklin would be happy about the child and would see to it she wasn't moved to the horrible abbey. But when she entered the room, she froze. Seated on the divan next to the king was the mother of his bastards, Clare. They were holding hands. Clare! What was she doing here? Tregan had seen her several times out in public with the king and his sons; after all, the boys lived with her, and she frequently accompanied them to the palace. Tregan had spoken to her a few times and found her to be pleasant and deferential. Clare had been invited to Franklin's last formal dinner, but Tregan had had the seat next to the king and Clare had been placed far down the table. Seeing the two of them together like this was shocking, as if she had walked in on them in the middle of lovemaking.

"Tregan, I'm glad you have come," Franklin said, not getting up. "You know Clare."

Tregan nodded, keeping her face neutral.

"You have news for me?"

"I do," Tregan said. She sat stiffly on the divan opposite the two of them, irritated that the king hadn't moved away from Clare when she came in. She had to make herself not stare at the king's hand on Clare's lap.

"I bear our child, Your Majesty."

"That is the news I have been waiting for," the king said, clearly not surprised.

"Congratulations, my dear," Clare said, clapping her hands with joy. She went over and sat next to Tregan, her strong perfume assailing Tregan's senses. "You have served the commonwealth well. Now for the fun part!" She put her arm around Tregan and squeezed her. Tregan tried not to stiffen. "There's going to be a lot of excitement, of course. You will be paraded around the city, invited to parties—"

"She is to be sequestered at the abbey," interrupted the king.

"What? I hadn't heard that," Clare said. "Whatever for?"

So Franklin knew! Tregan removed Clare's hand from hers. "I wish to speak to you about that. Perhaps when you are alone?"

"You may say whatever you have to say in front of Clare; she is most discreet."

"I see," Tregan replied, off-balance. What she had to say wasn't any of Clare's business. She gathered her thoughts, wary of the fire smoldering behind Franklin's eyes. "Per the terms of our contract, I am to be regarded as a member of the palace household, given free rein, and to be treated with the respect and deference befitting the king's royal mate and mother of the heir." She couldn't help but glance at Clare when she said 'king's royal mate.'

"Yes, and so you have been." The king raised an eyebrow. "Do you feel differently?"

"No, of course not. My court and I are comfortable here. I have made a few friends, and I am fond of your sons. I have enjoyed participating in the management of the house; I've even been welcome to help in the kitchen or work in the garden if I choose. But...Franklin, being sequestered in the abbey, a cheerless and solitary place at best, feels ... inconsistent with our arrangement up to now."

"It is only temporary, until the child is born."

"May I ask why?"

"For your safety, of course."

"Have I not been safe?"

"It's for the safety of the unborn child. The heir."

The irritation in his voice was growing, but she pressed him. "I don't understand. What do you mean?"

"Tregan, you carry inside you the commonwealth's most valuable possession. Nothing can happen to that child. Once the baby is born and the royal sigil is embedded in their shoulder, the protections the sigil provides will take over and you will be free to carry on as you choose. Surely you haven't forgotten why you are here."

The king was lecturing her as if she were a little girl. It made her want to scream. Her arms were trembling, and she pressed her elbows tight to her sides to keep it from showing. "I see." Her voice was ice.

"I don't think you do," the king replied, stone-faced.

"I see very well." Her cheeks were hot and tingly. "Before I became pregnant, I needed to be here, in proximity to you, available at any hour to receive the seed you were so eager to plant in me. Every attempt was made to keep me happy, compliant, even enthusiastic. But now that the deed is done and the seed is planted, I am nothing more than an oven, and great care must be taken not to slam the oven door so the bread won't fall."

"Oh, Tregan, that's not fair," Clare said, placing a hand on her arm. "Franklin speaks fondly of you."

"Be silent," Franklin snapped.

Clare's hand jerked back in surprise.

"You talk of contracts." Franklin rounded on her, his blue eyes cold. "Here are the terms that you agreed to. The child in your womb does not belong to you; it belongs to me. I say what happens to this child, where it happens, and how it happens. Per our contract, you are required to remain healthy and strong and safe. Once the child is born, you are required to stay with it and nurse it, providing it the nourishment it needs from your milk. Once the baby weans, you are free to remain here and participate in raising the child as would any other member of this household, or you may choose instead to return to your people, having performed your service. As you are well aware, your beloved desert province of Argonne receives many benefits from this agreement. Those are the terms of your contract. Do you disagree with those terms?"

Tregan sat straight as a poker, balling up her fists in her lap as she swallowed her anger. *I am not any other member of this household,* she thought. *I am Lady Tregan Anthelia of Argonne.* Only Clare's presence next to her kept her from saying this out loud. "No, my lord," she said coolly. "I agree those are the terms."

The king stood and went to the door. "An escort is waiting for you outside to take you to the abbey. You will remain there until the child is born and receives the sigil. And, Tregan, you will make sure that no one slams the oven door. You may go." He pushed the door open and stepped aside.

Tregan mustered her dignity and rose to her feet; she gave a slight nod to Clare and walked past the king, ignoring him, her escort following in her wake.

⚜

Once the door closed, Clare turned to the king. "Oh, Franklin," she sighed, twisting her kerchief.

"Leave me," the king said, turning his back on her and pouring himself some wine.

⚜

Spring arrived. Tregan pushed open her narrow window and looked down on the garden below. The pink buds on the cherry trees inside the abbey enclave had burst open into white blossoms, as if they were covered with snow. Newly minted translucent leaves pushed their way out of the woody grapevines climbing the abbey walls. She had been sequestered in these suffocating rooms for three months now. The abbey's stone walls seemed to absorb the light, but the morning air smelled fresh, and she took some joy in watching blossoms fall from the cherry trees onto the gray stone path below. Beyond the wall, the sun shone on the gilt dome of the palace in the distance. What was the king was doing over there? She hoped it was something unpleasant.

Life in the abbey was incredibly boring. When she'd first arrived, Tregan had been pressured to attend church services twice a day, listening to ignorant clerics tie every cloudburst that dropped rain in the valley to the mood of some dissatisfied, egotistical god. After letting out an audible guffaw in the middle of the bishop's homily, where he told the congregation that the many geysers dotting the Wess River were evidence that gods were subject to fits of rage, she was no longer asked to attend. She quickly learned that no one dared overly upset her, the mother of the heir, and she used that to her advantage.

A line of novices made their way to the chapel for meditation. *So much beauty in the world, and those young people don't get to see it; instead, they will spend the day kneeling on a cold stone floor.* She sighed and closed the window. She placed her hands on her belly and felt a soft flutter; that had been happening for a week now.

"How are you doing today, my precious love?" she whispered and patted her stomach. The baby was not due until harvest, which seemed ages away. She dreaded the idea of spending the hot summer months trapped inside these stuffy rooms, with their sparse un-upholstered furnishings and lack of indoor plumbing. Her one reprieve was that she was allowed to walk around the inside perimeter of the abbey enclave twice a day. Early on, Barton and Lowden had come to visit her, and she was permitted to give them pointers as they practiced with their staves as long as she remained seated on a bench. That visit was terminated when Gwyn happened to glance out the window and saw her sparring with the boys, swinging her stave and taking blows. Franklin's sons were banished from the abbey, and Gwyn took Tregan's stave and hid it.

Tregan wished she had her stave with her now. She had some heads to rap—first and foremost, the king's. She was still furious with Franklin, and he had not come to visit her, not even once. She hoped a geyser would erupt under him. At the same time, she missed him. He could be so warm when he wanted. And he was funny: no one had ever made her laugh the way he did. She had foolishly started to imagine that she would be the king's chosen partner, and together they would transform Caleddon into a beacon of light shining on all its citizens. It was sobering to think how naive she had been.

She had suffered through an awkward visit from Clare, and she endured daily visits from Bishop Rutter, who came to lay blessings on her unborn child and pray with her that she might someday find patience. Rence came and went (he was under orders from the king to report on her progress), and when he visited, he brought with him news of the outside world and much-welcomed fresh fruit and bread. She hardly ever saw Dax. He had moved into the apprentice's dormitory at the ministry of magic to continue his studies. She belatedly realized she had missed his fourteenth birthday. Had anyone celebrated it with him? He was still just a boy.

Merta sat by the tiny hearth, quietly knitting a blanket for the baby. She smiled when Tregan crossed over to warm her hands. Merta had moved to the abbey with her, and they shared the single bed. She was a tender and caring soul, and her gentle ministrations and soft caresses kept Tregan's stress levels down. Tregan enjoyed Merta's stories of growing up the child of seaweed farmers in the middle of the desert, told in whispers late at night under the quilts. She derived much comfort there.

There was a quick rap on her chamber door, and Gwyn, the healing woman, let herself in, tucking in a few wisps of sandy hair that had escaped her headscarf. "Good morning, my lady. How do you feel today?" She opened her bag and began pulling out her equipment.

"The baby moves a lot." Tregan rubbed her belly. She liked Gwyn. The healer was pragmatic and informative, she didn't overexplain things, and she rebuffed all the religious and magical interventions that were suggested by overbearing bureaucrats. Gwyn was Tregan's first line of defense.

"That's good! Come lie down and let's have a look."

Merta excused herself, taking advantage of Gwyn's appearance to go down to the kitchen and bring back something to eat. Gwyn latched the door for privacy, and Tregan loosened her robe and lay down on the bed. Gwyn rubbed her hands together to warm them and applied gentle touch to various parts of her body, her forehead, her breasts, the sides of her belly. She took her pulse, counting out loud while consulting a timer. "I'm going inside now," she soothed, applying oil to her finger. There was a quick pressure and then it was over. "Everything looks very good, my dear." She smiled. "Let's listen to the baby now and see what it's up to." She took out a glass ear cup and warmed it for a second in her palm. "Where do you feel the movements?"

"Here." Tregan placed a hand near her navel. Gwyn put the ear cup on Tregan's belly and placed her ear against it. She listened for a long time. Then she moved the cup lower and listened again.

"Is everything—?" Tregan began.

"Shhhh, everything is fine. Be very still please." Gwyn moved the cup again and listened, this time closing her eyes. After a few moments, Gwyn's arm inadvertently jerked, and Tregan stiffened up in response.

"Don't move now." She placed the cup higher and listened. Moved the cup to the other side of her navel and listened. And listened again.

"What is the matter? Can't you hear it? It's been kicking all morning." Tregan started tearing up, even though it was irrational.

"Yes, my dear, I can hear it." Gwyn stood up, pocketing the ear cup. She sighed and frowned. "I can hear them."

"What?"

"Tregan, I hear two heartbeats."

CHAPTER 2

Tregan grabbed the healing woman by the wrist and squeezed hard. "Listen again. Maybe my stomach churned."

"I heard them clearly, my lady. You carry two souls inside you." Gwyn's eyes welled up with tears, and she trembled in Tregan's grip.

"You're wrong! You've made a mistake." She pushed the healer away, got up, and paced across the room, clenching her fists. This couldn't possibly be true. It was a nightmare. And what was Gwyn going to do now? Her job was to prevent this very thing from ever happening. The healer remained silent, dabbing her eyes with her apron.

Finally, Tregan stopped pacing and sank into a chair, putting her face in her palms. This was a disaster. She was bonded to her baby. She had already decided she would stay in Weslynde and raise the child no matter what; she was in love. She had pictured herself holding it, warm and snug, smelling its hair while it suckled her breast. She had created stories of their life together, mother and child, filled with joy and laughter. And now this! A second child, also hers, forcing its way into her heart more and more as each second passed, begging to be wanted, to be held, to be loved. She had two children, each bright and beautiful and worthy of life. And what was she to them? Their mother? No, she was merely a prison cell, holding one child who would live and one child who faced certain execution. She wanted to scream out loud. To hit something. To run away. She wished Gwyn would stop looking at her; she couldn't stand her pity.

There was a sharp knock at the door. Tregan locked eyes with Gwyn and put her hand to her mouth. Gwyn moved slowly, casting a furtive glance at Tregan as she went to open the door. The door unlatched and swung open of its own accord as she reached for it. The healer was forced back as Gerard Mort filled the doorway, black robes swirling. Following behind him were Bishop Rutter and a thin novice wearing a drab gray dress.

"Good morning, my lady," the house mage said, taking in the room quickly. "I was in the abbey and learned you had an examination scheduled. I am here to inquire about the child's progress before I meet with the king. Why did you have the door locked? What if there were a fire?" He turned to Gwyn without pausing for breath. "My dear, are you crying?"

Tregan stopped breathing, trying to slow time, clutching at the seconds that remained before she heard the death sentence Gwyn would deliver.

Gwyn wiped her face with her hands and smoothed down her apron. "Yes, my lord mage, I am afraid so." She managed a weak smile and quickly glanced at Tregan. "You see...this morning we heard the child's heartbeat; it beat clear and strong —I never get used to that moment. I am just an old softie at heart, I imagine."

"That is wonderful news," Gerard Mort said. "The king will be so pleased." He turned to Tregan. "Congratulations, my lady, you serve the commonwealth well. But why do you look so grim? Are you not also pleased?"

"Of course, lord mage. I am pleased indeed." Tregan lowered her eyes. "I am...overcome with the significance of this moment." Her heart pounded in her chest.

Gerard Mort studied the two of them carefully. Tregan remained still, wondering if his magic somehow discerned truth or if her body language would give her away. She straightened her posture and gazed at him with what she hoped was an expression of calm.

Another moment of dreadful silence passed, then the mage spoke. "I'm going to supply you with one of the abbey's novices. This is Amilee." Bishop Rutter pushed the novice, a tiny waif with stringy hair and brown circles under her eyes, into the room. "Amilee will be your attendant when Gwyn can't be by your side. Do you have a spare bed?"

"I already have an attendant. Merta is her name," Tregan replied. *Could things possibly get any worse?*

"You have a maid," the mage said derisively. "What you need is someone who can minister to you, keep your spirits uplifted."

"There isn't space for her in this tiny room, and Amilee doesn't look like she could lift anyone's spirits." Tregan didn't care if she offended the girl or not.

The mage chuckled. "Ah, Tregan, you are always ready with a jest."

"We can make the necessary accommodations," Bishop Rutter assured him.

"Perfect. Then it's settled." Gerard Mort patted Tregan's stiff shoulder. "I must go. Congratulations again on the good news." He swirled out of the room, quickly followed by the bishop. The door closed of its own accord.

Amilee hugged herself into a corner, shrinking under Tregan's crushing glare. Silence hung in the air.

Gwyn was the first to speak. "Well then, Amilee. Why are you standing there? Make yourself useful; go and fetch us a pitcher of water, and get some fresh citrus from the kitchen; we need vitamins for the baby. Hurry!"

Amilee fled.

Tregan rose and went to Gwyn; they clasped hands. "What are you going to do?" Tregan asked, still confused by this temporary reprieve.

"I'm not sure," replied Gwyn. "All I know is these are your children, and you should have a say over what happens to them and when. I would want that if I were in your place."

"Thank you." Her voice shook.

"And understand this," Gwyn added, gently placing her hand on Tregan's cheek. "I will support you however you need me to. Do you understand?"

Tregan nodded as the tears began sliding down her face. Gwyn pulled her close and held her tightly.

⚜

Tregan and Gwyn did not speak of the twins again. They continued on as before, but now Tregan would not allow another physician to touch her.

To keep anyone from getting suspicious, Gwyn doubled down on her reporting, documenting Tregan's every statistic: weight, skin tone, nipple size, diet, sleep patterns, discharges, and mood changes. She made sure to share her notes with Gerard Mort as well as the other physicians in the palace. She flattered them all, asking for their opinions and insisting they remain close by, available at a moment's notice, in case she needed help. Tregan marveled at the healer's confidence and composure.

The weeks raced by, and Tregan's belly swelled. A closet was cleared out and a mattress placed inside for Amilee, who was obviously Gerard Mort's spy. She was easy enough to manage; Gwyn would not allow the girl to be in the room during examinations, telling her she might carry diseases, and Tregan took great satisfaction in sending the girl on countless errands. She kept the twins a secret from everyone, even Merta. She cringed one night when, as they lay in bed, Merta felt the babies kicking against her back. She had said it felt like an army in there.

By midsummer, Tregan had made up her mind that somehow, someway, both babies would live. She would need help to make that impossible feat happen, so she invited Rence, the smartest person she knew, to meet with her and ordered a light meal for two set out on a balcony near her room. It was shaded from the hot afternoon sun, and, like everything else in the abbey, it was small, so there wouldn't be room for anyone else but the two of them, especially Amilee. Rence arrived on time as always, holding his notebook as if he knew he would need to take notes.

"My lady, you look well; in fact, you look as if you are ready to give birth today!" He smiled as he buttered his bread.

"It feels that way, to tell you the truth." She paused, suddenly fearful that Rence would reveal her secret to the king. All would be lost if that were to happen. She was no longer hungry and pushed her plate away.

"What is it?" Rence asked, his butter knife poised in midair.

Tregan composed herself. It was either this or nothing. She leaned in and spoke softly. "Rence, we've not much time, and I have much to say that must remain private between us. I am aware you report everything to the king, but in this instance...I think you are my friend. Are you my friend? Can I trust you?"

Rence put down his bread and knife. "Speak freely. I am at your service."

She saw sincerity in his eyes and forged ahead. "A calamity has occurred. A calamity and a miracle." She froze for a moment, and Rence nodded, encouraging her. "Rence, I carry two children. I carry twins." She faltered again as Rence's eyes widened. "I know this is impossible, but both babies must live. I must save them. I must. I need your help."

"Does anyone else know?"

"Only my healing woman, and she has proven to be an ally."

"By the gods, my lady, this is sobering news indeed." He sat back and said nothing for what seemed an eternity, drumming his fingers on the arms of his chair.

Tregan started to despair, but then he spoke.

"How can I help?"

She realized she had been holding her breath. "I have a plan, but I don't know how to execute it. It will require support from you, Merta, and Dax."

Rence quaffed his wine in one gulp and placed his hand on hers. "Tell me your plan."

Tregan's idea was to be alone in the birthing room with Gwyn and Merta when the babies came. When the first baby was delivered, Merta would take it and leave Caleddon without being seen. Dax would be on hand to help her get the baby out of the city. They would take the baby far away where no one would ever find it, perhaps to Merta's home country of Cordel. The second baby would then be presented to the king as the only child, named heir, and raised in the palace.

"And where will you go? Which child will you follow?" Rence asked gently.

"My heart will be in both places at once. After I wean the baby, I think the best choice would be to return to Argonne, as is my right. Then, at some safe point in the future, seek out Merta and the first child and be its mother. My heart breaks at the thought of leaving the other one here, but it will be protected and raised well. Franklin is a good father."

Rence sat very still for a few moments, his eyes boring into hers. Then he picked up his fork and stabbed at his food, placed a bite in his mouth, and started chewing.

"There are a million things that could go wrong, of course," he said through a full mouth. "Not least of which is the fact that you are the most watched person in the world, and you live sequestered in an abbey, effectively under house arrest!" He poured more wine and washed his food down. "Then there are the logistics. Everyone must be in the right place at the right time for your plan to work, transportation at the ready, iron-clad cover stories in place."

Tregan smiled as he sawed at his meat, caught up in his enthusiasm.

"There can't be a leak. I daresay no one can breathe a word between now and when the babies are due, and then"—he waved his fork in the air—"the riskiest part of all is that these babies don't know the plan. They could be born anytime, any day, anywhere!"

"That's not the worst part," she said with a wry smile. "The worst part is the curse of the twins. When the babies are born, will there be a plague? Will the moon fall from the sky? Will the ground part beneath our feet?"

"There is that," Rence mused.

"I was joking."

"So was I. No serious academic believes in the royal twin curse, you know. Twins didn't send the salt sea into Weslynde. The volcano sitting underneath us burped; that's all. Earth tremors happen all the time. Dax studies them at magic school; he has to be able to locate the weak spots underground in order to pass his earth-magic training."

"If the curse is not true, then why would Franklin go along with it?" Tregan asked. "Why would he let his child be killed?"

"Because the church says it's true, and therefore, the people believe it. Franklin won't do anything that would jeopardize his control over the people, even if it means preserving a myth."

Though this wasn't a surprise to her, Tregan was stunned to hear it spoken out loud.

"The existence of twins would lead to a revolt," Rence continued. "And the king won't allow that to happen. Franklin can never know this."

"You don't offer much hope," Tregan said quietly.

"There's always hope, and you, my dear Tregan, are very strong," Rence said tenderly, reaching across the table and squeezing her hand. "Now, no matter what else happens, we must keep this information from ever making it to the church; they would burn the palace to the ground. And can you do something about that blasted Amilee? That girl is always lurking about, cleaning in the corners, rearranging the furniture,"

Tregan made a face that showed Rence exactly what she thought of Amilee.

Rence chuckled, then went on. "I will speak with Merta and Dax directly—do not communicate this news to them; wait to hear from me. By the gods, I hope your healing woman remains true." He rubbed his hands together. "Of course, our biggest problem is Gerard Mort, the house mage. He has the ear of the king, and he will exploit any weakness to his own advantage." He wadded up his napkin and threw it on his plate. "Now I must go; there is much to do. Stay strong."

They stepped over to the balcony door. Rence opened it on Amilee, who was standing behind it. She pushed in between them and began to clear the table.

How long has she been standing there? Tregan thought. *How loud were we?* She exchanged glances with Rence, but he winked at her and rolled his eyes skyward.

CHAPTER 3

F all came early to Weslynde. The few remaining grape leaves clinging tenaciously to the abbey walls turned red in protest. The air smelled of wood-smoke, and the nights brought frost that patterned the glass on the abbey windows. Tregan pushed open her narrow window as the morning sun touched the glass, letting the icy air into the stuffy room. It felt good on her face, and she took a deep breath; it froze the hairs inside her nostrils, but she didn't care. She was due in three weeks, but Gwyn had warned her to be ready—the birth could happen at any time. The babies kicked her in the ribs and made it impossible to sleep. She imagined they were fighting each other for the best position—not a pleasant thought.

It seemed to her a miracle that no one could tell she was carrying twins. She felt enormous. Rence had whispered to her that Dax and Merta were prepared, but her attendant had never spoken of it until two nights ago. As they'd lain in bed together, Merta had placed her hand on Tregan's belly and kissed her forehead, whispering, "I'm ready." They'd wiped each other's tears away in the dark. Amilee, whom they had assumed was asleep in the alcove, had risen up like a specter in the moonlight shining through the window and asked, "Is something amiss, my lady?"

Chilled by the memory, Tregan closed the window and pulled her shawl close. Merta was sitting next to the fire, fixing a hem. Amilee was kneeling in her alcove, praying to the stump of a candle. Tregan gave a slight shudder at the sight and took the other chair near the fire. She closed her eyes, thinking about the strange meeting she'd had with the king the day before.

Yesterday morning, there had been an unexpected knock on her door. A palace guard stood there, waiting to take her to the king. It was the first time she had been allowed out of the abbey and the first time she had seen Franklin since she had been sequestered. She nodded slightly when she saw the king and kept her face impassive, not giving him the satisfaction of knowing how she felt, while inside she raged and imagined hitting him with her bare knuckles.

Franklin acted as if nothing unusual were happening, took her unwilling hand, and ushered her into a small room. She was surprised to find Gerard Mort inside waiting for them. She took the offered chair, and the house mage presented her with a tray holding two metal rings, each about the size of a peach stone. They were sigils, infused with charms.

"One of these rings will be embedded in your child's shoulder, marking the child as the heir to the throne. The sigil will provide your child with enhanced abilities and protections befitting the sovereign." Gerard Mort held up the silver tray so she could examine the rings closely. Filling the space inside each metallic band was an intricate lacework of black metal symbols and words that seemed to float in the air like a spiderweb. The calligraphy woven into the mesh was stunning, created out of metal wires no thicker than a thread. When she looked closely, she could just make out how the metal mesh was attached to the bands themselves. "Once the ring is embedded, only the scrollwork suspended in the middle will remain visible on the surface of the skin."

Tregan had seen Franklin's sigil, of course, and had always thought that it was a tattoo inked across his shoulder blade. "Why have you made two of these?" Tregan asked warily, sensing danger in every corner.

"Two sigils are always made in advance," Gerard Mort explained. "One is forged with elements and laced with charms that are compatible with a male child, the other with a female. Whichever one matches the sex of the baby is embedded; the other is melted down and destroyed."

Tregan read the names that had been wrought into the scrollwork. "Jarin né Franklin. Sabrin né Franklin. Who chose these names?"

"They are named after my ancestors," the king said. "Both famous warriors in their day. Jarin for a boy, Sabrin for a girl."

Tregan picked up Jarin's sigil. It was cold and surprisingly heavy. She ran her finger over the black filigree suspended in the middle of the ring. It felt like a sieve you would find in the pantry. The band itself glittered green gold when she turned it; it was curious indeed.

"What metal is this?" she asked.

"It is from a meteor—a sky stone," Gerard Mort replied. "Sky metal has special properties that benefit the ruler bearing the sigil."

"These symbols and runes. What do they represent?"

"Each is a character trait written in old majik. The symbols were chosen by King Franklin. They stand for power, integrity, and courage."

"It is an interesting custom," Tregan said. "I like the words you chose, Franklin, but I might have added compassion and ... humility." She aimed this last word at Gerard Mort.

"It is more than a custom, my lady," Gerard Mort said icily, affronted by her apparent dismissal of the sigil's importance.

"The royal sigil provides the bearer with protections and also gives them power to influence those around them. It amplifies the bearer's natural gifts. This has proved to be a decisive advantage to the sovereign throughout Weslynde's history: when rallying troops before a battle, gaining consensus in the senate, responding to a crisis."

"I see." Tregan set the sigil back on the tray, not liking the mage's tone of voice.

"These two sigils were created by the high wizard in Riddien," the mage went on. "And they have been blessed by Archbishop Mellon, leader of the Church of the Commonwealth. His blessing means the ruler bearing the sigil has the trust and support of the church. Do you see the importance now?"

Tregan kept her face still while Gerard Mort berated her. She glanced over at Franklin for some support, but he was nodding along with the mage. Why did he always seem so passive in front of Gerard Mort?

"How does the ring get inside the baby's body? Tregan asked. "Will it hurt?"

"Only a handful of high mages have the power to fuse a sigil with a person's body. The high wizard of Riddien has the power, of course, as do I. I will embed the sigil when the baby is born. The ring will adhere to the baby's shoulder blade."

"But will it hurt?" she asked again.

"No, my lady. The baby won't feel a thing."

"Are we done here?" the king interrupted, scraping his chair back and standing. Gerard Mort nodded, and King Franklin abruptly left the room.

Tregan tried not to visibly react to Franklin's sudden departure. She thanked Gerard Mort for enlightening her and made her way back to the abbey, trailed by Amilee and another novice assigned to escort Tregan. She remained unsettled the rest of the day and lay awake all night. She kept picturing Gerard Mort's gnarled hand with its age spots and split nails on the back of her baby, pressing the metal sigil down into its shoulder blade. Would it burn? Would the baby cry out? And what about the second child, the secret child, who would receive no powers or protections? What was to become of that child? Of Tregan? Of all of them?

That was yesterday. Now Tregan sat by the fire, wrapped in her shawl, cheeks tingling from the cold, contemplating for the thousandth time what was to come. She shook off her gloom and stood in front of the hearth, rubbing her hands together.

"Merta, would you bring us all some tea?"

"I'll do it, my lady." Amilee sprang to her feet.

"Thank you, but no. I would like Merta to do this; she knows how I like it."

Amilee bowed her head, and Merta set her sewing aside and started to leave. Tregan bent down and put a log in the fire. As she straightened, liquid trickled down her leg.

"Oh," she uttered softly, startled.

"What is it?" Merta said by the door.

"Something ... I'm not sure; I think..." She held back her skirts; a small pool of liquid was expanding around her foot on the hearth.

"The baby!" Merta cried in alarm and put her hands over her mouth. Amilee saw her fear, and her eyes widened.

This won't do, Tregan thought. "Amilee, go now and find the healing woman. Do not stop and talk to anyone on the way."

"Yes, my lady."

"Stop for no one; talk to no one. You must hurry as if your life depended on it. Do you understand?"

Amilee nodded.

"Now go."

Amilee fled.

"My lady." Merta rushed over to Tregan and took her by the hands. "Oh, my lady, the babies are early; what do we do?" Panic filled her voice.

Tregan needed Merta to be calm. "Merta, look at me. If you do what I say, everything will be fine. Go find Rence and tell him the baby is coming. You must go as quickly as you can and return to me before the king and others find out the news from Amilee. She will squawk as soon as she is able."

"What about—"

"Go and come back to me quickly. I trust you, and I need you by my side. And, Merta, do not say the word 'babies' again. I am having one baby. One."

Merta kissed her hand and ran out of the room. Tregan shut the door, found a cloth, and wiped up the hearth. Then she went to the bathing room and washed herself off. She looked at herself in front of the mirror and placed her hands on her belly. "Give me the strength of the gods," she whispered. "I must save them or die in the attempt." She tied a fresh robe around herself and noticed her hands were shaking. She lay back on her bed and stared at the ceiling, and she was willing herself to remain calm when she was seized by a strong contraction.

"Curse the gods," she moaned, blowing out slowly.

Merta returned with Gwyn on her heels. The healing woman felt between her legs and said, "By the gods, you are almost fully open; it won't be but a few hours before you will need to push."

Merta gave her a slight nod in affirmation and a reassuring smile. Tregan's body flooded with relief. Rence had been alerted. The plan was in motion.

Gwyn and Merta went about preparing the tiny bedchamber behind Tregan's sitting room to serve as the birthing room. While they were propping Tregan up on the bed, the door to the front room opened and Tregan heard the king's voice. He appeared at the bedchamber door, followed by Gerard Mort, Bishop Rutter, and Amilee, but Gwyn blocked their way.

"Only the king," she instructed. She let Franklin enter and

glared at the others, shutting the bedchamber's door in their faces.

"My lord." Tregan smiled tentatively, suddenly afraid. Franklin was not part of the plan.

"My dear Tregan." The king sat beside her on the bed and took her hand in his. "You look lovely, and you will be wonderful at this."

Tregan didn't know what to make of this sudden tenderness. He'd been so cold for months.

"And don't worry; I am an old hand at birthing babies." He smiled affectionately. "Clare gave birth to Lowden in a tent while we were out hunting. It was just me and the healing woman there with her. I caught the baby in my hands. I promise you I won't leave your side."

"Oh, no, my lord," faltered Tregan, her plan crumbling into ruin. "I will be well attended by Merta and the healing woman."

"Nonsense. Nothing could drag me from your side."

Tregan attempted a smile and placed her hand on top of Franklin's. Gwyn continued to fold cloths and scrub tools. Merta stood in a corner in horrified silence.

"Well, it's going to be a while, Your Majesty," Gwyn said matter-of-factly. "I hope you brought something to read." Tregan marveled at her coolness.

A patch of sunlight slowly crossed the room as the contractions grew stronger and closer together. Tregan buried her panic deep inside while the women worked quietly, soothing her, helping her walk around the room, wiping her brow. Franklin sat on a stool and told her stories about his babies and gave her words of encouragement. The sun set behind the Cordel Mountains, and Merta lit a few candles that contained a soothing herb.

⚜

Outside Tregan's bedchamber, Gerard Mort began to prepare the sigils. He instructed the king's guards, who were positioned in front of the bedchamber door, to move a side table to the middle of the room. He covered the table with fine fabric and set the two sigils on a plate of gold in its center. Bishop Rutter led the small group in prayer and silent meditation, while Gerard Mort breathed slowly in and out, hands folded on his chest, summoning the calm and focus he would need to successfully modify the structures of the baby's flesh and bones.

⚜

Inside the birthing room, Tregan was starting to panic. She really needed to push. She locked eyes with Gwyn and fought back tears as another contraction doubled her over.

"I can't," she moaned.

"You can; you are strong." encouraged Franklin, smoothing her brow and kissing her hand. "When can she push?" he asked Gwyn.

"Not yet, my lord. Not yet." Gwyn's voice was calm and authoritative.

There was a loud knock on the bedchamber door. Merta went over and cracked it open. A strong hand pushed it open from the other side.

"Your Majesty." One of the house guards stuck his head in the room. "There is an emergency."

"What emergency?" hissed the king.

"A fire at the grain silos. A big one. The grain reserve is threatened, as are other supplies nearby."

Rence, Tregan thought. She exhaled slowly and reached for Gwyn's hand.

"Curse the gods," the king swore. "I am sorry, my dear, but I must go. I have no choice. Once things are secured, I will return to your side."

"Go, my lord. Save the grain; I will be fine." Tregan reached out her hand and squeezed his. "When you return, you will have an heir."

The king left the bedchamber, followed by the guard. Tregan let her head fall back against the pillow, exhausted.

Gwyn put her head out the door and told the room, "No one enters." She pushed back a protesting Amilee who was trying to enter and shut the door in her face and latched it. "Move Tregan to the birthing chair," she ordered Merta. "Quickly, there's no more time!"

Things happened very fast. Tregan dug her fingers into the arms of the birthing chair, finally able to push. She yelled as the pain and pressure overcame her.

"Very good my lady, very good. I can feel the head. Merta, get ready."

Merta pulled a large kit bag out from under the bed and laid out cloths and insulating blankets to receive the first child. Tregan yelled again.

"Push now, my lady; push hard," Gwyn said.

Tregan bore down and let out a deep groan. The healing woman squatted in front of Tregan and caught the child as she pushed it from her womb.

"A girl," she whispered.

Tregan mouthed, "Sabrin," helpless with fear as Gwyn quickly stuffed the newborn's mouth with fabric to prevent her from taking her first breath and making a noise. She handed Sabrin to Merta, who was waiting for her, holding out a clean wrap. Gwyn tied and cut the cord and helped Merta swaddle the baby and place her in the bag.

"Quickly, quickly," whispered Gwyn.

Merta cracked open the narrow window, too small for a person to get through; a shadow moved outside. Tregan craned her neck to try to see, her heart pounding as Gwyn reached into the baby's mouth and removed the fabric.

"Breathe," the healer whispered. The baby didn't move. Gwyn blew on her face, and after a tense moment, the baby reacted, inhaling and screwing up her red face to yell. Gwyn threw the flap across the top of the bag, muffling her cries. Merta lifted the bag onto the window ledge; it seemed too big to fit, but she pushed it forward. A shadowy hand grabbed the bag's handle, and then it was gone, vanishing into the night air. Merta closed the window and checked to make sure that nothing was disturbed.

Tregan wept openly, overwhelmed with loss. "My Sabrin. I didn't even get to hold her."

Gwyn hissed in her ear, "You will be with her soon. Now yell. Yell loudly. There can't be any gaps in sounds."

Tregan pressed down and released a guttural roar, bolstered by the grief that filled her soul.

"Good, good. Now this time push, my lady."

A few minutes later, Tregan delivered the second baby, a boy. "Jarin," she whispered as Gwyn laid him on her chest. "My son." She kissed the top of his head as he cried lustily and loudly.

Outside the chamber, clamors of joy and excitement went up. Gwyn tied and cut the cord as someone banged on the door.

"Present the child!" Gerard Mort yelled through the door.

"Take him," Gwyn ordered Merta. "I must stay and tend to Tregan."

Tregan reluctantly handed Merta the baby, who cradled him and took him out to the front room, wiping his face and body with a clean cloth as she went.

⚜

"Good people, the heir is a boy." Merta sobbed as she came out with the baby, her happiness and her sadness spilling out of her all at once. Amilee clapped her hands in joy, startling the baby, who flailed his hands and legs and started crying again.

"Bring him here and place him face down," Gerard Mort ordered. He took the girl's sigil from the plate, the one with Sabrin's name on it, and casually tossed it into the fire burning in the hearth. Then he took the plate still holding the other sigil, the one that bore Jarin's name, and held it aloft with both hands.

Merta placed Jarin face down on the table. The baby cried in protest, his naked body coming in contact with the cold stone. His arms and legs made spasmodic movements. She tried to comfort him, but the house mage elbowed her out of the way. She melted back into a corner by the hearth. The candles suddenly blew themselves out, and the light from the fire, the only light in the room, made dancing shadows on the ceiling. Everyone crowded around Gerard Mort and the table. Merta found herself pushed up against the wall. She noticed a shiny ring on the floor next to the hearth, reflecting the fire-light. The discarded sigil! It must have bounced off the logs in the fire and landed outside the hearth. Without thinking, she reached down and took it, stuffing it in her apron. Amilee was staring at her. Had she seen it? Merta turned away quicky, heart pounding.

⚜

Gerard Mort took Jarin's sigil from the plate and raised it in the air, blessing it with a chant in old majik, then placed it on Jarin's tiny shoulder. Behind him, Bishop Rutter said a prayer of consecration and began humming a dissonant melody; the others in the room joined in. Gerard Mort closed his eyes and pressed the heel of his palm onto the sigil. He shivered a little as he focused his energy and felt the baby's skin around the ring soften and separate, allowing the ring to sink through the skin into the body. The skin reformed over the ring, leaving the sigil's mesh symbols visible on the baby's skin. The baby Jarin grew quiet and seemed not to feel anything. The mage bent over and placed his forehead close to the sigil, willing the soft bone of the newborn's shoulder blade to rearrange itself around the ring and embed the ring deep into the bone. He felt a surge of energy pass through him into the baby. The fusion was complete.

Gerard Mort picked up Jarin and held him in the air. A perfectly round black emblem, the mark of the heir, stood out prominently against the baby's brown skin, like an intricate tattoo. The room let out a collective sigh. He handed Jarin off to Merta, who still stood by the fire. Amilee ran over and pressed up against her, marveling over the baby.

"Bring out the healing woman," the mage said.

Gwyn came out of the bedchamber, wiping her hands.

"Prepare to depart; we must present the heir to the king."

"I cannot leave the mother now." Gwyn scowled at him. "There has been some tearing that needs to be mended."

"Then you bring the babe," Gerard Mort ordered Merta. The guards closed in around Merta, who was still holding Jarin, and Amilee, who clung to her arm.

"And where do you plan on taking him?" Gwyn snapped, planting her feet in front of the mage. "Out in the cold night air with the buildings burning and all? And why are you still here? You're the house mage, aren't you? Shouldn't you be helping the king?"

Gerard Mort sputtered.

Gwyn went on, not pausing for breath. "You can tell the king to meet his son here when he is able—he's not going anywhere." She didn't wait for a response and put her hand on Merta's arm. "I need your help. And the rest of you lot need to leave us now;

the baby needs quiet." Merta, holding Jarin, followed Gwyn through the bedchamber door, and Amilee followed behind.

Gwyn stopped Amilee at the door. "No, no, dear. You stay out here and clean up."

"Woman, give the baby to Amilee," Gerard Mort ordered, dark eyes glittering. "The heir will remain in the sight of these guards at all times."

Merta somewhat reluctantly handed Jarin to Amilee.

Gwyn gave Amilee a motherly smile. "Lady Tregan needs you to watch the prince and keep him safe. You can sit in that rocking chair by the fire. We will call you when it is time for you to bring him to meet his mother."

Amilee went over to the rocking chair and sat down, beaming.

"No one comes in or goes out," Gerard Mort told the guards. "Amilee! Make sure that child remains safe and secure. Your life is forfeit if you don't." With a final look at the bedchamber door, he spun on his heel and left.

⚜

Gwyn closed the bedchamber door behind her, shutting herself and Merta inside with Tregan.

"Where is my baby?" Tregan asked anxiously.

"Outside the door with Amilee. He is safe," Gwyn soothed.

"The room is filled with guards," Merta whispered, taking Tregan's hand. "Amilee is suspicious."

"One thing at a time, child," Gwyn admonished. "Amilee won't harm the baby, and the plan is not yet complete. Now, I need both of you to help. The afterbirths need to be delivered. There are two because the twins are not identical. Merta, once they are delivered, I need you to dispose of them so that no one sees there is more than one."

Merta nodded and started pulling the soiled bedding into a pile.

"And drink this." Gwyn handed Merta a vial full of milky blue liquid.

"What is it?" Merta asked.

"It's a medication that will start your breast milk flowing. That baby girl will be hungry when you catch up to her."

Merta's eyes widened, and she swallowed it down.

"Merta, come here." Tregan reached out and took Merta's hand. "It's time for you to go. Promise me you will love her as if she were your own child. And tell her that I love her too and that someday I will be with her again."

"I will, my lady; I promise." Merta's face broke. "I wish you were coming with us."

"I do as well, but the game must play itself out. Oh, but my heart is breaking. Now go, while you still can."

"What about Amilee?" Merta asked.

"We'd best not let her out of our sight," Gwyn replied. "Whatever she suspects, she mustn't have an opportunity to share it with the mage." She delivered the second afterbirth and wiped her hands on a cloth. "Well done, my lady, well done."

Merta gathered up the birthing tissues inside a sheet, rolled the sheet in a ball, and stuffed it in a pail. She hugged Tregan one last time, then went to the door and invited Amilee to bring the baby in. Merta picked up the pail and started to slip out behind Amilee, but one of the guards had followed Amilee through the door and pushed Merta back inside. He closed the door and stood in front of it, arms crossed. Merta's eyes were bright with fright. Gwyn patted her arm, signaling her to wait and be patient.

Amilee handed Jarin back to Tregan, who folded him into the crook of her arm. "My baby, my Jarin," she crooned, kissing his fuzzy black head again and again. The baby nuzzled against her, and silent tears of joy ran down her face.

There was loud knock at the door. The guard opened it and stepped aside. Another guard entered.

"We have new orders from the king," he said. "You are to be moved to your rooms in the palace. Immediately. A carriage awaits; gather your things."

"A few more minutes are needed here," Gwyn said, firmly.

"You have five."

Amilee started to follow the guard out the door, but Gwyn stopped her.

"Stay and help, Amilee. We need you to carry the baby." She smiled sweetly. "You are so good with him."

Amilee lit up and took the baby from Tregan. Merta quickly gathered up the things they needed to bring, and Gwyn helped Tregan, who was still a little wobbly, to her feet. The healing woman ordered the two guards to carry Tregan to the carriage waiting outside the abbey. Once Tregan was aboard, several more guards who had been waiting for them formed a circle around the carriage.

Amilee handed Jarin up to Tregan and then climbed up and sat next to her, taking the only empty seat.

"I'll walk beside the carriage, then," Gwyn muttered, rolling her eyes. "The exercise will do me good."

Tregan's anxiety grew stronger as each minute slid by. It was past the time for Merta to meet up with Dax, who was waiting for her somewhere out there with Sabrin. She tried not to dwell on the fact that she had entrusted the life of her baby girl to a fourteen-year-old boy, magician's apprentice or not. She shot Gwyn an anxious frown, and Gwyn nodded back.

"Merta!" Gwyn exclaimed, as if she had suddenly remembered something, loud enough for the guards to hear. "I need you to run to the abbey kitchen as quick as you can and fetch some tea leaves—the dark ones infused with the peppermint. Tregan will need them to help her milk come in."

"I will go," Amilee volunteered, jumping down off the carriage.

"No, my dear," Gwyn said, grabbing her by the shoulder. "You stay here with Jarin. You are so good with him. Merta can do this."

Merta bobbed her head. "I will return with them shortly."

"No," Gwyn insisted. "Send one of the kitchen staff back with them. You have been on your legs all day, and I need you fresh in the morning so that I can get a rest. Stay here in the abbey tonight and get some sleep."

"But—"

Tregan reached down and squeezed Merta's hand. "That's an order from me. Amilee will take care of all our needs." She smiled reassuringly. "Don't worry; I will see you soon."

Tears welled up in Merta's eyes. She let go of Tregan's hand and pushed between the guards surrounding the carriage.

The gods keep you safe until we meet again, Tregan thought as Merta disappeared through the abbey door. *Take good care of my little girl for me*. She kept her face composed and turned back to Jarin, who was fussing in her arms. As she did so, she caught sight of Amilee talking to one of the guards.

"Amilee!" she shouted in alarm. "Come here and help me with this baby. You can't run off like that. I need you by my side at all times!"

CHAPTER 4

A homing lizard slithered under the door, darted across the dormitory room, and scrambled up Dax's leg, wrapping itself tightly around his arm. He unwound the lizard and unfolded the message tied to its neck. It contained only one word: "now." He stroked the lizard's head with his finger and whispered, "Good girl." He slipped it in the cage with the others, and it settled on the hot water pipe, turning a rusty brown to match it. Dax made sure the room was empty (his roommates had gone to dinner and he was about to join them). Then he knelt down, grabbed his pack out from under his cot, and pulled out the inky-black cloak he had stolen from the armory.

It hadn't been that hard to steal. The armory door had an old mortise-style lock, and when he'd put his hand on the knob and closed his eyes, it had been easy to suss out the inner mechanism. Once he'd had the shape of it in his head, he'd put his finger over the keyhole and concentrated, listening as the deadbolt slowly slid back. He'd slipped in, pulled the cloak over his shoulders, and slipped out again. A few months ago, he had discovered that if he concentrated hard enough, he could move small objects with only a thought, something very few magicians could pull off, especially one as young as he was. He hadn't told anyone and had been practicing in private, improving his skill.

Dax put on the cloak and hood. He untied the soft mask hidden under the hood and pulled it down over his face. He quietly slipped out of his dormitory room and ghosted down the hallway toward the exit. An instructor, a master in earth magic, appeared out of a side hall, and Dax quickly pressed himself into a corner. The instructor didn't see him as he passed by, even though he was no more than an arm's length from Dax.

Six concealment cloaks had been created by the high wizard of Riddien. One had been lost to fire and five remained. No other wizard or mage had ever been able to summon the magic required to recreate the cloaks. The cloaks didn't make the wearer completely invisible; it made them unnoticeable. They were made out of light-absorbing tenebrous plant fibers and strengthened with charms, tricking the eye into thinking they were seeing something else. They were one of Caleddon's great treasures, and permission to use them was granted by the king himself. The one Dax had stolen would be discovered missing before long and the dorms would be searched. He intended to be far away from Caleddon before that happened.

Dax made his way out of the dormitory and zigzagged down through the city's many side streets to the abbey, avoiding the more populated areas. Once there, he scaled the rock wall surrounding the enclave, sussing out cracks he could use as handholds and toeholds. There was a heart-pounding moment when a stone came loose in his hand and he had to scrabble around frantically for a new handhold, but once he reached the top, he made his way unnoticed across the rooftops to the window outside Tregan's room. There he made a harness out of the rope he had brought in his pack, wrapped it around a sturdy chimney pipe, and lowered himself down next to her window. It was fully dark now, and there was no moon. The cloak concealed him from anyone who might have thought to look up three floors. He tied himself off and waited.

While he hung suspended in the air, Dax thought about the last time he had seen Tregan; it had been after Rence had told him about her twins and Dax's part in the plan to save them. He had passed Tregan in the abbey courtyard while running an errand for Rence. When Tregan saw him, she dismissed the novice who was with her and pulled him into a small prayer garden. She took him by both hands and looked deep into his eyes. He was startled by the urgency he saw there.

"Dax, I charge you with the care of my children," she had said. "I charge you to live and die in service to them. Swear to me you will."

She had a quaver in her voice he'd never heard before. She had been so good to him, and he wanted to protect her any way he could.

"I swear, my lady," he whispered fiercely. "I swear it gladly. I would give my life in service to you."

Tregan folded him into her arms and squeezed him, then held him out at arm's length. "I don't know when we will meet again," she said. "Don't be afraid of your power, Dax. Use it. You are stronger than you realize."

"My lady?" The novice who had been walking with her had entered the garden.

"Goodbye, my young friend," she whispered and broke away, linking elbows with the novice and strolling away down the path, laughing carelessly about something he couldn't hear.

The rope was beginning to cut off the feeling in his legs when the narrow window next to him opened outward with a creak and a kit bag appeared on the ledge. It was too dark for him to see who was pushing it. He kicked off the wall and swung over to the window. He grabbed the bag by its handle and yanked. It resisted at first then scraped free. He kicked off again and swung out in the air, bag dangling from his hand. He held his feet out in front of him, and when he touched the wall again, he steadied himself in place. He fastened the bag to his shoulder strap and began rappelling down the abbey wall. When he reached the garden below, he put both hands on the rope and sussed the knot he had tied around the chimney pipe above, closed his eyes, and concentrated. The rope fell free, making a thupping noise as it coiled at his feet. He turned around quickly to be sure no one had seen him and sighed in relief.

As Dax stuffed the rope into his pack, muffled cries grew louder from inside the kit bag. He had no idea what to do about it other than make sure that air was getting in, so he loosened its straps, grabbed the bag by the handle, and sprinted across the garden, past the meditation fountain, to a side gate that opened to the abbey's orchard and fields beyond. The gate was locked, but he had been expecting that. He put his hand on the gate handle and sussed the locking mechanism, but the spring was broken and the cylinder had rusted shut. He couldn't unlock it. He rattled the gate and tried again, but it was point-less. He fought down his panic and considered climbing over the wall but didn't think he could manage a rope free climb with the baby.

Dax looked around wildly and saw that he was not far from the main gate, which was standing open, but unfortunately, two clerics loitered in front of it in the torchlight, talking. He placed his trust in the cloak and crept silently along the wall toward the gate. The clerics continued chatting and laughing. They were oblivious to his approach, but he knew he couldn't get past them without being seen. The baby started to fuss, and they would hear it if he moved any closer. Beyond the clerics was an apple tree growing inside the wall, late apples still clinging to the branches. Maybe he could knock one loose somehow and make a noise. The tree was pretty far away, and he had never tried to reach that distance with his mind, but he couldn't think of anything else. Heart thumping in his chest, he tried sussing the tree, but he couldn't make it out. He squeezed his eyes shut and tried again. It didn't work. Now he was trapped, and to his dismay, the baby started to wail in full-throated anger from inside the bag.

"No no no no," he whispered into the flap as the baby's wails grew louder. One of the clerics turned at the sound, and Dax panicked. His body stiffened, and his mind sent out an involuntary pulse, causing all the trees in the courtyard to shake and snap violently, sending every apple and even a few branches crashing to the ground. He stood open-mouthed in shocked surprise as the two men ran off to investigate. Seeing his chance, he sped through the open gate behind them and tore up the pathway toward the palace where Rence waited for him.

⚜

Rence was waiting for him on the terrace outside his office. Holding a finger to his lips, he motioned Dax to follow him inside. They moved to an inner room with no windows. Rence closed the door and lit a candle.

"Well done." Rence smiled and squeezed his shoulder. He took the bag from Dax and opened it, letting the baby's lusty cries ring out.

"Ooh, you are mad and I don't blame you." Rence picked up the baby and cradled it, making shushing noises to calm it. "Let's see what we have here." He laid the baby down on the table and unswaddled it. "A girl! A fine healthy girl. Ten fingers, ten toes. Red hair? Well, that is something unexpected."

Dax noticed something else. Tregan's complexion was very brown, darker than an acorn. Franklin's skin was pale and freckled, but this baby was the color of snow. Her skin was translucent, and a lattice of faint blue veins traced paths beneath its surface. Her eyes were an uncanny shade of blue. The baby's face and chest flushed pink, and she started to wail again.

"Here, Dax, you hold her," Rence said, handing him the baby. "That's right, like that. Put your finger in her mouth and let her suck on it. Is it clean? No matter, just do it. Sit down, boy, sit down!"

Dax sat and held the baby out stiffly. She felt like a wobbly sack of potatoes, and her head lolled back. He cradled her head with his hand and narrowed his eyes suspiciously at Rence, then put his forefinger in her mouth. She quieted and started sucking on it. It felt very weird, and he was slightly embarrassed.

"She's an albine," Rence said. "That portends something good."

"An albine?"

"Her white skin. That is rare. Albines are thought to be blessed. Some think them equal to saints."

"She's so little." Dax ran a finger through her bright red hair.

"Your life is about to change, my lad," Rence said. "Now listen to me carefully. Moments ago, I received word that Tregan and the other baby, a boy, by the way, are coming here, to the palace. It is time for you to go." He took the rope out of Dax's pack and loaded supplies into it, including a parcel that held a travel pass and a substantial amount of money.

"You aren't coming?" Dax asked, even though he knew the answer. The whole thing was starting to become overwhelming.

"You need to make your way to the wine train. It leaves for

Cordel at first light. I have secured passage aboard it for you, Merta, and the child. Merta will meet you there. The story is you are traveling with your half-sister and her baby, returning home to your family before the pass closes for the winter." He took the now sleeping baby from Dax and laid her back in the kit bag with some changing cloths and another blanket. Her white face shone in the candlelight, and then Rence closed the flap.

"Go now. Merta will join you shortly. And, Dax—be well. It may be a long time before we are together again." Rence pulled the hood up on Dax's cloak, opened the door to the terrace, and ushered him out. Dax took one last backward glance at Rence, hoping for more guidance, but Rence had already shut the door.

Dax made his way through the city center to meet the wine train. He had to pass by the city's grain silos on his way. One of the silos was ablaze, lighting up the area for blocks, and teams of men and women were trying to put out the fire and keep it from spreading to the other silos. He thought he saw the king standing on a platform, shouting orders. He snuck behind some crates and wagons, skirted around the area, and ran on until he found the wine train, a wagon caravan so named because it carried great casks of Weslynde's prized wine over the Cordel pass. This was the last wine train scheduled before the pass closed for the winter. It consisted of six large wagons pulled by a mighty team of massive four-horned oxyn, twelve animals in all. Large casks of wine were tightly packed into the wagons, and there was not much room for passengers, but Rence had secured a space for Dax and family among the casks. Dax stowed his pack and nestled the kit bag securely between two casks and peered down the road anxiously for any sign of Merta. A short while later she appeared, backlit by the glow of the fire, hurrying toward the train. He jumped down and helped her aboard. She crept down among the casks and opened the kit bag.

Dax ran forward to the lead wagon. "What time do we leave?" he asked the wagon master, a great bear of a man who was frowning at Dax behind his bushy beard.

"We leave now, young sir; we were waiting for you. We need to get far away from that blaze. LOAD UP!" he yelled. His crew moved into position; four climbed aboard the wagons, and two jumped astride their mountain ponies, leading the oxyn by ropes tied to their snout rings. The oxyn strained forward, wheels creaked, wooden slats squeaked, and they were on their way. Dax crawled down among the casks next to Merta.

"What took you so long?" he asked her.

"I had to hide in a kitchen cupboard," Merta said, trembling slightly.

"What happened?"

"Guards came looking for me. I hid in the cupboard until they left. I think that novice, Amilee, suspects me and sent them after me."

"Did they see which way you went?" Dax asked, worried now that they might be discovered before they left the city.

"No, no one saw. I'm sure of it." Merta lifted the baby out of the kit bag.

"How is the baby?" Dax whispered.

Merta moved the blanket that was covering her face to show Dax. "Still asleep, thank the gods. She's a pretty one, so pale."

"Rence says she is an albine."

"Truly? Maybe she is a saint." She smiled and sighed. "And that hair, so red! I have never seen the like."

They talked quietly together, sharing their adventures. Not long after they left the glow of the city behind, the baby woke up and started to fuss.

"I'm going to try to feed her," Merta said. "The healing

woman gave me something to make me have milk. Will you help me?"

Dax sat down behind her with his legs apart to form a sort of chair she could rest against. Merta leaned back and opened her blouse. After some trial and error, the baby latched on and began sucking.

"Ow."

"Does it hurt?" Dax asked.

"Not bad; I'm just not used to it. I think it's working."

Dax gathered a blanket around the three of them, and they relaxed into one another, slowly falling asleep to the creaking sounds of the wagon.

⚜

Dax woke to the sound of rushing water. Sunlight streamed down between the wine casks, warming his face. He jumped off the wagon and joined the crew, who were standing around a fire, warming their hands and tending a pot of coffee. The oxyn wandered loose nearby, cropping the dried grass, their silver-tipped horns shining in the cold thin air. They had stopped in a high meadow next to a tumbling stream that fell rapidly away toward the valley far below. Dark green conifers blanketed the mountains all around them.

"Where are we?" Dax asked the wagon master, who was smoking a pipe near the fire.

"That there is the Wess River, believe it or not, where it comes out of the mountains," the wagon master said. "We put some good miles behind us last night. We follow this road up over the Cordel Pass. With any luck, we will cross the pass before nightfall."

The road above him switched back and forth up the side of the forested mountain. Where the snowline met the forest, the road disappeared between two peaks. "Is that the pass?"

"It is," the wagon master replied. "It's farther than it looks. Once we cross, it's all downhill into Cordel. It's a beautiful view from up there, but the weather can get a little tricky. I'll be happy when we're over."

Dax carried a mug of coffee back to Merta. She took it gratefully. They chewed on bread and chatted quietly. Then Merta asked him to watch the baby while she tended to herself. She stood to go and brushed her apron off, and her hand stopped over her pocket. "Oh, I forgot I had this." She pulled out a metal ring. It glinted in her hand.

"What is that?" Dax asked.

She handed it to him. "It's the royal sigil; an extra one, I think. I was there when the house mage put one like it in the boy baby's back. It was very strange. They put out all the candles and the bishop was chanting. The house mage took the ring and sort of pressed it into the baby's back with his hand. The baby didn't cry or nothing."

"How did you get this one?"

"The house mage threw it in the fire; I think to melt it. It must've bounced out. I saw it and picked it up. I forgot about it until now." She swung her leg over the side rail. "I'll be back in a bit." She climbed down the side of the wagon and set off a distance from the others to attend to herself.

Dax held the sigil up to his face. The ring glittered green gold in the sun. Sky metal. He'd seen sky metal once before at the ministry of magic and he could tell exactly what it was; there was no other metal like it. It came from a stone that fell from the sky. There were traces of sky metal in the snout rings put through the noses of every domestic animal, including the great chameli. The snout rings contained charms, and that was how magicians sent commands to the animals. The sigil was very heavy for its size. He didn't understand the symbols woven across the filigreed mesh but recognized Sabrin né Franklin written in common script. "*Sabrin*," he mouthed; it must be a name. He closed his eyes and felt power radiating off the metal. It buzzed in his hand; it felt like the charms inside a chameli's snout ring, but the sensation was greatly amplified. He was curious, and before he realized it, he sank his mind inside the ring and started to work out the charm. The sky metal was intertwined with a very powerful magic. The ring felt alive, and he was instantly drawn into it.

The baby stirred and started to fuss. He picked her up, still holding the sigil, and put her over his shoulder. She quieted, but she was strong; her little arms pushed on his chest, and her head lifted up for a few seconds at a time.

"You're a fighter," he said, moving the hand holding the sigil across her back to support her head. Power surged out of the sigil as it brushed against the baby's skin. He pondered this new sensation, then, without much thought, he moved the blanket away and set the sigil gently on the baby's back, above her tiny shoulder. A bolt of energy flowed unbidden down his arm and into his fingers. His eyes went wide and his mouth fell open, but he didn't pull away. Holding the baby against him, he had a sudden compulsion to press down on the sigil with his fingers. The baby stiffened but didn't make a sound. His legs started to tremble, and, still holding her tightly, he dropped to his knees and put his whole hand over her back, pressing the sigil down with his palm. The feeling was very intense now; he could suss the different aspects of her body: her muscles, her bones, her little heart, fluttering like a bird. He could sense the elements inside the sigil reaching out of its ring to intertwine with the tiny bones in the baby's shoulder blade. Suddenly the ring itself sank through the baby's skin and disappeared, leaving only the filigree of words and symbols on the skin's surface. He felt more and more power leave his body and enter the baby's sigil. He got scared and tried to pull away, but he couldn't disconnect himself. His eyes started to roll up in his head.

"WHAT ARE YOU DOING?" Merta stood on the wagon bed, fresh from the stream, wet hair dripping on her blouse.

Dax jerked up and snatched his hand away from the baby's back. "I don't—I just—"

Merta grabbed the baby from Dax and examined her, touching the mesh of the sigil for any sign of trauma. The symbols and runes glittered green-gold on the baby's back. All the jostling made the baby start to cry again.

"—It just happened," Dax stammered. "I had to."

"It's the royal sigil! It belongs to the heir. This can't be allowed; take it out." Merta was horrified.

"I can't," Dax cried. "I don't know how I put it in."

"Take it out!" she insisted.

The wagon master popped his head over the side of the wagon, interrupting them. "Dax. I need you. There's weather coming. You need to give us a hand if we're to make the pass before it hits."

Dax scrambled over Merta and the baby and jumped down.

"Dax, come back!" Merta cried. He glanced back at her and saw the alarm in her face. He frowned and hesitated, then started to climb back up onto the wagon.

"DAX!" yelled the wagon master. Dax gave Merta a last look and dropped to the ground.

The crew was attempting to pull one of the huge oxyn into the yokes, and the great beast was balking. The men were no match for the bovine's great strength and couldn't budge him. Dax pushed his way between them, reached up on tiptoes, and grabbed it by the snout ring. The oxyn reared its head, lifting him off the ground, but he hung on, the snout ring buzzing in his hand. He shouted a few words of old majik he had learned at school, and immediately the great oxyn calmed down and allowed itself to be put into the yoke and harness.

"Are you a magician, then?" the wagon master asked, eyebrows raised.

"Apprentice," Dax said, patting the oxyn on the leg.

"More than an apprentice with that skill. Do the others, then, and hurry."

Dax led the rest of the oxyn into their harnesses, and the crew strapped them in. A breeze ruffled Dax's hair.

"Storm's moving in west out of Riddien," one of the crew said. "Straight across Weslynde valley—moving fast too."

"I read the sky this morning!" another said. "No clouds and clear sailing. This shouldn't be happening."

"Let's move," the wagon master shouted and snapped the reins. The two men on the shaggy ponies tugged the ropes tied to oxyn's snout rings, and they started up the hill. Sparks jumped from the oxyn's metal-shod hooves when they struck a rock. Dax ran alongside the wagons, throwing pots and other items that they had taken off during the stop up to those already on board.

They made good progress throughout the morning and were nearing the top of the pass when a sudden gust of wind swept over them. The menacing clouds racing across the valley had overtaken them and now roiled directly above them. Dax climbed up on the wagon and piled blankets over Merta, holding the baby, crouched down between the casks of wine. Moments later, the sky filled with large wet snowflakes that stuck to everything and everyone. The road up ahead quickly turned white and faded in the gloom.

One of the crew shouted, "Should we turn around?"

"It's too late—we're near the top," the wagon master yelled back. "If we make the pass, there's caves for the oxyn; we'll be safe there."

They lumbered forward. Snow piled up until it was scraping the axles on the wagons. The snow got too deep for the ponies, and the horsemen fell behind, following along in the wagon ruts. The great oxyn lowered their heads and began swinging them back and forth, their massive horns clearing away swaths of snow in front of them. Dax had climbed forward and was sitting next to the wagon master now. He took courage from the oxyn. They made slow but steady progress until they rounded the last turn and could see the pass a mere one hundred yards in front of them. But between them and the pass a great wall of snow had drifted across the road, higher than the wagon, and the oxyn could not push through. The road behind them was already covered and trackless. The wine train slowed to a halt. They were trapped.

Dax glanced at the wagon master. His hair and beard were coated with ice, and his face was very grim.

"What do we do?" Dax asked.

The wagon master sat quietly staring at the huge wall of snow. After a moment, he said, very softly, "Can you move that drift, magician?"

Dax was taken aback, and he stammered when he spoke. "I'm only an apprentice. I'm not sure if a high mage can move snow. It's not like a rock. It's made up of a million little pieces of ice."

"I don't need the details, young apprentice. I just need to know if you can move it. Will you try?"

There was fear behind the wagon master's eyes, and it shook Dax. "I will try."

He climbed down and stomped through the snow to the edge of the drift without a clue what to do. He asked a couple of the crew to lift him up, and he waded up onto the top of the drift. The snow had already packed down, and he found he was able to stand. He gazed up at the mountain above him as wet splats of snow smacked against his face. He felt helpless. He had never done anything remotely like this.

He blew out his breath and shook his cold fingers and tried sending feelers out underneath the snow. It wasn't working. Desperate, he sank to his knees and closed his eyes. His thoughts focused, and he was able to suss the ground deep under the snow. A door in his mind opened, and he was sobered by the massive weight of all that snow above him straining to come down. The ice crystals were barely holding together, and the earth's pull was coaxing them downward toward him.

It scared him badly. The snow was too much, too messy, too chaotic for him to exploit or control. And at the very peak, a ridge of snow had blown up from the other side and was cresting over like a giant wave, unstable, shifting. It wouldn't stay there for long. Heart hammering, he took several deep breaths through flared nostrils and reached out again. Up. Under. Underneath the crest of snow, he sussed a large boulder resting against smaller rocks and old tree roots. It may have been there for a hundred years, but the roots holding it in place had grown weak.

He went lower. Under. There. At the base of the boulder, a dead tree lay on its side. If he could break it...but no. He was not strong enough. He sat back in defeat. Then, inside his head, he thought he heard a baby crying and a voice, Tregan's voice, whispering in his ear.

I charge you with the care of my children. I charge you to live and die in service to them. Swear to me you will.

He reacted on impulse, and he sent his awareness into the dead tree, the tendrils of his skill winding through the fibrous strands that held it together.

Protect my children.

He pictured Merta holding the baby, trying in vain to keep her warm until the snow covered them up and they froze where they lay. He cried out in anguish and a pulse left his body, radiating upward into the dead tree at the top of the mountain, snapping it in a dozen places, releasing the large boulder it was holding in place. The boulder began to roll, and the crest of snow above it fell forward, cascading swiftly down the mountainside. All the snow above and around it came loose and roared downward, picking up speed as it went. Too late, Dax realized his error. He had just enough time to see the crew's surprised faces before the avalanche hit him, sending him down into the abyss below.

⚜

The wagon master sat stunned on the wagon's bench. As the clouds of snow dissipated, he saw the road start to appear, a clear path all the way to the pass. A couple of his crew ran forward and peered over the edge for any sign of Dax, yelling his name.

"NO TIME," yelled the wagon master. "TAKE YOUR POSI-TIONS!" He jumped down from the wagon and grabbed the dominant ox by its snout ring and pulled. "FORWARD NOW!" The great beast bit its hooves into the ground and strained forward, the others followed its lead, and the wagons broke free from the snow. The train started up the road again. A short time later, they crossed over the pass and made it safely into the caves on the other side.

⚜

Merta stood at the entrance of the cave, waiting for Dax to appear. He must be helping with the oxyn, she thought. He always liked animals more than people. The snow had stopped, and the clouds were breaking up. The sun, a dull red ball, appeared below the clouds in the west, turning the snow on the peak above her orange. Around her, the wine train crew were unharnessing the oxyn, wiping the ponies down, and throwing hay from the storage tunnels that dotted the walls of the cave. When they caught her looking at them, they turned away.

Finally, the wagon master came up and stood quietly beside her. He towered over her. *He must have some Argonnian blood in him*, she thought, noting his weathered brown face and curling dark hair. He lit his pipe and puffed on it.

She pushed a strand of hair behind her ear and asked, "Where is Dax?"

"The magician?" The wagon master sighed. "He's gone, little one." He studied his pipe carefully. "He saved us, but we could not save him."

She stood silent for a minute, letting the shock pass through her, and paused until she could speak again. "What happened?"

"He brought the whole mountain down—that's what happened. All the snow. Never seen the like. He cleared the road for us. We'd all be dead but for him."

She waited to hear the rest of the story, willing herself not to cry.

"The avalanche he conjured up took him down with it. He was there and then not there. It were straight down where he went over."

She put her hands over her face.

"Now don't you worry, little one; you've safe passage with us. We will take you as far as Sudo Bay, and I will send someone along with you to take you to your family. We owe you that much."

She left the wagon master standing in the entrance and headed back to the wine train.

We are doomed, she thought. *It's the curse of the twins, and Dax was its first victim. We can't escape it.*

She climbed up on the wagon and threaded her way between the casks to the sleeping baby. Dax's pack leaned against a cask nearby. She opened it and went through its contents: dried meat and fruit, a water jug, a fire starter, a spare tunic, a length of twine. In the next pocket she found a book of poems, their travel papers, and a brown envelope. She took the envelope out and opened it. Inside was quite a large sum of money, given to him by Rence, no doubt, from Tregan's account. Well, it belonged to the baby now. She dug down and found a flap at the bottom of the pack. She felt a bundle of cloth underneath and pulled it out. The fabric was so dark she couldn't quite make out the cut or design. *This is special,* she thought, stuffing it back in the pack along with everything else. She closed the pack, wrapped her arms around it as if it were Dax, and cried.

CHAPTER 5

Rence was out in front waiting for them when Tregan arrived at the palace. She handed Jarin to Amilee so Gwyn could help her step down from the carriage. Tregan searched Rence's eyes for news. He gave her a subtle nod and a wink. She kept her expression neutral, but inside her heart skipped a beat.

After months in the abbey, her old rooms felt warm and welcoming. Her bedchamber had been set up with a cradle. Fresh tapestries hung on the walls, and a crackling fire was burning in the hearth. Tregan sank down gratefully into the new cushioned rocker. Amilee put Jarin in her arms and she cradled him, stroking the fine black fuzz that covered his head. He even had hairs on the top of his ears! He was so small and his hands were so tiny. He squeezed her finger with his fist when she touched him and she gasped, delighted. His skin glowed golden-brown, and he was so soft. She lifted him up and smelled his fuzzy head and kissed it. He startled, squeezing his eyes tight and wrinkling up his forehead. He bashed his face with his little fists, making her laugh in delight.

"My precious little Jarin," she cooed, gently tucking his arms inside his blanket.

At the sound of her voice, Jarin opened his bright blue eyes and looked up at her. She fell heart-first into them.

"I will never ever leave you," she whispered as a tear stole down her cheek. All her previous plans now seemed hopeless. When the tea leaves arrived a few minutes later, she was already asleep, Jarin feeding at her breast.

⚜

Gerard Mort stood beside the king, staring at the smoldering ruins of the grain silo. A few fire fighters remained, turning the ashes over, putting out embers. The morning sun broke through the smoky haze and shone on their sooty faces. The amount of grain lost could have fed the entire city for two months, but even so, it could have been much, much worse. The blaze had burned so hot and grown so fast the walls of two other nearby silos were scorched black. It had been a near thing.

Franklin stood next to the mage, face smudged with soot. "I need to know how this could happen, Mort—today!" He wiped his face with a dirty cloth. "I have to go now and meet my son."

The king stomped away, stiff-shouldered. Gerard Mort had seldom seen Franklin so angry. The mage shouted out new directions to the fire fighters, instructing them to start searching for clues. While the workers began picking through the burned timbers and twisted support beams, Gerard Mort clasped his hands together and stood silently for a moment, composing himself. Then he rested the tips of his fingers on his forehead, muttered a phrase in old majik, and reached out with his skill. His mind quicky traversed the silo platform and felt every timber and nail of it. He discerned fire damage on one of the beams supporting the platform. He climbed down and tossed his black robe on a railing, then crawled under the platform to examine the damaged support beam. He rested his palm over the dirt below the beam and sifted through the element that made it up, one by one. Ash, iron, rock, oil. Oil! He dug his fingers into the dirt. There was a dark patch that felt greasy. He rubbed his fingers together and smelled them. Distilled pine resin. Highly flammable. The remnants of a fuel-soaked rag lay nearby. Someone had deliberately started this fire.

Who? he thought. *And why last night, the night of the baby's birth? Was the king pulled away from that event on purpose? A diversion of some kind? Did someone attempt to harm the baby?* He pulled on his robe and headed for the abbey.

Bishop Rutter met him at the gate. "Lord Mage." The bishop bowed. "Lady Tregan and the baby are no longer here. The king ordered them moved to the palace last night."

"I am fully aware of that," Gerard Mort snapped. "Step aside, Bishop. I left something behind in the lady's rooms."

"Of course, my lord. I will escort you."

"I know the way." The mage gave the bishop a look that said *don't follow* and pushed past him.

Tregan's room had not been cleaned, and he searched through it for anything that might link the fire to Jarin's birth. Everything seemed drab and ordinary, just an empty room. The gold plate that had held both sigils was still sitting on the table. Both sigils! He should retrieve the second sigil. He used a fire poker to sift through the ashes in the hearth, but he couldn't locate the second ring. He sussed the hearth, but it wasn't there. The fire would not have been hot enough to melt sky metal. Where was it? He closed his eyes and sussed the rest of the room; there was no sky metal anywhere. It was gone. Someone had taken the second sigil! He put the clues together. Someone had started a fire to draw him and the king away from the abbey. They must have intended to harm the baby but failed. But now they had the sigil, which meant they had a weapon they could use, perhaps to challenge Franklin's child and lay claim to the throne. It must be recovered. It wouldn't be hard to retrieve; he would get a list of everyone in the room and use his magic to search them, starting with that self-important healing woman.

As he was on his way out of the abbey, a guard, one of the men he had left with Tregan to protect the baby, came running up the road.

"My lord," the guard said, breathing heavily. "I have information."

"Is the baby safe?" Gerard Mort asked, alarmed.

"Yes, my lord. The babe and his mother are under guard inside the palace."

"What is it, then?" the mage asked, relaxing a little.

"Your novice, the one called Amilee, informed us that Lady Tregan's servant woman stole a gold ring she says belongs to you. We searched the abbey grounds but can't find her anywhere."

Merta! Gerard Mort thought. *She must have taken it.* He remembered she had traveled north with Tregan. She must be a spy for Argonne.

"Block all roads leading south toward Argonne," he ordered the guard. "The woman must be found immediately."

"At once, my lord." The guard bowed and raced away.

Gerard Mort headed to the palace to report his news to the king.

⚜

Tregan was propped up in bed, holding Jarin in her arms, when King Franklin arrived to meet his son. The sunlight streamed in through the window, bathing the room in a soft light. The healing woman and the novice moved about the room, quietly attending them. Franklin sat down on the bed next to her, and she handed him the baby.

Franklin lifted the blanket from Jarin's head. "He's been baked brown, like his mother." His eyes crinkled with mirth as he stroked his son's fuzzy black hair. "I see we have created a little Argonnian baby. That will please the southerners. What's this, hair on his ears? Is he a wolf cub?"

"That will fall away," Tregan assured him. "He has your eyes, my lord, and he's bossy as well. That didn't come from me."

"Bossy, eh? Good, good. He's very small, though; you looked like you were going to give birth to a steppe-horse. Where's the rest of him?"

"He's all there."

"Let me see." Franklin pulled the blankets away. "Ten fingers, ten toes. Oh, and a big pair of ox balls, like his father. Yes, he's all there." They laughed together. "So, tell me, my dear Tregan. Will you stay and raise this child with me?"

"I..." Tregan paused. Franklin was being so tender, and his invitation surprised her; she had given up thinking of the two of them as partners. "I love him so much; it would surely break my heart to leave him, but...do I have to decide right now?"

"Of course not," Franklin muttered, his smile disappearing. "You have your contract. I will not alter the terms." He caressed Jarin's head with his big hands and added, softly, "But it would make me happy if you were in his life, in our lives."

Tregan studied the king's face, marveling at his gentleness with the baby. Who was this person? How was it possible that this man speaking so lovingly was the same man who had placed her under house arrest for the last six months? She ached to stay. How could she ever leave Jarin? She was so in love with him. But the girl child, little Sabrin. Out there some-where. Was she cold and hungry? Alone in the dark? She needed to find her, protect her. She trusted Merta more than anyone, but still it tore at her that she had abandoned her daughter. What an impossible choice. An unwanted tear slid down her face.

The king wiped her tear away with his thumb. "You look so sad. What is it?"

"It's nothing. I'm overwhelmed a little; that's all."

There was a loud rap on the door, and Gerard Mort stepped through without waiting for an invitation. "Your Majesty."

"What is it now, Mort?" The king scowled, clearly irritated. "You are always interrupting."

"I have information on the silo fire." The mage gazed coldly at Tregan.

The sun went behind a cloud, turning the room dark. A sudden gust of wind blew hard against the window, slamming it open. Leaves flew into the room, and Jarin started to cry. Tregan took him from the king and sheltered him with her arms while Gwyn ran to the window and closed it. Tregan pulled Jarin close against her and noticed his back felt hot. She turned him over and lowered his blanket. The black runes on his sigil had begun to glitter a weird green-gold. She pulled the blanket back up and cuddled him to her chest.

"By the gods, what was that?" the king said. The window continued to rattle violently.

"A big storm moving in, Your Majesty," Gwyn said. "Came out of nowhere."

Gerard Mort placed his hand on Franklin's shoulder. "Your Majesty, I have news. It won't wait."

"Eh? What?" the king said. "Oh, yes, the silo. Tell me."

"Better we talk in the next room." The mage guided the king out of the bedchamber.

As the door closed, Tregan overheard Franklin say, "What? Who started it?"

What had Gerard Mort discovered? She replayed the sequence of events from last night in her head. Everything had gone as planned. She didn't know for certain if Rence was behind the fire, but she thought he was; the timing was too perfect. She hoped in her heart that Merta had met up with Dax and that she and the baby girl were already far away from the city. There were so many things that could have gone wrong.

"Gwyn?" she began, her anxiety spilling over.

"Hush now," Gwyn said, glancing sideways at Amilee, who was lurking nearby as always. Big splats of wet snow began spattering against the window.

The king came back in the room, followed by the mage. The warm light was gone from the king's eyes.

"You all stay in here," he said. "Something foul is afoot."

"My lord, what is it?" Tregan asked, suddenly afraid.

"Your servant woman has proved false and has fled. You are not to leave this room."

"What do you mean false? Merta is loyal to me!" Tregan sat up quickly, raising her voice in protest. Then she felt a sudden twinge, like something had snapped deep inside her. "Oh..." she exclaimed. "Amilee, take the baby."

She handed Jarin to the novice as a terrible cramp struck her so hard it made her bend over. She crossed her arms over her belly and groaned.

"Something's wrong," she said. A widening pool of dark red blood was staining her gown between her legs. Her head felt suddenly light, and she collapsed back against her pillow.

The window burst open again, sending streamers of wet snow into the room. A gust of wind swept across the chamber into the fireplace, blowing embers and ashes on everything and everyone. Gerard Mort sent a command to the window, slamming it shut and dropping the crossbar over it.

Gwyn jumped onto the bed, put her hands between Tregan's legs, and pressed down hard. "Bring me cloths," she yelled over the storm. "I need to stop the bleeding."

Amilee set Jarin, who was wailing, down in the cradle and

ran to Gwyn with a roll of clean gauze. The king stood by helplessly.

Dizzy now, Tregan found could no longer raise her arms. A panic was growing inside her. This couldn't be happening. She needed to stay strong. She had to save her babies.

Gwyn stuffed gauze between Tregan's legs to staunch the flow. "Massage her belly with your fingers; do it now," she screamed at Amilee.

Amilee climbed on the bed and pressed down with her fingers. The women furiously worked on Tregan for a few minutes, then the air in the room grew close.

Gwyn sobbed in despair. "I can't stop the bleeding. It won't stop coming."

Tregan turned her head weakly and held out her hand. "Franklin?" The king took her hand and bent close to her face. "Franklin. Tell Jarin I love him. More than anything. Please tell him."

"I will," choked the king.

"Tell him I didn't want to leave him; I had to make a choice..." She trailed off and closed her eyes.

"I don't understand...Tregan?" The king rubbed Tregan's hand gently. "What do you mean?" Tregan did not answer.

"Healing woman? Help her." Franklin's voice shook.

Gwyn pressed her ear against Tregan's chest. She felt her neck for a pulse, listened again for a heartbeat, then slumped back on her heels. "She's gone."

A gust of wind hit so hard it shook the palace walls. Gwyn put her hands to her mouth and stared helplessly at the others: the king, the house mage, the novice. They all seemed to be frozen in place. Jarin wailed from his cradle, unnoticed.

Someone banged on the door. Gerard Mort opened it on a group of worried house staff.

"We need permission to free the king's horses from the paddock; the snow is getting too deep for them."

"Of course, you fool, do it," Gerard Mort hissed.

"The kitchen roof has collapsed. What do we do?"

"Use your heads. Find the general and the fire chief—GO!" He slammed the door and swirled back into the room. "Your Majesty, the storm worsens. We must address it."

"The contract is broken," Franklin muttered, gray-faced.

"What?"

"We agreed to guarantee her safety. The contract is broken. Find my lawyer and bring Rence to me. We need a plan."

"That can wait, my lord," the mage began. "The storm—"

"Find them now!" Franklin raged. "The Argonnians will be infuriated. They will blame Weslynde for her death and make a martyr of her. At least my son is safe. He looks Argonnian. We can leverage that. Tell them to meet me in my office in one hour. And bring the House Chaplain as well. GO!"

Gerard Mort started to object, thought better of it, bowed, and went out.

Gwyn stared at the king, afraid of what he might do or say next.

"Clean up this horror and give her some dignity," he ordered her. "And make sure nothing happens to my son. Your very life depends on his safety." He left the room.

Gwyn sat on the edge of the bed, absently wiping her bloody hands on her apron over and over.

"Tell me what to do?" Amilee was crying and rocking Jarin in her arms. "He won't stop crying and his back feels hot."

Still dazed, Gwyn slowly willed herself back under control. "Put the baby back in the cradle. Then go and find someone to help clean this up. Bring a mop."

Amilee set Jarin down and ran out. Gwyn pulled a clean

coverlet over Tregan's body and went to the cradle; the unhappy child lay there, red-faced and screaming.

"What have we done, Tregan? What have we done?" The window rattled against the crossbar. She looked from the window to the body on the bed and back down at the baby. She'd known all along what she should have done, but now it was too late. The king had said this baby must live if she were to keep her own life. Because of her actions, or failure to act, both twins lived and the curse had fallen. She picked Jarin up; his back did feel hot. Probably a reaction to that damn sigil. The filigreed symbols on his back seemed to glow; she hadn't noticed that earlier. *Must be a trick of the light*, she thought. *Who knows what putting that thing in his body did to him?* She cradled Jarin gently, and he turned his head toward her, instinctively seeking out her breast. He became more and more frustrated until finally she closed her eyes and sighed, walked over to her bag, pulled out a vial of milky blue liquid, and drank it.

"Don't worry, little prince. Dinner is coming."

PART II

THE TALE OF SAINT CERISE

CHAPTER 6

Cerise balanced on the gunwale with one hand lightly resting on the rigging, monitoring the harvesting fleet dotting the bay. The harvester's jib crane was hoisting another bundle of seaweed into its hold, and a flotilla of smaller boats surrounded it, bobbing up and down on the blue-green water. She checked her crew's positions; they were all in place, posted around the deck and up on the mast, scanning the sea's surface for predators. Lyon seals routinely patrolled the seaweed beds and were not above snatching the occasional diver. Cerise focused her glass on the divers floating in the water, their clear head bubbles disappearing under the surface as others popped back up. The sea was starting to get choppy; streaks of foam were running down the waves, and the harvester's captain would soon call everyone in and head to shore.

A flag unfurled on the harvester's mast, and its horn blasted twice across the water. Cerise relaxed and jumped down to the deck. "Prepare to sail," she yelled. Her women jumped into action, pulling in the drag line and readying the mainsail.

Cerise very much loved her job. She was nineteen and already pilot of her own vessel, the *Flying Fish*, a sleek privateer commissioned to protect the Sudo Bay seaweed fleet. She was trim and muscular and stood six feet tall. To protect her blue eyes from the sun's glare, she outlined them with a large amount of eye-black in a cat's eye pattern. She painted her lips the same color. She kept her shock of cherry-red hair pulled back against her head in a Cordelian warrior's knot. A tight seal-skin jerkin with a brimmed hood and sleeves that that extended down over her wrists kept the sun off her albine skin. She wore lightweight leggings down to her ankles, but on board she went barefoot, as did her crew. A protective cream kept her feet from burning.

Janis called down from the mast, "Cerise! There's a sea dragon northwest, at a hundred yards."

Cerise held up her glass and saw the streamlined reptile heading directly for the fleet, porpoising through the waves. She felt a rush of excitement as she always did at these moments. "Alert the harvester," she shouted.

The privateer's horn sounded the predator alert before she even finished her command. She swung her glass toward the flotilla; most of the boats already had their divers aboard and were hoisting their sails, but one boat was farther out than the rest and the crew aboard was motioning at something in the water. They were encouraging a diver to swim faster.

"Intercept the dragon," she yelled. "Fire the accelerator."

Tar, the first mate, swung the wheel, and Mae Linn, the youngest member of the crew, unfurled the gennaker; it ballooned in the breeze. Tar fired the accelerator; a cloud of black smoke belched from the stern and the cutter leapt forward, skipping across the choppy waves. Cerise grabbed the railing and hung on; it would be close.

Cerise leapt onto the starboard harpoon pedestal and glanced across the bow. Luce, who was by far the best shot, was already stationed at the port harpoon, ready to fire. Cerise didn't need the spyglass any longer to see the sea dragon; it was closing in swiftly, diving through the waves, its emerald body glittering as it shed water from its flanks. She marveled at its power and beauty even as her concern for the seaweed diver grew. It arched its long neck gracefully, and it kept its four flippers tucked close to its body as it leapt and dove.

The sea dragon, so named because its fins and spines resembled the creature of myth, was a big one, at least eighteen feet long. It appeared to be alone, which was a good thing, but the swimmer had no chance if it caught him in the water. Though their mouths were small, sea dragons were known to grab a diver's arm or leg and drag them down into the depths, drowning their victim then eating them at their leisure.

The *Flying Fish* was closing the gap, but the dragon was closer; it would reach the diver in moments. Cerise aimed her harpoon and calculated the distance. She should cut the accelerator and turn sharply to avoid plowing into the seaweed boat, but if she did that, she wouldn't be able to make her shot. *I have to fire now,* she thought. *Luce is the better shot, but I have the better sight line.* She pulled the levers that moved the platform, aimed slightly ahead of the beast to account for its speed, and fired. The spear whistled through the air and struck the water inches in front of the sea dragon's nose. The dragon startled and dove straight down, disappearing under the choppy water.

"Curse the gods!" she muttered, angry with herself, knowing she should have let Luce take the shot. The *Flying Fish* hurtled toward the seaweed boat; she could make out the alarmed faces of the divers. "Cut the 'rater! Hard to port and lower the sail!"

Tar spun the wheel. The gennaker fell and the *Flying Fish* swung around, tilting over almost to the edge of her gunwale. The wake they raised with the sudden maneuver crashed into the side of the seaweed boat, rocking it violently. The *Flying*

Fish broadsided against it with a loud boom, knocking the crew of the seaweed boat off their feet. They quickly regained their footing and threw up ropes to the *Fish*, lashing the two vessels together.

Cerise jumped down onto the seaweed boat's deck, adrenaline pumping. "Where's the diver?" she yelled.

"There." One of the sailors pointed. "He's caught in a line."

The diver had lost his head bubble and was struggling to keep his head above water. *He's going to drown,* she thought. A surge of energy went through her body. She threw off her sealskin jerkin, exposing her body to the sun, and dove over the gunwale into the water.

The diver's foot was caught in a seaweed net, and it was dragging him under. Cerise pulled her knife from its sheath and cut the net away. It came apart easily, and she felt the diver kick free and swim toward the boat. She came up for air, took a deep breath, and went back under, scanning the depths for the sea dragon. Sea dragons always came back to investigate. She held still, heart pounding, but saw nothing but shafts of sunlight diffusing into darkness. She waited another moment to be sure it was gone, then relaxed, sheathed her knife, and started to swim back.

Her body tingled in warning, and suddenly she was flying through the air. The sea dragon had come up directly below her and head-butted her into the sky, a behavior it used to stun prey. She hit the water hard with a stinging slap and rolled over face down, crouching into a ball and holding her knife in front of her, jerking it back and forth so it glinted in the light like a lure. The beast would try to grab her arm or leg and take her deep, and she needed to be ready.

She saw it a split second before it reached her, its jaws agape. She thrust her knife into the top of its mouth. The dragon yanked its head back, but she managed to wrap her arm around its neck, and before it could shake her off, she sliced its throat open. Ignoring her bursting lungs, she hung on until it stopped thrashing, then let go and watched it sink in a cloud of blood. She kicked back to the surface, gasping for air. Coughing and choking, she grabbed the float the seaweed farmers had thrown to her, her body still tingling as the crew towed her in. The seaweed divers made a circle around her as she climbed aboard, breathing hard, knife still in her hand, water streaming off her half-naked body: a marble statue gleaming in the sun.

"The white angel!" cheered a sailor. "Saint Cerise!" yelled another. The sailors raised their arms and yelled enthusiastically.

Cerise cringed hearing the names they had created for her.

"Saint Cerise? That's a new one," Luce commented as she helped Cerise back into her jerkin.

"I've heard it before and I don't like it." Cerise pulled the sleeves down over the tops of her hands. She was no saint and didn't want to be thought of as one.

"Your skin is going to blister if you keep taking your clothes off, Your Holiness," Luce said with a wry smile.

Cerise clenched her jaw. She didn't appreciate Luce's teasing in front of the seaweed divers. "Take Skua and check the *Fish* for damage."

Luce looked up and winked at her crewmates, who were leaning over the railing of the *Flying Fish,* grinning down at the two of them. Cerise ignored them and stomped off to check on the diver she had rescued.

⚜

The port master was waiting for them when they docked. His presence meant there must be news. Cerise jumped down onto the wooden pier and strode over to him.

"Port Master Aki," she said in greeting. "It's a good day to be alive."

"It is that. I heard you had some excitement on the water."

"We did indeed; a sea dragon came for a visit. All crew and cargo are accounted for."

"Excellent service as always. Your wages are in the port office, along with a bonus for your crew." Aki extended his hand.

"Thank you." She shook his hand. Cerise enjoyed working with the port master. She had known him ever since she was a little girl and harvested seaweed beside her parents.

"I have another job for you, if you're interested." The port master stroked his thin moustache.

"Always interested if the coin is right," she replied, curious what he had in mind.

"There's a shipment of seaweed and salt fish leaving for Isidima tomorrow aboard the *Dreike*." Aki nodded toward the tall-ship anchored out in the harbor. It had arrived from Argonne two days ago.

"The *Dreike*? That's a small ship for a cargo run."

"Speed is important." Aki lit his pipe. "It's what they're picking up in Isidima and bringing back with them that's the real reason for the trip. That's also why we need a privateer to escort her."

"What's the important cargo?" she asked, intrigued.

"A senatorial delegation from the Western Commonwealth. They are coming to meet with the Premier of Cordel."

Cerise had never taken a job like this before. *Why do they need an escort?* "Are you expecting trouble?"

"Nothing like that. Let's say the premier wants to guarantee their safety. Weslynde-Argonne politics being what they are these days."

"Why not send a navy vessel?" she asked. She didn't know much about Weslynde's dispute with Argonne, only the gossip at the local pub, and she always steered clear of politics. Choosing a side meant fewer job opportunities, and she had her parents to think of—they were too old to work in the factory now.

Aki raised an eyebrow and knocked his pipe on a piling. "The premier asked for you. Seems your reputation is getting around."

She was surprised the premier of Cordel even knew who she was. "Reputation? That's ridiculous," she scoffed.

The port master re-lit his pipe and blew smoke out toward the bay. "They're offering twice the usual fare for your services. Will you take it?"

The extra money could greatly benefit her family, and a voyage to Argonne sounded exciting. "Yes, we'll take the job."

"Good, good. Be ready to go when the *Dreike* departs. I'll inform Captain Tayjal the white angel will flank them."

Cerise frowned at the "white angel" comment. This was getting out of hand. She was tired of the attention and the stares; she wanted to be left alone and to do her job. She said goodbye and headed off to the port office to collect her fee while Port Master Aki quietly chuckled behind her.

⚜

Cerise joined her crew at their favorite pub to give them their wages and the port master's bonus. The smoky common room was packed with sailors, and the fire in the corner made things cozy if not a little too warm. The women hailed her when she came through the door and raised their mugs. They were all there except Luce, who had first watch aboard the *Flying Fish*. Cerise would meet her later, and she smiled at the thought. Luce always made her feel better.

Cerise's crew of six had been sailing with her for almost two years, ever since she'd acquired the *Flying Fish*. Cerise had known Dee, Mae Linn, and Skua since childhood. They were native Cordelians, short and wiry, olive-skinned with long jet-black hair. Their families were all seaweed farmers, and growing up, they had spent more time on the ocean than on land. Tar and Janis were her lieutenants. Tar, the first mate, was also Cordelian. She was older and more experienced than the others and looked out for the younger sailors. Solid and muscular, the no-nonsense Tar had piloted the *Flying Fish* long before Cerise acquired it and knew the cutter like the back of her hand. Freckle-faced Janis was a Weslynder. She had traveled to Cordel when she was fifteen because she had always dreamed of life on the sea. Her relaxed nature and disarming smile disguised the fact that she was, in fact, a trained soldier and fierce fighter. Luce had been born in Riddien and had the yellow hair and creamy skin of her people. She was the best harpooner of the group and was unmatched with a crossbow. Cerise was fiercely devoted to all six of them, and the last two years sailing with them had been the happiest in her life.

"Long live the dragon slayer!" shouted Mae Linn.

"Here's to the naked angel, raising lascivious sailors' hopes everywhere!" Dee raised her mug high.

They all laughed and made room for Cerise at their table. The pub's proprietor handed her a foamy mug as she walked by.

"You wouldn't've had to jump in naked if you had let Luce fire the harpoon," teased Janis.

"I agree! We all know she's the better shot," Tar chimed in, lighting her pipe and grinning as she blew out the smoke.

Cerise ignored the ribbing, but it bothered her that she had missed her shot. She really should have let Luce take it.

"I have your wages, and Aki threw in a bonus for each of you. He says to tell you job well done." She tossed bags of coin on the table.

"To Port Master Aki!" Dee toasted again, sloshing her ale over the rim of her mug.

"You might want to slow down a little, Dee. The port master

has a new job for us. Starts tomorrow." Cerise sipped her ale, feeling the warmth of it spread down her chest.

"What's the job?" Tar asked, always ready to get down to business.

Cerise told them about escorting the *Dreike* down to the port of Isidima in Argonne. Everyone was immediately excited. Tar and Janis had been there before, and they described Isidima as exotic and worldly, very different from sleepy Sudo Bay.

Cerise sipped her ale and listened to them talking over one another, sharing tales of the desert province. Was the city really carved out of a volcano? Was it true it never rained in Argonne? Did Argonnian men take multiple wives? She stretched out her legs under the table, at home among these women who were her family.

Pretty Mae Linn started flirting with two Argonnian men sitting at a table across the room. They were sailors and must have come into town aboard the *Dreike*. They were handsome and exotic looking with their gold earrings and braided hair, and their well-muscled arms were on full display outside their vests. Mae Linn flashed her eyes and smiled coyly.

Cerise smiled to herself while the other women prodded Mae Linn to go say hello. The men finally stood to go, rising to their full seven-foot height. One of them winked and blew a kiss to Mae Linn as they ducked under the door. Tiny Mae Linn squealed and pretended to faint, fanning herself with her hand.

"Forget it, Mae Linn," ribbed Skua. "You would need a rope and a ladder to climb one of those trees." Everyone laughed.

It was time for her to go, and she went to pay the proprietor. He waved her off, telling her it was on the house. She ignored him and put a sizable stack of coins on the bar and pushed it across to him.

"Everyone be back on board the *Fish* by noon," she ordered.

"Yes, Saint Cerise!" Dee stood and saluted, more than a little tipsy.

"Don't ever call me that." Cerise's voice went dark and her eyebrows furrowed.

Dee sat back down, embarrassed.

Cerise flushed. "Well...goodnight, then," she said awkwardly, regretting her overreaction. Why did that name, Saint Cerise, get under her skin like that? She realized Dee was kidding, but it irked her. It had all started with the church. The local cleric had been obsessed with her for years because of her albine skin. Her parents had done their best to shelter her from him while she was growing up, and she'd thought it was behind her, but then, recently, someone had shouted, "Saint Cerise," when she walked by. It had happened a few more times since then. *Let it go,* she thought. She ducked out the door and headed up the road past the seaweed processing plant, glad to be out in the open air.

Sudo Bay was a busy port town wrapped around the bay of the same name. It was also the capital of Cordel. The Premier's fortress rose above the rest of the town, and it was the first thing ships saw when they entered the bay, its ornate rooflines stretching above the stately conifers that surrounded it. The seaweed processing plant dominated the town center, and even at this hour, it was still bustling with activity. Fog was rolling in across the bay and the lights in the town's windows took on a hazy glow as Cerise set out, eager to get home. Her stomach growled at the thought of Maemae's cooking.

About a mile from the town, a gravel lane veered off into a small, wooded, valley full of ferns. A cluster of neatly maintained thatch-roofed cottages were nestled along a cheerful creek, their windows shining in welcome. She entered the farthest one, ducking under the door to the smell of savory ginger rice.

"It's me, Mama."

"You're back just at the right time." Cerise's mother, Maemae, a small woman with twinkling black eyes and streaks of gray in her long black hair, smiled at her as she scooped food from a pot into a bowl. "Sit down—eat it while its hot. Baba will be in shortly." She placed the bowl of steaming rice, dotted with chunks of fish, seaweed, and wild onion tops, on the table and placed chopsticks and a bowl of dipping sauce next to it.

Cerise pulled off her boots and poured some clear wine from a pitcher into a mug.

"How was your day?" Maemae brought another bowl and sat across from her. "Did you stay out of the sun?"

"I picked a fight with a sea dragon." Cerise stabbed a piece of fish with a chopstick and looked Maemae in the eye slyly. "I won."

Maemae swallowed her dismay and countered, "Will there be a rematch?"

Cerise talked through her food. "Not this time. It was the final round."

Maemae gave a little sigh of relief.

The door opened and her father, Min, came in. "Hello, hello, my little one!" He always called Cerise his little one even though Cerise stood a good foot taller than her parents, both of them bent over from years of bundling seaweed down at the processing plant.

Cerise waved her chopsticks at him, still chewing.

Maemae filled a bowl for Min and placed it on the table next to hers and poured him some wine as he put on his slippers. Min kissed her and sat down, then went to work with the chopsticks.

"How was your day?" he said. "Did you stay out of the sun?"

Cerise nodded her head. "We got a bonus today, Baba—here." She tossed a sack of coins on the table. "For the new cart."

"Oh, wonderful, wonderful," Min said.

Maemae frowned. "We don't need this; save it for something important." She handed the bag to Cerise. Min took it from Cerise and handed it back to Maemae.

"No, we don't need it," Maemae protested.

Min motioned for her to put it in a jar on the shelf, and with a huff, she complied.

"Baba, Mama—I have news. I start a new job tomorrow; I will be gone several weeks." Cerise scooped more rice from the pot into her bowl.

"Are you going north with the fishing fleet?" Min asked.

"South. To Argonne. We're escorting a shipment of seaweed to Isidima, then escorting some commonwealth senators back here."

"Any Weslynders?" Maemae asked casually, poking at her rice and holding her face still.

"Yes, three senators: one from Weslynde, one from Argonne, and one from Riddien. They are coming here to meet the Premier of Cordel. They asked for me by name."

"What are Weslynders doing in Argonne?" Min asked. "They don't like each other, and the young prince doesn't seem to be making things any better. Why didn't they come over the pass? It would have saved them weeks."

"Don't know, but it's good coin. It will be my first time in Argonne in command of my own ship." Cerise rinsed her bowl, went to the door, and pulled on her boots.

"You have to go so soon?" Min asked. "Your uncles are on their way."

"I need to get back—we have an early start tomorrow. Say goodbye for me."

"Say hello to Luce for us." Maemae smiled knowingly.

Cerise rolled her eyes. "I will." She kissed them both on the tops of their heads and went out into the night.

⚜

Merta waited until the door had closed behind Cerise and put her hands to her mouth.

"Maemae, it's nothing," Min said.

"They asked for her by name." Merta shook her head doubtfully. "Why would they do that? I should warn her."

"About what? What would you say? 'By the way, Cerise, you are a stolen princess from Weslynde, so be extra careful. Maemae, no one in the world even knows she exists!"

"It doesn't feel right. Why would they ask for her in particular?" Merta started clearing the dishes.

"Do you listen to the talk in town? Shippers fight for her services. The girl is a hero! Remember when she saved those sailors in the cave? Word gets around. Do you know what they call her?"

"What?"

"The white angel. She's a natural leader; be proud."

"She's only nineteen," Merta said, wiping her hands.

"She's a grown woman, in charge of her own future. And I'll tell you this. She's a far better person than that prince in Weslynde, from what I hear. They say all he does is drink and cause trouble everywhere he goes."

"Min!" Merta put her hand on his mouth. "You are not to mention the prince of Weslynde. Ever."

Min took her hand and held it. "You have done your job well. Now let her go."

Merta would never stop protecting Cerise. She would keep the promise she'd made to Tregan as long as she had breath in her body.

⚜

When Merta had arrived in Sudo Bay nineteen years earlier, carrying a blanket-wrapped bundle, the Aikawas, her extended family, welcomed her in. She introduced herself as

Maemae, the pet name her parents had called her as a child. The elder Aikawas remembered her mother and father from their younger days before her parents had gone to Argonne, and they embraced Maemae as one would a lost child. Merta explained that the baby in her arms was the result of a brief encounter she'd had with a merchant from Riddien. She was roundly admonished for not using birth control, but everyone agreed that having an albine in the Aikawa family meant nothing but good luck.

Merta named the baby Cerise because of her cherry red hair. She fretted about the sigil on the baby's back, which clearly identified her as Sabrin né Franklin, the daughter of the king. It was as big around as a peach stone and easy to spot against the baby's snowy skin. She kept Cerise covered up head to toe, using the baby's sensitivity to the sun as an excuse for not letting her be seen naked.

When Cerise was four months old, Merta met Min, who was a foreman at the seaweed processing plant. Her aunt arranged for the two of them to find themselves alone during a large family gathering, and, despite all the meddling from the relatives, the two fell in love and were married shortly after.

There was no hiding the baby's sigil from Min, and Merta took him into her confidence and told him who she really was. He was instantly supportive and pledged to keep her secret and protect Cerise from anyone who might want to harm her. It was his idea tattoo a birthmark over the top of the sigil. Before he did it, however, he got out his calligraphy tools and painted a detailed copy of the sigil's runes and symbols onto a piece of parchment. He hid the parchment in a safe place where no one would find it, knowing at some point the child would want to know her legacy. Then he filled his tattoo pen with ink-root and blacked in a birthmark that Merta thought resembled a flying fish.

Cerise grew up headstrong and carefree and was adored by

all the Aikawas. Her first love was always the sea, which was as wild and unpredictable as she was. Nothing made her happier than sailing out of port at dawn balanced atop a railing, ocean spray on her face. By the time Cerise was thirteen, Merta and Min no longer talked about the day they would tell her who she really was. It no longer seemed important.

CHAPTER 7

Luce lay on the bunk next to Cerise, watching the sky grow pale through the porthole. The sound of waves thumped softly against the hull. She stretched, then traced the outline of the birthmark on Cerise's shoulder. "Your skin feels rough here —lumpy."

Cerise shifted on the bunk. "Maemae says it's always been that way. I can't reach it, so I don't really notice."

Luce cherished these early mornings with Cerise. It was the only time she could get her to actually talk; it was like she hadn't put on her armor for the day yet. Luce rubbed her thumb back and forth over the birthmark. "There's something underneath your skin here, sort of a roundish ridge. Does it bother you?"

"No. It's strange though. It tingles when things get intense: when I shout an order, or like yesterday when I fought the sea dragon. Some kind of muscle spasm." She chuckled softly. "Baba says the spirit of the flying fish lives inside my heart."

Luce smiled. That sounded like something Min would say. "Does it hurt?"

"No, the opposite. I feel braver if that makes sense, and my knife arm feels stronger... It's all in my mind, of course." Cerise rolled over and pinned Luce beneath her. Her golden hair came loose from its leather tie and cascaded across the pillow. "You've fallen in love with a madwoman!"

Their laughter filled the tiny cabin.

"That's for certain," Luce said as she wrapped her arms around Cerise's neck and kissed her softly.

⚜

While her crew prepared the *Flying Fish* to sail, Cerise rowed out to the *Dreike*, which was anchored offshore. She was both excited and nervous to meet the captain of a tall-ship for the first time. Most tall-ship captains had a reputation for being intimidating or tyrannical. Captain Tayjal certainly looked the part. He was an imposing Argonnian with white hair, gold teeth, and skin the color and texture of a raisin. It only took a few moments, however, to discover they spoke same language, the language of the sea. He spread out a map of the coast and plotted the course with his finger.

"The detail on this map is amazing," Cerise said with respect. "Is this your work?"

"My navigator gets most of the credit," Tayjal replied. "I just filled in some blanks."

Cerise smoothed the map out with her hand. The route from Sudo Bay to the Port of Isidima had been well charted, and the map was covered with notes and sketches that Tayjal had added over the years. Cerise loved maps, and the two fell into an easy rapport, discussing the challenges of this voyage and their past experiences at sea.

"I plan to make this voyage an uneventful one for you," Cerise said as they returned to the deck.

"No voyage is ever uneventful, as you no doubt know," Captain Tayjal said. "But I welcome having you as my escort.

Port Master Aki speaks highly of you, and your record speaks for itself. It is good to finally meet you, Cerise Aikawa."

Hearing praise from the captain did not engender the same feelings of irritation she usually experienced receiving compliments. Maybe it was her respect for his position, or maybe it was because he called her by her real name. They wished each other good sailing, and Cerise paddled back to the *Flying Fish*, even more excited about the upcoming adventure.

The two ships set sail under a clear sky, taking advantage of the ebbing tide. Cerise held the *Flying Fish* several lengths in front of the *Dreike*, scanning the sea for rocks and other vessels. The wind was favorable and the sea remained calm throughout the journey south. Only one ship came within hailing distance of the *Dreike*, a fishing vessel harvesting spider crabs. Cerise steered the *Flying Fish* next to her and hailed the captain for permission to come aboard. Once on board, she examined the fishing vessel's papers and traded weather reports with the captain. This was followed by a shot of whiskey and stories of the big one that got away. As she reboarded the *Fish*, one of the sailors shouted, "Saint Cerise."

How has this name followed me all the way out here? she thought.

They were twenty days out from Sudo Bay when they reached the Serpent's Tail, a series of steep island peaks that jutted out of the ocean like the spines of a giant underwater sea creature. The islands were a natural barrier separating the ocean from the Bay of Argonne. Narrow water passages ran between the islands with currents that were greatly affected by the tides, making them dangerous to navigate. The largest of these gaps, known as the Sluice, was used as a shipping channel by some of the more seasoned cargo haulers because it cut several days off the journey to Isidima. Ships could only pass through the Sluice at high tide, and even then only when the tide began to shift, or else the currents became too strong. The Sluice had carried many an unlucky vessel into the sharp rocks surrounding the islands.

Cerise climbed aboard the *Dreike* and consulted with the captain before making the run.

"I've piloted the Dreike through the Sluice many times," Tayjal said. "It can be risky, but not if you follow the steps I've given you."

"I understand," Cerise said.

"My desire is to run the Sluice, but I am willing to take the longer voyage around the Serpent's Tail if you think your crew is too green. They all seem very young."

Cerise stiffened at his comment. "They are more than ready," she avowed. Her crew was unmatched, and she couldn't wait to prove him wrong.

A multitude of seabirds circled the white-streaked cliffs looming above the Sluice, their harsh cries easy to make out even over the boom of the waves against the rocks. When the high tide reached its zenith, Captain Tayjal moved the tall-ship into position. Cerise held the *Flying Fish* in the open water until the *Dreike* started her run. When the current shifted, the *Dreike* unfurled her sails and entered the channel. The captain held her close to the north island as he'd said he would, knowing the current would pull them toward the south island. The *Dreike* slipped through, picking up speed as the current grew stronger. They sailed out of the island's shadow and into Argonne Bay, white sails shining in the sun.

When they started their run, Cerise took over the helm from Tar, not wanting to leave anything to chance. They entered the Sluice when the *Dreike* was halfway through. The current was very strong, and it sucked the *Flying Fish* forward into the channel. She steered for the north island, following the

Dreike's path, and the *Flying Fish* sliced through the water. The current was stronger than she anticipated, however, and she felt it start to pull her ship sideways. She adjusted course, knowing she had no choice but to turn the cutter's nose in the direction of the current to gain back control. They arrowed southward, picking up speed, and white spray cascaded in great sheets over the south island's rocks in front of them. Her pulse quickened as she considered what to do.

"Cerise, we are too close to those rocks!" Tar yelled from the bow.

"I see them," she yelled back. "Hold fast."

They were caught in the current, and Cerise realized she had started her run too late. Wolf seals dove off the cliffs into the water in front of her, and boat wreckage was strewn among the rocks.

"Fuck the gods," she whispered, angry at herself for her earlier boasting with the captain. She would not allow this to happen. She set her jaw, and her shoulder blazed hotly.

"Drop all sails," she roared. "Raise the keel." The crew jumped at her command. The sails fell with a boom, and she felt the change in the boat's stability as the keel went up inside the hull. The *Flying Fish* suddenly felt like a leaf spinning in a stream. She turned the wheel sharply and pointed the bow away from the rocks, sideways to the current.

"Secure yourselves," she bellowed. "Luce, fire the accelerator—now!"

Luce pushed the plunger, and the accelerator's explosive charge rocketed the boat forward and sent it skipping across the waves like a flat stone across a pond. With the keel raised, they cleared the rocks submerged below and shot out into the sun and calmer waters of the bay. The women whooped and raised their fists in the air. Cerise exhaled in relief and looked up at the *Dreike* to see if the captain had been watching. The *Dreike's* crew was lined up along the rails yelling and waving their hats. Up on the helm, the captain raised his hand to her briefly, then resumed shouting commands to his crew. She wondered if she had passed his test.

"Lower the keel and raise the mainsail," she yelled, adrenaline subsiding from her body.

Tar took the wheel back from Cerise. "Was this trip not exciting enough for you?" she asked sarcastically, piloting the *Fish* into the glittering blue waters of the bay.

⚜

Three days later they reached Isidima. The ancient city filled the skyline, towering over the harbor. The women marveled at the wonder of it; Isidima's buildings wound up and around a pillar of volcanic rock like vines growing around the trunk of a tree. Rose-colored stone structures with needlelike spires clung to its sides like corals. Gardens filled with exotic flowers and palm trees spilled over the roofs of buildings like verdant waterfalls, spreading onto the abundant terraces beneath in riots of color. The city's iconic ziggurat, carved out of the extinct volcano's summit, formed the city's crown and dominated the view.

The harbor was teeming with fishing boats of all shapes and sizes and ports of origin. Several tall-ships that plied their trade between Cordel to the north and the island nations south and west across the ocean were anchored in the bay.

Captain Tayjal informed Cerise the *Dreike* would be fully loaded for the return trip and would leave with the tide the following day. That meant she had today to explore the city, and only the gods knew when she might return to Argonne. Cerise put Tar on watch, since she had been to Isidima before, and dismissed the rest of the crew, all of whom excitedly fanned out into the streets. She grabbed Luce and headed for the market square, excited to share their day together.

The square was bustling, full of foods they did not recognize, the air redolent with spice and the smells of grilled meats. The aisles were packed with towering, slender Argonnians, majestic in their fresh white linens and golden baubles, dark skin glistening in the sun. Cerise was amused to find that she felt short moving through the crowds here, whereas in Sudo Bay, she sometimes felt like a giant. She saw many islanders, and a smattering of blond Riddiens and Cordelians mixed in the throng, but only one person of Weslynde lineage.

Cerise's white face and cat makeup drew a lot of stares as they pushed through the crowded aisles. She pulled the brimmed hood of her jerkin forward self-consciously and bought a wide conical hat that shaded her face and cut down on stares as well.

Luce found a silver-wrought hair clip for her long blond hair and modeled it for Cerise.

"It's a pretty thing," Cerise said. "You should have it."

"You should get something pretty for yourself." Luce held up some tiger stone bracelets that had caught her eye.

"I have no need for such baubles," Cerise replied. "Besides, I have my new hat."

"You look like a mushroom."

"Ah! The disguise is working."

They strolled through the market holding hands. Cerise enjoyed the way Luce bartered with the vendors. She was quite striking with her high cheekbones and golden hair, and her laugh was charming; street vendors seemed to want to give her things for free.

They picked up a couple of trinkets to take back to family and wandered out of the square and up the steep paths toward the ziggurat. Halfway up the volcanic mount, they came to a large terraced garden that had a stunning view of the bay. It was filled with statuary, and a fountain gurgled at its center.

Bougainvillea spilled from large ceramic urns placed around the perimeter.

"This is lovely," Luce exclaimed. Cerise had to agree.

The view of the bay far below was beautiful, and the sea breeze cooled the intensity of the sun, so they found a bench in the shade and ate the fish rolls they had picked up in the market. Cerise stretched her legs in front of her and rested her head against the garden wall.

"Oh, look, it's you!" Luce exclaimed, pointing at a statue. She jumped up and crossed the terrace to a marble bust of a woman on a pedestal. "It really does look like you," Luce shouted back at her. "Come and see."

Reluctant to move from her comfortable spot, Cerise sighed and strolled over to the sculpture. "It's only because it's carved from white stone. This is clearly an Argonnian woman." Cerise read the inscription: "Tregan Anthelia." She looked back up at the statue's face. There was something familiar about her mouth and the shape of her jaw.

"Wasn't Tregan Anthelia Prince Jarin's mother?" Luce asked. "She was an Argonnian."

"I'm not sure. I don't follow Weslynde politics."

"I heard she was killed shortly after the prince was born."

"Killed?" Cerise found this surprising.

"By someone in Weslynde. A lot of Argonnians think so anyway. They say it's why the provinces don't get along."

"She's a pretty one anyway." Cerise touched the statue's cheek again, and something strange tickled the pit of her stomach. She shook it off. "Let's get back."

On the way back down to the harbor, they passed a huge mural painted on the side of a building. It was a portrait of Tregan Anthelia, wearing a fierce expression and dressed in a gleaming metal vest. She was holding a stave over her head in a fighting stance, surrounded by Argonnian men and women with their fists in the air.

"She must be a hero to these people," Luce said, impressed.

Something about the way the muralist had painted Tregan's expression drew Cerise in. So strong. So...full of conviction. Cerise's arms prickled with gooseflesh, as if someone had blown on the back of her neck.

⚜

That evening Cerise boarded the *Dreike* to introduce herself to the senators she would escort to Cordel. Luce suggested she change out of her weather-stained jerkin and into a clean outfit before she met them. Cerise changed but refused to remove her eye makeup. She also kept her red hair tied in its warrior's knot, explaining to Luce she didn't want to look soft.

Captain Tayjal did the introductions. "Cerise, this is Senator Kresh of Riddien, Senator Wilmount of Weslynde, and Senator Anthelia of Argonne. Senators, I would like to introduce Cerise of Cordel, the pilot of the *Flying Fish*. She will provide escort for us when we sail."

She bowed respectfully and clasped each senator by the arm in the formal manner of the commonwealth.

The senators were traveling to Sudo Bay to meet with the Premier of Cordel. Their official business was to renew treaties and trade agreements, but Captain Tayjal had pulled Cerise aside before the meeting and explained that the true purpose was to dispel growing rumors of friction among the provinces, especially between Weslynde and Argonne.

In addition to the three senators, the delegation also included Weslynde's house mage, Gerard Mort, and Archbishop Mellon of Riddien, the leader of the Church of the Commonwealth. Cerise grimaced when she discovered the head of the church was present. Ever since she was a child, the church had harassed her, intruding in her life and trying to get her to join them because she was an albine.

The senators peppered Cerise with questions. She had to describe her boat's capabilities and her crew's worthiness, and they made her swear an oath.

"Do you swear to protect this delegation from all harms?" Senator Anthelia asked her.

"I do," Cerise replied without hesitation. "With all my strength and abilities."

"Even if it puts you and your crew in harm's way?"

"Even if it means I die in the attempt." She stood tall and put her shoulders back proudly.

"Well said." The Argonnian senator seemed satisfied.

Cerise was good at this kind of scrutiny and always found it easy to talk about her crew. She felt she'd won the senators over by the time that the wine was poured.

As she was preparing to leave, she was approached by the archbishop and Weslynde's house mage.

"Might we have a word with you?" Archbishop Mellon asked.

"Of course," Cerise said with an inward sigh, figuring it was inevitable that the archbishop would want to fill her ears with stories of the famous albine saints of the past, something she had heard a thousand times before. The three went out into the cool night air above deck. The lights of the city reflected prettily in the harbor.

"News of your triumphs have reached my ears," Archbishop Mellon said.

"Triumphs?" Cerise asked. "What do you mean?"

"Your humility shows your good character, Cerise," the archbishop said approvingly.

"I am sorry, but I truly have no idea what you are talking about." She glanced over at Gerard Mort, who appeared to be sizing her up. It put her on edge.

"The church has been aware of the good deeds performed by the white angel of Cordel for some time now." The archbishop pressed his palms together and pointed them skyward. "The sacred text says we should turn to the sea for a savior clad all in white."

"Clad in..." This was too much for her. "You think because I'm albine I'm some kind of holy person?"

"There have been albine saints, it is true, but I am talking about your deeds of service, not just the color of your face."

"You do realize I am a privateer; I work for the best pay, not because I have a good heart." Cerise wanted to end this conversation. "Some might call me a mercenary. None would call me a savior."

Gerard Mort spoke for the first time. "Cerise, you do yourself a disservice. At fourteen, you rescued your schoolmates from a burning building. At fifteen, you led a team into an underwater cave and freed five sailors trapped inside. No one knew how you found them. Not one seaweed harvester has lost their life since you began protecting the fleet. The captain of the *Dreike* told me this morning that you killed a sea dragon with your bare hands."

Cerise's cheeks grew hot. The mage made her feel off-balance. "How do you know these things?" she sputtered. "Have you been following me?"

"You are famous. I hear the sailors call you Saint Cerise," the mage replied.

Cerise frowned. *That name again!* It was maddening. "Who is spreading these stories?"

Archbishop Mellon smiled even more broadly. "These stories are told and retold by the church-faithful. They have spread far beyond your sleepy town of Sudo Bay and have reached my ears all the way in Riddien."

Riddien? she thought, completely surprised. *That's practically across the world.*

"Children ask their parents to tell them stories about 'Saint Cerise' at bedtime." He leaned in closer and spoke in a conspiratorial voice. "Tell me, is it true that you can fly over the water like a flying fish? And turn saltwater fresh?" He chuckled at his own joke. "We have many stories about you."

Cerise writhed inside. It was bad enough to hear it on the streets of Sudo Bay. But from Riddien's archbishop? And why would the house mage of Weslynde be interested in this conversation? She glanced his way, but his face was unreadable. No matter. She'd had enough.

"I don't listen to bedtime stories," she said. "Tell me what it is you want."

"Want?" The archbishop placed his hand on his chest, shocked. "We don't want anything. We only wanted to meet you and extend our offer of support."

"I am sorry to disappoint you, but I don't subscribe to the church's worldview. I don't believe in the gods. I'm not the saint you think I am." She started backing away. "Sirs, I thank you for this informative and...flattering conversation. Rest assured I will do my utmost to protect you on your voyage to Cordel."

"We are most grateful, and we look forward to speaking with you again." The archbishop held out his ring to be kissed. Not sure what to do, Cerise took his hand and shook it. The archbishop withdrew his hand and gave her the slightest of nods, then returned inside the ship. Gerard Mort continued to stand between her and the gangplank.

"Is there something else?" Cerise asked, unable to get by without pushing him, which was a tempting idea. The mage was scrutinizing her face. She resisted the urge to brush something off of her nose.

"I have a favor to ask you," the mage said.

"Name your favor." Cerise went on alert.

"I'm looking for someone. A woman."

"A woman?"

"Yes. During my visit here, I learned she may be in Sudo Bay. She has something I would like returned."

"What does she look like, this woman?"

"She would be a middle-aged woman of Cordelian descent. Dark eyes, dark hair, olive skin, small of stature."

"You just described every woman in Sudo Bay. What is her name?"

"The woman's name is Merta," Gerard Mort said. "She used to be in service to Lady Tregan Anthelia. Perhaps you have heard of her? Tell me where she might be found?"

Tregan Anthelia again? Cerise thought, remembering the bust and the mural. *Twice in one day.*

"I don't know anyone like that. I'm sorry." She tried to step around him, but he didn't move.

There was a long awkward pause while the mage studied her, as if he was searching for flaws, cracks in her armor. Cerise returned his gaze firmly and fought down the impulse to slap him.

"No matter." He finally broke off and stepped out of the way. "I will say goodnight and let you retire. If you remember something, please let me know."

"Of course." Cerise bowed and hurried down the gangplank. She felt his eyes on her back the entire way down the dock.

Cerise was in too much turmoil to sleep. She found this Saint Cerise business more and more disturbing. Did children really tell stories about her in Riddien? Maemae had warned her that she would always have to deal with zealots because she was albine. But what was really keeping her awake was the house mage. The way he looked at her, like she was hiding something. And who was this woman he was seeking? Merta was a common enough name in Cordel, but this Merta he was searching for had once served Tregan Anthelia, Prince Jarin's long-deceased mother. It was so strange. She'd seen the bust of Tregan Anthelia this very day and Luce had said it resembled her. Maybe Maemae or Min had heard of this Merta woman.

When it was Janis's turn to watch, Cerise took her place instead, staring out at the sea the rest of the night.

⚜

The return trip to Sudo Bay took longer than the voyage down to Isidima. Captain Tayjal directed Cerise to escort them around the southern end of the Serpent's Tail, deciding against running the Sluice. He wasn't taking any risks with the senators on board.

They were two weeks out from Sudo Bay when the *Dreike* was attacked. The tall-ship had rounded Sparrow's Point and was sailing close to shore, searching for a sheltered cove to drop anchor for the night. The breeze was light, making it slow going, and it grew dark before they could find a suitable location. The *Flying Fish* was sailing on the inland side of the tall-ship and Cerise had her crew on high alert, scanning the coastline for possible threats. The sea was smooth and glassy, and the conifer forests along the shore were black silhouettes against the evening sky.

Janis was on the mast, scanning the sea with her glass, when a shadow separated itself from the forest's reflection and headed toward the *Dreike*.

"Incoming! Forward starboard," she shouted down to Cerise. "It's a boat, coming in fast."

Cerise sprang up on the gunwale and saw a small black boat skimming past their bow, oars furiously scooping the water, attempting to get around the front of the *Dreike* in order to put the tall-ship between it and the *Flying Fish*.

"Alert the *Dreike*," she ordered, gripping the rigging tightly.

The warning horn sounded, and she saw the *Dreike's* crew

react, scattering across the deck. They spotted the boat, and the captain did what Cerise hoped he would do—he turned hard to port. The *Dreike* couldn't avoid contact with the small boat, but the maneuver would give the *Flying Fish* time to intercept. Skua unfurled the gennaker, even though the wind was light, and Tar steered toward the *Dreike*, intending to put themselves between it and the unknown vessel. It was frustratingly slow, and the mystery boat had the advantage. Cerise held off using the accelerator. It only had one charge remaining and needed to be timed for best effect.

She cupped her hands around her mouth and yelled loudly, "Unknown vessel, put your oars up and stand down." There was no response, and the boat continued to press forward. Cerise had to act. "Crossbows," she barked. "Luce, ready the harpoon. Prepare to board."

Her mission was clear: stop the boat and allow the *Dreike* time to escape, and that meant engagement. The mystery boat changed course and headed directly for the side of the *Dreike*. Did it intend to ram the tall-ship? That would smash the small boat and not do much damage to the *Dreike*. It seemed like suicide. Did they carry explosives? They were close enough now that she could make out crouching figures holding wooden shields above them, keeping low to avoid arrows.

The crew of the *Dreike* stood along the railings, watching the small boat come in, preparing to fire their crossbows. The boat would reach the tall-ship before the *Flying Fish* could get between them.

"Luce," Cerise climbed up onto the harpoon platform next to her. "Aim for the bow and try to pierce the boat's hull. Fire now!"

Luce pulled the trigger and the harpoon whistled away, piercing the boat's hull three feet from the nose. Screams echoed across the water as the spear met its mark.

"Perfect! Now reel it in! Fast!"

Luce hit the spring-loaded winch, and the rope recoiled. The harpoon jammed against the inside hull of the attacker's boat, jerking it away from the *Dreike* as the winch pulled it toward the *Flying Fish*.

"Be ready; here they come," Cerise warned her crew as the attackers were reeled in.

Two dark silhouettes aboard the small boat suddenly jumped up and fired crossbows at the *Dreike*. The crossbows were fitted with hooks and ropes, and the hooks lodged on the tall-ship's gunwale. The two attackers swung across the water and climbed up the hull. Dee fired her crossbow and took the first one out; he fell screaming into the water. The second made it to a porthole, but Janis fired before he disappeared inside. The figure slumped, hanging halfway out of the hole. The *Dreike*'s crew rained arrows down on the remaining attackers, who held their shields over their heads as the tall-ship pulled away. The attacker's boat was rapidly approaching the *Flying Fish,* and Cerise counted four figures on board. She pulled her sword from its sheath.

"Get down," she yelled to Luce, who was standing on the harpoon platform, monitoring the winch.

Seconds before they collided, the attackers threw down their shields and stood, firing arrows wildly at the women. Cerise ran forward and leapt across the six-foot gap into the attackers' boat, slashing with her sword.

Dee and Janis shot two of the assailants, and Cerise sliced the neck of the third. The fourth charged her with a knife, but she sidestepped and pulled him off-balance. She stabbed the back of his leg and he fell, writhing in pain. She put a knee on his back and used a rope inside the hull to lash him to the deck. "Now we find out who you are." She pulled back his hood, and his eyes blazed at her defiantly. His dark lip was pierced with a gold ring, and beads were woven through his black braids. He was Argonnian.

Cerise looked back at the *Fish*, quickly scanning for injuries. Luce was still standing on the harpoon platform, her back against the mast. Cerise didn't comprehend at first, but then she saw. An arrow had pierced Luce's chest and lodged itself in the wood, pinning her to the mast. Luce was struggling, trying to dislodge the arrow and pull herself free.

"Gods, no." A groan tore from Cerise's lips. Her ears filled with noise as she leapt across to the *Fish*. She scrambled over to Luce, trying to figure how to lift her up, how to remove the arrow.

"Cerise," Luce moaned quietly. "I'm sorry...I didn't listen."

"Hush," Cerise ordered. She had Janis and Tar hold Luce's arms while she yanked the arrow hard. She couldn't dislodge it, and Luce cried out in pain. Shoulder tingling, Cerise closed her fist around the end of the shaft and snapped it off where it entered Luce's chest. Janis and Tar lifted Luce off of the shaft and laid her down on the deck. Tar pressed her hand down on the wound to stop the bleeding. Blood pooled out on the deck beneath her.

Cerise knelt over her, kissed her on her hands and face, and whispered. "Please, please, don't go. Stay with me."

Cerise's shoulder grew hot while she held Luce, but then the warmth slowly dissipated, and finally ice spread throughout Cerise's body. Luce was gone.

The surviving attacker was taken on board the *Dreike* to be questioned. Captain Tayjal invited Cerise to participate in the interrogation, but she declined, taking the *Flying Fish* farther up the coast about a mile and dropping anchor.

The captain didn't learn much from the prisoner before he died. Gerard Mort expressed regret that the interrogation techniques he applied might have hastened the prisoner's demise.

What was learned was that all six attackers were Argonnians. Glass vials full of a deadly gas were found sewn inside their clothing. The gas would have killed the attackers as well as the victims if they were smashed open, making it a suicide mission.

The captain gathered the senators together and informed them that they were the target of an attack. Gerard Mort singled out the Argonnian senator, Tregor Anthelia, for additional questions.

"Senator," the mage said. "Forgive my insensitivity, but given the circumstances, does your prime minister condone this Argonnian assassination attempt?"

"Of course not," Senator Anthelia shot back. "Does your king condone your insulting line of questions?"

"I meant no disrespect," the mage said coolly.

"Oh, I think you did." Senator Anthelia pushed his chair back and left the cabin.

⚜

Gerard Mort made his way below deck and knocked quietly on Archbishop Mellon's cabin door.

"Enter," the archbishop called out from within. The mage entered and closed the cabin door behind him. The archbishop was finishing a late meal; a stained napkin covered his ample belly. He poured whiskey into an empty glass and pushed it across the table. Gerard Mort swallowed it in a single gulp and poured himself another.

"What was learned?" The archbishop shoved his plate aside and wiped his greasy hands.

"The captain believes the attackers were part of an Argonnian group that is plotting to secede from the commonwealth. Their goal was to kill the senators, thereby sowing further dissension among the provinces. Unfortunately, the prisoner started to share information that might have complicated our plans, so I had to...um...shorten the interrogation."

"Are we compromised, then?"

"No. The captain thinks they acted alone." Gerard Mort chuckled. "I did upset the Argonnian senator though. I suggested the Argonnian prime minister might be behind the attack. That comment alone should further strain relations with Weslynde."

"Tregor Anthelia? He's a powerful senator. Your insult will no doubt find its way back to the prime minister." The archbishop sipped his whiskey. "Isn't he Prince Jarin's grandfather?"

"He is."

"That might soften his feelings toward Weslynde. What is his relationship with the prince?"

"I would say that Senator Anthelia is ... disappointed in his grandson."

"Interesting. What now?" Archbishop Mellon asked.

"We proceed as before. This incident plays into our plans nicely. The albine thwarted the attack as I predicted she would. I will continue to befriend her and gain her trust. You and your clerics will spread this new tale of Saint Cerise, how she singlehandedly saved the leaders of the commonwealth from the treachery of Argonnian non-believers."

"You are putting a lot of effort into creating an alliance with this girl," the archbishop mused. "She seems wild and unpredictable and, by her own admission, is not at all aligned with the church. Are you sure she will get us what we want?"

Gerard Mort thought back on his brief encounter with Cerise. Everything the archbishop said was true. She was defiant and would be hard to manage. But her brave deeds spoke for themselves. The people of Cordel loved her—they called her the white angel—and she had easily foiled the attack on the *Dreike*. If he could enlist her, give her a reason to fight the Argonnians, she could put him and the church in power.

She was bold, charismatic, and there was something else about her. Something strangely familiar that he couldn't quite figure out. He wished he could see her without all that face paint she wore.

"King Franklin does not support the idea of including the church as part of his government," the archbishop grumbled.

"Leave the king to me. When the time is right, he will make the necessary change."

"He will not be king forever. What happens after he dies?"

"Are you speaking of the ridiculous Prince Jarin? He is nothing, a buffoon. He spends his time drinking, gambling, and sleeping with the servant boys. He will be easy to manipulate."

"Still, it will be hard to get the royal family to pay fealty to the church," Archbishop Mellon said. "That could take generations."

"All you need is a savior, and I think we have one." Gerard Mort raised his glass in a toast.

The women held a ceremony for Luce on board the *Flying Fish* at dusk. Cerise kept silent, letting the others pay tribute. She was afraid to speak lest her grief overwhelm her and flood the boat. One by one, each woman laid an item that meant something to Luce on the wrapped body and shared a memory. Cerise placed the silver hair clip Luce had found in Isidima on the shroud. Her fingers trembled as she let the clip fall from her hand. When the sun touched the rim of the ocean, painting it orange, Dee broke into a sailor's lament in her sweet soprano. When the last speck of sun disappeared under the horizon and the sea went dark, they lowered Luce's body over the side and let it sink into the depths. Then they held on to each other and sang songs about sailing until the stars shone thickly overhead.

The seashell fossil that Luce had worn hung around

Cerise's neck now. She sat on the deck and absently rubbed it, going over and over the events of the attack in her mind, cursing herself for not doing the things that might have kept Luce alive. When dawn came and Tar took the watch, Tar found Cerise still sitting there and had to coax her below.

The *Flying Fish* sailed into Sudo Bay a full day before the *Dreike*. Captain Tayjal had asked Cerise to proceed ahead and alert the port master of the tall-ship's pending arrival. Cerise dismissed the crew and briefed Port Master Aki on the events of the voyage. After that there was nothing left for her to do. She stood on the dock, unable to move, unable to think, unable to breathe. She was only dimly aware that her feet began to move on their own, step by step, leading her home.

Min was working in the garden and knew by the way Cerise walked up the lane that something had happened. He waited for her, leaning on his rake until she stopped in front of him. He touched the seashell fossil hanging around her neck and went into the house, returning with a bottle and two glasses. They made their way down to the creek and sat on a rock next to a small waterfall. They drank in silence and listened to the water burble over the stones as evening turned to night.

CHAPTER 8

The seaweed harvest was over and the bonito migration was still a month away. The empty fishing boats rode the gentle swells in the harbor, masts nodding back and forth like a field of dry grass. The crew of the *Flying Fish* found odd jobs in town while waiting for their next mission.

Everything on board the *Flying Fish* reminded Cerise of Luce, so she moved in with Maemae and Min. She re-thatched her parents' cottage roof and helped them bring in the early summer fruit. She was in the orchard, picking cherries with Min, when Maemae brought out some rice balls wrapped in seaweed. They sat in the shade of a sour-cherry tree to eat.

"I saw something odd in town yesterday," Maemae said.

"What did you see?" Cerise asked, taking a rice ball.

"Three women wearing novice robes, like the ones they wear at the abbey."

"What's odd about that?"

"The robes were red, not the traditional gray. And their faces were painted white."

"White?"

"You know, painted like they were in a play. And their eyes

were all lined with black paint." She traced a finger around her eyelid to demonstrate. "Exactly the way you paint your eyes."

Cerise's stomach did a little flip. "Saint Cerise," she whispered under her breath.

"What?" Min asked.

"Oh, nothing—it's just something I heard. Some of the workers down on the dock called me Saint Cerise as a joke, and then on the trip to Argonne..." She trailed off, reluctant to mention anything about that trip.

"What about the trip to Argonne?" Min asked. "Go on, tell us." He gave her an encouraging nod.

"I met the Archbishop of Riddien and the house mage of Weslynde," Cerise said. "They were aboard the *Dreike*. The archbishop said that children in Riddien tell each other fairy tales of a hero named Saint Cerise, about her good deeds."

"The archbishop said this?" Maemae asked, taking pinches from her rice ball.

"Yes, he thinks the stories are about me. He says there's a prophecy about a white saint who comes from the sea. Isn't that crazy?"

"Albines are considered good luck," Min said. "That's well known."

"My luck has not been good."

Everyone sat in silence for a few minutes. Cerise dug in the dirt with a stick.

"What is the house mage of Weslynde doing in Cordel?" Maemae asked casually, gathering up the food remnants. "Cerise?"

"Oh, um—he came with the commonwealth senators meeting with the premier. They have been here for two weeks now." Cerise suddenly remembered the other news. "And he's looking for someone."

"Who?" Maemae asked sharply.

"He's searching for a woman named Merta. He thinks she

might be in Sudo Bay. This Merta has something that belongs to him."

"Did you tell him about me?"

Maemae's question struck Cerise as odd. "Why would I do that? Anyway, he said this Merta spent time in Weslynde in service to Prince Jarin's mother…" She broke off. Both her parents were staring at her with shocked faces. "What's wrong? What did I say?"

"What is the name of the house mage?" Min asked.

"Gerard Mort."

"Oh." Maemae stood up and clasped her hands together. "Oh," she said again. Min put his arm around her.

"What's going on?" Cerise had never seen Maemae so upset.

"Oh," Maemae said again.

"Everything will be fine," Min said to Maemae. "Sit down, sit down." He guided her to a log next to the tree.

"Mama, what is it? Tell me." Cerise didn't like the fear in her mother's eyes.

"We're not safe here." Maemae picked up the food tray and walked away, heading back to the house.

"Mama, wait." Cerise gently took her arm and stopped her. "Do you know who Merta is?"

"It doesn't matter. It's not important. We have to go." Maemae pulled her arm loose and went inside the house. Cerise watched her go.

"Baba? Tell me what is happening."

"Cerise, sit, please." He motioned to the log next to him.

It must be serious, she thought. She sat.

"This will be hard to explain," Min said. He took her hand.

"Tell me."

"Your mother used to serve Prince Jarin's mother, Lady Tregan Anthelia. When Tregan died, your mother fled and has been hiding in secret all these years."

"Is Maemae the Merta the mage is looking for?" Cerise asked, dumbfounded.

"Yes. No one here knows her true name."

Cerise's mind was swirling. "I don't understand. What happened in Weslynde? Why is she hiding? Gerard Mort said she took something that belongs to him."

"She took something, but it doesn't belong to Gerard Mort."

"What did she take, Baba?"

"You, Cerise. She took you."

⚜

Cerise sat stunned while Min told her the story of her birth —that she was the daughter of King Franklin of Weslynde and Tregan Anthelia of Argonne and that she was the twin sister of Prince Jarin, the heir to the throne. He told her how Merta had spirited her out of the palace to save her life and how she came to be his beloved daughter. When he finished telling the story, she said nothing, and left him sitting on the log by himself. She went down to the harbor and boarded the *Flying Fish,* telling Janis and Tar she wanted to test the rigging. They spent the rest of the day sailing around the bay.

Her mind was in turmoil. Why hadn't they told her? She had the right to know. And how was she going to come to grips with the fact that she wasn't the daughter of Cordelian seaweed farmers but was actually the daughter of the king of Weslynde? She wanted to laugh out loud; the whole story was so preposterous. Looking back over her life, she realized there had been clues if she had bothered to look for them. At eleven, she'd already been taller than her mother, and she didn't have any of Maemae's Cordelian features. She had always assumed that she must resemble her birth father, a native of Riddien, according to Maemae. But a Weslynder? And Argonnian? She never would have believed she had Argonnian blood. But then Luce had pointed out that bust of Tregan in Isidima. Luce had seen the resemblance immediately, and admittedly, so had Cerise.

As she piloted the *Fish* across the placid swells of the bay, she began to accept the possibility that the story might well be true. King Franklin was her birth father and Tregan Anthelia her birth mother. She had a twin brother in Weslynde, Prince Jarin. A twin, by the gods! But then who was she, really? The white angel of Sudo Bay? Saint Cerise of the church? A Weslynde princess? Most disturbing of all was learning that she was a twin. That she and her brother Jarin both lived. What would the church do if they found out that their precious Saint Cerise was a cursed twin? If Gerard Mort found Merta, would he realize who Cerise really was and try to kill her? And whom could she talk to about this? No one. She fingered the seashell fossil, wishing she could tell Luce about it.

⚜

The sun was well on its downward arc toward the sea when the *Flying Fish* finally headed back to port.

"You've a visitor," Tar shouted up to Cerise as she moored the ship. "What do you think he wants?"

Gerard Mort was standing on the wharf, arms tucked inside his black robes. Her heart sank. "He wants me to confess."

"Confess? Is he a cleric?" Tar asked, confused.

"Worse. A magician."

"I don't understand."

"It's nothing." This moment could not be avoided. "Will you secure the *Fish*, Tar? I need to get this out of the way."

"Of course. G'night, Cerise."

Cerise jumped off the cutter and walked down the dock to Gerard Mort. *He stands so still*, she thought. *Like a snake waiting to strike.* She stopped in front of him, arms crossed. "Good evening to you."

"Ah, Cerise," Gerard Mort said. "I was hoping to see you tonight. We sail back to Isidima in a few days. The port master told me you took your boat out, and I wondered if you would return."

"Why wouldn't I return? This is my home."

"Yes, of course, of course it is," the mage said contritely. "How silly of me." Then he asked, "I would like to ask you a few questions if you have the time?"

"Let's get a drink." Cerise headed for a dockside pub, not waiting for him to follow. It was crowded, but they managed to squeeze into a small table next to a window. The pub master brought them two foaming mugs.

Cerise swallowed half her drink in one gulp and thumped the mug on the table. "What's on your mind, magician?"

"You are a very direct woman."

"I am a privateer. It pays to be direct."

Gerard raised his mug to her in salute. "And a very capable one. Indeed, you have already taken command of this conversation." He smiled.

She did not return his smile, suspicious of his casual demeanor. "You are hoping I have information about this woman you seek. This Merta."

"Direct indeed. Very well. Have you learned anything?"

"Before I help you, I need to understand your motives. I am Cordelian and feel bound to look out for my fellow citizens."

"I honor your loyalty to your country." The mage studied her face for a moment. "Well then, let me be frank."

Cerise took a swig from her mug. *Here it comes*, she thought. *The story of the stolen twin.*

"The woman I am looking for was once in service to the Lady Tregan, mother of the heir to the throne, Prince Jarin. Have you heard of Tregan Anthelia?"

"I am aware of who she is."

"Was. She died years ago."

"I heard she was killed."

"There was indeed some sort foul play surrounding her death. Argonnian separatists objected to her union with King Franklin. We suspect they were involved."

"Argonnians?" Cerise was caught off guard; this was not the conversation she had been expecting.

"Cerise, I am here in Cordel seeking justice for Tregan Anthelia. She was a great lady. I recently came across information that suggests Merta may know what actually happened to her. I want to question her and learn what she knows."

"Why do you think this woman, this Merta, was involved?" Cerise asked.

"There was an Argonnian plot to kidnap Tregan's baby, Prince Jarin, and take him to Argonne, perhaps hold him for ransom. The plot failed, but the same night Tregan gave birth to Prince Jarin, Merta disappeared and was never seen again. We believed she fled to Argonne."

"Argonne? Why aren't you searching there? Why are you looking for her in Cordel?"

"On my recent journey to Isidima, I discovered that Merta's family name is Aikawa."

Aikawa! Cerise thought. *Oh, no. Does he realize I am Aikawa?* She kept her face blank.

"Merta's parents lived in Argonne, but they were originally from Sudo Bay. The Aikawas own a seaweed factory here, and I think she may have come here to be with her family."

"The Aikawas are a huge family," Cerise countered. "Every third person in Sudo Bay is related to the Aikawas. As a matter of fact, my own surname is Aikawa." Cerise saw no surprise in his eyes and realized he had been baiting her. "You already knew this." Cerise felt the noose tightening.

"That is why I came to you. As you are an Aikawa, you must have an idea where this woman is."

They both sipped their ale. Cerise looked out the window at

the lights on the water, taking this moment to regain control. When was he going to say he knew who she was? She fingered her knife under the table.

"There is more to this tale than you have told me, Gerard Mort. The kidnapping plot failed. Prince Jarin is alive and well in Weslynde. So why do you still look for this woman? You said she has something of yours?" Cerise had to know. She closed her hand around the hilt of her knife.

"Ah, yes." The mage set his mug down. "Alright, then—I'm going to tell you everything I know, but I hope that you will keep this to yourself."

"I will decide once I hear."

"As I said, Merta was a spy, working for Argonnian separatists. I discovered she planned to kidnap the heir once he was born and flee to Argonne. The truth is, the Argonnians planned to make him king of Argonne and break away from Weslynde."

"This is hard to believe."

"The kidnapping plot failed, as you said, but Merta escaped. And when she fled, she took a very important artifact with her. An artifact the Argonnians could still use to lay claim to the throne."

"An artifact?"

"The royal sigil, a ring that identifies the wearer as the legitimate heir to the throne."

"She took a ring?"

"The royal sigil."

"She took Prince Jarin's sigil?"

"No. This was a second sigil. One that was made in case the child born was female. It had different...charms inside it. Two are always made. It should have been destroyed. Someone in possession of this sigil could claim to be the heir and cause chaos. That is why I need to find this woman Merta. She must know where the sigil is."

"What will you do once you find her?" Cerise's heart beat a little faster.

"I hope to retrieve the sigil, prevent war between Weslynde and Argonne, and save the monarchy. Nothing more. Will you help me?"

"I am not an agent for Weslynde."

"This affects Cordel as well as Weslynde, and that is why I am asking you. People trust you. If you ask a question, you will get an answer that a stranger would not."

Cerise weighed her options. The mage did not appear to know that there was a second child, a twin. He didn't realize who she really was. This was a relief, but he thought her mother was a spy for Argonne. If he found her, Cerise would not be able to protect her. And this story of a sigil? Min hadn't mentioned that. If Maemae still had it, maybe there was a way to return it to Gerard Mort without revealing more. If not, they would have to leave Cordel! She needed to buy time.

"I will help you." Cerise pushed back from the table. "I'm not convinced your story is true, but it should not be hard to piece together some family history with the Aikawas and learn if such a woman exists. I will need some time."

Gerard Mort nodded his head. "I thank you. The *Dreike* leaves in three days, and I will be aboard."

"You will hear from me before you leave." Cerise tossed the pub master a coin and had him refill Gerard Mort's mug before departing through the door.

Brew in hand, Gerard Mort followed Cerise outside as she made her way down the dock to the *Flying Fish*. Laughter rippled across the water as she greeted her crewmates. The sun had slipped below the horizon, and when Cerise climbed aboard the cutter, her silhouette was captured perfectly against the crimson sky. Backlit the way she was, her profile reminded him of Prince Jarin, tall and slim, with the same straight-backed regal bearing the prince had inherited from his mother Tregan.

Prince Jarin! Both times he had met Cerise, she had reminded him of someone, but it was so hard to tell what she really looked like behind all that face paint. It was obvious she wasn't a native Cordelian—she was much too tall—but did she have some Argonnian in her? And the resemblance to Jarin. Was she somehow related to the Anthelias? Startled, he inadvertently jerked his arm and sloshed ale over the rim of his mug. He wiped his hands on his robes and crept a little closer to the cutter, standing behind a lamppost as she went below deck. One of her crewmates jumped off the ship and walked down the dock toward him. He kept to the shadows, and she didn't notice him as she passed by.

The harbor was quiet now. The only sounds were the cries of seabirds and wooden boats knocking against the pylons. Gerard Mort's heart thumped in his chest. A revelation was pressing on his mind. It was almost there, becoming clearer.

The mage called up his magic. He closed his eyes and focused his energy, reaching out across the water and sifting through the interior of the *Flying Fish*, searching for something, anything that might unlock this mystery. Casting such a wide net was exhausting, but he persisted; he had to understand. Wood, canvas, rope, and foodstuffs filled his awareness, along with a generous amount of smokeless powder, which he assumed must be for the ship's accelerator. Then something unusual tickled the back of his mind. He started over and sussed only the metal on the ship. There it was. A strange metal, unlike any other. Just a small amount. It was moving through the cabin; Cerise must be carrying it with her, in her pocket perhaps. It was sky metal! He recognized its unique signature immediately.

He leaned back against a piling, his magic draining away.

He was stunned by what he'd found. The sky metal must be the royal sigil; nothing else made sense. Cerise had the missing sigil with her! But how? He thought about the way she'd looked at him when he'd mentioned it. There had been no reaction from her, no hint of recognition. Her blue eyes were like armor. Blue eyes! He'd seen those eyes before. Where? The king! He hadn't seen it until now because of all that cat makeup she wore. The king's eyes! Jarin had them too. And now he saw Tregan's profile in her face, her jawline, her nose. *By the gods,* he thought. This woman, this Cordelian he had been promoting as Saint Cerise was the child of King Franklin and Tregan Anthelia, and she carried Sabrin né Franklin's sigil in her pocket! But how could that even be possible? The king and Tregan had never met each other before she came to Weslynde. There wasn't time for a second pregnancy before Tregan died.

Then the pieces fell together. A silo fire the night Jarin was born. He and the king torn away from the birth. Merta and the healing woman alone in the room when the baby was born, and then Merta never seen again. By the gods! Tregan had given birth to twins, and Merta had stolen one of the babies. Royal twins. And both alive. The implications! If the truth came out, there would be chaos.

Gerard Mort realized that he'd revealed his cards to her; she had the upper hand now. She knew he was looking for the sigil. *She must know who Merta is and where she is; by the gods, her own surname is Aikawa.* How could he have been so blind? Did Cerise realize she was the daughter of the king? She must. Why else would she have the sigil? He started down the dock to confront her but then stopped, reconsidering, the beginnings of a new plan forming in his mind. A plan to turn Cerise to him. To put her on the throne instead of Jarin and then use her to put himself in power. He wasn't sure exactly what he was going to do, but he would have to act fast. And now he could use the sky metal to track her, and she would lead him to Merta.

The mage melted away into the shadows to wait.

⚜

Cerise spent the night on the *Flying Fish*. When Skua came aboard at first light, Cerise hurried home, detouring down a side street, taking care she was not followed. She slipped unnoticed into her parents' cottage, surprising Merta and Min, and quickly told them about her conversation with Gerard Mort, how he was searching for Merta because he believed she had taken the royal sigil. She also told them that the Mage had not mentioned anything about twins and perhaps her secret was still safe. Merta clutched her apron tightly while Cerise spoke.

"Mama, do you have the sigil?" Cerise asked.

Merta opened her mouth but no words came. She turned to Min for help answering; he patted her arm reassuringly and made her sit down. Then he went into the back room and reappeared with a box. Inside the box was a scroll tied with a leather strip. He undid it and spread the crinkled paper out on the table. It was an exquisite calligraphy of a royal crest, filled with symbols and words in a language Cerise didn't recognize. Ringed around the outside of the crest, in common script, was the name 'Sabrin né Franklin.'

"Is this a drawing of the sigil? Is this the ring?" she asked, touching the image on the paper.

"Yes," Merta said. "This is what it looks like. It was tossed into the fire the night you were born, but it bounced out. I found it and kept it."

"Where is it now? Perhaps we can return it. Maybe the mage will leave us alone."

"You carry it on you," Min said.

Cerise frowned. "I don't understand."

"A magician embedded it into your shoulder when you

were only a day old." Merta gently traced the round ridge under Cerise's birthmark with her finger. "Can you feel it?"

"Feel my birthmark?"

"The birthmark is only a tattoo to cover it up. Baba inked it on your skin to hide the sigil from view."

"When were you going to tell me?" Cerise sat, stunned by surprise after surprise.

"Our hope was to never have to tell you," Min said.

"Can you take it out?" Cerise asked, reaching over her shoulder, pressing her fingers on the ridge.

"I wouldn't know how," Merta said. "It's part of you. Perhaps a magician could remove it."

"I was hoping to use the sigil as a bargaining chip," Cerise said. "Give it to the house mage so that he would leave you in peace." She rolled up the scroll and retied it. "Mama, the mage thinks you are a terrorist from Argonne. I don't think he will stop looking for you. I bought us a couple of days, but it's not safe for you here anymore."

"We're not going anywhere. This is our home," Min said, planting his feet apart. "We can fight him."

"And you would lose, old man," Merta said, pushing him back down by his shoulders. "Cerise, your mother put a life charge on me to protect you, and while I live, I intend to do that. If that means we have to leave this place, then so be it."

"We need to go now." Cerise paced the room and thought for a moment. "We can go aboard the *Flying Fish*—she is the fastest vessel in port right now. I can take you to Argonne or farther south to the islands, someplace safe. I don't have a lot of coin, but we can make a living as we go, live on board the *Fish* if we must."

"I have something set aside for a day such as this," Merta said, going to the pantry shelf. She tiptoed on top of a stool and reached a faded pack tucked on a high shelf in the back. She took a leather purse out of it and turned it over. A large sum of money spilled out on the table. "This belongs to you. It was given to me to use however I needed to make sure you were well cared for."

"This is a fortune, Mama." Cerise laughed in amazement. "Enough to buy a small property and still have money to live."

"We could have bought a new cart," Min said, scraping the coins into a pile.

Merta slapped his hand. "It came from your mother, the Lady Tregan. It belongs to you."

"You are my mother," Cerise said. "My mama. And you are my baba." She hugged them both and kissed them, then proceeded to push the coins into her pack, along with the rolled-up calligraphy. "I am going into town to alert the crew, get the *Fish* ready to sail, and buy provisions. Gather what you need and be ready by dusk. I will return for you. Only bring what you can carry in a pack. We sail tonight." Cerise grabbed her pack and went out.

Cerise hastily gathered her crew aboard the *Flying Fish*. "Be ready to sail when it is fully dark."

"Can you tell us what's happening?" Janis asked.

"Not with any clarity," Cerise replied. "Some bad people are hunting for my parents and I'm afraid they will hurt them. I need to take them to a place far away where they will be safe—Argonne, maybe, or the southern islands." She realized with a pang that she might be leaving Sudo Bay for good. "To be honest, I don't know when I will come back, if ever. If you want to remain in Sudo Bay, I will understand."

"Our home is with you." Tar held her hand out, palm down. The others laid their hands on hers.

Cerise held back her tears and placed her hand on top. "Together."

"Together forever," her crew chanted in response.

Cerise gave Tar money for provisions and a bribe for the port master. If anyone asked, he would say they were headed north to prepare for the bonito run. Then she headed back up the road to fetch her parents. As she turned up the main street, she saw the senate delegation she had escorted to Sudo Bay heading her way. They saw her and beckoned to her to join them. There was no avoiding them, so she strode over to greet them, hoping the conversation would be quick.

"Senators." She bowed.

The senator from Riddien, a pale woman with yellow hair in plaits, held out both her hands. "We were never properly introduced—just that absurd grilling we gave you on board the *Dreike*. I am Senator Kresh, of course, but please call me Lenora."

Cerise took her hands in hers and bowed again. "Lenora, I am at your service." She glanced up the road, anxious to be on her way.

"You saved us from those dreadful pirates, and at great personal cost," Lenora went on. "We are in your debt." She extended her arm toward her companions. "You remember Senator Wilmount from Weslynde and Senator Anthelia from Argonne."

Tregor Anthelia stepped forward and bowed. He stood almost seven feet tall. His piercing eyes danced, and he had a charming smile, which he flashed frequently. His white braids framed his dark face; they were strung with beads and hung down his back almost to his waist. "Call me Tregor, and I am also at your service."

Cerise bowed in response.

"Fedor Wilmount." The senator from Weslynde bowed stiffly, looking somewhat uncomfortable, she thought.

Senator Anthelia spoke again. "You seem to be well known

here in Sudo Bay; in fact, we have seen several people out walking with faces painted to resemble you."

"Several people?" Cerise asked, discomfited.

"Indeed, look over there." He pointed. Three young novices stood a respectful distance away, round-eyed, hands clasped at their waists. They wore traditional novice garments, but they were made of red cloth instead of gray. Their faces were painted white, and their eyes were thickly lined with black paint to resemble cat eyes. They bobbed up and down respectfully and hurried off down the road, giggling.

This has gotten out of hand, Cerise thought as they scurried away.

"People here call you Saint Cerise, but I prefer the white angel," Tregor said, laughing. "And, Cerise, this may surprise you, but I feel as if we have met somewhere before. Do you feel the same?"

"I don't see how that is possible," Cerise replied. "I have only been to Isidima once."

"Well, whether we have or have not, I hope to see the white angel and her fellow guardian angels on board the *Flying Fish* sailing beside us when we start south next week. You stopped those barbarians in their tracks and saved us all."

"Hear, hear," Lenora Kresh chimed in.

"I will speak to the captain of the *Dreike* about that," Cerise assured them, knowing she was leaving Sudo Bay that very night. "I apologize, but I must take my leave now. It was a pleasure meeting you again."

"We will meet again soon; I am sure of it," Tregor shouted after her. "You and your women warriors."

⚜

Cerise headed up the hill quickly, hoping not to be stopped

again. She made sure no one else was nearby and turned down a narrow lane between two buildings that led to a footpath that went through the middle of a bamboo thicket. *Why did Tregor Anthelia think we had met before?* Then she remembered that he was the father of Tregan Anthelia, and she stopped in surprise. The senator was her grandfather. He must have seen her resemblance to Tregan. She wanted to turn around and go back and speak with him and ask him questions about her family. She shook her head at this new twist and hurried down the path through the bamboo.

She met back up with the road not far from the lane leading to the cottage and noticed smoke rising over the conifers. Too much smoke for a chimney. Alarmed, she sprinted up the gravel path to the little cluster of homes. The roof on farthest one, her parents' cottage, was in flames. The neighbors had formed a bucket brigade and were trying to put it out, to no avail.

Fear flared up inside her. She pushed through the crowd, shouting, "Mama, Baba!" She grabbed one of her neighbors by the arm. "Have you seen my parents?"

"No, Cerise, I have not."

Someone yelled, "Look out," as the thatched roof fell in on itself with a crackling roar. A torrent of angry sparks flew high into the air, and the cottage walls were quickly engulfed in flames. People were yelling over the top of one another, telling everyone to stand back, to save the other houses. They ran to the cottage next door, beating out sparks with brooms and shovels and pouring water on the embers.

Cerise ran around the burning cottage, trying to find a way in. There was none, not even a recognizable door or window. She got as close as she could until the heat was searing her face. She ran from person to person, asking if they'd seen her parents. None had. She screamed at the fire, "Mama! Baba! Where are you?"

⚜

By the time the last embers were doused, night had fallen. The nearby houses had been saved, but nothing remained of Cerise's home except the stone chimney. Cerise walked slowly around the smoky ruin, looking for any clue that would suggest what had happened to Min and Maemae. She couldn't accept that they'd died inside the cottage. A few neighbors joined her, holding torches to light her way. She widened her circle and walked through Maemae's vegetable garden behind the house. There, among the purple squash, she located a pack, ripped open, its contents strewn across the soil. She knelt and picked up a worn leather tobacco pouch. It was Min's. Not far from there, she found his quilted jacket lying in the dirt. He had escaped the house, but there had been a struggle. Who would do this? Was it the house mage? Had he found Maemae? Were they alive?

A few steps farther, she came across a border stone with a dark stain on it; it felt sticky. She sniffed her fingers. Blood. She wiped her eyes furiously and growled to keep herself in control. At the far edge of the garden, she found more footprints in the soft soil and followed them to the lane. She lost them once they reached the packed gravel of the road, and she clenched her fists in agonized frustration.

She decided to bring back her crew to help with the search and started down the lane toward town. As she did so, the rector from the local parish came running up the lane in her direction, holding a lantern, leading a group of novices in red robes. The rector hailed her when he saw her. The novices clumped around him like baby chickens.

"Word of the fire reached us in town," he said. "Are your parents safe?"

"They are missing. I think they were taken." She was tired

and didn't have time to deal with this. "I'm sorry, rector; I have to go."

"Taken? What do you mean?"

"I found this in the garden." She held up the tobacco pouch. "It belongs to my father. He must have dropped it. There were signs of a struggle. There was blood. I'm afraid they've been hurt; I must find them." She pushed past the rector. The novices parted like sheep.

"Cerise, wait!" The rector held out a sealed envelope. "This arrived at the parish a short time ago. Maybe it will tell us something."

She took it from him. The envelope was addressed to Saint Cerise.

"Who brought this to you?" she asked.

"It was found on the ground by the gatehouse. I was taking it to your ship when we heard about the fire."

Cerise slid a thumb under the seal and broke it open. The message inside was written in native Argonnian, and she couldn't read it. Below the words, someone had drawn a picture of a trident. "I can't read what this says."

"May I?" the rector asked. He translated the message out loud. "'White Devil. A life for a life. You have been warned.' Below the trident it reads 'Freedom for Argonnians.'" The rector shrugged. "A life for a life? I don't understand what that means."

Cerise didn't answer. She couldn't without screaming. Had the Argonnians done this to her? Was this the same group that had attacked the *Dreike*? The captain had said they were part of an Argonnian terrorist group. She crumpled the note in her fist.

"Cerise. Let the church help you," the rector said. "We have prepared for this moment."

"What moment? What are you talking about?"

"You are destined to wage a holy war against the evildoers who seek to harm you. It has been foretold. And we, the church-faithful, will be your warriors." The novices fell to their knees behind him, pressing their palms together and bowing their heads. "Saint Cerise will triumph over the darkness and crush those who oppose her," he said with passion, a fierce light in his eyes.

✦

Tar and Janis raced to help Cerise when the tragic news reached them, leaving the others to finish preparing the *Fish*. The three women searched throughout the night, combing every inch of ground around the destroyed cottage with torches, looking for anything that might lead them to her parents. A short distance down the lane, Janis discovered fresh wagon wheel ruts in the soft earth. A wagon had veered off the road down a small side trail through the woods. The tracks led them back into town, disappearing on the stone road near the wharf.

Shortly after dawn, a novice, red robes flying, came running toward Cerise, who was questioning some fishermen about the Argonnian vessels currently in port.

"Saint Cerise! Saint Cerise!" the novice cried.

"Don't call me that." She wheeled on them. "What do you want?"

"We found something behind the seaweed factory. Come quickly." The novice ran off the way she had come. Cerise whistled to Janis and Tar, and the three of them raced to catch up with her.

The rector was waiting for Cerise, sober-faced, in front of an open shed door. Two novices in red knelt beside him in prayer. The rector glanced at the open door and stepped to one side. Behind the door was a black void that Cerise did not want to enter. She steeled herself and slipped through, taking a moment to let her eyes adjust to the gloom. A wagon-wheeled cart was parked near the back of the shed, and someone was lying in the wagon bed, one arm cradling their head as if sleeping. She stepped closer and recognized Min, the back of his head dark with blood. She put her hand on his face. It was cold.

"Oh, Baba, who did this to you?" Cerise whispered as a tear slipped down her face. "Who, Baba?" She stroked his hand and leaned in next to his ear. "I will find them. And I will kill them. I promise." She kissed his cold cheek and rested her forehead against his. A few dust motes drifted down through a shaft of sunlight that broke through the shed's roof.

"Look down here, Cerise." Tar, who had crept in behind her, put her hand on the wooden slats of the wagon bed. Someone had scraped a crude trident symbol into the wood with something sharp. It was fresh. It was the same as the one drawn on the message the rector had given her.

"What does it mean?" Tar asked.

A shadow blocked the door. "It's the symbol of the Argonnian terrorists." It was Gerard Mort.

In a flash, Cerise had her knife in her hand. "What are you doing here?"

"I came as soon as I heard," the mage said, stepping backward, palms outstretched. "I am here to help you, however I can. Please, I am a friend."

"A friend?" Cerise gripped her knife harder. "How so? You were looking for Merta. She had your damned sigil. Who told you to come here?"

Janis and Tar drew their knives and moved next to Cerise.

"The archbishop. The rector told him, and I came as soon as I heard."

Cerise was trembling. "This Merta you are seeking. She's not an Argonnian spy, do you understand? Tell me you understand."

"I understand," Gerard Mort said. "I was mistaken."

Cerise did not back away. Her knife arm blazed.

"Cerise," the mage pleaded. "Listen to me now. I know who you are, who Merta is. I can help you find her."

"You know?"

"What is he talking about?" Tar asked, shifting her knife.

"May we speak privately?" the mage asked, eyeing Tar's weapon.

"I have no secrets from Janis and Tar." Cerise's tone was dark. She badly wanted to stab the mage, but he'd said he could find Maemae.

"I see. Well, then, we should talk away from the ears of the church," the mage said. "Will you come with me?"

"I have to find my mother." Cerise's voice shook.

"No stone will be left unturned, I promise. Come. It won't take long." He led Cerise and her lieutenants to a quiet spot away from the others.

"Do you trust these two?" the mage asked.

"With my life. Now speak!"

"Very well. Cerise, you are the daughter of King Franklin and Lady Tregan. I believe you know this too."

"Cerise, what is this?" Janis asked.

"That's crazy," Tar said at the same time.

Cerise didn't take her eyes off the mage. The two women stared at her.

"I realized who you are when we spoke at the pier," the mage continued. "I can feel the sky metal you carry with you. It is the sigil of Sabrin né Franklin, isn't it?"

"How does knowing this help me find my mother?" Cerise gripped her knife harder.

"Cerise, I want to help you."

"Tell us what he's talking about," Janis insisted. "Why did he call you the daughter of the king?"

Cerise quickly glanced at Janis's and Tar's confused faces, then back at the mage. Gerard Mort held his palms open in a gesture of submission. She decided not to kill him...yet. She sheathed her knife.

"I learned who I am only yesterday," she told Gerard Mort. "It's true. Maemae, my mother, is the Merta you seek. She stole me out of Weslynde the day I was born because I am Prince Jarin's twin sister and would have been put to death if people knew I existed." She ignored the gasps coming from Janis and Tar. "Merta is not a terrorist, do you hear? She has raised me as her own and kept me safe. She means everything to me. I have to find her." She wiped back an angry tear. No one spoke, and finally she muttered in a low voice full of hurt, "What happens now?"

"I will keep your secret until you are ready to share it," Gerard Mort replied. "May I see the sigil?" He held out his hand.

"You can't. It's inside me."

"What?" The mage's eyes went wide. He reached his arm toward her and closed his eyes. Cerise took a step back and again put her hand on her knife, watching him warily. A few seconds later, his eyes flew open.

"Your sigil has been embedded in your shoulder blade. All its charms and protections are in place. By the gods, how is that possible? Who did this to you?"

"A magician—when I was born."

"What magician?"

"I don't know." She was frustrated now. "This talk solves nothing. You can either help me find Maemae, or you can crawl back in the dark hole you came from. You're a magician, aren't you?" She spun on her heel. "Janis, Tar, let's go."

She made herself go back inside the shed. The novices were tending to Min's body, wrapping it in a tarp so that they could transport her father to the parish. Cerise went over to him while Janis and Tar combed through the shed, looking for clues.

"Goodbye, Baba." Cerise leaned in close to his face. "I will find Maemae; I promise you. If you know where she is, please give me a sign." She kissed his forehead one last time and allowed the novices to cover his face and lift him from the wagon.

"Cerise, over here." Gerard Mort had followed them back to the shed. He bent down inside the door and picked up a small object and held it out in his gnarled hand.

Cerise took it from him and brought it out into the sunlight. It was a round pewter button with a seagull engraved on it. It was from Maemae's jacket.

"She was here." Her voice cracked.

The mage closed his eyes and focused. "There is another, in the dirt outside the shed. Over there in the shadow."

"Here it is," Janis said, bending over to pick it up. "They must have taken her down this path."

Three sets of footprints went down a path behind the shed. The trail led a short distance down to a rocky ledge overlooking the sea. Waves crashed against the rocks below. The soil here was loose and had been kicked about. There were clear signs of a struggle at the edge of the cliff.

"Cerise," said Tar, pointing to the footprints on the ground. "Three sets of prints come down the path to this point, but only two sets continue forward from here."

Filled with dread, Cerise stepped to the edge of the cliff. The waves below thundered in, sending up spray over the rocks and driftwood jumbled up below. Clinging to a piece of wood was a scrap of cloth, the same blue color as the jacket Maemae wore. Cerise scrambled down the steep path and made her way back over the slippery rocks below the cliff. She could not reach the strip of cloth, but sticking out of the pebbles beneath it was a smooth white object. She picked it up and recognized the hair stick, made of whale bone, its end carved to resemble a flying fish. Min had carved it, and Maemae always wore it in her hair. A ragged sob escaped her. The waves were rolling in, and it would not be long before this whole area would be underwater. Cerise had to find her.

"Mama!" she shouted as the next wave curled toward her. "Mama!" Her voice was drowned out by the sound of a wave buffeting the rocks. It overwhelmed her and knocked her backward, but she regained her footing and started to wade out into the surf, the water eagerly sucking at her feet as the wave receded. She lost her balance again, but Tar, who had followed her down, grabbed her and forced her back to shore, dragging her to higher ground.

⚜

Tregor Anthelia poured out a glass of spirits and gestured for Cerise to sit at the little table in his cabin on board the *Dreike*. Cerise swallowed the strong liquor, and Tregor refilled her glass.

"I am very sorry to hear this," Tregor began. "Your father?"

"Murdered," Cerise said.

"Your mother?"

"Drowned."

"This is indeed a tragedy; I grieve for you." Tregor sat silently while she traced her finger around the rim of her glass, then he prompted her. "Tell me, how can I help you? You sought me out for a reason."

"Senator, my parents were killed by Argonnians. I was hoping—"

"Argonnians!" Tregor interrupted. "What makes you say that?"

"I was given a message, a warning."

"Show me the message." Tregor held out his hand. Cerise pulled the crumpled note out of her bag, smoothed it, and handed it to him. He took it and quickly scanned it, then folded it and returned it to her.

"Nothing about this makes me think an Argonnian wrote it. You have been deceived."

"How can you think that?" Cerise asked, bewildered. "Argonnians did this! When I found my father, a trident had been carved into the wagon next to his body. The same symbol as the one inked on this message."

"No one in Argonne has a reason to attack a poor seaweed farmer and his wife," Tregor snapped back, clearly irritated at her. "That is not the Argonnian way."

"I meant you no insult," Cerise said, caught off guard. "I came to ask for your help."

"Because I'm Argonnian?" the senator said, voice tight. "Did you expect me to tell you where to find all the Argonnians hiding out in Sudo Bay?"

"No. I meant...if you heard anything."

"From my spy network? Cerise, who do you think I am?" Tregor set down his glass with a thump.

Everything she said seemed to make him more upset. "Senator—I'm not sure what I'm looking for—what I'm looking at." Cerise pushed the letter toward him. "The trident—"

"You have been set up," Tregor interrupted. "There are no Argonnian terrorists in Cordel."

"But the attack on the *Dreike*," Cerise insisted. "Those were Argonnians. Do you deny it?"

"You may recall that attack was against me, not you." The senator walked to the door. "I am truly sorry for your loss, but Argonne has nothing to do with this. I can't help you." Tregor opened the cabin door and ushered her out.

"But I thought... You being my..." She stopped herself from revealing she was his granddaughter. She was not ready yet to open doors she wouldn't be able to close.

"Your friend?" Tregor paused and softened his tone. "I'm

sorry for my overreaction. I hope you find what you are looking for. I truly do." He shut the door, leaving her standing alone in the *Dreike's* cramped passageway.

Cerise left the *Dreike* confused by his reaction. Were all Argonnians this prickly? The senator's response had done nothing to change her thinking that Argonnians were responsible for Min's murder; in fact, it increased her suspicions and dislike for Argonnians in general. Did the senator have something to hide?

Cerise spent the rest of the day searching through the city, talking to everyone she met. The few Argonnians living there knew nothing and, like the senator, took great umbrage at the implication that an Argonnian would attack anyone in Cordel. When night fell, she met back up with the rest of her crew. No one had found anything. Cerise went on board the *Flying Fish* and spent the night staring out at the dark sea. Mae Linn brought her something to eat, but her plate remained untouched.

⚜

The next morning, Gerard Mort was on the dock, seated on a seaweed crate, waiting for her. She wanted nothing more than to push him into the ocean, but there was no avoiding him. Maybe he brought some news. She jumped down off the *Fish* and sat beside him.

"Your mother is alive, Cerise; I can feel it," the mage said. "Don't give up hope."

His kind words called up unwanted emotions. She was so tired of crying. She rolled up the pain and stuffed it away. She wouldn't lose control now, not in front of the mage.

"You're a strange man, Gerard Mort. Just when I am done with you, you say something nice like that." She started to break down but shook her head angrily, regaining her composure. "No, she is not alive. There is no hope." She pulled Maemae's whale-bone hair stick from her pocket and held it up as evidence.

Two gulls were fighting over a scrap on the boardwalk. The winner flew off with the scrap; the other followed behind, screaming his displeasure.

"Cerise, listen to me," the mage said. "You may not want to think about this right now, but it's important. You are the child of King Franklin and Lady Tregan, most likely Franklin's firstborn."

"Stolen at birth so I wouldn't be murdered by the king. Not a welcoming family."

Gerard Mort ignored her comment. "If you are firstborn, that means you are the legitimate heir to the throne, not Prince Jarin. You need to go to Weslynde and claim your birthright."

"Why would I want to do that?" Cerise scoffed. "Have you forgotten the curse? I am a royal twin."

"The curse is a fiction," the mage said dismissively. "Listen to me. Claiming your right as firstborn puts the power and might of Weslynde at your fingertips. As princess, you can demand reparations from Argonne, the province that took your family from you."

Cerise had not considered this before. A path to justice. A way to make those who hurt her pay. Someone should be punished.

Surprised by her vehement reaction, she quickly tamped down her anger and tried to let reason guide her.

"Prince Jarin might object," she said.

"Prince Jarin is a fool. He wants nothing more from life than to carouse with miscreants and drink himself into oblivion. He doesn't want to lead. Trust me, the prince is not a problem."

"Even if that were true, there is the king. Why would he choose me over his son?"

"King Franklin admires strength and boldness, which you

have in abundance. Jarin disappoints him; he longs for an heir worthy to continue his legacy."

"But this is my home." Cerise gazed out at the ships floating in the harbor.

"Not any longer," the mage replied. "You have been cheated out of the life you were supposed to have, and you deserve to have it back. Your loved ones have been wronged, Cerise. You have been wronged. Wronged by Argonne. There is nothing more you can do here in Sudo Bay to fix it. But if you go to Weslynde, you can make things right. You can have justice."

"That sounds impossible. How would I even—"

"I can grant you entrance to the palace and access to the king; he listens to my counsel. You can do this, Cerise."

Cerise held his gaze, seeking hints of deception. She saw genuine desire inside him to help her.

"What about the curse of the twins?"

"We can deal with that fairy tale once you are on the throne. Cerise, you deserve to be the leader you were born to be."

She could be queen. She allowed herself to imagine it. She could put Argonne in its place, demand justice. Make sure they never hurt her or her loved ones again. She imagined herself leading an army of crusaders, beating down her foes. Foes dressed in black. Foes dragging her parents away.

Cerise focused on her ship. Mae Linn and Skua were cleaning the deck. The sun still shone brightly over the blue water. The storm in her heart quieted. This was her home. Her crew was her family. She couldn't leave them.

"My crew?" she wondered out loud.

"Bring them with you," the mage replied.

They would follow her; she knew that for sure. And something was happening inside her, a certainty that this was the right choice. She had always felt destined for something more, something bigger than sleepy Sudo Bay.

"I will consider what you have said," she finally answered.

"Good. I will help you do this. In the meantime, tell no one who you really are. There are many who would exploit you or try to harm you. Take the rest of your crew into your confidence if you must, but make them swear an oath."

"I will. I have no desire for this to get out."

"Cerise—I leave tomorrow on the *Dreike*. When I arrive at Isidima, I will travel straight to Caleddon and prepare the way for you. You will have justice for your loved ones. I promise."

"How will I contact you?" Cerise asked.

The mage stood and dusted off his robe. "I will contact you. And, Cerise, remember that you have an army here, ready to do your bidding. Ready to go to war for you."

"You mean the church? I want nothing to do with them."

"Do not be afraid to use them to your advantage. You are Saint Cerise."

"I never wanted that."

"Claim it! Be the hero you were destined to be. This is your time, Cerise. You are the princess of Weslynde." The mage bowed and left her standing alone on the dock.

I am Sabrin né Franklin, princess of Weslynde, she thought. *I'm returning home to claim what's mine. And if I need her, Saint Cerise will be there to help me.* A squadron of pelicans glided across the bay, floating mere inches above the water. *Who am I fooling? I might be returning to Weslynde, but I'm not returning home. My home is out there, with them.* The pelicans dipped behind the crest of a wave and disappeared from view. She headed back to tell her crew.

PART III

THE PRINCE OF WESLYNDE

CHAPTER 9

The chamber door slammed open, startling Jarin awake. He opened his eyes on Rence pulling the thick curtains aside. Shards of bright sunlight fell across his pillow.

"Fuck the gods," Jarin groaned, head throbbing. He threw an arm over his face. What was Rence doing in his room? Why didn't he knock first? The old steward knew very well Jarin expected his privacy to be respected.

"Get up," Rence ordered. "Get dressed." He began laying out Jarin's clothes.

Two palace guards had entered behind Rence and took position on either side of the open door. *That's not a good sign,* Jarin thought. He eyed them suspiciously. Memories of the night before came flooding back, and he cast a furtive glance at the pillow next to him. There was no one there, thank the gods. He slid his hand across the mattress—*still warm.*

Various house folk hurried past the open door. "What's going on?" Jarin said, rubbing his sandy eyes. He rolled over and took a swig from the wine bottle next to the bed, swished the dregs around his mouth, and spit into a bowl.

"Your father wants to see you. He's waiting for you on the balcony outside the grand hall. Now start moving."

His father! A surprise summons from the king was seldom pleasant. What had he had done this time? Missed a council meeting? Some boring farmland dispute? The thought of facing the inevitable lecture was disheartening, but not going would be worse. Jarin knew better than to keep his father waiting. "Will you at least close the door?" he yelled to the guards, swinging his long legs to the floor and stepping naked from the bed. "Rence, do I have time to bathe?"

"No, you don't," Rence replied, holding out his pants for him.

Jarin's legs were shaky, and he had to hold on to Rence's shoulder as he stepped into his leggings. What could his father want? He had plans to meet his mates at the pub and hoped this wouldn't take too long.

"Bend down so I can reach you," Rence grumbled, holding out his shirt. "You are even taller than your mother was."

Jarin bent forward and fought his way into the sleeves. He raised his head up too fast, and spots danced before his eyes. How much had he drunk last night? He fumbled with the buttons on his vest until Rence knocked his hands out of the way and finished buttoning for him.

He ran his hands down the fine fabric. "This is my formal vest! What's happening, Rence?"

"Here are your stockings and your boots," Rence replied, ignoring the question. "Put them on. You are late."

Rence sounded uneasy, and Jarin's stomach gave a small flip. This was not like Rence at all. He worked his foot into a boot while Rence hurried to the wardrobe and brought out his sash and ceremonial sword. He handed them to Jarin.

"Go. Now!"

"My hair?" Jarin asked, smoothing the mass of tangled curls away from his face.

"No time!" Rence barked as he pushed him out the door.

The guards pulled him down the hall. He cursed at them

loudly, hopping on one leg while he struggled into his other boot.

"Let go of me, you fools, before you run me into a wall!" He wrestled his arms free of their grip and pushed them away, glaring daggers at them while he yanked up his boot.

⚜

The prince harangued the guards until they disappeared around the corner. The boy so reminded Rence of Tregan, his mother. He was not quite as dark-skinned as she had been, but his Argonnian ancestry was plain to see. He was well over six feet tall and reed thin. And he had Tregan's regal bearing (when he wasn't tripping over his big feet). He wished Jarin had also inherited some of her poise and tact and hoped he would deport himself well in front of his father.

The king had been in a volatile mood since those strange women had arrived from Cordel. He needed to find out what was going on, and quickly. He stepped back inside Jarin's door, closed it, and leaned against it. He frowned, addressing the tapestry that hung down beside Jarin's bed.

"You may come out now." The heavy fabric rustled and a young man wearing nothing but chagrin stepped out from behind the tapestry and started grabbing up his clothes (the new page assigned to Jarin, Rence noted). "You may go," Rence said stiffly, opening the door. The page fled, not waiting to dress.

⚜

The two guards hustled Jarin down the corridor, boots drumming on the stone floor. House staff nodded deferentially and quickly stepped out of the way as they sped by. Jarin had a suspicion that whatever was amiss went beyond his usual infractions. The doors to the grand hall stood open, and their footsteps echoed loudly as they passed under the golden dome and out onto the balcony. Jarin tried to rake out his snarled curls with his fingers and squinted when the bright sunlight hit his face. His mouth felt fuzzy, and he badly needed to take a piss.

His father was standing at the parapet, looking toward the snowcapped mountains that formed the border between Weslynde and Cordel. King Franklin was wearing his uniform and was flanked by his general and the chief of security. Jarin surmised from their presence that some sort of military action was imminent. What could it be? Cordel was a country of seaweed farmers, the most peaceful country on earth. He glanced around to take in who else was with the king and saw Gerard Mort, the house mage, standing next to the balcony doors. The mage closed the doors behind Jarin, and he felt the hairs on his arms rising.

"Jarin. Come to me," the king said, not turning around. The others backed a polite distance away. Jarin walked warily to his father's side, anticipating the reprimand.

People in the courtyard below were bustling back and forth like ants. Soldiers were loading crossbows and other armaments into supply wagons. Two gigantic carrier beasts wearing battle armor and personnel platforms stood waiting to be harnessed to the wagons, tails lashing and tongues flicking. What were they preparing for? It must be serious if they'd dragged a chameli out of the hot caves. There weren't any drills planned that day. He shaded his eyes and followed his father's gaze over the palace walls and across the fields and vineyards to a line of geysers misting along the Wess River. Nothing seemed out of the ordinary, but he didn't comment, recognizing the look on his father's face, the set of his jaw, the throbbing vein on his neck.

"Who was in your room last night?" the king asked, still staring into the distance.

Jarin swallowed hard. It was to be a reprimand after all. His father looked at him darkly and raised an eyebrow. "A page," Jarin confessed, then quickly added, "I'll have Rence reassign him."

"You stink of rut." His father pressed his finger into the telltale love bite on his neck. It hurt. "Next time bathe before you see me."

Jarin rubbed his neck. They had argued over his indiscretions with the staff before, but he had never been rousted out of bed for it. Something else was going on. Something far more important than a tryst with a page. "Father, why am I here?"

The king put his hand on Jarin's shoulder and guided him out of earshot of the guards. The house mage followed behind them, Jarin noticed with some consternation.

"She's coming. She's almost here." The king gazed out across the valley.

"Who? Who's coming?"

Jarin saw worried apprehension in his eyes. "Your sister. Your twin."

Jarin stifled a laugh. Was he joking? He glanced back at Gerard Mort to make sure. The mage's expression remained somber, and that scared him.

One of the carrier beasts bellowed in the courtyard below, unhappy with its harness. Its handler calmed it by grabbing its snout ring and whispering into its earflap. Jarin's own ears filled with a rushing noise. He had no sister, not even a half-sister. That was impossible. Every child sired by the king was identified and cataloged. Royal lineage was public record, and he'd been required to memorize the family tree at a young age. His father had two bastard sons and no daughters. But that wasn't what shocked him. The king had said he had a twin. If that was true, it meant catastrophe.

"A twin?" Jarin scoffed in disbelief. "That's not possible. Why are you saying this?"

"I received a package from Cordel," the king said, frowning at Jarin in a way that made him cold inside. "It was delivered to the palace by two women wearing strange face paint. I welcomed them in as is our custom and offered them food and rest. Inside the package was a letter, a letter revealing an arrangement made by your mother before you were born. Your mother had discovered she carried two babies and could not bear to have either killed. She ignored Weslynde law and kept the twins a secret, and she schemed for someone to take and hide the weaker twin when it was born. Now an adult, the taken child is laying claim to the throne, stating that she is the firstborn twin and the rightful heir, not you."

Jarin found this unbelievable. "Anyone could write that letter," he said. "There are no twins in Weslynde; there haven't been for hundreds of years. Why would you believe this fairy story?"

"In addition to the letter, the package included a calligraphy done in ink. It was a rendering of our family sigil, down to the tiniest detail." He reached in his jacket and handed Jarin a rolled-up piece of parchment. It was old and stained around the edges. Jarin unrolled it and examined the artwork painted on the surface. It was the royal family's sigil, identical to his father's and the one embedded in his own shoulder. All the intricate filigreed patterns and symbols on the ink drawing matched in perfect detail. The only difference was the name inscribed on the sigil. Instead of his name, Jarin né Franklin, which was emblazoned on his shoulder, the sigil on the ink drawing read *Sabrin né Franklin.*

"Sabrin?" he asked.

The house mage lifted the scroll from Jarin's hands and rolled it up. "No one could have copied the intricate filigree of the house sigil in such exact detail without direct access to the original. I have examined it thoroughly. It is an exact copy in every way."

"And the name Sabrin," the king added. "I chose that name for a girl child and told very few about it." He took back the scroll and tucked it away. "The image is identical in every way to your sigil, mine, your grandmother's, and her ancestors before her."

"A drawing on a piece of paper is not evidence," Jarin protested. The whole story was absurd. "It could have been done by someone inside the palace, by anyone who sees us without a shirt. A masseuse, a consort."

"Granted, but unlikely. The house staff is vetted and loyal... and consorts are supposed to be screened." The king poked Jarin's neck again.

"Ow." Jarin flinched. "But still..."

"Then yesterday, this happened."

Jarin watched, confused, as the king took off his jacket and handed it to Gerard Mort. He pulled open his shirt and turned his back to Jarin, exposing his left shoulder. Jarin had seen his father's sigil many times. It was identical to his own in every way except for the name written on it, Franklin né Rosin. It appeared to be a tattoo, but the words and symbols were not done in ink and were, in fact, thin filaments of metal. A ring of sky metal lay underneath the skin, fused into the bones of the king's shoulder blade, exactly like the sigil in Jarin's own body. But what he saw on the king's shoulder this time was different. Very different. The filigree and symbols visible on Franklin's skin, normally a dull black, glittered green and gold as if they were made of polished metal, lit by the sun.

"Why is it glowing like that?" he asked.

The house mage moved closer. "Take off your shirt, Jarin. Let the king examine you."

"Why?" He glared at Gerard Mort, taking a small step backward. Jarin had never liked to be touched by the mage, even as a little boy.

"Take it off." Gerard Mort put his hand on Jarin's arm, and the prince felt a sudden urge to comply with his command. He tore off his vest and pulled his shirt over his head. He craned his neck but was unable to see the sigil on his own shoulder.

"Your sigil glitters as well," confirmed the king, fastening his jacket back together. "It glows like a falling star."

Jarin reached his fingers over his shoulder and felt the sigil. The filagree was rough to the touch, and it felt as if needles were pricking his fingers. He snatched his hand away.

"It burns! It's never done that before. What does it mean?" Jarin asked.

"It means," King Franklin said, "that this woman claiming to be your twin must have Sabrin's sigil. It was made of sky metal like yours, and her sigil is interacting with our sigils."

"It burns because the charms in her sigil are not compatible with yours. They are resisting each other," Gerard Mort added.

Jarin had no idea what he meant.

Franklin turned to face Jarin; arms crossed. He frowned and sighed deeply. "We must investigate her claim," he said flatly. "And, Jarin, if you are twins, only one of you can remain alive." He signaled to the house guards and waved them over. "Take the prince and lock him in his rooms."

Jarin's mouth fell open in shock. Had his father threatened to kill him? Before he had a chance to react, the guards grabbed him by the arms and yanked his sword from its sheath.

"What are you doing?" Jarin cried.

"I'm sorry, Jarin," the king said. "There is no other way."

The balcony doors boomed shut behind Jarin as the guards pulled him away.

⚜

Jarin was too stunned to resist the guards as they yanked him back to his rooms. They pushed him through his door, and he staggered over to a chair.

"You are to remain inside these rooms until further notice," the guard ordered. "Guards have been posted outside this door and the door to your terrace. If you need anything, have us call for Rence, and he will assist you." He stepped out and closed the door behind him.

The bolt slid into the cylinder. Jarin flung himself against the heavy wood door and pounded on it with his fist.

"What are you doing? This is madness! I am the prince of Weslynde! I'll have you banished! Put in prison!" He ran across the room and yanked on the terrace doors. They were locked and bolted, and he could make out two guards through the windows. He went back to the chamber door and pounded again. "Bring Rence to me. Bring Rence at once, do you hear? I command you." There was no response.

He thought for a second, then dashed to his closet and found all his weapons had been taken: his sword, his knife, and his stave. The whole thing had been planned! He picked up a stone statue from the table, intending to throw it through his window, but realized it would be pointless—the guards were standing right outside, and it might result in him being moved to a prison cell. He spun around in helpless fury, then slumped in the chair and put his head between his legs, trying to calm his breathing. Why would his father lock him up? It made no sense. Whoever this woman was, she could be dealt with. She wasn't his twin. This had nothing to do with him. He only needed to wait for Rence. Where was he? What was taking him so long? Rence would help him figure something out. Rence had always been there when times were rough. Agitated, he stood up again and went to the side table and uncorked a bottle of wine.

The day passed very slowly. Jarin finished one bottle of

wine and opened another. He banged on the door from time to time, demanding Rence be brought to him, but got no response from the guard outside the door. It grew dark, but he didn't bother to light the candles. He opened another bottle of wine to blunt his growing despair.

⚜

Rence crept silently through Jarin's room, seeming to appear out of thin air. The setting moon made soft blue squares of light on the floor. He found Jarin slumped in a chair, legs splayed out in front of him, wearing only his silk lounging pants. The prince was staring half-lidded at the flickering hearth, an empty bottle of wine dangling from one hand. Drunk again. Rence did a quick sweep of the room and listened at both doors. Then he went over to Jarin and softly touched his arm. Jarin stared blankly at the fire.

"I thought you were my friend."

"Jarin, I'm sorry," Rence said quietly. "I didn't realize what the king planned to do."

"I don't believe you." Jarin's words were slurred. "You're the king's man. Always spying on me. You're a spy, aren't you? How did you get in here anyway? Where have you been? Why didn't you come?"

Rence took Jarin's sullenness in stride. He had experienced the boy's sulks before. "I have been...busy."

"Why would my father do this? I am the prince! His son, for gods' sake." The prince sank lower in his chair and muttered, "He loves me. I know he does. I think he does."

Rence studied Jarin's tortured face. *The king thinks only of himself*, he thought.

The moonlight faded, and a flash of silent lightning lit up the windows, momentarily highlighting the mountains on the horizon. Rence went to the window and peered out. It was starting.

"We have to get you out of here. Now. You have to get away from this place." He hoped the message he had sent earlier had found its recipient.

Jarin rose unsteadily to his feet. The empty bottle slipped from his fingers and rolled away under the bed. "I'm not going anywhere. This is my home. Go get my father and explain it to him. Now. I command you." He lurched forward unsteadily, reaching for the bed post.

Rence grabbed him and held him upright. "Jarin, there is much you do not understand, and I do not have the time to explain it to you. You are going to have to trust me."

"Trust you! You're the king's man! How can I trust you?" Jarin swung his hand around, knocking over a water jug and sending it crashing to the floor.

Rence put his finger to his lips and stared at the chamber door in alarm.

At the same instant, the sound of thunder rolled up around them, low at first but then increasing to the point where Rence couldn't hear his own voice. The stone floor vibrated. It lasted longer than thunder normally did, roiling in his ears then slowly fading out. The air in the room grew thick, damp, and warm, the pressure closing his ears.

"That's strange," Jarin said, rubbing his ears. "It's not monsoon for two months yet." He turned away. It was then that Rence saw that the sigil embedded on Jarin's shoulder was glowing a weird greenish-gold. Before he could mask his surprise, Jarin swung back around and saw his face.

"What is it? Jarin whispered.

"Your sigil, it—it—"

"It's glowing, I know. It feels hot, like needles."

Rence's alarm grew. If the charms in the sigil were active... The windows were black and opaque. He had to get the prince to safety. "Jarin, listen to me. The king is acting as if he believes the curse of the twins, and your glowing sigil and that storm outside are giving him all the proof he needs that it's real." The sky flashed again. "You have a twin. And if you want to live, you have to go. You have to leave the palace. You probably need to leave the province."

"Leave the—? Are you crazy? The curse of the twins is ox shit. This is my home."

"Not anymore." Rence's voice was firm. He had to get through to Jarin somehow. "No more talk. It's time to sober up. Now gather your things. I have arranged for someone to guide you to safety." He led Jarin by the arm to the wardrobe and pulled out a pack.

"Guide me where? What are you saying?"

"Hurry! The storm will alert the clerics. They will come for you and kill you."

"My father would never let that happen."

"Your father will send them," Rence hissed.

Jarin's eyes went wide. *That finally got through*, Rence noted with satisfaction.

The thunder boomed again, this time suddenly and massively. Both men jumped. Rence rushed to the terrace doors and peered through them. A shrouded figure stood outside. Rence sighed in relief and opened the doors. The dark figure stepped inside, blending into the shadows of the room.

"Those doors were locked," Jarin said. "I checked them. And who is this?"

"This man is a magician," Rence explained. "A friend. He will guide you out of the city. Go now."

"I'm not dressed!" Jarin protested, gesturing at his silk lounging pants and slippers.

"No time. They're coming." The prince had to leave now; they were out of time.

The magician held out an inky black cloak in front of Jarin.

"Put it on," he ordered. "It's a concealment cloak. It will make you hard to see."

"Rence?" Jarin asked, stumbling away from the hooded man. "Who is this man?"

Footsteps sounded in the hall. Rence snatched the cloak from the magician and threw it at Jarin.

The magician ran to the chamber door, brought the interior crossbar down, and bolted it. He placed his hands over the bolt and muttered under his breath, binding it with a holding spell. "It won't hold long," he warned.

"Jarin!" Rence's voice shook. "Go now! Before it's too late."

Jarin wrapped the cloak around him and fumbled his hands through the arm slits. Rence fastened the clasp at his neck.

"Put on the hood; cover your face with the mask," Rence hissed.

Jarin pulled up the hood and found a soft face covering sewn inside it. He pulled it down and followed the magician to the terrace door.

The latch on the interior chamber door rattled. Someone pounded on it. Jarin pushed up his mask and locked eyes with Rence.

"You're not coming with us? What will you do?"

"I will be of more use here." Rence gave him a tight smile and readjusted the mask over his face. "Go with the gods, my prince."

The magician grabbed Jarin by the arm and pulled him out onto the terrace. Rence closed the terrace doors behind them and bolted them from the inside. He pressed his ear against the wood and listened as the magician charmed the outside lock, sliding it into place. He peered through the small windows onto the terrace but could not make out the prince or the magician, only a brief flicker of shadows along the wall. The chamber door behind him boomed and shook. He spun around and saw the bolt slide open and the crossbar lifting on its own, the spell breaking.

By the gods, Gerard Mort must be on the other side of the door! Rence sped through the adjoining bathing room and slipped into a storage closet, shutting the door behind him. He felt around at the back of the closet and found a slight bump in the corner. He pressed it, and the back wall of the closet pushed open. He stepped through and closed the wall behind him.

The wind was coming up fast, and it billowed Jarin's dark cloak underneath him. A few large drops of rain smacked hard on the flagstones around him. He turned back to say goodbye, but Rence had already closed the terrace doors behind them. The magician muttered a few unfamiliar words, and the bolt on the terrace door slid home. The magician took his hand and pulled him across the terrace. Two guards were slumped on the ground. Jarin wrested his hand free and bent over to check if they were alive, but the magician jerked him up by the arm and pulled him down the terrace steps. Halfway down the steps, the magician suddenly shoved Jarin into a shadow and pressed up against him, covering his mouth. Three palace guards clattered up the steps, mere inches from where they stood. Jarin closed his eyes, waiting for the guards to grab them, but they passed them by unnoticed. Once the guards had passed, the magician vaulted over the stair rail and sprinted across an adjoining rooftop, motioning Jarin to follow. When he reached the far edge of the roof, he jumped, disappearing over the side.

Jarin clambered over the stair rail and stepped gingerly onto the roof ridge, his slippers sliding on the wet tiles. He held his arms out for balance and staggered across, the cold rain stinging his face. He stopped at the edge of the roof, windmilling his arms. It was a twelve-foot drop to the garden below, and the magician seemed to have vanished altogether.

"Jump," the magician hissed, suddenly appearing out of the darkness below. "Now."

Jarin cautiously bent down and grabbed the edge of the roof, attempting to lower himself over the edge. His feet slipped and he hung on by his hands, feet dangling in the air. When it was clear he was losing his grip, he closed his eyes and let go, tensing up for the pain of hitting the ground. Instead, to his surprise, he landed gently on his side in the soft grass.

"This way," whispered the magician, pulling him to his feet.

Jarin realized the magician must have slowed his fall. He ran after him around a corner of the palace wall and there, tethered to a tree, were two scout beasts, their long low bodies writhing like snakes in the grass, tongues flicking, their red side stripes visible in the light streaming through the palace windows. Scout beasts were chameli, but unlike their giant cousins, the carrier beasts, scout beasts were no more than ten feet long from their nose to the tip of their long twitching tail. They were very fast and they could climb anything. Jarin had trained on one a few times but hadn't come close to mastering the art of riding this animal. The magician was already stretched out atop his beast, his arms and legs hooked in the saddle restraints. He looked back at Jarin.

"Hurry, you fool! Do you wish to die today?" He bent his head close to his beast's earflap and spoke a word. It bolted away, leaving Jarin and his beast behind.

Jarin cautiously swung his leg over the beast and lay down on its back. The beast felt his uncertainty and skittishly turned in a circle. Jarin hung on and managed to hook the backs of his knees under the saddle clips and got his ankles into the foot clips. He slid his arms into the arm restraints and grabbed the tethers. Not knowing what else to do, he whispered to the animal, "Follow your mate."

The chameli turned its head and inspected its rider up and down. It felt the air with its tongue and then took off at a rapid clip in the direction of the other scout beast.

It was raining harder now, and Jarin's water-soaked hood kept falling over his face. He dared not let go of the tethers and rode somewhat blindly through the gardens, catching a glimpse of his surroundings from time to time. His scout beast soon caught up with the magician, and they sped toward the outer palace wall without slowing down. When they reached the wall, the chameli scaled up its vertical surface, footpads adhering to the smooth stone. Jarin was sure he was going to fall off as they headed face first down the outside of the wall, but his knee and ankle restraints held him in place.

Once outside the palace walls, the magician steered them through parklands away from the city. They stayed clear of roads and snaked through the underbrush, skirting along tree lines and fences, occasionally darting across small clearings after the magician determined no one was about. They continued like this for some time, and the constant jostling turned the wine in Jarin's stomach sour. He couldn't yell at the magician or make his beast stop; all he could do was turn his head and vomit as they crashed through the brush and bracken.

Jarin's arms and legs felt like fire. He thought it must be past dawn by now, but the sky was still dark and the rain continued to pour down. When would the magician let them rest? They were now crossing through the many vineyards that carpeted Weslynde valley. At one point, lightning lit up the clouds, highlighting millions of frozen raindrops falling from the sky. A deafening crash of thunder followed a split second later, shaking the ground. The scout beasts froze and camouflaged their skin to match the ground and could not be coaxed to move. More lightning lit up the trees and farm buildings around them. Jarin was stroking the beast's neck, encouraging it to move, when he felt something hard strike his back. A hailstone. More hail, the size of acorns, hit the ground around him.

"This way. Quickly." The magician leapt off his beast and led it by the snout ring into a nearby hay barn.

Jarin slid off and led his beast after him, splashing through the mud. The hail stung his neck, and his scout beast bleated in discomfort. He made it through the open barn door just as the skies opened up and unleashed their fury. The hail grew to the size of turtle eggs, and the hammering on the barn's roof became deafening. Jarin sank to the floor, body shaking from exhaustion. The magician dropped to his knees in front of the scout beasts and placed a hand on their snout rings. The two beasts climbed into the rafters and disappeared under mounds of hay.

The hail grew louder, and one huge icy stone punched a hole through the barn roof and smashed into the ground near where Jarin lay. Others began to splinter the wooden roof above him. The magician pulled him to his feet and pushed him into a corner of the barn, underneath some heavy timbers stacked there. More hailstones broke through the roof, splintering the wood and thudding into the dirt floor. With each new breach, the men flinched and tucked themselves further underneath the logs. Jarin put his hands over his ears to lessen the roar and became aware of a tingling sensation on his shoulder; it was as if angry bees were dancing there. He rubbed his back against the wood, but it didn't abate. He reached around, trying to scratch it, and noticed the magician looking at him strangely. Embarrassed, he lowered his arm and tried to ignore the discomfort.

After what seemed an eternity, the hail decreased, then stopped, replaced once again by rain. The buzzing in Jarin's shoulder also abated. The men crept out from under their hiding place. Outside the barn door was a scene of devastation. The nearby copse of trees had been stripped of all its leaves, and the ground was littered with branches. A few trees had snapped and were lying on their side. Piles of hail were stacked up like snowdrifts, changing the landscape from summer to winter. The rain continued to fall, and a torrent of water was running down the middle of the nearby roadway, carrying leaves and bits of bracken in its wake. The drumming on the barn roof gradually lessened to the point where they could talk over it.

The magician stepped over to the wall and urinated against a post. "We must move on at the next break in the weather. Rest."

"Where are you taking me?" Jarin asked, wiping his face with his cloak.

"East. Away from the palace and the mountains, as far and as fast as we can."

"Why east?"

"The threat is in the west. Your twin is coming from Cordel. We must gain some distance from her to be safe."

Does everyone know about this supposed twin but me? Why do we have to move away from her to be safe? Nothing that was happening made any sense to him.

The magician opened a pouch full of fruit leather. "Eat this for energy."

Jarin took a strip and sniffed it. His stomach flip-flopped, and he put it down. "Who are you? Tell me your name."

The magician pulled back his hood. He had a smooth pale face, piercing green eyes, and straight black hair pulled back in a long braid. His nose had been broken at some point in the past, and an old scar ran down his forehead, through his right eyebrow, and down his cheek. "I'm called Dax." He took a swig of water from his waterskin and handed it to Jarin.

"Why are you helping me?" Jarin sipped some water, swirled it around in his mouth, and spat it out in the hay.

"Your mother charged the members of her court to protect you after you were born. Rence was part of that court, as was I."

"You knew my mother?" Jarin asked, astonished.

Dax didn't answer him; his focus was on the barn door. A momentary shaft of sunlight had broken through the clouds and streamed in through the barn door.

"There is a break in the storm," Dax said, smelling the air. "We must go now."

He whistled to the scout beasts, who popped their heads out of the hay, making Jarin laugh in spite of everything. The beasts slithered down the barn poles and presented themselves to Dax, who gave them each a strip of fruit leather and then knelt, touching their snout rings and whispering instructions. Jarin groaned at the prospect of another ride, but he pulled up his hood and climbed onto the back of his beast, wrapping his arms and legs under the restraints. Dax tested the weather one more time, then signaled the beasts, and they dashed out of the barn, splashing down the muddy road.

Traveling by scout beast was extremely uncomfortable, and the low-slung chameli were not suitable for more than a short surveillance mission. Scout beasts were trained to respond to directional commands (such as "head for that outcrop") but the chameli chose the best path to get there. They ran low to the ground and ducked under obstacles, meaning their riders were subject to encounters with whatever bush or low-hanging branch lay in their path. Jarin ducked his head and hung on the best he could; his arms and legs were soon covered with scratches and bruises. They continued on for what seemed to Jarin an endless amount of time. His body grew numb, and just as he could no longer hang on, the drizzling rain stopped and the clouds began to lift. Dax blessedly called them to a halt.

⚜

Dax had stopped them at the edge of a large open field. He had spotted a group of farmers standing between them and the far side, picking through the hail damage.

"Take the scout beasts and hide behind those bushes," he ordered Jarin. He was happy to see that the prince, even as tired as he was, was responding to directions now and taking matters seriously.

The farmers didn't appear to notice them, but Dax did not want to take any chances while they were still so close to Caleddon. His focus was erratic—he had expended so much magic getting the prince out of the palace—but he closed his eyes and blew his breath out slowly, focusing his energy on a tree on the other side of the field that had been weakened by the storm. He muttered a few words under his breath and sent a pulse, splitting the tree down its center with a sharp crack, causing it to fall across a pasture fence. While the farmers rushed to keep their oxyn from escaping, the scout beasts, carrying Dax and Jarin, raced across the pasture unseen and into the woods beyond.

By late afternoon, the clouds broke up, and for a few moments the sun lit up the woods and fields in a golden light before setting behind the Cordel Mountains, now in the far distance behind them. Dax again commanded the beasts to stop and dismounted. Jarin slid off his scout beast and lay on the ground beside it like a dead animal. Dax had no pity for him and instead focused on the two chameli that had carried them so far in such a short amount of time.

"They're exhausted," Dax said, stroking the panting scout beast's head. "We can't make them take us any farther tonight." He briefly closed his eyes and reached out with his mind, searching for shelter, then smiled. "There is a river nearby; we can shelter there for the night." He nudged Jarin with his foot. "Get up, Jarin. It's not much farther now." He headed off downhill, leading the two tired beasts, leaving Jarin to find his way to his feet and follow on his own.

Evening overtook them, and shortly before it grew too dark to see clearly, Dax heard the sound of running water and led them through some scrub willows to the bank of a wide river. A large rock outcropping extended out over the water. Underneath it was a sandy embankment sheltered from the elements and from any prying eyes nearby.

"We'll be safe here for the night." Dax pulled some dried meat from his bag and handed a strip to Jarin. The scout beasts drank heavily from the river, then dug themselves into a sandbank not far away from the two men. Once he made sure they were safe, he finally gave in to his post-magic fatigue, rolled his cloak up in a ball for a pillow, lay down on the sand, and closed his eyes. Within seconds, he was fast asleep.

Jarin lay on the sand, listening to Dax's soft snores, still holding the strip of jerky in his shaky hand, too exhausted to even chew it. His brain was in a fog; his entire world had been upended. He briefly considered rousting one of the beasts out of the sand and returning to the palace, but what fate awaited him there? After a few minutes, he rolled onto his side and curled up in a ball, tucking his arm under his head as he listened to the river flow past in the dark. He ached with muscle soreness and with loss and wondered if he would ever sleep on the soft mattress in his bedroom again. His exhaustion overtook him, and the jerky slipped from his hand.

Jarin woke to the smell of a campfire, not remembering where he was. He sat up quickly, instantly regretting it. He pressed his fingers against his pounding forehead and rubbed grit from the corners of his mouth. The morning sun glinted off the river and onto his face, forcing him to shade his eyes. He scanned the nearby beach and saw a man with a long dark braid not far from him, sitting naked in the sun next to a fire, cooking fish. He slowly remembered it was the magician, Dax. The events of the previous day came flooding back. A black hole of despair opened up in his heart.

Dax's clothes and cloak were drying on poles, and his boots were propped close to the flames. Jarin slowly limped over to him, every muscle on fire.

"Good morning, my prince," Dax said cheerfully. "Take a swim and get the mud off you. The scout beasts have caught us some breakfast!" He held up a fish skewered on a stick. "It is a fine day in Weslynde."

Jarin grimaced. "It is not a fine day in Weslynde," he grumbled. His head was screaming in pain, his stomach was in knots, every joint ached from the long ride then sleeping on the ground, and his arms and legs were scratched and scabbed over. Was the magician a friend or another captor?

The broad green river in front of him was totally unfamiliar; he had no idea where he was or even which way to run should he decide to try to escape. He shuffled down to the river's edge in his ragged slippers and scooped some water into his mouth and rubbed his face with his wet hands. He noticed that the two scout beasts were swimming far out in the middle of the glassy water, rolling over and over each other like enormous otters, splashing and diving. Fish scattered out of the water in front of them like fireworks. Jarin undid his cloak and peeled off his mud-caked lounging pants and waded in. The water was cold but felt good on his scrapes. He swirled his clothes in the river, and clouds of mud lifted off them. He squeezed the water out of the fabric, set the cloak and his pants on a rock, then dove into the river, swimming away from the bank.

The scout beasts spotted him and raced over, swimming circles around him and nudging his arms and ribs. Annoyed at first, Jarin finally gave in to their antics and grabbed one of the beasts by its harness and let it pull him across the water, sending up a large sheet of spray. Invigorated, he whooped and hollered while the other beast followed, leaping from the water like a seal, barking and hooting. Refreshed, Jarin swam back to shore and carried his clothes to the drying rack. Dax handed him a stick with a charred fish speared on the end.

"Thanks." Jarin took a tentative bite and realized he was starving. He found a rock to sit on and inhaled his fish, then took another.

"You are nothing but skin stretched over bones," Dax said. "You take after your mother's people. Tall as a tree and scrawny as a flagpole."

Jarin frowned at Dax's description of him. He suddenly felt exposed sitting naked in front of the magician. Dax was a fine-looking man, fit and lean, well-muscled with broad shoulders and slim hips. Dark hair dusted his chest and arms. He had the image of a snow cat tattooed on one arm. Jarin imagined that he himself must resemble a skinny brown scarecrow sitting there in front of Dax, his ribs showing through his hairless chest and his black hair kinking up into a wavy cloud around his head as it dried. He tried pushing it back, but he had nothing to tie it back with. In fact, he had nothing at all. His current situation sank back in, and he was no longer hungry.

"How did you get that scar?" Jarin asked, studying the jagged line across Dax's face.

"Snow cat."

That explains the tattoo, Jarin thought.

Dax took another fish from the pole and ate in silence, offering no further information.

"You knew my mother?" Jarin finally asked the question that was looming large in the front of his mind.

Dax said nothing in response, picking bits of meat off his fish bones. After a minute, he dusted off his hands and said, "We travel at night now. Get some rest."

Jarin was stung by the rebuff. The magician hung the remaining fish on the drying rack next to their clothes and instructed one of the beasts to keep watch. Then he lay down on a flat rock in the sun and fell instantly asleep. Jarin lay back, staring at the sky, thinking of possible ways he could strike out on his own and return to the palace. He thought if he could talk to Rence and meet with his father at a better moment, all would be restored and this stupid panic over a mythical twin would blow over. The warm sun overtook him while he was thinking this, and he drifted off to sleep.

When he woke up, Dax was dressed. Jarin stretched in an attempt to work out some of the kinks and pulled his silk lounging pants off the drying rack. They were in shreds, and his slippers were falling apart. He pulled on the tattered pants and hurled the slippers into the river with a bitter curse. Any escape plans he had formulated vanished along with the loss of his shoes. Three days ago, he'd been carousing with his mates in the streets of Caleddon, dressed in the finest fashion, well fed and adored by all: the future king. Now he was nothing more than a half-naked fugitive. A fugitive with an uncertain future, one that included a possible death sentence. Everything seemed to rest in the hands of this mysterious magician, whom he knew nothing about, who refused to tell him anything, and who seemed to dislike him.

"Where are you taking me?" he asked Dax.

Dax pointed upriver and said cryptically, "We go that way."

Another unhelpful answer, Jarin thought, even less certain than before.

CHAPTER 10

"Tell me more," Jarin demanded, tired of evasive answers. He pointed up the river to where it turned and disappeared. "What's that way?"

"Nettle Falls," Dax replied calmly, raising an eyebrow at Jarin's change of tone. "We need provisions."

"I can't take another torture session on the scout beast," Jarin snapped. Napping on the flat rock had only further stiffened his muscles.

"Unfortunately, we can no longer ride them. But don't fret. It's only a two-day hike from here to Nettle Falls."

"Two days?" Jarin remembered his bare feet. He was regretting his prior outburst. "Maybe the scout beasts won't mind taking us a little farther."

"Scout beasts are trained for short surveillance trips. Be happy they tolerated the long journey here."

"What will happen to them?" Jarin didn't like the idea of losing them.

"We can't send them back to Caleddon. Any magician worth his wages would be able to discern where they've been and send a pursuit party. We must discharge them."

Jarin wouldn't miss riding them, but he'd grown fond of

their comical behavior. After their romp in the river, they were the closest thing he had to a friend right now. He followed Dax over to the two chameli, who were draped across each other, sunning on the rocks.

"Thank you for bearing us here." Jarin bowed to them. "And thanks for the fish. Good fortune to you both." One of them opened an eye and shut it again. Jarin grinned at Dax, and Dax smiled back.

The magician removed their saddles and harnesses and knelt in front of the chameli. He placed his hands on their snouts and said, "I release you from service. You are no longer scout beasts. Return to the wild." He closed his eyes, squeezed the snout rings, and whispered a few words of old majik under his breath. The seemingly solid rings snapped open, and Dax unthreaded them from the chameli's nose flaps. The animals rubbed their faces with their front paws, licked the air, and bolted away, climbing up under the rock overhang until they were hanging upside down over the water. They flattened their bodies against the rock and blended into the tan sandstone until they were indistinguishable from the rock.

"They must like this place," Dax said. "That pleases me."

Jarin sighed and flexed his bare toes, thinking about the two-day trek facing them and wondering how he would manage it without shoes. He scanned the shoreline they were going to follow; it appeared to be mostly sharp rocks and thick brush. He noticed a long piece of ironwood wedged in some rocks at the river's edge and pulled it free from the other drift-wood. It was as tall as he was and was more or less straight. The smooth gray wood was heavy in his hands, and he thought he could make a decent stave out of it or at least a staff to help him walk. He brought it to Dax, who took it in both hands and closed his eyes. Jarin had not spent much time around any magicians other than Gerard Mort and found Dax's stillness and concentration fascinating to watch.

"This is a good length of ironwood." Dax rubbed his hand along it. "I sense no imperfections in the grain. It could handle quite a blow without breaking." Dax handed it back to Jarin and then looked him up and down critically. "Where we are going, you are going to stand out like a palm tree in a field of yellow wheat."

Jarin pulled at his hair self-consciously.

"There's really no way to make you blend in, but perhaps we can make you look more Argonnian and less like a fugitive prince. Those blue eyes of yours are going to be a problem, though."

Dax cut some dried reeds, then handed his knife to Jarin so he could use it to shape his walking stick. "Sit," he ordered.

Jarin sat cross-legged on the sand, and Dax sat on a stump behind him. As Jarin whittled the ironwood, removing bumps and side branches, Dax worked on his hair. He started by twisting Jarin's unruly curls into locs often worn by Argonnians, then intertwined the locs with the reeds he had collected, plaiting them against his head and down the back of his neck.

"Where did you learn to do this?" Jarin asked.

"I told you. I was in service to your mother. She had hair like yours. I had to help Merta braid it sometimes." He paused. "You look like her."

Dax's sudden candidness surprised Jarin. No one had ever really told him much about his mother, and who was Merta?

"What was she like, my mother?" he ventured, coaxing Dax to say more. "No one talks about her."

"She was brave...protective...I was only a boy, so I don't remember much. She was good with a stave." He tapped Jarin's staff. "I used to practice with her, until ..." He dropped off.

"Until what?" Jarin persisted. "Until she died and left me alone?" *Until she was murdered?*

Dax didn't answer. He tied the reeds together at the nape of

Jarin's neck and let the hair at the ends stick out in a haphazard ball of fuzz.

"It will have to do," Dax said, examining his work. "Perhaps the people of Nettle Falls will think you are from a region of Argonne not familiar with style." He picked up the leather saddle he had pulled off one of the scout beasts. "You need shoes, and we need to get you out of those Weslynde rags. For now, keep your cloak on."

For the next hour, the two worked together fashioning simple sandals out of the scout beast's saddle and tethers. Jarin laced them on his feet and walked about. They seemed solid enough and would work for now, but he'd need real boots soon. He put the concealment cloak on inside-out, so that the gray lining was visible, and tied some of the harness leather around his waist and cinched it tight.

Dax buried the rest of the scout beasts' tack in the sand, wrapped their remaining fish in some leaves, and filled the water-skin. They set out upriver when the sun went behind the hills. They walked through the night and in the morning hid under some tree roots, resting during the hottest part of the next day. The river trail they had been following broadened into a path, and the path soon became a narrow lane rutted by wagon wheels. Late in the afternoon, they topped a rise and got their first good view of the landscape in front of them. The river meandered across a fertile plain filled with orchards and vineyards, separated by occasional woodlands. A mile south of them, a smaller river tumbled out of the hills and merged with the river they had been following.

"The smaller fork is the Nettle River. It will lead us up to Nettle Falls," Dax said. "This big river we've been following is the Darno. We cross over up ahead." He pointed to a stone bridge spanning the Darno River in the distance.

The dirt lane they were following ended at a wide road, paved with bricks, running east to west. A few wagons pulled by oxyn and a handful of men and women shouldering packs traveled along it. "This is the Great Weslynde Highway. It runs all the way from Caleddon to Nettle Falls, and from there is crosses into Riddien through the Riddien Gap."

"I've never been to Riddien," Jarin said.

"That's where I am taking you."

"How long before we return back home to Caleddon?"

Dax didn't respond. Jarin knew Dax well enough by now not to bother asking again and let his eyes wander westward down the highway until it disappeared in the distance. That way led to Caleddon, his home. A home he wasn't sure he would ever see again.

They followed the highway over the stone bridge spanning the Darno River. Clustered around the bridge on the far side were several buildings and a small inn. A couple of barges were tied to the riverbank, and several wagons were parked outside the establishment.

"I think we can risk getting a meal," Dax said, nodding at the inn.

"What if I'm recognized?" Jarin asked, fingering the new braids in his hair.

"It's time we learned if people are searching for you. Try not to draw attention to yourself."

The sign outside the brown wood building read Broadwater Inn. A bell tinkled when they entered the dark smoky room, and Jarin had to duck his head under the lintel. Several men and women were sitting at long tables or standing at the bar. They called out a greeting to the newcomers, then turned back to their business. Most were freckle-faced Weslynders, but there were a few Riddiens mixed in (easy to spot with their bright blond hair and plaited beards). There were no other Argonnians present, and Jarin stuck out like a giant. A short middle-aged woman with a round freckled face and an even rounder belly waved them over to a table with some open spots on the bench.

"Sit, sit, rest your legs. Some ale for you?" she asked. "Or a bowl of stew?"

"Yes to both," Dax said, handing her a coin from his pocket. "Our thanks."

Jarin sat on the bench next to Dax and nodded to the two men and the woman sitting next to him, feeling very conspicuous.

"Traveled far?" one of the men asked. His face was leathery and his clothes rough and stained.

"We came north from Argonne," Dax volunteered. "We're going to Nettle Falls for medicinals."

"I thought your young friend here was Argonnian," the woman said. "He has the look about him, what with the dark skin and hair all knotted up." She elbowed Jarin and gave him a friendly, brown-toothed grin. "Do you live in Isidima, young fella? I hear it's a pretty place, a real oasis, they say."

"No, I don't." Everyone waited for him to go on, and Jarin had to scramble for something else to add. "I'm, um, from a small village in the desert, not anywhere near Isidima."

"Well, you don't sound Argonnian, that's for sure; you don't have that funny accent," the woman said. "You sound like you've been schooled."

"You sound like one of them university graduates from Caleddon," the leathery man said. "All high up and full of airs. You ever been to Caleddon? Been inside the golden palace?"

Jarin gaped at them, open-mouthed, unable to think of how to respond.

"Tuval spent a year at university in Caleddon, studying earth science," Dax calmly interjected. "He hopes to be a miner."

"Ahhh, that's it!" The group seemed satisfied.

Tuval? Jarin thought. *Where did that name come from?* He

realized he should have figured out a back story before they'd entered the inn.

The innkeeper brought mugs and bowls. Jarin gulped the ale down in one swallow and handed the mug back to the innkeeper for a refill, even before she had a chance to set everything down.

"Here, now," the innkeeper admonished him. "Don't they teach you manners in Argonne? I'm not your wife."

"Sorry," Jarin stammered. He was used to people jumping up to do his bidding. "When you have a moment, then?"

The innkeeper raised an eyebrow and crossed her arms, waiting.

"Please?" Jarin's apologetic smile was charming, and the innkeeper nodded with a grunt.

"My name's Dax," the magician went on. "My people are from Saltbank. I've lived in Argonne for some years now."

Why does he get to remain Dax? Jarin thought to himself. *Why doesn't he need a new name?*

"Saltbank!" the woman said. "Good people come from Saltbank. Salt of the earth, you might say." Everyone groaned. "I'm Merith, this here is my lazy husband, Garthe, and that is his good-for-nothing brother, Northe." Her men took no noticeable offense; they smiled and raised their mugs in greeting. "We traveled east from Caleddon."

"What's the news in Caleddon?" Dax asked casually.

"Here's the story," Merith said, leaning in. "There's strange things afoot." Garthe and Northe nodded sagely. "We were getting provisions in the city, the royal city, mind you, five days ago, and there was all this commotion in the market square. Supplies coming in and supplies moving out. Soldiers taking those giant carrier beasts they got there from the hot caves to the stables. Everything in the produce and meat booths was being bought up by folks bearing the city emblem. No one was saying anything, but they were getting ready for something, something big."

"I couldn't get my favorite smoked fish," complained Northe. "They was all taken."

"Who's telling this story, you or me?" Merith scolded, glaring at Northe.

The innkeeper set a foaming mug in front of Jarin.

"So, we sets out," Merith went on. "On our way to Riddien, we were, through the gap. The weather was fair, nothing in the air, not a cloud. We set up camp for the night and then suddenly, out of nowhere, BOOM!" She slapped her hand on the table. Others in the inn turned at the noise. She had an audience now and stood up. "I'm telling you: it weren't natural. These black clouds rolled in from nowhere. Rain started falling like buckets was being dumped out on us. Lightning hit the ground all around us."

"It hit a tree not fifty paces from us," Northe chimed in. "It split in two."

"We scrambled under the wagon in the nick of time, right before the hail —"

"Hail the size of your fist!" Northe interrupted.

"The size of your fist," Merith repeated, "started falling on us from everywhere."

"She speaks truth," an older man at another table shouted. "We got hit as well. One of our goats was killed by the storm."

"Our barn collapsed. The wind took it," another man said. Everyone started talking, sharing stories of the storm.

Jarin drained his second ale and waved at the innkeeper.

"And then it stopped," Merith said, eyes wide. "All at once. It was spooky. I'm just saying it weren't natural is all."

"Maybe that wizard in the palace conjured it up," someone chimed in from the bar.

"Wizards can't change the weather," another shot back. "Everybody knows that."

"Maybe it's worse than that," Merith said ominously. "Maybe someone birthed a pair of twins." Everyone groaned and started talking over the top of each other, offering further conspiracy theories.

The mention of twins rattled Jarin. "The curse of the twins is ox shit!" he shouted, banging his empty mug loudly on the table. Everyone suddenly stopped talking. Jarin realized he had drawn attention, and his cheeks flushed.

"We should go." Dax put his hand on Jarin's arm and started to get up.

"I've got another mug coming." Jarin jerked his arm away. Dax was not his warden, and he was still the prince.

"Leaving so soon?" the innkeeper asked, handing Jarin a third mug. "Stay and sit a spell; we're barely getting to know you."

"We must be in Nettle Falls by tomorrow night," Dax said. He turned to Jarin. "We should go now and get some rest."

Jarin took another swig in defiance.

"Nettle Falls! That reminds me," Northe said, grinning lewdly, "they got all that medicine and whatnot up there. While you're there, can you pick up a bag of stiffening powder for my brother Garthe here? His cock's been having trouble standing up lately and poor Merith ain't being serviced proper."

The men at the nearby tables jeered.

Garthe raised his head up from his drink and spoke for the first time. "Don't you go worrying about my Merith; I know how to please my woman." He stuck out an incredibly long tongue and moved it up and down. The room howled, and Merith blushed and slapped his arm.

Dax used the distraction to yank Jarin off the bench and head for the door. Jarin held on to his mug, protesting under his breath. The innkeeper followed them to the door.

"Hold up now!" she said. "I've not got any free rooms

tonight, but there is a dry loft in the barn if you need a place to sleep."

"Thank you," Dax said, "that will serve us very well." He handed her another coin. She stepped outside with them.

"There's one more thing you should know," she said, wiping her hands on her apron and leaning close to Dax. "There was a wagon driver came in earlier from Caleddon. He said there's a rumor going around that the palace is looking for the whereabouts of the prince." She nodded pointedly at Jarin and raised an eyebrow. "A lad of nineteen, dark skin, blue eyes, very tall."

Jarin's heart beat faster. He had exposed them. He was a fool.

"'Course, your young friend here clearly ain't no prince," she went on. "He don't smell like one at any rate, but you would do well not to draw more attention to yourselves. Once folks think there's a reward, they'll be grabbing up every boy in Weslynde between ten and thirty and painting him brown." She held up her hand to Dax, rubbing her fingers and thumb together.

Dax reached in his bag and gave her several more coins. She pocketed the money, took Jarin's mug from him, and went back inside the inn.

"We're leaving for Nettle Falls," Dax said.

"What about a place to sleep? The innkeeper said—" Jarin protested.

"We leave now!" Dax roughly shoved him into the barn behind the inn.

Dax's voice had an edge to it, and Jarin realized his carelessness had cost them any chance they might have had to rest. He stopped arguing and put up no further resistance. Once Dax was sure no one was watching, they crept out the barn's back door, cloaks wrapped around them, and faded into the countryside.

⚜

Dax planned to stop in Nettle Falls only long enough to get clothes and boots for Jarin and then continue on to Riddien before news of the prince's disappearance traveled any farther. He was worried since the news had already reached the inn, and he set a brisk pace, pushing Jarin to keep up. They walked throughout the night, stopping only to re-knot the straps of Jarin's sandals, which were quickly wearing out. He ignored Jarin's protests, and eventually the prince stopped grumbling and settled into a rhythm that matched his own. After that, they made good progress.

The road they were on followed the curves of the Nettle River, climbing steadily into the foothills of the Saddle Mountains, the border between Weslynde and Riddien. The road was empty of travelers this late at night, but they kept their cloaks on anyway, and anyone who might have been out would not have seen them, perhaps only shadows flickering in the moonlight. When the sun rose, they passed several groups of travelers coming down from the mountains, including a few tall Argonnians. Dax grew more comfortable and returned the nods of travelers who greeted them. He stashed his cloak in his pack and had Jarin turn his inside-out and belt it. The road got steeper and veered away from the river, which had disappeared into a deep gorge. As they climbed the switchbacks, willows and oaks were soon replaced by huge conifers. Dry needles crunched underfoot, sending a sweet piney smell into the air.

They climbed steadily most of the day and reached the road's summit by late afternoon. They sat on a log and shared Dax's waterskin, breathing a little heavier in the thin air.

"I hear something up ahead," Jarin said. "A roaring sound."

"You hear the falls," Dax replied. "We have arrived."

Dax followed Jarin around the next bend in the road and was rewarded with a view of the cataract for which the town of

Nettle Falls was named. A cascade of crystal-clear water spilled over the edge of a cliff and dropped down in long white sheets into the gorge below. Clouds of mist billowed up from the bottom and coated every tree and rock along its sides with sparkling dew. The surrounding canyon walls echoed with the thunderous roar of falling water. Jarin's mouth hung open in happy surprise, which made Dax smile, and even though he had seen it before, it still took his breath away.

Seemingly suspended in midair at the top of the waterfall was the town of Nettle Falls. On either side of the river, buildings were stacked one on top of the other and leaned out over the river, right to the very edge of the cliff. A few even clung precariously down the sides of the gorge. Most were made of squared-off logs, and their steeply pitched roofs were covered with slate shingles. Colorful banners hung from balconies and windows, waving in the misty air. Spanning the river, right at the lip of the falls, was a large wooden bridge that connected the town's two halves, brightly painted with the symbols of all three commonwealth provinces. The bridge itself was an open market filled with carts and stands, and it was packed with people.

"It's wonderful." Jarin grinned. "I've always wanted to come here but never had the chance."

Mineral-rich hot springs bubbled out of the rocks behind the falls and vented steam into the water from top to bottom, creating a unique climate that was home to several healing plants, including analgesic nettles that grew nowhere else. The town's public baths were also famous, and many traveled there to bathe in the therapeutic waters.

As they marveled at the view, two gorgeous blue and red birds flew across the gorge below them, feathers shining in the sun. That type of bird wasn't native to the falls, and Dax quickly sussed them. They were wearing leg rings.

"Courier birds," he said, his caution returning. "They may

be bringing unwelcome news from Caleddon. We need to move quickly and quietly. Be careful now."

⚜

As they pushed their way through the crowds, Jarin spied several Argonnians and felt less conspicuous. They stopped at a booth, and Dax handed him a leather vest and a white linen wrap skirt in the Argonnian style. At the next stall, Jarin spied a fine pair of boots—it was a good thing, since the disintegrating straps on his homemade sandals had raised a blister on his heel. He also grabbed a linen shirt to wear under the leather vest and some sturdy leggings for the cooler weather he was sure they would encounter in the frigid steppes of Riddien. The leggings didn't quite reach down to his ankles, but he could tuck them into the boots. He couldn't wait to try them on and toss his flimsy rags.

They crossed over the bridge, filling out their needs as they went—a pack and waterskin for Jarin and several days' worth of food: nuts, flatbread, dried fruits, and even some hard cheese. Jarin found a pair of tinted-glass eye-shades to hide his bright blue eyes. At the blacksmith's shop, Dax bought Jarin a large hunting knife. "I can't always be looking out for you," he said.

The knife had a nice weight to it, and it felt good hanging from his hip. Jarin stood a little taller leaving the booth. "Where did you get all this money?" he asked, chewing an apple as they pushed through the crowd.

"Rence gave it to me for such a time as this. Your mother must have given it to him, long ago."

Jarin had learned to recognized these rare moments when Dax would open up and pressed him. "Dax? Why are you helping me?"

"Rence and I have a charge on us for life."

"A charge?"

"We made a promise to your mother to protect you. We are bound to you and to each other."

"You and Rence?" Jarin asked. He had never really thought of Rence as anything more than his steward, and it was very clear that Rence answered to the king, not him. "I can't remember a time when Rence wasn't with me. He has gotten me out of trouble more times than I can count, but I think it's mostly to keep my father from being embarrassed by me. But you and Rence? He never mentioned you. I didn't even know you existed."

"Rence thought it best I remain hidden. He had good reasons."

"You serve Rence, then?"

"I served your mother before I met Rence. I was only a boy when Rence came to Argonne to meet us." Dax's expression turned soft. "Your mother was a great lady."

"How did my mother die?" Jarin asked, not wanting to waste this opportunity. "My father won't discuss it with me, and Rence is evasive. And why did she place this charge on you? Did she realize she was going to die?" Dax had gone silent, but Jarin had to know. "Dax. Please tell me what happened to her. I've heard so many stories. Even stories she was murdered."

"I don't know any more than you. I never saw her after you were born."

Jarin could tell Dax had closed off again. He wouldn't say anything further.

The magician found them a small room they could rest in and told Jarin to be ready to leave in three hours. Then he lay down on the bed and immediately fell into a deep sleep, not even bothering to take off his boots.

How does he fall asleep so fast? Jarin thought.

Jarin was restless in spite of walking all night, his mind churning over his mother's fate and his supposed twin sister lurking about. The tiny room was stuffy, and Dax's snores were annoying. A strong drink and a soak in the baths would calm him and help him think. He reached into Dax's pack and took a few coins, telling himself he would be careful and Dax wouldn't even miss him—he'd be back in plenty of time. He grabbed his new Argonnian clothes and closed the door softly behind him, setting out to find the baths. On the way, he ducked inside a pub and downed three fingers of hard spirits, savoring the familiar burn that radiated through his chest.

The baths at Nettle Falls boasted a large thermal pool ringed with submerged benches. There was an entrance to a steam cave along the back wall, and massage tables lined the perimeter. Jarin secured his new clothes in a locked bin and stripped. What remained of his silk lounging pants went into the refuse box, along with his tattered homemade sandals. He sat on a low bench while an attendant quickly scrubbed the dirt off him with a soapy sponge and poured hot, clean water over him. Once clean, he sank slowly into the thermal pool, allowing his body to acclimate to the heat. He found a bench and settled back, letting his head fall back on a headrest carved into the pool's edge. He started to feel like himself again.

Jarin soaked for a while, attempting to relax, but his mind continued to race. A nice-looking man waded over to him and flashed him a smile, but Jarin ignored him. Another time he would have flirted back, even taken the man back to his room, but he knew Dax wouldn't approve. Why did it matter what Dax thought about him? The magician was so gloomy and bossy.

Still restless, Jarin climbed out of the pool and went over to a massage table and lay down on his stomach. An elderly attendant got up from her chair and came over with a pitcher of warm oil. She drizzled oil on his body, then set the pitcher down and began to work the oil into his muscles. She was excellent. Jarin began to unwind, sinking down into the table. She found knots and kinks he didn't know were there and kneaded them into oblivion. She worked on one arm and shoulder, then the other. It was bliss, and he began to get drowsy.

"What's this, then, a tattoo?" she asked, rubbing her thumb over his shoulder blade. "It feels rough."

Jarin stiffened. His sigil. He hadn't even thought about it. Everyone in the palace had seen him naked; he'd never had to worry about hiding his sigil from view.

"Ooh, relax, young man," she soothed, patting him on the arm. "I was curious is all; I didn't think it would set you off that way. You're going to undo everything I did—ooh, you are so tense." She rubbed her hand over the sigil. "What do the words say? My eyes are so bad." She pressed her fingers into his shoulder. "It's strange though—it doesn't feel like a tattoo. It feels like you've something under your skin, something round."

In a panic, Jarin pushed himself off the table. "I'm sorry, but I must go. I have an appointment. Thank you. Thank you."

He backed away from her, then ran over to the bin that contained his clothes. He fastened his new wrap skirt around his waist and shrugged into his vest. The boots seemed to take forever to lace, and he grew more and more anxious as the old woman went over to talk with her fellow masseurs sitting along the wall. They all started glancing his way and whispering to one another. *Oh, gods*, he thought. *I have exposed us again. What will Dax say?* He fled the baths and raced back to the room they had rented.

"You did what?" Dax cried, aghast. "You are supposed to be wearing a disguise, not removing it! Why not hold up a sign for all to see? I'm prince Jarin."

"I know, I know. It was foolish. I didn't think about the sigil."

"The courier birds we saw! News will have come. We must

leave now." Dax gave him a frustrated glare and started shoving items into his pack. "Grab your staff." He cracked open the door to their room and peeked out. A crowd of people walked past the door.

"Let's go," Dax said.

They slipped into the crowd and headed down the street toward the bridge. As they started across, Jarin saw two hefty men wearing official-looking tunics behind them at the top of the street, heading their way. Constables! They were pointing at him.

"Dax, look!"

"Get down and move quickly," Dax hissed.

They ducked low and threaded their way across the bridge, dodging people and vendor carts. When they reached the far side, the men were already starting to cross.

"They're still following us," he said. "What do we do?"

Dax turned and stared hard at something on the middle of the bridge. His forehead wrinkled in concentration, and then a chorus of yelling sprang up. A cart full of melons had fallen sideways right in front of their pursuers. There were cries and curses as the men stumbled over the fruit. Dax grabbed Jarin's arm, and they sprinted off the bridge and up the road that led to the Riddien Gap. Once out of sight of the bridge, they ducked down a side lane and hid behind a shed, putting their backs against the wall.

"I don't think they're following us anymore," Jarin said.

"But they'll report this back to Caleddon," Dax said angrily. "And they have a full description of you, right down to the mole on your ass."

"I'm sorry. I have never been on the run before." Jarin's cheeks flushed at the criticism.

"You are making this very hard," Dax scolded. "I was taking us to Riddien, but now I think we make for Argonne. It's in a different direction than we've been going, which might throw them off, and it's clear we need to be some place where you blend with the locals."

As he said this, the two constables pursuing them rounded the corner of the shed, surprising them. One of the men shoved Dax against the shed before he had time to react, knocking the wind out of him and pinning him to the wall by the neck.

The other man grabbed Jarin's arm and yanked him away from the wall, shouting, "Got you!"

Jarin had his staff in his free hand and punched the end of it into the man's stomach. The constable let out a surprised 'oof' and bent over in pain. Jarin raised his staff and cracked it down hard on the man's head. As the man slumped forward, Jarin spun around and struck Dax's assailant across the back of his neck. That man fell as well. Dax staggered back against the shed, rubbing his neck and gulping air. Jarin grabbed him by the hand and pulled him away, leading him down a side path that disappeared into the pine forest.

CHAPTER 11

Jarin crouched next to Dax on a rock overlooking a steep ravine. The magician was on his knees, hands splayed out on the ground in front of him, determining the best way to get down. Dax had given up his plan to cross into Riddien because of what had happened in Nettle Falls, and they were now heading south to Argonne. They had spoken little since the incident, and Jarin regretted his actions deeply.

After a few moments, Dax opened his eyes and sat back on his heels, stretching his arms over his head. "You've some skill with that staff," he said. "For which I am grateful. Where did you learn that?"

The tension in Dax's voice had broken. "I served a year in Drissen's security force when I turned sixteen," Jarin said.

"Yes, of course."

"I like the stave because it's all about balance and leverage. You don't have to have the arm strength you need to wield a broadsword or mace." He picked up a stone and examined it. "Also, it was my mother's weapon."

"You are very quick," Dax said. "Like she was. She was quite an expert with the stave."

Jarin threw the stone into the ravine. They listened to its

echoes as it bounced off the rocks far below. "When I was small, I imagined someday I would fight her in the ring and punish her for leaving me." He laughed at the notion. "That's silly, of course. A child's ravings."

"Do you think Tregan abandoned you?" Dax asked.

"Sometimes. It feels that way even more now that I've learned I have a twin sister. My father told me my mother died giving birth to me, but that can't be true, can it? If she hid a sister from me, what else did she hide? Maybe she wanted Sabrin to live instead of me." It hurt him to say it, but it felt good to share it with Dax.

"She loved you, Jarin."

"Love." Jarin gave a bitter laugh. "What is love? My father locked me up the moment he learned he had a daughter. He's never loved me. He's told me more than a few times that I'm a failure and I don't deserve the crown. Maybe I'm better off in Argonne."

Dax kept silent.

"Which way down?" Jarin finally asked, clearing a lump in his throat.

"Over there. Those rocks are the most secure."

Dax and Jarin clambered slowly down the ravine, navigating ledges and avoiding loose tree roots and scree. They reached the bottom without incident, and from there the land became easier to traverse. The conifers thinned out and were replaced by oaks and other leafy trees. By the time they reached the broad river basin, the trees had given way to meadows and river willows.

They rejoined the Darno River several miles upriver from the inn they had stopped at two days ago. Dax hailed a barge being pulled upriver by two oxyn lumbering along a well-beaten tow-path on the far shore. A man steering the barge saw them and launched a small rowboat and paddled over to meet them.

"Keep those blue eyes covered," Dax warned Jarin.

Jarin pulled out the eye-shades and put them on.

"Well met and thank you for stopping," Dax called out as the man drew near.

"Who are you and where you be heading?" the man asked, keeping the rowboat a few yards from shore.

"I'm called Dax, and this is Tuval from Argonne. We're returning to Isidima. We've been to Nettle Falls to get medicinals for Tuval's cousin. We're hoping for a ride. We can pay."

"You look fit enough. Can you pole a barge?"

"We can. I hail from Saltbank and know my way around a boat."

"Saltbank! Why didn't you say? We set out from Saltbank three weeks ago. Come aboard, then!"

The man, whose name was Dysan, owned the barge. He was traveling with his wife, adult daughter, and her husband. They saw nothing unusual about two men carrying medicinals home from Nettle Falls and wanting to hitch a ride.

They set off upriver, plodding along at the pace of the two oxyn, and Jarin quickly grew bored. It seemed like they weren't moving at all, and he resented the way Dysan ordered him around, making him pole the barge, scrape snails from its sides, and clean the fish they caught for their meals. There was hardly room to turn around, and he knocked his shins on crates several times. Sleeping on the wooden deck left him cranky and achy, and he never felt clean, even after swimming in the river.

Jarin noticed that Dax seemed to slide easily into the routine of barge life. He helped apply new pitch to the decking and used his skills as a magician to sense underwater snags that would have trapped the barge if they had struck them. The barge family made much of him, and Jarin felt useless by comparison.

Dysan strictly rationed out the small cask of ale he kept on board, and Jarin obsessed over his limited share. After being chastised for knocking a crate overboard, Jarin gave in to temptation and broke into the cask when it was his turn to watch. Dysan found him snoring on the deck the next morning with his arm draped over the empty cask. He kicked Jarin awake and threatened to throw him overboard. Dax had to intercede and pay for the loss of the ale. He yanked Jarin away from the others during a stop on shore.

"I don't care if you are the future emperor," he scolded. "You have been putting us in harm's way since the night I met you. If not for the promise I made your mother, I would turn you over to the king myself."

Jarin was surprised at the vehemence in Dax's voice. He apologized and stopped complaining about everything, and for the next few days made a conscious effort to help out more, making things easier for everyone.

Jarin had to admit it wasn't all bad. He did enjoy sitting by the fire in the evenings, listening to the family sing traditional songs of adventure, love, and loss. He greatly enjoyed walking alone, leading the two massive oxyn up the tow-path. They were gentle beasts, in spite of the four formidable horns that sprouted from each of their foreheads. When they passed close by an orchard, he knocked fruit from the trees with his staff and fed it to the gentle bovines. After a few days like this, his stiffness and aches went away and he began to sleep more soundly.

They poled upriver for two weeks until one particularly bright and sunny morning they reached Gwindell Station, a tiny village and loading dock marking the southern end of the river's trade route. The oxyn were turned out to graze, and Dax and Jarin helped the family unload empty crates and reload the barge with stacks of late summer fruits and vegetables for the return trip downriver to Saltbank.

Dax was stacking apple crates along the station wall and sussed that one of the slats making up the crate was weakened and about to break. He set the crate aside and went about replacing the slat.

Dysan approached Dax while he worked. "You could tell it was broken even though you couldn't see it," he said. "And that business on the water, finding those snags before we hit them. You be a magician, then?"

Dax gave a slight nod.

"We haven't seen one of your kind in ten years or more. It would be right nice to have a magician on board. Do you want to join us? We live a simple life but a pleasant one. You can even bring the skinny giant with you if you want. He's not that horrible once you get used to him."

"He gets his grouchiness from his father," Dax said with a smile. The thought of floating leisurely down the Darno was appealing. "Another time I might have taken you up on your offer, but the medicinals we carry won't wait."

"That's alright, then, but you won't find anyone like yourself south of here. Magicians don't come this way no more. Rumor is the great mage that lives in the golden palace, that Gerard Mort fellow, won't let magicians travel to Argonne."

This disturbed Dax. He remembered meeting a few magicians in Argonne when he was a boy. They were essential in creating the human-animal bond with the great chameli that were so central to Argonnian culture.

They shared a final meal with the family and wished each other safe travels. Then Jarin surprised Dax by bringing forth snail shell necklaces as gifts for the family. He must have woven chains of the iridescent shells together as he led the oxen along the banks. Dax stood next to Jarin as the barge, riding low in the water, drifted back down the broad river and vanished around a bend. He imagined himself on board, traveling home to Saltbank, and sighed wistfully. He put his arm on Jarin's shoulder and gave him a rough squeeze. Jarin glanced at over at him with a grin. Dax clapped him on the back and then set off to find shelter for the night.

⚜

Dax and Jarin remained at Gwindell Station, hoping to hitch a ride across the desert on the next caravan passing through. On their second day there, they got lucky and joined a train bound for Isidima. The caravan, made up three wagons in a line hitched to a carrier beast, was driven by two young Argonnian men, Timeer and his cousin Tevin. To earn their ride, the Argonnians put Jarin and Dax to work loading wine casks and textiles onto the wagons. Then they wrestled a heavy barrel of water they would need while crossing the Argonne Desert into place.

"The water is for us," Timeer explained. "The carrier beast won't need to eat or drink until we reached Isidima."

The Argonnians were quite impressive. Lean and roped with muscle, they were both seven feet tall, and their smooth hairless bodies had been burnished an even deeper ebony by the sun. Jarin was shorter by half a foot, and he felt scrawny and pale around them. The Argonnians wore nothing but wrap skirts and sandals, and they tied their long black hair back in braids strung with beads and charms that hung down the middle of their backs. Even more beads adorned their necks and wrists. Within two minutes of meeting Jarin, they determined he wasn't from Argonne and teased him about everything.

"You must live underground like a cave lizard," Timeer said. "You are so pale."

"And who created that terrible bird's nest in your hair?"

Tevin added. Both of them found this extremely funny and laughed long and loudly, picking at the reeds that Dax had woven into Jarin's curly hair.

Their first night together, they sat around a fire and discussed their plans for crossing the desert.

"We travel by day until we reach the dunes," Tevin said. "Then we switch to night." He passed around a pipe filled with an herb that made Jarin relax and smile.

"Tell us of your people, Tuval," Timeer said. "Where are you from? You got some Weslynde blood mixed inside you, that's for certain."

"I grew up near Saltbank," Jarin improvised, enjoying the buzz in his head. "My father is a shrimp farmer, my mother...is a baker." He handed the pipe to Dax.

"You talk educated for a shrimp farmer," Timeer pressed.

"I went to university in Caleddon. I studied earth science."

"Oh! You're a miner, then, not a shrimp farmer?" Timeer asked. "And why are you traveling with a magician?"

"I'm not a miner," Jarin said, taking the pipe back and beginning to get confused. "And who told you Dax is a magician?"

"Everybody stop now," Tevin interrupted and broke into a wide grin. "We know who you are. You are Prince Jarin."

Jarin choked on the pipe and started coughing. He glanced at Dax in alarm.

"We knew right away," Tevin continued. "You look exactly like your mother. There are portraits of Tregan Anthelia all over Isidima. She's a legend, you know, and so are you. Why don't you take off those silly eye-shades so we can see your pretty blue eyes. You realize it's strange to be wearing shades at night, don't you?"

Jarin slowly pulled off his glasses, still gripping the stem of the pipe.

"But what we don't understand is this," Timeer said, gently

extracting the pipe from Jarin's clenched fist and taking a puff. "Why is the prince of Weslynde in disguise, and why is he traveling with a magician down to Isidima?"

"And taking the long way round?" put in Tevin. "It would have been a much shorter trip to Isidima from Caleddon if you had sailed down the Endelas Lake."

"We figure you're on a secret mission," Timeer added. "Maybe you are meeting with the Argonnian senate, plotting some sort of—"

"You are right," Dax jumped in. "We are on a mission. You are very perceptive."

"You see?" Timeer said to Tevin. "I knew it!" They slapped each other's palms.

"Are you going to report us?" Jarin asked. His staff was leaning against the wagon, out of reach.

"Report you?" Timeer asked. "To whom would we report you? You are the prince! We are your people! Now tell us the plan."

Relief spread through Jarin's body. "The plan? Oh, yes, the plan." He glanced at Dax, hoping for inspiration. "Tell them the plan, Dax."

Dax cleared his throat. "Prince Jarin is on a quest to find out, once and for all, what really happened to his mother. He has a better chance of finding the truth if he remains undercover."

"Of course." Timeer slapped his leg. "All of Argonne wants the answer to that question."

"There was never even a funeral for her, you know," added Tevin. "I say she's alive."

"No, she died," Timeer corrected him. "But the question is how. I heard she was poisoned."

"The king sent her body to Isidima for burial, and they say it got lost." Tevin spoke with skepticism. "How do you lose a body?"

"They didn't lose it; they got rid of it," Timeer scoffed. "They didn't want anyone to see the body because then they could find out how she really died."

"I think she is still alive and will bring Argonne back to glory," Tevin said with certainty.

"She is a hero, no matter if she is alive or not," Timeer summed up, "and Prince Jarin here is the one to avenge her."

"And we will help you do it!" Tevin crowed. Timeer agreed.

They passed the pipe again and discussed ever more outlandish theories late into the night. Jarin and Dax smiled their encouragement until the Argonnians finally passed out, snoring against one another by the fire.

When Jarin opened his eyes the next the morning, Tevin was sitting next to him, waiting for him to wake up. He said his first task was to make Jarin look like a true Argonnian. He retrieved a box of beads from the wagon and spent the better part of the morning fixing Jarin's hair. He pulled out the reeds, then braided and beaded it tight against his scalp in the traditional Argonnian style.

While Tevin worked on his hair, Timeer informed Jarin that a few days in the desert sun would turn him a proper shade of brown. He helped Jarin out of his vest and tunic and rubbed palm-oil all over his skin. Then he presented Jarin and Dax with spare sandals they had stashed on board, a better choice for desert travel than the thick leather boots they wore.

"What are we to do about this sigil?" Timeer asked as he rubbed oil into Jarin's back. "Your hair's not long enough to cover it."

The Argonnians puzzled over it until Timeer remembered he kept a bottle of tattoo ink in his pack. An agonizing two hours later, bolstered by frequent puffs from Tevin's pipe, Jarin boasted a pair of raven wings across his shoulders, effectively masking the sigil.

They set out the following morning atop a platform

strapped to the carrier beast. The heavily loaded wagons creaked and squeaked behind them. Few Weslynders lived this far south, and the terrain before them was wild and empty. As they traveled, the landscape changed from grassland to rocky ground sparsely dotted with scrubby brush. In spite of the arid conditions, animal signs were everywhere, and Jarin spotted a huge herd of camel deer in the distance, sending up clouds of dust. *They must number in the thousands,* he thought, awestruck.

They stopped each evening when the sun touched the horizon, giving themselves time to hunt or practice martial arts. The Argonnians were delighted to see Jarin's skill with a stave, and the three of them would spar until it grew too dark to see. They behaved like giant children, bouncing up and down, knocking each other to the ground, swearing crudely and laughing hysterically. Jarin hadn't had fun like this in months.

Timeer and Tevin both had women waiting for them in Isidima. They had boasted of their women's beauty and their lovemaking skills many times around the campfire and couldn't wait to be back in their arms. Timeer even had a son with his mate whom he was very proud of. So Jarin was surprised and startled when one night he rounded the wagon to get water and stumbled into the Argonnians, pressed up tightly against one another. Tevin's arms were wrapped around Timeer's neck and Timeer's hand was underneath Tevin's wrap skirt.

"My pardons," Jarin said, backing away. "I didn't see you there…" His face grew hot.

"Don't worry," Timeer said. "You're not bothering us."

"It makes the days go faster until we are home with our women," Tevin said, looking over Timeer's shoulder with a grin.

"Do you want to join us?" Tevin extended his arm, beckoning Jarin to join their embrace.

"No. I don't need— I will leave you now."

Their laughter followed him as he hurried back to Dax,

who was tending the carrier beast, rubbing its snout and whispering to it.

"Everything alright?" Dax asked. "You seem...rattled."

"I'm fine, really," Jarin said, bringing himself back under control. "I'm learning a lot about Argonnians." It had been a long time since anyone had held him like that. He glanced sidelong at Dax, imagining what he would have done if the magician had opened his arms to him. He stood silent and stroked the side of the beast absently to distract himself. Its cheek spots glowed in response.

"She likes you." Dax smiled.

Jarin pulled his hand away, suddenly frustrated. "Dax, what are we doing here? I mean, besides hiding out."

"My charge was to keep you safe. I am keeping that charge. You should be safe in Argonne. We can find work, blend in."

"But then what?" Jarin asked. Was this who he was now? A half-naked peasant lurking about the desert pretending to be a caravan driver? He felt alone and unloved.

He followed Dax back to the campfire, and Dax poured them both some wine from the cask.

"What do you want to happen?" Dax asked. "Where do you want to go?"

"I want to go back home." As soon as he said it, he knew it was true. "I want the life that was promised me."

"You wish to be king?"

"I never wished to be king; it's just what was going to be." It wasn't about being king for Jarin. It was more than that. It was about everything working the way it was supposed to. He wasn't sure he could explain it. "I've trained for it, you know. Politics, economics, military defense. I attended four years of law school, for the gods' sake. I can't plant a grapevine, but I can negotiate a binding contract."

"Argonne needs lawyers," Dax offered, throwing a stick in the fire.

"And now this... It's like a nightmare. I'm on the run. I have a sister I never knew I had, who may have ransacked the palace by this time. My own father tried to kill me, Dax. I'm only a commodity—expendable now that someone better showed up. And this curse—the royal twin curse." He laughed sarcastically. "A bedtime story told to me by my nurse. Dax, do you think it's real? Do you think I'm cursed?"

"There was the hailstorm—"

"Which abated, like all storms do. Humans can't change the weather, not even magicians."

Dax looked thoughtful, as if remembering something else. "What about the changes to your sigil—you said it glowed the night we met, remember? What about that?"

Jarin reached over his shoulder and rubbed the ring under his skin. "It's the same as it always was. Maybe I imagined it. Maybe I have no sister. Maybe I'm a fugitive for no reason."

"What is it you really want, Jarin? Down deep."

Jarin had really never stopped to think about this before. His life had been so easy. His wants were nothing more than food, drink, sex, a good time with his mates back in Caleddon. All those things had been at his fingertips with a single command. Did he even care about anything else? What kind of a man had he turned out to be?

"I want to know who I am."

They shared a pipe and gazed up at the stars. After a while, lyons started calling to each other in the distance. Tevin and Timeer joined them and said the lyons must be following the camel deer. The chameli was too big to be prey for the lyons, so Timeer put out the fire and had everyone climb on top of the beast's platform. Jarin found himself unable to sleep, so he took the first watch, smoking the rest of the pipe and staring up at the crescent moon.

The days grew hotter the farther south they went. Rose-colored sand dunes appeared over the horizon. Timeer said they would switch to night travel after their next stop, a desert spring well known by the caravanners. When they arrived at the spring later that day, they unhitched the giant chameli from the wagons and removed its carrier platform, and it lumbered out into the deep water and vanished in its depths. Tevin said it would come up for air in about four hours and they would retrieve it then.

The spring itself was beautiful—an oasis surrounded by protective rock ledges and filled with date palms. Azure water welled up through fissures deep underground and filled the wide pool. The men stripped naked and dove in the cool water —so clear it seemed like they were flying through the air.

Jarin swam away from the others and floated peacefully on his back. Daily exercise and constant exposure to the sun had baked his skin a deep mahogany, and new muscles rippled on his thin frame. A hawk circled above him high in the sky, and he decided living the life of a caravan driver would not be so bad. Doing simple work in pleasant surroundings was decidedly preferrable to Rence shouting at him that he was late for some grievance session with flax farmers.

He climbed out on a rock in the middle of the spring and sat, arms around his knees. The Argonnians and Dax had returned to shore and were digging a fire pit in the sand. They were going to roast the runner-bird they'd shot the day before.

Dax was piling rocks at the edge of the pit, and Jarin could tell he was laughing at something Tevin said. Jarin's feelings for the magician had changed. The two had spent many nights together on watch, sitting and talking by the campfire under the stars, and they had fallen into an easy rapport. They enjoyed being with each other, but Dax had never shown Jarin any interest beyond being his protector. Dax was not very forthcoming about his personal life, but he had shared a few things, funny attempts at failed magic, his affinity for animals, and memories of being part of Tregan's court when he was a child. Dax moved a couple of rocks into place. Jarin enjoyed the play of muscles across his bare shoulders and imagined what it would be like to kiss him. He started to stiffen in response and dove in the water to cool off.

Jarin swam back to shore in time to help the others lower the runner-bird into the pit and cover it with rocks. As they were setting the last rocks in place, another caravan, pulled by two carrier beasts, arrived from the same direction they had been traveling. The other caravan set up a respectful distance down the shore and unhitched their carrier beasts, who vanished in the water as theirs had done earlier. The driver of the caravan hailed them, and Tevin waved him over.

The driver's name was Sten, and he was traveling with his two brothers, his wife, and their daughter Breen. They had come from the grasslands of Riddien and were bound for Isidima, hauling a great load of wheat and other grains. The ruddy-faced men had plaited beards and blond hair shorn at the shoulders. The women's hair was pulled back in double braids that fell down their backs to their waists.

Jarin knew a fair bit about Riddien but had never been there. It was mostly vast stretches of grassland that grew right up to the edge of the northern ice sheet. Massive herds of antelope and steppe-horses were said to roam wild across the province. The people of Riddien were proud and fierce. They had been the last to join the western commonwealth and brought with them a fierce religion, now called the Church of the Commonwealth, that had swept through Weslynde. Jarin regularly attended services and had adopted many of their rituals. He scowled at Riddien's association with the church now, knowing the church was responsible for propagating the myth of the curse of the twins.

Timeer invited the Riddiens to share their runner-bird

roast, and they gratefully accepted. They brought with them bread, cheese, and some fresh apples. Tevin tapped a cask of wine while Jarin and Timeer pulled the runner-bird from the pit and carved it up. There was plenty for all; it was a feast! When the stars appeared, they sat around the fire and swapped stories of aggressive lyons, marauding bandits, and long days on the road. Timeer broke out his pipe and was passing it around when the Argonnians' carrier beast resurfaced with a lot of splashing and hooting. Dax led the chameli to a flat rocky area away from the others and proceeded to rub it down with oil.

Jarin couldn't help but notice that Sten's daughter, Breen, a striking young woman with big blue eyes and white-blond hair, had been watching Dax all evening. He was dismayed when she left the fireside and went to join Dax by the carrier beast. She openly flirted with Dax, smiling and laughing and occasionally touching his arm while Dax rubbed the beast's skin with a cloth. She took his hand and whispered something into his ear, then walked off toward the other caravan, glancing back occasionally. Dax wiped his oily hands, nodded goodnight to the beast, and followed her. Jarin's cheeks flushed, and he rose to his feet when they disappeared into a tent together. He looked back at Breen's parents, who seemed unperturbed.

"What are ye gawking at, Tuval?" asked Sten. "Is our caravan on fire?"

"No. It's nothing," Jarin said. "Everything's fine."

Jarin's jealousy was obvious to all.

"Breen chooses who she chooses, Tuval," Sten said. "You're a fine-looking young man, and it's no reflection on your manhood. Now come back over here and join us. We hear you've been to Caleddon; tell us more about that."

Jarin grabbed his mug and refilled it with wine from the cask. He gulped it down and filled it again, then flopped back down on the sand next to the fire. Breen was a scrawny, pushy wench as far as he was concerned. He kept his mouth set in a line, silently fuming.

"Ah, to be young again." Sten chuckled. "Hot-blooded and full of spunk." He put his arm around his wife and kissed her cheek. His brothers laughed and clinked their mugs together. Jarin drained his mug and filled it again.

❖

The two caravans started across the high desert, traveling in tandem, crossing over the smaller sand dunes and threading their way between the larger ones. They traveled only at night after the air cooled. Each morning, they set up white tents that reflected the intense sun. Dax sheltered with Breen inside her tent, leaving Jarin to bunk with the Argonnians. Jarin found it hard to sleep and frequently borrowed Timeer's pipe to try to relax. He drank copious amounts of wine and would finally pass out late in the day. He had to be kicked awake in the evenings to break camp, head pounding and mouth like cotton. He found ways to avoid Dax, choosing different watch schedules, walking when Dax rode, sitting apart during meals.

The caravans were nearing the far edge of the dunes and had stopped to camp when Jarin felt a sudden pressure in his ears. He noticed an orange tint in the sky he hadn't seen before.

"Sandstorm," Tevin yelled down to the others from atop the beast. "It's a fair size and it's coming fast."

The two caravan teams worked together, lashing canvas over the wagons and settling the three giant chameli in a line, head to tail, sideways to the wind. Tevin threw a rolled-up tarp down to Dax and Jarin, who were helping arrange the chameli.

"What do we do with this?" Dax asked.

"It's to cover yourselves," Tevin shouted over the wind. "You need to stay with our beast, Dax. She gets skittish in a storm.

Make her go dormant and dig out a shelter for yourselves on the lee side of her body."

Jarin started to join the others, but Tevin stopped him.

"Jarin, you stay here with Dax. Take the tarp and tie one side of it to the carrier platform and then get under it. Once you're under, tie yourselves to these hooks." He showed Jarin a series of hooks underneath the platform. "And you need this." He threw down a long black hose from the beast's platform. "It's for air." He disappeared off the other side of the beast.

Sand and grit stung Jarin's face as he lashed the tarp to the beast's platform and anchored the loose side in the ground, forming a shelter. Dax put his hand on the great beast's snout ring and murmured in her ear flap until she closed her eyes, nose, and ear flaps, going dormant to wait out the storm. Then he crawled under the tarp next to Jarin, took one of the ropes Tevin had given them, wrapped it around his chest, and tied the other end to the hook on the platform. He started to help Jarin with his, but Jarin rebuffed him and did it himself. They pressed their backs up against the beast as the wind howled and the canvas flapped above their heads. The tension between them filled their little space.

"We've not talked much lately," Dax began. "How are you faring?"

"How should I be?" Jarin snapped. "I'm not here by choice."

"We are close to Isidima. Things will be better there." Dax positioned the air hose so the end would reach above the drifting sand. "We will blend in and find work and learn what is happening in Weslynde and get news of your sister."

"She could be dead for all we know." Jarin frowned. "Or maybe she killed my father and burned down the palace. Either way, I did not stay and fight for myself. I was a coward and I ran. I ran away because my butler told me to. My butler," he said in disgust.

"Jarin, you are alive because of Rence. And now you have

the gift of time to make a good plan and return when you are ready. You will make things right, and I will help you."

"How? You spend more time with your precious Riddien girl than you do with me."

Dax did not respond to that. It grew steadily darker, and they lay back against the side of the chameli, listening to the wind.

"What work will you seek when we get to the city?" Dax asked, breaking the silence.

"I don't know," Jarin muttered, exasperated that he would have to find work. "What will you do?" he countered.

"I can work for the miners finding metal, or I can train chameli to be carrier beasts. Isidima is the breeding center for all the chameli: the mining beasts, carrier beasts, scout beasts, messenger beasts."

"You know a lot about lizards."

"Chameli," Dax corrected softly. "And yes, I know a lot about them. They only breed here in the desert. Think of that. Argonne supplies all the beasts to the other provinces. Caleddon has to keep theirs in hot caves so they don't get sick. They are smart, but they are not like people. Maybe that's why I like them. They don't let things get to them; they only care about the now: food, water, shelter—"

"Fucking," interjected Jarin.

"Yes, that too," Dax acknowledged quietly.

They lay against each other in the dark, shoulder to shoulder, listening to the wind grow fainter as sand covered the tarp. Once it was quiet, Dax spoke again. "Breen is a welcome break in the storm for me, but that is all. You are more than my charge, Jarin; you are my friend."

Jarin stared up into the darkness, and tears formed in the corners of his eyes. He was afraid to speak, lest his trembling voice give him away. He listened to Dax breathing next to him, and after a while his breathing changed to soft snores. Jarin lay awake in the dark, resisting the urge to reach over and intertwine Dax's hand with his own.

⚜

The sandstorm stopped sometime during the night. The next morning, Dax told Jarin to tighten the rope around his chest, and then he shouted a command to the chameli. The beast lumbered to its feet, pulling the men up out of the sand and into the bright morning sun. It was sudden and exhilarating. They laughed and cheered as the other two beasts emerged, sand streaming off of their sides, the Argonnians and Riddiens dangling from their hooks like a row of smoked fish in the market. They stowed the tarps and cleared off the wagons and set off soon after. Jarin ended his sulk and pitched in with gusto, making things easier for everyone.

Three days later, they reached the ancient city of Isidima. Dax realized that it was anniversary of the day the twins were born; it was Jarin's twentieth birthday. If Jarin remembered, he didn't mention it.

CHAPTER 12

When Weslynde and Argonne had joined together and formed the Western Commonwealth, many had argued that Isidima should have been named its capital. Isidima was older, larger, and grander than Caleddon. The official reason Caleddon had been chosen over Isidima was because it was a center of knowledge and learning, home to the famous universities of magic and science. Although Isidima's contributions to the commonwealth's economy were considered less important by some, every Argonnian knew that the great carrier beast King Franklin rode down Caleddon's boulevard and the gold that clad Caleddon's glittering palace dome both came from Argonne.

Jarin was astonished when they topped the last dune and Isidima came into view. "By the gods!" he exclaimed. "It's magnificent! I've never seen anything like it."

"Close your mouth or flies will get in." Timeer laughed. "Welcome to the home of your ancestors, Tuval."

The city was squeezed into a thin strip of land between the desert and the ocean. It soared into the sky, towering over the dunes, its many shops and dwellings carved into the sides of an extinct volcano. Houses festooned with balconies and trellises clung to its steep sides like mussels on a rock, overstuffed with exotic trees, tropical flowers, and cascading vines that spilled from the terraces of one building down onto the roofs of the buildings below like some verdant waterfall. The entire city was a garden. A forest of spires and minarets spiraled up around the volcanic core. At its peak, a four-sided pyramid dominated the view.

"That building at the top. What is that?" Jarin asked.

"That is the Ziggurat," Timeer said. "The prime minister lives there. The volcano under the city is hollow, and its caves go all the way down to the ocean. The sea breeze blows up through the caves and keeps everything cool even on the hottest of days."

The caravans pushed their way into the packed market square, which was filled with the smells of savory food mixed with pungent animals and ringing with the sound of people shouting and merchants haggling. Jarin and Dax helped Timeer and Tevin unload their cargo off to merchants excitedly waiting for its arrival. When they rolled the last barrel of wine off of the wagon bed, Dax told Jarin it was time to leave.

"I haven't said goodbye!" Jarin spied Tevin at a nearby booth, talking to another Argonnian man. The man glanced in Jarin's direction and hurried out of the square.

"Tevin!" Jarin yelled, waving his arm.

Tevin flashed a big grin and came trotting over. "Tuval, I will miss sparring with you." He laughed and wrapped Jarin in a tight hug and swung him around. He started to say more but was happily distracted by the arrival of his mate. He ran off to greet her, leaving Jarin standing breathless, ribs crushed from the strong embrace.

"Tuval!" shouted Timeer, leading a pretty woman and small boy by the hand. The child was a miniature copy of Timeer. "Come over here; I want you to meet my son."

Jarin crouched down so he was eye level with the boy.

"Tij, this is Tuval. Tuval is a very, very important man."

"I am honored to meet you, Tij," Jarin said, holding out his hand.

The boy took his hand shyly. "Why do you wear those funny glasses?" he asked, then wrenched his hand free from Jarin's and ran to go play with another boy in the square. Jarin stood up and smiled after him.

"I am Tegreena," Timeer's mate said, slapping Timeer on the arm for not introducing them. "I hope our men provided you safe passage to Isidima."

"Tegreena, it is my great pleasure to meet you." Jarin gave her a royal bow and kissed her hand.

"So polite!" Tegreena said. "You could learn manners from this one, Timeer." She burst into giggles as Timeer wrapped his arms around her and hugged her to him.

Dax spent several minutes telling Timeer's and Tevin's women about their men's unmatched strength and leadership, especially during the harrowing sandstorm. The Argonnian men glowed with pride. Introductions complete, Dax and Jarin shouldered their packs and thanked the Argonnians several more times, politely refusing their offer of lodging and a night on the town.

As Jarin turned to go, Tevin put his hand on his shoulder and said in his ear, "We are all at your service, and we will meet again soon. I promise you."

⚜

Jarin and Dax threaded their way through the throng. As they neared the exit, Dax saw Breen, surrounded by three young Argonnian men smiling down at her with rapt attention. She was laughing and playing with the beads on the neck of one of the men. Dax stopped to watch for a moment, then trotted to catch up with Jarin.

"She won't be missing you, then?" Jarin asked, the corner of his mouth twitching.

"It doesn't look that way," Dax sighed. "She's got bigger toys to play with here in Isidima, much bigger." They both laughed.

"Where are we going?"

"I want to pay a visit to the chameli caves and training center," Dax said. "I think I can find work there as a trainer. It would be a good place to gather information as well."

"I want to explore. Isidima is amazing."

"We shouldn't split up. It may not be safe for you."

"I won't go far. I will look for a place we can get a room. We can meet back here at dusk. I will be careful, and I'm in disguise." Jarin lowered his eye-shades to prove his point.

Dax hesitated. He was distracted. Ever since they'd arrived, he had sensed the bundled energy of dozens of great chameli emanating from the nearby training center. He looked Jarin up and down appraisingly. The prince was no longer the skinny pampered royal dressed in silks he had rescued in Weslynde. His body was harder, he stood taller, and he carried himself with confidence. His stance was relaxed and his staff balanced easily in his hand. He blended in with the diverse throng filling the streets in both appearance and dress. He pushed down the twinge in his stomach.

"Alright, then. We meet back here at dusk. Don't engage with anyone, and for the gods' sakes, keep your clothes on."

"I will." Jarin laughed. He tossed his staff from one hand to the other, then twirled it over his head and trotted happily out of the square. Dax gave him a last searching look, then headed off to find the training center, eager to meet the remarkable animals he would find there.

⚜

Jarin headed up the main avenue, which wound its way

around the slopes of the great city. He stopped at an open-air pub to quench his thirst. Two mugs of potent cider later, he continued up the road, marveling at the many sights and sounds of Isidima, now enhanced by the pleasant buzz inside his head. As he climbed, the residences became larger and grander and he began to pass offices and lecture halls. He didn't really have a plan of action, but now that he was nearing the peak, he imagined it would be a good place to seek a position as a scribe or accountant and do some digging.

Jarin had put on his shirt and vest and switched his road-stained wrap skirt for a pair of leggings before setting out, but he still felt like a dusty caravan boy and doubted anyone would take him seriously should he inquire for work. The tall Argonnians he passed were dressed in fine linens and mostly ignored him.

The road led around to the side of the volcano that faced the ocean, and a welcome breeze that carried with it the tang of ocean brine met him there. He wandered onto a large terrace with a fountain bubbling at its center and leaned against a railing overlooking the bay. The busy port below was full of ships bobbing up and down in the shimmering blue-green water. It was beautiful and peaceful, but the desert sun overhead was fierce, so he moved back into the shade next to the fountain, peeling off his vest and stuffing it in his pack.

"Jarin?" a voice called out. Jarin wheeled around and saw an older Argonnian man with white braids and dressed in elegant clothes, staring at him in astonishment.

"I am sorry, sir; you have made a mistake. My name is Tuval," Jarin said cautiously, backing away. Then he faltered. He recognized the man. He pulled off his eyeshades and cried out, "Grandfather!"

"Jarin né Franklin! What are you doing here?" Tregor Anthelia clasped Jarin by his shoulders, then pulled him in, wrapping his arms around him and holding him tight. "My boy, my boy. We feared you were dead. It has been months since anyone has heard from you."

"I'm still alive," was all Jarin could say as his grandfather hugged him. He hadn't seen Tregor in years, not since an Argonnian delegation had traveled to Caleddon for a summit. Their conversation back then had been terse; Senator Anthelia had lectured the sixteen-year-old Jarin on the responsibilities of his office and the importance of the Argonnian legacy he represented. Jarin remembered he had been drunk at the time and had ditched a state dinner in his grandfather's honor. Tregor had stumbled in on him having sex with a server boy in the pantry.

Tregor took Jarin firmly by the elbow and steered him off of the terrace. "Come with me; you can't be seen here. There is a price on your head."

"What are you talking about?" What had his grandfather heard?

"Follow me. Quickly. We will talk more when it's safe." The senator led him through a vine-covered iron gate Jarin hadn't noticed before and down a narrow stone path to a small side door to one of the more ornate buildings. Tregor produced a key from his pocket and unlocked the door. A blast of cool, moist air hit Jarin's face. Once inside, they headed down a narrow hallway and up a staircase. At the top of the stairs, Tregor unlocked a second door, and they quietly stepped through into a grander hallway marked by columns of sunlight streaming down from skylights in the ceiling. The door snicked closed behind them, and Jarin noticed that the edges of the door disappeared into the carved stonework around it.

"My private entrance." Tregor smiled. He guided Jarin down the hall and opened the door to a richly appointed room containing an ornate desk, upholstered guest chairs, and a massive bookcase overflowing with books and papers. Thick curtains framed a deep inset window.

"Welcome to my office. Come in quickly." His grandfather locked the door behind them. He poured water into two glasses and handed one to Jarin.

"Jarin, this is a miracle. Where are you lodging? Did you come alone? Please tell me everything."

"You said there's a price on my head?" Jarin asked warily, still standing in the middle of the room.

"It's best if I show you. This arrived a month ago." Tregor went over to the desk and picked up a message scroll and handed it to Jarin. Jarin unrolled it, noting King Franklin's seal on the paper. It read:

By order of King Franklin né Rosin, sovereign of the Western Commonwealth.

Any and all information regarding the whereabouts of Prince Jarin né Franklin is to be brought to the king's attention immediately. The prince is implicated in a plot to overthrow the monarchy and is armed and dangerous. A substantial reward will be given to the citizen who delivers the prince alive to the Weslynde Royal Guard.

Prince Jarin has Argonnian coloring and characteristics. Blue eyes are a distinguishing feature. A sigil bearing the name Jarin né Franklin on his left shoulder provides positive identification.

A silkscreen of Jarin's face and upper torso, dressed in formal palace wear and with hair in loose waves to his shoulders, was inked below the message. Jarin did not recognize himself in the image.

"None of this is true. What are you going to do with me?"

"Nothing," Tregor said. "Except ensure your safety."

Jarin did not believe him, and he knew his face betrayed him.

"Jarin, trust me. That message scroll was delivered directly to the prime minister and has not been distributed to anyone outside her inner circle. You are safe here." Tregor sat behind his desk and motioned for Jarin to take a chair. "Now sit down and tell me what has happened. Why have you left Weslynde? Why are you here in Argonne? I mistook you for an Argonnian, by the way: your clothes, the beads in your hair."

Jarin cautiously sat in one of the upholstered chairs, beginning to relax a little. "It's a long story," he said, deciding to leave out any mention of a twin. "A contingent from Cordel marched into Weslynde. They sent my father a message stating that their leader had a claim to the throne, and my father had me locked up. I still don't know why. I was warned that he planned to have me killed, so I made my escape and came here, hoping to hide out until I can find out what is happening in Weslynde, why I'm being hunted. Do you know anything?"

Tregor took a sip of water before answering. "We received a report from Senator Intsimi that the king has welcomed a delegation of religious extremists into the palace. They hailed from Cordel and are led by a warrior woman known as Saint Cerise. Her followers famously dress in red and wear black and white war paint." Tregor leaned forward. "I must tell you, Jarin; I have met this Saint Cerise before, and she is hostile to Argonne. Apparently, she now lives inside the palace, and the king appears to be collaborating with her. Senator Intsimi is the only Argonnian remaining in the palace, and since that first report, he has sent us little else. I fear the king may be intercepting his communications."

"Senator Intsimi is a good man. I hope he is safe," Jarin mused. Inwardly, he was reeling at the information his grandfather had shared. Was this warrior, this so-called Saint Cerise, his twin?

Tregor took the scroll back from Jarin. "Jarin, why have you come here, to Isidima of all places?"

"I thought I could hide here. Blend in as an Argonnian until I can figure out what to do." He remembered the story he and

Dax had told Timeer and Tevin. "And maybe find some information about my mother. My father said she died when I was born, but there are rumors she is alive and fled Weslynde. Some even say she came back to Argonne." As he said these words, he realized how deeply he needed to know.

"Your mother never came to Argonne. She never left Weslynde. We think she was murdered."

"Who would do that? Why?"

"Politics. The Church of the Commonwealth was never happy about the union of Franklin and Tregan. They had long petitioned for an heir with ties to Riddien, the seat of the church."

"But that's crazy. Why would anyone—?"

"Power, Jarin. The church has long been angry with Argonne's resistance to adopting it as its official religion. They have been spreading lies that Argonne is planning an insurrection to overthrow the crown. With Tregan out of the way, I think they assumed they could turn you to the church and, when you became king, move the seat of the church to Caleddon."

"That's ox shit." Jarin said, but his grandfather's words made him realize all the ways the church had been immersed in his daily routine growing up—constant rituals, prayers, invocations to the gods.

"I believe the church plans a move on Weslynde and is using Saint Cerise as their weapon. I don't know what leverage this woman has on the king, but she has something. And she has a large following. I have even seen her acolytes here in Isidima, dressed in red robes and wearing white face paint."

Jarin slumped in a chair. Was his twin a weapon for the church? "Do you think the church is behind the death of my mother?" he asked.

"Yes, I do," Tregor said somberly. "I think they murdered your mother. My daughter."

"Oh, gods." Jarin tried to process this new information. If Saint Cerise was his sister, she had a claim the throne! She had to be stopped.

Jarin noticed a painting hanging above the fireplace. A portrait of Tregan Anthelia in battle gear, staff in hand. He had never seen a tribute to her like this in the palace back home. She was fierce and intelligent. He stepped closer to it.

Tregor came up behind him. "She was a great lady. You look like her, you know."

"Why did she ever go to Weslynde? Why did she agree to have a baby with Franklin?"

"Tregan was...unique. Extraordinary. She always did what she believed to be the right thing, never the selfish thing. She thought their child would bring greater legitimacy and status to Argonne, strengthen the bond and repair the rift that had grown between Argonne and Weslynde." He paused. "And I pushed her to do it, which I will always regret. In her letters to me, she wrote that she believed someday her child, you, would ride into Argonne next to her and restore honor to the province."

"I wish I had met her."

"I wish you had too," Tregor said. They regarded the portrait for a few more moments. "Jarin, I'm curious—how did you manage to escape the palace?"

"A magician helped me."

"A magician?"

"He served Tregan as a boy."

"Dax?" Tregor asked in surprise.

"Yes. Do you know him?"

"Dax is alive? This is a day filled with miracles. Where is he?"

"He's here, in Isidima. He's been my traveling companion since I left Caleddon."

"This is great news. You must bring him to me. He may know what happened to Tregan."

"He knows no more than I do," Jarin said. He let his fingers slide along the painting's frame. "Grandfather, I wish I could avenge her."

"Many feel the way you do," his grandfather said. "Jarin, there are some people I think you should meet."

⚜

Senator Anthelia summoned a page and asked her to assemble the high senate. He then led Jarin to a small room dominated by a large table. Thick tapestries hung on the walls, and sunlight entered through a single shaft centered above the table. Two older Argonnian women and a blond Riddien man with a thick plaited beard entered the room shortly after they arrived.

"Tregor, what's going on?" the Riddien man asked, looking quizzically at Jarin, who remained near a wall in the shadows.

Tregor put a hand on Jarin's back and guided him forward. "Jarin, I would like to introduce the high senate of Argonne. Senators Tvetha Talani, Trillian Eg, and Boreth Vanger. Boreth came to us all the way from Riddien." Tregor smiled proudly. "My friends, I would like you to meet my grandson, Jarin né Franklin, the prince of Weslynde."

The senators gasped and rushed over to Jarin, peppering him with questions.

"A moment, a moment," Tregor said. "Please sit down."

The senators pulled up chairs around the table. Jarin took the empty chair next to his grandfather. He studied the senators' expectant faces with some trepidation.

"Jarin, these are my trusted friends. Please share with them what you shared with me."

Senator Eg, an imposing woman with black beetle eyes,

spoke first. "The king of Weslynde has issued a warrant for your arrest. Tell us why."

"There is trouble in Weslynde." Jarin threaded his words together carefully. He was not going to tell anyone about his supposed twin. The specter of the curse loomed over everything. "The king has aligned himself with a religious group hostile to Argonne, and I was forced to flee."

"Why? What did you do?" Senator Eg asked, her voice full of suspicion.

"I did nothing. It all happened very suddenly," Jarin said. "The king had me locked up, but I managed to escape. Today I learned there is a warrant for my return."

Tregor nodded encouragingly.

Senator Vanger, the Riddien, spoke next. "We have heard reports that a woman called Saint Cerise, a religious fanatic, has moved into the palace and is influencing the king. My contact in Riddien says the church is planning a move on Weslynde, and this warrior is their champion. They intend for the church to take over the monarchy."

Senator Eg jumped in. "That is an unfounded rumor, Boreth." She trained her brittle eyes on Jarin. "The king's warrant says it is you, Jarin, who is plotting to overthrow the crown."

"That is a lie," Jarin shot back, surprised at the harshness of his own voice.

"I wonder if you were confined because of your Argonnian blood," Senator Talani pondered. "It's no secret Argonne opposes the church."

"There is more to this story than the prince is revealing." Senator Eg frowned. The senators began to argue with each other.

Jarin raised his voice a notch. "The story I want told is the one my grandfather told me. The story where the Western Commonwealth is united by more than name. A story where

Argonne and Weslynde are equals and there is no talk of separation or insurrection or a takeover by the church or by some warrior woman. That was my mother's dream, and it is my dream as well." He could not name the feeling inside him, a sort longing for something he had lost.

"Well said!" Senator Talani clapped her hands. "You give me hope I haven't had for a very long time."

Senator Eg continued to gaze at him with narrowed eyes. *Well, she has good reason,* Jarin thought to himself. *I am a fugitive, after all.* "Tell me about my mother, Tregan Anthelia." His voice caught when he said her name out loud. He cleared his throat and continued, "I want to know who she was and everything she tried to do."

⚜

The senators promised to keep Jarin's presence in Isidima a secret and to meet again soon. Jarin left the meeting with a new sense of purpose. He no longer felt like a refugee. Tregor escorted him back to the terrace where they'd first met.

"I will prepare a room for you at my villa," Tregor said. "My staff is discreet, and they have no reason to know who you really are."

"I need to tell Dax what has happened," Jarin said. "We were to meet at dusk." He glanced at the sun, which hung low above the ocean.

"Of course, of course," Tregor said. "Dax needs to be part of every plan. Go, my boy, and bring him back here to my office. I will wait for you there, then we can go together to my home. I can't wait to see him again. Where are you meeting him?"

"At the entrance to the market square."

"Ah, that could be dangerous for you. There are so many people from different places. There is a side path to the market, one that is not so well traveled so you will have less of a chance of being recognized." Tregor took him to a flight of stairs descending off the terrace. "When you get to the first landing at the bottom of these stairs, take the path to the right that leads through the hedge garden. It will put you on a stairway that goes straight down to the square."

"Thank you, Grandfather." Jarin clasped his hand and put an arm around his shoulders. "I won't be long."

"Wait," Tregor said, gripping Jarin's arm. "Let me provide you with an escort."

"I'll be fine." Jarin let go and put on his eyeshades to demonstrate. Exhilarated, he flew down the stairs and found the path through the gardens. On the far side, a narrow opening appeared between two rows of tall buildings. The passage went straight down in a series of staircases. There was a square of light at the bottom and what appeared to be the flat open space of the market beyond. He trotted down the stairs into the cool dark, passing by doors and windows and the occasional person panting up the stairs in the opposite direction. It grew darker, so he took off his eye-shades and put them in his pack. He continued down until he came to the bottom of the stairs. Instead of the market, the stairs ended at another small street, not much more than an alley, that split in two directions. He hesitated for a moment, unsure which way to go. The wider lane forked off to the right. Three men leaned against a produce cart in that direction, laughing and smoking. Their dog ran up to Jarin, tail wagging.

"Hey, there," he said, bending down and patting the dog. "Which way to the market square?"

"Headed to the square, are you?" asked the largest of the men, a bald man with pierced eyebrows. "You best take that street there." He pointed to the left lane, a narrow alley that dwindled into darkness.

"That way?" asked Jarin. The hairs on his arms rose, and his shoulder grew warm.

"It will put you out where the wagons unload," the man said.

"Thank you," Jarin said. "But it's getting dark, and I have no light. I think I'll try the other way." He set off jogging down the wider street, veering around the men.

"Take him down, dog!" the bald man yelled as he passed by them.

The dog sprang forward, fangs bared and snarling. Jarin spun around, instinctively grasping his staff with both hands. It whistled as he cracked it across the side of the dog's head. The dog yelped and went spinning across the ground. The three men leapt into action, pulling out knives and a club as they charged him. Jarin moved into a fighting stance and swung his staff again. He caught one of the men across the arm and heard the bone snap. The man fell, holding his arm. Jarin spun on his heel and ran as fast as he could down the street, the remaining two men close behind him. He gained ground, but as he rounded the next corner, he was confronted by two more men holding knives and blocking his path. He skidded to a stop and brought his staff back up, but before he could act, he was grabbed from behind and overwhelmed. He was thrown to the ground and rolled over in time to see the bald man raising a club over his head. Flashes of light filled his vision, and he knew nothing more.

⚜

Someone was whispering his name. Jarin opened his eyes. A woman in a battle vest bent over him. She held a long stave made out of silver. "Wake up, wake up, my son," she soothed. Her voice was silk, and her smile radiated love.

"Mother? You're alive?" He reached up to hug her but found he couldn't move his hands. "Where have you been? Where did you go?"

"I never left you." She bent and pressed her soft lips on his forehead. Her face slowly dissolved into the flickering shadows.

"Don't go. Don't leave me." Tears slid down his face.

The flickering light grew brighter, and his surroundings slowly came into focus. He was sitting in a chair in a small low-ceilinged room. Candles sputtered in sconces on the stone walls. His head was pounding. Every inch of his body ached. He tried to move his arms and found that they were bound to the chair back behind him and that his feet were tied to the chair's legs. His leggings were torn and his knees were bloody. The rest of his clothes were gone. His left eye was blurry, and he could taste blood in his mouth.

A table stood in the middle of the room. There were no windows and only one door. His staff was propped against the wall in the corner. That was something; maybe he could get to it. Voices approached outside the door, and he struggled to free his arms, but the ropes were too tight. The door creaked open, and the bald man who had clubbed him on the street entered, followed by a skinny man with bad teeth.

"You're not dead," the bald man said. "That's good."

"We're expecting a substantial reward," the skinny man said. "So you best not be thinking about dying on us. It says they need you alive." He leaned his face next to Jarin's; his breath smelled like rotten fish. "Let's start by making sure you are who we think you are. Tell us your name."

Jarin didn't speak. The bald man casually backhanded him across his blurry eye. Pain exploded in his head.

"Let's try again," fish breath continued. "My name is Togg. And your name is...?"

"Tuval," Jarin muttered through a split lip. His mouth was dry, his tongue thick. The bald man struck Jarin again, causing him to cry out.

"We think you have another name." Togg grinned. "Want to try again?"

"Water," Jarin mumbled.

"Where are our manners?" Togg exclaimed. "Tahoneh, get the lad some water."

The bald man filled a mug from a pitcher on the table and grabbed Jarin by the hair and pulled his head up. He poured the water into Jarin's mouth, making him choke and cough. Somewhat revived, Jarin shook his head defiantly.

"Let's try something else," Togg said. He picked up a scroll from the table and unrolled it. It was a copy of the king's warrant for Jarin, identical to the one Tregor had shown him. Togg held it up so that the image of Jarin was in front of his face. "Look familiar, Prince Jarin?"

Jarin glared at him.

"Nothing to say? Why don't you open those pretty blue eyes and have another look."

"He's not going to talk," Tahoneh said. "Let's find the sigil. Maybe we didn't search in the right place."

Tahoneh pulled a knife from his belt and cut the cords that held Jarin's arms and legs. He hoisted Jarin up by an arm, but Jarin's legs gave out beneath him, and he sank to the floor. Both men grabbed an arm and dragged him over to the table and dropped him face-first onto it. Jarin's head struck the tabletop, and he groaned. He tried to push himself up with his arms but had no strength. He closed his eyes and lay across the table, gasping like a fish, limbs splayed out. Tahoneh lashed his wrists and ankles to the leg posts.

"It says it's on his left shoulder," Tahoneh said, examining the scroll. "Which one is the left?"

"This one, fool," Togg pointed.

"There's only a big tattoo—a raven wing. Nothing else."

"He's covered it up. It must be here." Togg crouched over Jarin's back, examining his left shoulder closely. "Here, this part is darker." He touched Jarin's shoulder blade and poked at it.

"His skin is rough here, and I feel something underneath." Togg's finger pushed hard into his shoulder blade. "It's here."

"I can't make it out," Tahoneh said. "I don't see any words."

"It's under the skin. Let's cut it out," Togg said.

"No, wait," Jarin groaned weakly. "I'll tell you what you want."

"Oh, now you start squawking, my chicken. Well, you're too late. We need the proof." He stuck his knife into Jarin's shoulder.

Jarin screamed and bucked up and down on the table.

"Hold him down, Tahoneh."

Tahoneh lay across Jarin's back while Togg continued probing. He dug the knife down to pry the ring loose. Jarin screamed in agony, vomited, and then fainted.

⚜

Togg jostled Jarin by the arm, but the prince didn't respond. "Don't worry. He's still breathing." He tried to pry loose the sigil from Jarin's body a few more times but couldn't.

"It's lodged in the bone somehow." In frustration, he dragged the edge of the blade across the rough patch of skin on Jarin's shoulder, scraping the top layer away. Blood ran down Jarin's side and pooled on the table. The blade exposed the sigil's filigreed metalwork, and Togg crowed in triumph. He grabbed the king's warrant and pressed it down onto Jarin's shoulder. When he peeled it off, the bloody impression of the sigil was clearly visible next to the picture of Jarin's face.

"We have him!" he said with glee. He blew on the paper to dry the blood. "Tahoneh. Pour some whiskey on that wound and put a rag over it. We wouldn't want to hurt the lad."

CHAPTER 13

The sights, sounds, and even the pungent smells of the chameli training center brought with them a flood of memories for Dax. He'd only been ten when he'd first arrived in Isidima, having been expelled from the university of magic in Caleddon for lack of talent. The head magician had sent him south to "tend the dumb beasts," telling him he had utterly failed at his attempts at earth magic and was good for nothing else. Dax had found he enjoyed caring for the chameli and thrived in the training center. Tregan Anthelia had found him there, taken him under her wing, and cared for him the way a loving aunt might. She had brought him home to live at the Anthelias' villa, and he'd become her devoted servant from then on.

The training center was as impressive as he remembered, set back in an enormous box canyon surrounded on three sides by towering rock walls. The vast floor was a sandy arena with stone holding pens near the back. A broad ledge ringed the canyon halfway up the walls, along which caves were carved into the rock, providing housing for the trainers and handlers who tended the beasts.

Two Argonnian trainers were working with a great chameli

in the center of the arena. They were attempting to harness it to a wagon, and the giant animal was resisting, lashing its tail and huffing in an aggravated manner. When Dax approached the trainers, the chameli raised its head, and its cheek spots changed from an irritated red to a peaceful blue. The two men noticed the change and turned to see Dax standing there.

"Good day to you," the older trainer said, patting the beast's leg. "You seem to have attracted his attention." The chameli rumbled and sidestepped back and forth restlessly.

"I didn't mean to interrupt," Dax said. He could sense the beast's anxiety and was eager to jump in. He knew exactly what to do. "May I?"

The trainer frowned, then nodded. Dax stepped forward and grabbed the beast's snout ring, uttering a few words in old majik. The chameli calmed immediately and backed into the wagon's traces. Another word from Dax and it settled on the ground.

"You're a magician!" the older trainer exclaimed, surprised. "And you clearly have experience with the beasts."

Dax nodded and rubbed the chameli's eye ridge. The beast rumbled in appreciation.

The younger trainer piped up, "Old Angus put the charm in that one's snout ring but not one of us can give it a proper command. He's losing his touch, he is."

"Angus?" Dax asked. "Is he your magician?"

"Aye," the older trainer grumbled. "He's responsible for this chaos."

"He's going on a hundred," the younger trainer complained. "Things've been getting tough around here. The newer beasts can't tell their earflaps from their assholes."

"Hush now, Tymm," the older trainer admonished. He held out his hand to Dax. "I'm Tonga. I supervise the handlers working with the beasts. This one flapping his jaw here is Tymm, my apprentice."

"I'm Dax. I recently arrived from Weslynde by caravan." He shook Tonga's hand. He was about to say more when the chameli stood up and shook in its traces, knocking the wagon backward. Dax grabbed its ring again and put his other hand on its flat snout. He closed his eyes and spoke a word under his breath. A calming energy flowed from his core, down his arm, and radiated into the chameli. The beast settled back down, cheek spots undulating from blue to green to blue again.

"Try it now," he said to Tymm. Tymm took the ring and spoke to the beast. It stood and took a few steps forward, gently butting its giant head against the young man.

Tymm spoke another command, and the beast settled. "That's amazing." He laughed joyfully. "We was losing control of this one."

"He should be fine now." Dax rubbed the beast's chin. "He's still a pup and only wants to play." He gave the beast a final pat, happier than he had been in weeks. "Tonga, I'm looking for work. Where can I find your magician?"

"Angus would be up there." Tonga pointed to the ledge high above them.

"He'll be waking from his second nap of the day and heading down to dinner before bedtime," Tymm added sarcastically.

"Tymm, close your trap and take Dax to meet the magician. Get him some food while you're at it." Tonga turned to Dax. "Truth be told, we could use your help. We need someone to put proper charms on those rings. We'd be glad to have you."

✢

Angus, the center's head magician, hailed from Riddien. He was a small man with leathery skin and was bent with age. His long white hair and plaited beard made him look like a wizard out of a storybook. After introductions, Angus invited Dax to join him at the cooking pit. They grabbed bowls of corn chowder and flatbread and found a place to sit at one of the long tables. Dax offered up his experience as a magician's apprentice and shared that he had worked with chameli in Isidima as a boy. Angus seemed more interested in reminiscing about the old days than he was in Dax's qualifications.

"You were at Caleddon's university of magic, then?" Angus asked.

Dax nodded. "For a short time. I left when I was ten."

"You must have known old Lady Trimble—she was the best at earth magic and steam."

"She was retired by the time I got there," Dax said.

"Oh, that's too bad. She could make water move, you know. I never knew anyone else who could do that. There was the time she stopped a geyser from coming up in the middle of the queen's summer lodge. It was an impressive feat, I tell you." He stared off into space for a moment. He shook whatever vision he was having out of his head and asked, "How is Queen Rosin? She's a pretty one."

"She's passed on, I'm afraid. Franklin is king now."

"Franklin! That arrogant sod. Always looking out for himself. He and that gods-cursed magician friend of his, Gerard Mort. I hope they found a jail cell that could hold that mage." He paused for a moment, then said, "Mort was good with locks though, too good by half."

"Gerard Mort is Caleddon's house mage now," Dax said, blowing on his chowder. He was secretly pleased that Angus shared his low opinion of Gerard Mort.

"He is? Gods curse him. He's the reason I left Weslynde and came here. Mort pushed out any magician who wanted to learn more than how to locate a vein of copper. He didn't like the competition." The old magician waved his spoon in the air. "He didn't have time for animals, I tell you that. You'd be hard-pressed to find a decent homing lizard in Weslynde these days."

Angus leaned in conspiratorially. "I'll tell you a secret. Mort spent all his time trying to figure out how to control people. Even experimented making snout rings for humans. It was an abomination. He's no good, I tell you...no good." He trailed off, then yawned. "Well, it's getting on nap time. It's been a pleasure talking with you, er, what did you say your name was?"

"Dax."

"Dax. Oh, yes. That's right. When do you travel back to Weslynde, uh, Dax?"

"I'm not going back. As I said earlier, I'm looking for work. I would like your permission to assist Tonga in the training center, setting charms and teaching the handlers to work with their animals."

"Are you a magician, then?" Angus asked, surprise in his eyes. "Where did you get your training?"

Dax observed Angus thoughtfully. The old magician's mental faculties were clearly failing him. No wonder the trainers were in disarray. He asked gently, "Where are the other magicians who help you?"

"Other magicians!" scoffed Angus. "There are no other magicians. Only a few field witches. That blasted Gerard Mort saw to that. He stopped letting trained magicians come to Argonne a few years back. Not even to work in the mines, and gods know we need them there! I haven't seen a young magician in Argonne since...since...um, well I can't recall." The old magician scraped his empty bowl with his spoon, then brightened with a new thought. "Say, are you looking for work? Why don't you talk to Tonga? He runs the training center. He can always use an extra hand. Tell him that Angus wants you on the team."

"I will, thank you." Dax smiled.

"Now if you will excuse me, I have some research to do up in my room. It was a pleasure meeting you, er, em..."

"Dax."

"Dax. Of course. A pleasure." He took Dax's hand and squeezed it.

"You as well—and thank you; I won't let you down."

"Oh, they always do, son, they always do." Angus headed up the stairs, holding his robe up to keep from tripping.

Dax watched him go, pondering the stories Angus had shared. Gerard Mort had been stirring up unrest between Weslynde and Argonne longer than he'd thought.

By the time Dax made his way back to the market to meet Jarin, the sun had set behind the city's peak. He was elated from his day with the animals and was looking forward to sharing his news with Jarin. The prince was not there waiting for him, however, and he felt a slight pang of dismay. He pushed it down, but his alarm grew as the sky darkened and there was still no sign of him. He rushed around, questioning the vendors closing up shop, but none of them remembered a young Argonnian wearing eye-shades. Dax cursed himself for being such a fool. How had he let himself be distracted from his mission? What had possessed him to allow Jarin to wander off on his own? He found a quiet corner and sat cross-legged and let his mind expand out, searching for traces of sky metal, hoping to sense the spark of heat he always got from Jarin's sigil, but he sensed nothing and the effort left him exhausted, his magic drained. Kicking himself, he set out toward the city center as the lamps were being lit along the thoroughfare, and he searched throughout the night, trying to think like his young charge, asking in the pubs, visiting the baths and brothels. No one had seen anyone like that, and his panic steadily grew.

Bleary-eyed and anxious, Dax made his way back to the training center as the eastern sky started to lighten, having promised Tonga that he would meet him there. He begged Tonga's forgiveness, shook off his fatigue, and set out on new search. As he was leaving the arena, he noticed a well-dressed white-haired Argonnian standing near the entrance. He walked past him, but the man motioned for him to come over. Something about his face was familiar.

"Hello, Dax, I am very happy to see you again," the man said with a broad smile.

"Have we met?" Dax asked, curious now. "How is it you know my name?"

"You were indentured to my daughter as a child. You used to play kickball in my courtyard."

"Senator Anthelia!" Dax cried out joyfully. He grasped the senator's outstretched hand. "Why didn't I recognize you?"

Tregor put his other hand on Dax's shoulder and drew him close. The men hugged each other warmly.

"I have changed a little bit over the last twenty-odd years, as have you." Tregor smiled, appraising Dax, his eyes tracing over his scar. "You have had some adventures, I see. You are no longer the shy little boy always hanging back in the corners."

"How did you find me?"

"Jarin told me you were traveling with him, and I heard the center acquired a new magician. I put the two together."

"Jarin!" Dax's heart leapt with hope. "Is he with you? Is he safe?"

Tregor's brows furrowed. "That's why I came to see you. I was hoping you would tell me. He went to find you and to bring you to my villa last night. You haven't seen him?"

Dax was crushed anew. "No. I've searched all night. He's vanished."

"That is troubling news indeed. I sent him straight to the market."

"Straight from where?"

"From my senate office. I told him which path to take."

"Can you show me?" Dax asked.

"Of course. We go this way." Tregor led him out of the center at a brisk pace. A carrier beast penned nearby gave an alarm call as Dax passed by.

Tregor led Dax up the road he had told Jarin to follow to get back to the market. Dax focused his mind on their surroundings as they went, trying to sense anything that might be a clue. They climbed briskly until they came to a flight of stairs.

"He would have come down these stairs here," Tregor said.

Dax sensed a strong connection to a pile of rubbish against a wall. He sifted through it and picked up a pack. It was Jarin's. He recognized it immediately: the tattered edges, the knot holding the strap together where it had frayed and broken during their journey south. Heart sinking, he put his thumb on a dark stain that could only be blood. He cursed himself again for being such an idiot, for forgetting his promise, his pledge to protect Jarin even if it meant his own life. How easily he had cast it aside.

"This pack is Jarin's," Dax said grimly. "There is blood."

"By the gods," Tregor said. "Why did I let him go by himself?"

"That is my crime as well," Dax said. *One that can't be forgiven*, he thought. He bent low and searched the ground for other artifacts. Near the foot of the stairs, he came across the body of a dog, dead less than a day. The dusty bricks next to it showed signs of a scuffle, and he spied a long knife wedged between two loose bricks. He picked it up and showed it to Tregor. "There was a fight here; there were several involved. I think Jarin was ambushed here."

A sudden clatter of footsteps echoed on the stairs above them. Two Argonnian men appeared out of the gloom. They stopped short when they saw Dax and Tregor. Menace radiated off them.

"Here now, that's my knife you're holding," the taller man growled. He was bald and had pierced eyebrows. He pulled a short sword from his belt and brandished it. "Give it back if you don't want to die."

Senator Anthelia took a step back and reached into his robes, taking out a long knife he had hidden there. Dax stood his ground, gripping the knife he had picked up off the ground.

"You met a friend of ours here last night," Dax said, inwardly seething but outwardly calm. "Where is he?"

"The prince," whispered the shorter Argonnian.

"Shut your stupid mouth, Togg," the bald man hissed, cuffing him. He turned back to Dax. "I have no idea what you're talking about. We didn't meet your friend. But you did pick the wrong alley to wander down." With a sudden flip of his wrist, he sent his knife spinning toward Dax.

Dax sussed the knife in midair, making it wobble. It flew by his leg and clattered harmlessly on the bricks. A sensation he had no control over suddenly surged through his body, a potent mix of magic, anger, fear, and guilt that had been building inside him since the moment he'd realized Jarin was missing. He threw his head back and screamed, the cords on his neck straining. He clenched his fists in rage, and a pulse of energy flew out of his body and struck the two Argonnians, knocking them backward. The piles of crates stacked nearby shattered and splintered into the air. A wooden beam holding up a rusty balcony above them cracked and snapped, and the entire structure broke free of the wall and crashed down on top of the two Argonnians, pinning them under the debris. Dust roiled up and filled the air around them.

Senator Anthelia stood frozen in shock. "By the gods, Dax. Did you do that?"

"Apparently," Dax said, knees trembling. He could barely stand, and it hurt to talk.

"Only the high wizard has that much power."

An image of Jarin lying somewhere nearby bleeding and broken came into Dax's mind, and his anger surged anew. Adrenaline poured back into his limbs, and he grabbed the bald man by the arm and pulled him out from under the wreckage. He picked him up and shoved him against a wall.

"Take me to this prince you spoke of. Do not hesitate, or I will break both your legs beneath you."

The bald man nodded in fear and stumbled down the dark alley. Dax and Tregor left the other Argonnian buried under the fallen rubble and followed. A short distance away, the bald man pointed out a thick wooden door set back in a recessed alcove along the wall of a large building. A large padlock secured the latch on the door.

"Open it!" Tregor demanded.

"I don't have the key," the bald man muttered.

"Where is it?" Tregor grabbed the man and put his knife under his chin.

Before the bald man could answer Tregor, Dax put a finger on the padlock on the door latch and it burst apart, shards of metal clattering to the ground. Tregor lifted an eyebrow, keeping his knife on the man.

Dax stepped inside the room. It was dark and still. A box of candles sat by the door. Dax lit one and moved into the gloomy space. A table stood in the middle of the room, and a chair lay on its side next to it. Smears of blood streaked across the table-top. Dax touched it; it was still sticky. His hands shook as he lifted the candle above his head. Jarin's staff was leaning against the wall. He lifted it and detected Jarin's essence in the wood, soaking into his hand. He stepped out of the room and showed it to Tregor.

"Yer too late." The bald man grinned. "They've taken him to Weslynde for the reward. We'll all be heroes, I expect."

Dax pushed Tregor aside and shoved the bald Argonnian hard against the building. He pressed Jarin's staff into his neck, choking him.

Tregor placed his hand on Dax's shoulder. "Don't kill him. We need him."

Dax growled in frustration and released the pressure. The bald man bent over, coughing and rubbing his throat. Dax grabbed him by the collar and threw him into the dark room and slammed the door, letting the latch drop into the catch. He put his hand on the latch and whispered a few words of old majik, jamming the inside handle. The door could no longer be opened.

"Let me out of here," the man yelled, his voice muffled by the thick door.

"Maybe your friends will come back for you," Dax wheezed bitterly. "You know, the way heroes do." His magic was spent, his legs trembled uncontrollably, and he put his hand on the building to keep from falling down. Spots danced before his eyes.

"Tregor," he gasped hoarsely. "This trail grows cold. If they are indeed taking Jarin to Weslynde, how best would they get there?"

"Crossing the Endelas Lake is the fastest way," Tregor said.

"Show me the road that leads to the Endelas Lake."

"Not a road. To get there, you take a boat up the coast."

"Take me to the harbor."

"The shortest way to the harbor is through the mountain itself."

Tregor put Dax's arm over his shoulder and helped Dax up the lane to a large iron door set in the side of the volcano. Tregor spoke to the guards posted at the door, who joined them. They entered a massive lava tube, one of many that ran throughout the extinct volcano's core, Tregor explained. By this time, Dax had regained his footing, and they raced down polished ramps and descended long winding stairways. A strong ocean breeze blew over them, and Dax could hear waves crashing into rocks in some subterranean cavern far below. Not long after, they came out of the mountain through another iron door that opened on the south end of the main harbor.

Tregor was now winded and held his side. "You go on," he gasped. "Take these men; I will catch up with you."

With the two guards escorting him now, Dax pounded down the boardwalk. Hundreds of boats tied were up in the harbor, and at least a dozen small craft were floating out in the bay.

"He could be anywhere," one of the guards said.

"I'll alert the harbor master," the other yelled and ran off.

Dax's head pounded and his muscles were screaming; he wasn't sure he had any skill left, but he had to try. He fell to his knees, and he put both hands on the wooden walkway, letting his head hang down below his shoulders.

"Are you all right?" The guard touched his shoulder. "You're looking wobbly."

"I'm fine." Dax waved him away. "Leave me be." He shook his head to clear it, took a deep breath, then closed his eyes and focused, sending his power down the wharf and across the floating docks. He ignored the flood of information that poured into his consciousness, snatches of earth elements, copper, timber, oil, fish... he was searching for one thing: sky metal. It would lead him to Jarin if he was anywhere within a hundred yards. He sussed as far as he could, but he felt neither a spark nor a glimmer.

"I can't feel him," he said out loud in despair.

"Try again," the guard encouraged, not really understanding what it was that Dax was doing.

Dax clenched his teeth and redoubled his concentration,

expanding his reach down the pier to its farthest section. There. On the farthest floating dock, a spark. Barely a glint, but enough. He opened his eyes. A small boat, tied to the dock, was bobbing in the waves. He could make out two figures throwing ropes, getting the boat ready to sail.

He grabbed the guard by the arm and pointed. "He's on that boat."

The guard helped him to his feet, and together, they thundered down the pier and leapt down onto the floating dock. The two men on the boat turned at the sound, then quickly untied the boat from its mooring and pushed away from the dock. They hoisted the sail, and as it unfurled, it caught the breeze and the boat began to glide away. It was thirty feet from the dock and moving fast by the time Dax and the guard reached the far end of the dock.

"Now what?" the guard said. "We can't swim that fast."

Dax stretched out his hands one last time and closed his eyes. His heart pounded in his chest. He made a fist, and the boat's mast shattered and the sail fell across the deck. Next, he sussed the tiller, jamming it hard to port, turning the boat in a circle. The guard kicked off his boots and dove into the water. Dax jumped in after. The two men on board the boat lowered a small dinghy into the water and paddled away.

The guard reached the boat first and pulled Dax aboard. Dax yanked opened the cabin door and leapt down the three steps. Jarin was lying on his side on a pile of sailcloth in the corner, naked except for the remnants of his tattered leggings. His body was bruised and bloodied, and his skin was the color of wet ashes in the light of the cabin's oil lamp. A dirty cloth was wrapped around his chest and shoulder, stained dark with blood.

Dax knelt over Jarin and put his hand on Jarin's forehead. He was burning up. Dax untied the bandage and pulled it back. An open wound on his shoulder the size of an egg oozed pus and blood. Jarin's shoulder bone and part of his sigil protruded from it. He put his finger on the sigil, but the metal was cold. He didn't feel the spark of energy he should have. Jarin was dying.

I'm too late, he thought in panic. *Too late.*

Footsteps creaked on the deck and clattered down the steps, and then Tregor was there. He knelt at Jarin's side.

"He needs a healer immediately," Dax choked out. "His body is full of infection. I can't feel his life force."

"He still breathes, Dax," Tregor said. "There is hope. We will take him back to my villa." He yelled out the hatch, "Harbor Master, I need two men to lift this man, and we need a cart to transport him. And fetch me a messenger beast." He stomped up the steps to give directions.

Dax found a jar of water and poured some on a cloth and dabbed Jarin's caked lips. "Hold on, my friend. Hold on." He bent down and pressed his lips on Jarin's forehead.

Jarin's eyes fluttered open, and he whispered hoarsely, "Dax, you found me. I knew you would." He coughed weakly. "I let you down. I'm sorry..." His eyes closed again, and his head lolled to the side.

"It's alright." Dax knelt over him, cradling his head in his arms and dabbing his forehead with the cool cloth. "I have you now. I have you."

PART IV

THE AMBASSADOR FROM CORDEL

CHAPTER 14

King Franklin gazed across the ruined flax field, sobered by the view. Drifts of hail still huddled in the shady areas. Meltwater ran down in furrows between rows of broken flax stalks, and blue petals littered the ground. The leaves had been stripped from the surrounding trees, and the young grapevines in the nearby vineyards had been pounded into a pulp. In the distance, seemingly floating above the mist rising from the wet earth, farmers were working on a barn roof damaged by the storm. They paused in their repairs and pointed at his security force; the king had no doubt they must be wondering why a host carrying his banner was crossing their fields.

The day had not started well. In addition to reports of injuries and hail damage coming in from all over the city, Gerard Mort had brought him the unwelcome news that Prince Jarin had somehow escaped from his room and that the guards stationed outside Jarin's terrace door had been drugged. He had summoned Rence, along with the palace guards posted outside Jarin's chamber door, and they all confirmed that no one had entered or exited Jarin's room from the hallway. It was a puzzle made more confounding because Jarin's terrace door was locked from the inside as well as the outside and there was no sign of forced entry. The king had had his security team comb the city, and he'd had sent messages to the nearby villages with orders to find and return the prince as quickly as possible. If Jarin was not found soon, it would greatly threaten his ability to control the situation facing him.

The patches of fog started to break up, and the assembly from Cordel suddenly appeared out of the mist on the far side of the flax field, banners rippling in the freshening breeze. The king could make out at least fifty individuals, most wearing red robes, which made them seem more like clerics than soldiers. They were too far away for him to determine what types of weapons they carried, but he saw no shields. A trio broke away from the Cordel line and picked their way across the sodden field toward Frankin and his soldiers. The hooded figure in the middle wore a sword, and the other two carried spears. A white cloth was tied to one of the spears.

"They wish to parley," Gerard Mort said. He, along with General Drissen, head of Weslynde's armed forces, stood next to Franklin on a hillock overlooking the flax field.

At least they are not stupid, Franklin thought with grim satisfaction. He had sixty seasoned fighters from his royal guard stretched across the field behind him, and two carrier beasts flanked the contingent, each carrying six soldiers with crossbows. He liked his odds if it came to a conflict.

"Your Majesty," General Drissen said in a low voice, pulling Franklin's focus away from the Cordelians crossing the field. "The Archbishop of Riddien approaches."

Franklin turned around and saw the archbishop gingerly walking up the muddy road behind them, holding up his robes, followed by a long procession of clerics and novices in gray robes.

"By the gods, what is he doing here?" Franklin grumbled. "No one invited the church." He glowered at Archbishop

Mellon slogging up the slope to join him. The archbishop's followers fanned out across the field behind Drissen's soldiers.

"What did I miss?" the archbishop asked, puffing and mopping his brow.

"What are you doing here, Mellon? You were not invited."

"It's always wise to have clergy on hand when one negotiates," the archbishop said. "Keeps things calm."

"It fucks things up." Franklin scowled. He didn't like the way Mellon spoke to him; it sounded patronizing. The archbishop had gotten much too comfortable lately. "Next time ask first. And keep quiet unless I request your advice. We don't even know what they want."

"Of course, my king." The archbishop gave a slight bow and glanced quickly at Gerard Mort. The mage did not pay him any notice.

When the Cordelian truce party was two-thirds of the way across the field, the hooded figure in the middle handed off their sword to one of the spear carriers and continued alone toward the king.

"It is as you said," General Drissen murmured. "Cordel has sent an emissary with a message. Something egregious must have happened, and from the look of those red robes, something involving the church, I'd say."

"Mmmm," the king murmured. No one but himself and Gerard Mort knew about the message he had received from a woman claiming she was his child and heir to his throne. Franklin scanned the far side of the field. The woman was likely standing somewhere among the line of Cordelians. He took a deep breath and blew it out slowly. He wiped his sweaty palms on his tunic.

The messenger stopped about twenty feet away and pulled back their hood, revealing she was female. She was unusual looking: tall and thin, her face so white it shone in the sun. Was she wearing makeup? Black paint had been smeared around her eyes and on her lips. Her cherry-red hair was pulled back into a warrior's knot.

"By the gods," General Drissen spouted next to him. "It's the albine, the one the church calls Saint Cerise."

Behind Franklin, Archbishop Mellon clapped his hands, and an audible sigh went through the novices standing behind the soldiers.

Franklin's eyes went wide. What was she doing here? The heroic exploits of Saint Cerise had been spreading through the palace recently; it was a favorite dinner party conversation. He hadn't quite realized she was a real person. Why, of all people, was she the messenger? And what was her connection to this woman claiming to be his daughter? Had his supposed daughter enlisted her help? If the stories about Saint Cerise were true, his daughter had a powerful ally.

"Everyone stay here." The king slid down the muddy hillock to meet her, wishing to remain out of earshot from the others and keep the secret of his daughter as long as possible. He slogged through the furrows until he was face-to-face with the tall red-haired woman. Neither spoke at first.

The king finally broke the silence. "You are the one they call Saint Cerise."

"I am called that by some," said the woman, holding his gaze. Her alto voice was soft but powerful, and her blue eyes seemed to pierce through him, daring him to challenge her.

He studied her face. In spite of her alabaster skin and face paint, the shape of her nose and mouth and the blue of her eyes seemed familiar—much like Jarin's, in fact. A shock of recognition hit him hard in his stomach. "You're the one claiming to be my daughter," he gasped.

"I am your daughter. I am Sabrin né Franklin," Cerise said evenly.

"Sabrin." The king's knees trembled, and he fought to bring himself back under control. He would not lose the upper hand now. He forced a condescending scowl. "You have proof of this?"

"I bear the sigil."

"That will need to be verified. What is it you seek, woman?"

"I am your firstborn, and I am here to claim my rightful place as heir to the throne of Weslynde."

The audacity! thought the king. She had placed herself, unarmed, in the middle of a field, surrounded by his soldiers, who would shoot her instantly if he said but a word. She was foolhardy but, at the same time, brave. He couldn't imagine Jarin ever making a move so bold. It was time now, however, for him to shut her down.

"I already have an heir, and you have heard of him. Jarin né Franklin will take the throne after I pass."

"Where is my brother?" Cerise demanded, looking past the king at the crowd behind him. "Produce him. I wish to make my position clear to him as well as you."

Calling Jarin her brother caught him off guard. "You are in no position to make demands of me. You rise up out of nowhere, claiming to be my child, threatening to take my crown, leading this bizarre religious cult. Tell me why I should not strike you down here in this field?"

"Because I'm your daughter," Cerise said unflinchingly. "And I came here to help you keep the commonwealth secure, for the benefit of the people of Weslynde."

"For Weslynde's benefit? Or for yours?" King Franklin asked, angry at her impudence. "Return to your followers now before I take you into custody. I will send an envoy to verify any claims you have made, then you can petition the crown like any other commoner." He signaled to his security detail, shouting, "Guards, escort this woman back to her worshipers." He turned away, purposely dismissing her.

"Your Majesty, a word!" Gerard Mort called out from the hillock, holding up his hand to stop the advancing guards.

Franklin scowled, but Mort usually said something important to know. He nodded his assent, and the mage picked his way through the stalks.

"This man is Gerard Mort, my house mage," Franklin told Cerise when the mage reached his side.

Gerard Mort tripped slightly on a flax stalk and grabbed Franklin's left shoulder to steady himself. He caught his balance and leaned in close to the king's ear and whispered in a soothing voice, "Your Majesty. You would be better served to bring this woman directly inside your palace for talks. You can introduce her as Ambassador Cerise Aikawa and avoid revealing any news of twins." As he talked, he let his fingers trail over the king's sigil. "Better to gain an ally than create an unnecessary foe."

King Franklin relaxed. He closed his eyes, trying to remember why he had been so agitated. He shook his head to clear his thoughts and opened his eyes. It was as if he were seeing Cerise for the first time. She was Ambassador Aikawa, representing Cordel, an important ally.

"Perhaps you are right. We are not fighting a battle today." He gave a respectful nod to Cerise, then shouted back to his general, "Send word to the palace. Have quarters set up for Ambassador Cerise Aikawa from Cordel, and make room in the barracks for her delegation. We will address Cordel's concerns in the Grand Hall."

General Drissen splashed forward in consternation. "Your Majesty. Is this wise? None of these people have been vetted; we don't know their intentions. Perhaps an encampment outside the city walls would be more appropriate?"

"Your king has spoken," Gerard Mort interjected and gestured to the crowd behind the king. "Look behind you, Drissen."

General Drissen turned around and saw that Archbishop Mellon's followers had turned their gray cloaks inside out. A wave of red robes now met his eyes, the same robes the Cordelians wore. He shot Gerard Mort an angry look.

"It appears we all want the same thing." The mage smiled evenly.

"Your Majesty, do you see this?" General Drissen gestured at all the red robes.

Franklin scoffed dismissively. "Gerard Mort is right. I see no enemies here. We will escort the ambassador's delegation to the palace.

"But if I might—" the general implored.

"You have your orders. Ambassador Aikawa is to be welcomed in the palace." Franklin furrowed his brow. "Drissen, your priority is to find Prince Jarin, not tell me how to conduct my business. I want my son found and brought home before the day is out. Is that clear?" He frowned, daring Drissen to object again.

General Drissen anxiously regarded the host of red robes surrounding them, nodded curtly, and stomped back through the broken flax stalks, shouting orders to his troops to prepare to march.

⚜

Cerise observed this exchange with some interest, noting the king's sudden mood swing. She was pondering her next move when the king leaned close to her and whispered, "Breathe not a word of who you are to anyone for the time being, do you hear? Not a word. News of twins could spark a riot."

Caught off guard, Cerise nodded her assent. She splashed back through the mud to her contingent. Tar and Janis met her mid-field.

"What happened?" asked Janis.

"We proceed to the palace," Cerise said, still marveling at the ease of their encounter.

"They had their archers trained on you the whole time," Tar grumbled. "One shot, curse of the twins solved."

"It was on my mind, believe me," Cerise replied. "But the mage came through like he said he would. The king listens to him. Gerard Mort has some sort of influence over him. I don't understand what it is."

"Are you sure you want to go through with this?" Tar pressed. "I don't trust Gerard Mort the way you do."

"We've come too far to turn back now."

"So, you are Princess Sabrin now?" Janis asked. "Just like that?"

"No. Not exactly. I agreed to keep Sabrin a secret...for now. At least until the prince is found. I am now Ambassador Aikawa. Apparently, no one but the king and the mage know about Sabrin."

"But you came here to claim your right as heir," Janis said.

"I know." Cerise frowned. "But it seems wise to honor the king's request, at least for now. He has the upper hand, so we will have to wait for his next move before we make a challenge." She needed the king in her camp if she was going to ask him for help finding the Argonnian terrorists who had attacked her family. It wouldn't do any good to fight him. She hoped that Gerard Mort would continue to influence him on her behalf. He had proved true on everything he had promised so far.

"You said Prince Jarin has gone missing?" Tar asked. "How do you lose a prince?"

"I overheard the king telling the general to find him."

"Why is finding him important?"

"The king said news of twins could cause a riot. I imagine the king wants to keep control of the situation. If the prince doesn't fall in line and keep the secret, that could be a problem."

"We are walking into a dragon's den without any armor," Tar groused. "Saint Cerise protect us."

"Not funny," Cerise grumbled. Tar was right, of course, and the sight of the red-robed church-faithful that ringed the field did not provide her any comfort.

⚜

The procession wound its way back to Caleddon, led by King Franklin riding atop one of the huge carrier beasts. Cerise and the assemblage from Cordel fell in line behind him and were surrounded by the general's army. The church-faithful in their red robes trailed behind.

The king released a homing lizard announcing their approach, and by the time they proceeded up the main boulevard of Caleddon, the palace gates were already open wide and a line of palace staff waited to meet them. The archbishop had also sent messengers, and crowds of people lined up along the street, obviously hoping to catch a glimpse of Saint Cerise. They cheered and shouted her name. One woman held up her baby to be blessed. Cerise was embarrassed, and it was all she could do to nod as she went by.

Once they reached the palace gates, the palace handlers led the chameli away, and the delegation from Cordel, with the exception of Cerise and the crew of the *Flying Fish*, was escorted to the nearby army barracks. Cerise and her crew passed through the palace gates into the courtyard. A burly man with a ginger beard was waiting for them on the steps in front of the Great Hall, surrounded by a dozen well-armed men and women, all wearing red and gold. He knelt on one knee when the king approached.

"Father, I was not informed of your sortie this morning. I came as quickly as I could."

"Get up, Barton," the king ordered his bastard son. "You were not sent for."

Barton glowered suspiciously at Cerise and her crew. "Who is this woman, and what does she want? Is she from the church? We received no warning of a delegation arriving."

"This is Cerise Aikawa," replied the king. "She is an ambassador from Cordel, and her business is with me and me alone. There was no need to inform you since she is not your concern. Is that clear?"

Barton's face turned red, and his discomfort radiated from him. "Yes, Father." Barton swallowed his resentment as he turned to face her. The anger in his face remained clear to see.

"Ambassador Aikawa. I am at your service." He bowed curtly.

"And I at yours," Cerise replied calmly, returning his bow.

"Barton," the king interjected, fingering the hilt of his sword in agitation. "The prince is not in the palace. Do you know where he is?"

This clearly caught Barton by surprise. "Jarin? No, Father."

"Is he at your brother's estate?"

"No, I have not—"

"He has not been seen since the storm began," the king interrupted again. "Why haven't you checked on him?"

"Your Majesty. Father. Why would I—"

"I need to you to take your brother Lowden and find Jarin before another night has fallen. Have you forgotten that you swore an oath to protect him with your life?"

"No father, I have not forgotten." Barton's speech was clipped and his face was bright red.

"See to it that you never do. Now find him," the king ordered. "You may go."

Barton started to say something, thought better of it, signaled to his men and left.

If the King dies without an heir, the throne passes to Barton,

Cerise realized. Having Jarin out of the way might be to Barton's advantage. And once Barton discovered who she was, having her out of the way might be to his advantage as well. She would have to figure out a way to make him an ally, not an enemy.

"You there," Franklin said to a palace staffer standing in the line by the door. "Take Ambassador Aikawa and her party to the guest wing and have my office set up for a private meeting." He began pulling off his gloves. "Ambassador Aikawa, my chief of staff will escort you to my office in one hour. Bring no one with you. Until then." He tossed his gloves to a person in the line and left Cerise standing in the middle of a group of expectant palace staff members.

Like a piece of driftwood in the middle of the ocean, she thought. She was out of her element, and she knew it.

Cerise sat on a cushioned chair next to a small fire crackling inside a massive hearth. Caleddon palace was unlike anything she had seen before. The king's office was larger than her parents' entire cottage. The beamed ceiling above her soared away into darkness, and the room's marble floors were so well polished they reflected the flames from the fire. Carved sculptures and painted pottery adorned the side tables and bookshelves. Thickly woven tapestries and oil paintings lined the walls. A large hand-painted map of the commonwealth filled the space over the mantel, and she gazed wistfully at the line on the map representing the road that led from Caleddon back over the pass to Cordel. The king was sitting in the chair across from her, studying her face, and the house mage loomed behind his chair, looking every bit like a wrinkled scavenger bird. Both men had changed into clean outfits and groomed their hair. Cerise had been given barely enough time to scrape the mud off of her boots. She felt both unwashed and common.

A server handed her a goblet of wine she had not asked for and silently backed away into the gloom.

"Tell me your story," King Franklin commanded her. "Leave nothing out." He remained silent as she recounted what Maemae had told her about her birth and spoke about her life since then, growing up in Sudo Bay, the child of seaweed farmers. It was hard to speak of Maemae, but she forced herself to keep talking. When she finished, she realized her hands were shaking.

"The sigil, may I see it for myself?"

"It is hidden underneath a birthmark Min tattooed on my shoulder," Cerise replied.

"It is embedded and fully active, Your Majesty," Gerard Mort remarked. "I can feel it from here."

How can he feel it? she wondered. *What does he mean by that?*

Silence filled the room. The king's blue eyes bored into hers. Cerise gazed back at him, masking her discomfort. Should she say more or wait him out?

"She is who she says she is." The mage broke the silence. "She is your daughter, and I believe she is your firstborn."

The king sat back and rubbed his palms on his legs. "Sabrin," he sighed. "You are a child who should not exist. The fact that you do puts us all in danger. You, me, the prince. What do I do with you? If anyone should discover who you are..." He shook his head unhappily, then leaned forward, hands clasped, elbows on his knees. "Why did you risk coming here knowing what you know? What is it you want from me?"

There was a sadness in his voice, and Cerise decided to be candid with him. "Everyone I love has been taken from me. My mother, my father...someone else I cared for deeply." She had to stop for a moment to recover herself. "Taken from me by violence, even though I had caused them no harm. Then I discover the life I was born into and should have lived was denied me, again through no fault of my own. Maybe if I had grown up here, with an army at my side, I could have protected my family and stopped those who harmed them, but it's too late for that. Now I want justice. I want the power of Weslynde that comes with my birthright. I want to find and punish the enemies who have torn my world apart.

"I see." The king sat back and sighed. "You only want revenge."

"I suppose that is true, but you also have reason to care about this." Cerise spoke urgently now. "These are the same enemies who wish to tear you down. Rogue Argonnians seeking to destroy Weslynde and the commonwealth. Simply put, you and I have the same foes, Your Majesty, and with your help, I can stop them." She took a breath. "More than anything, I want my family back." She stared into the flames while she pushed the emotions building up inside her back down where they could not get in her way. "But I can't have that. So give me this."

Franklin sipped his wine slowly. A log snapped in the fire.

"We should go hunting," he said finally, setting down his wine glass. "Get to know one another better."

"I'll have it arranged," Gerard Mort said.

⚜

Cerise met Janis and Tar in the palace courtyard in front of the gate as the eastern sky was turning pink. The palace handlers had a trio of shaggy gray horses waiting for them, already saddled and bridled. Others joining the king's hunting party were stowing their gear and joking with each other. The morning air was crisp and cool, and the mood was festive.

"I'm not climbing on one of those hairy beasts." Tar said, warily scrutinizing the horses. "I can smell them all the way over here, and I don't like the look in that one's eye. Are you sure the king wouldn't rather go fishing?"

"I rode Weslynde ponies as a child," Janis said. "They don't bite. But you can stay behind and dig for worms. Maybe try your luck fishing in the plaza fountain."

"I'd prefer it," Tar shot back.

"You don't have to come," Cerise said. "Go explore with the others."

Tar looked relieved and retreated quickly.

Cerise faced the shaggy beast in front of her. She'd never ridden a horse, but it didn't seem that hard. She marched briskly up to the horse, causing it to shy away a couple of steps.

"Other side," whispered Janis out of the side of her mouth.

Cerise pivoted and approached the animal's left side.

"Grab the pommel, put your left foot in the stirrup, and swing your right leg over his back," Janis instructed. A handler held the reins and waited expectantly for her to mount the horse.

Cerise had no idea what a pommel or a stirrup was, but by watching the others, she had a pretty good idea what to do. She grabbed the saddle, got her foot into the stirrup, and swung herself up. She almost overshot, but the handler was there to stop her, and she righted herself.

"Steer with these," Janis said, handing her the reins. "Pull back to stop. Kick the horse to go."

"Kick the horse?"

"Just stay close to me." Janis mounted her horse and guided it through the palace gate, indicating Cerise should follow. Cerise's horse did not move.

The king appeared next to her, riding a large white horse. "Ride next to me." He smiled then shouted, "Let's move!" He slapped Cerise's horse on the rump. The hunting party trotted out of the gate.

Cerise's head jerked back as her horse suddenly jumped forward, and she listed a little before gaining control. *It's no different from riding the waves,* she thought, and she had no more trouble after that.

They roamed through the open woodlands west of Caleddon, hunting for striped forest deer. By mid-morning, they came upon a small cabin next to a rushing stream and tied up the horses, proceeding from there on foot. The king beckoned Cerise to come ahead with him to look for deer sign. She pulled her crossbow from the saddle hook and followed him.

"What am I looking for?" Cerise asked.

"Animal sign. Broken plants, droppings — and hoofprints, of course," whispered the king, holding his finger over his lips. "Speak softly. The deer have exceptional hearing."

"Something like this?" Cerise whispered, pushing aside a tuft of grass, revealing a fresh hoofprint in the damp soil.

"You have sharp eyes," the king said. "It's a striped deer. See the split hoof and dew claw? It's a big one, heavy. Now show me your tracking skills and tell me which way it went."

This is a test, Cerise thought. She noted the direction of the print, but there were no others nearby; the ground was too rocky. Then she noticed a few bent reeds near the streambed.

"That way." She pointed.

"Excellent," the king replied. They crept silently to the edge of the stream and crouched among the river willows.

Cerise caught a movement out of the corner of her eye and touched Franklin's forearm. "Over there," she mouthed. A large deer with massive antlers had raised its head not far from where they were hidden. Its striped hide had blended into the tall grasses, concealing it from view.

The king placed his head next to her ear and murmured, "Wait for a clear shot and aim for the heart, behind its front legs. Make no noise, not the slightest sound."

The deer cocked an ear toward them, and Cerise held her breath. She remained frozen for several minutes until the deer relaxed and stepped tentatively into the meadow. Its cinnamon and cream-colored stripes gleamed in the sunshine. She slowly raised her crossbow and silently released the safety with her thumb.

A branch behind them snapped and the deer bounded away, soaring over the stream in one impossibly long leap. Cerise sprang to her feet and released her arrow, piercing the deer behind the shoulder mid-flight. The deer crashed into the ground on the far side of the stream and lay still.

"Well shot!" crowed the king. Janis and the others had come up behind them while they'd been stalking the deer. "You lot are louder than a herd of carrier beasts," the king yelled back at them. "Go away and fetch the horses. Be quick."

Cerise followed the king down to the stream's edge. It was too swift to wade across, so they made their way upstream to find a better crossing. They found a spot where the channel narrowed. A large tree had fallen across the gap, broad enough that they could walk across it. Foaming rapids boiled underneath them. The king went first, holding out his arms for balance. Cerise followed.

When he was halfway across, the king stepped on a patch of loose bark, and his boot slid off the side of the log. He bent sideways and flailed his arms, trying to regain balance.

Cerise was right behind him and quickly grabbed his arm, holding him in place until he regained his footing.

"Are you recovered?" she asked, continuing to hold him by the arm.

"Yes, yes, I have it now," the king puffed. "That was a near thing."

"Let's cross over," she said, keeping a hand on his shoulder as he made his way forward and jumped off the other side. Neither mentioned it further as they made their way back down to the deer.

Without waiting to be told, Cerise pulled out her knife and began to field-dress the animal. The king joined her, and they had it completed before the others returned with the horses. While they worked, Cerise sensed a change in the king's demeanor. He was smiling now and was no longer watching her every move.

When the others arrived, the king opened a bottle of wine he had stashed in his horse's pack, declaring to all that the hunt had been a great success. Food was brought out and everyone tucked in, hungry from the morning hunt. Afterward, they packed up the horses and started back to Caleddon.

Franklin insisted Cerise ride by his side. She found him easy to talk to and told him stories of past adventures on the ocean that she shouldn't have survived but somehow had.

"Where did you learn to shoot like that?" King Franklin asked.

"On my ship, the *Flying Fish*," Cerise replied. "My crew and I are privateers for hire in Cordel. We are very familiar with crossbows and also harpoons, which are sort of like giant crossbows. We mostly hunt sharks and other serpents that threaten sea vessels."

"That shot was one in a million." Franklin grinned.

"My crew are all better shots than me," Cerise replied. "Luce was the best; she could—" Her voice faltered, a sharp pang of grief spreading through her chest.

"Luce?" Franklin asked.

"My ship's gunner," Cerise forced herself to say. "She handled the harpoon better than anyone. If you will excuse me." She reined in her horse and went back to ride next to Janis for the remainder of the trip.

⚜

The next morning, Cerise gathered her crew to compare notes and find out what they had learned. Skua and Mae Linn were already chafing to be free of the palace.

"When do you become queen?" Mae Linn asked. "When do we fight the Argonnians?"

"Patience!" Cerise said, lifting an eyebrow. Mae Linn was teasing her, but she could tell the crew was experiencing the same intense pressure she was. "I'm still learning about King Franklin. The hunt yesterday was helpful, but it's clear he hasn't made up his mind about me. I need to make more inroads with him, get him on my side. And they still haven't found Prince Jarin, which is concerning."

There was a knock at the door. Tar opened it on a young page standing in the hall.

"I have a message for the ambassador." The page tried to enter, but Tar pushed him back.

"Let him come in," Cerise said.

The page bowed low and pulled a message from his belt.

"Ambassador Aikawa of Cordel. While you are in residence, you are expected to attend the king's daily council meeting." The page handed her the message, then added, "I'm supposed to wait for you and take you there."

"Lead on," Cerise said, surprised by this invitation. Perhaps she was making inroads after all. "Tar, Janis, find us something to eat," she yelled over her shoulder as she trotted to catch up with the page. "The rest of you go out and get the lay of the city."

The page took Cerise back to the king's office. A heated discussion had already started but broke off when she entered the room. Several important-looking men and women sat around the table, including, she noted with some consternation, one Argonnian. The king introduced her and told the council she had been sent by the premier of Cordel to discuss recent trade disruptions, possibly stemming from a growing Argonnian insurrection. Cerise noticed the Argonnian man's reaction to this, and it seemed as if he was going to say something, but he held back.

"Cerise Aikawa!" A handsome woman with long blond hair greeted her fondly. It was Lenora Kresh, the senator from Riddien. Cerise recognized her and smiled.

. "So good to see you again," Senator Kresh continued. "Congratulations on your promotion to ambassador. It appears even the Premier of Cordel has recognized your considerable talents! You remember Fedor Wilmount, of course, senator of Weslynde, and this is Toberon Intsimi, senator from Argonne."

The Argonnian senator glared at her through hard eyes. Cerise extended her hand, but he frowned and raised an eyebrow.

"Tell your premier that stories of an Argonnian insurrection are overblown," he said with obvious derision. "I welcome your support in tamping down this false rumor." He turned back to the person next to him, effectively dismissing her.

Yet another haughty Argonnian, she thought. *Are they all like this? No wonder there's a rift in Weslynde.*

General Drissen and Gerard Mort rounded out the council. She shook hands with them both and took a chair. The ensuing discussion was frank and open, if not a little boring, but she noted that Senator Intsimi was openly defensive when it came to any issues involving the province of Argonne. She could hear the irritation in King Franklin's voice start to grow as the meeting went on.

After twenty minutes, the king abruptly adjourned the meeting and stood up to leave. As he was walking out the door, he stopped and turned to Cerise.

"Ambassador Aikawa, I would like you to sit by me as I adjudicate petitions brought by the citizens of Weslynde. Follow me." He continued out the door, not turning to see if she followed.

Cerise's stomach growled as she hurried to keep pace with the king. She should have eaten something earlier. They entered the great hall, passing under marble columns that supported the ceiling far above. Their footsteps echoed under the golden dome. Huge paintings of men and women wielding swords or riding giant chameli into battle ringed the walls. The elegance of the hall took her breath away. She realized her mouth was hanging open and closed it quickly.

A small knot of Weslynders stood in the corner of the hall, waiting to petition the king. A palace staffer let two men step forward and approach the table where Cerise now sat next to the king.

"Hurry up. Don't make me wait all day." King Franklin waved the men over.

Both men were visibly nervous. Cerise noted they had soot on their faces and their clothes. She assumed they must be farmers or winemakers.

"Your names?" the king asked.

"Nimit," said the first farmer.

"Shad," said the second.

"What is your petition?" Franklin asked. "Speak up."

The farmer called Nimit cleared his throat, his knees shaking. "My family has been making wine by the river for generations. My neighbor Shad here set a fire to clear brush away, so he says, and the fire spread from his vineyard onto mine and burned up this year's vines and destroyed my processing house and most of last year's barrels I'd put up. I've nothing to sell at auction and no way to feed my family."

"Is this true?" the king asked Shad, who was hanging his head and twisting his hat in his purple-stained hands.

"A freak wind came up," Shad said. "There was nothing I could do."

"There was no freak wind or nothing," Nimit protested as he rounded on Shad. "You've done this before. You light a fire and then leave it alone to do its mischief."

"Please, Your Majesty," cried Shad. "I'm a poor man. I've got no money and no way to fix this. I'm scraping by as it is."

"You can give me your vineyard," declared Nimit. "Then we're even."

"Enough!" The king rapped the tabletop with the massive ring he wore. The men stopped arguing and meekly hung their heads. Franklin studied them both closely then turned to Cerise. "What would you recommend we do?"

Cerise was caught off guard. *Another test*, she thought. She composed herself quickly, considering what she would do in this situation. "Winemaker Shad's actions caused the loss of winemaker Nimit's vineyard, accident or not. He must make amends." That much seemed clear.

"But I've no money, no means," wailed Shad. "Please don't take my vineyard. I won't survive."

Cerise glanced over at Franklin, but he waited, arms crossed and stone-faced, for her to respond. She cleared her throat to give herself a moment to think. An idea came to her.

"Do you have workers on your land?" she asked Shad.

"Only my family. My cousins come in for harvest. There's no one, really."

"Your harvest will be good? The fire did not touch your crop?"

"It's not much, but yes, this year is good."

Cerise was quiet for a moment, then said, "You will set aside some of the money you get from harvest, enough to feed winemaker Nimit's family for the next year. You will also rebuild his processing house and replant his lost field."

"But I have no crew and no means to hire one." Shad slumped to his knees and held out his palms. "I am lost."

"I have a crew," Cerise said. "A crew in need of something to do. Anything to do. We will help you rebuild the processing house." She glanced over at the king, whose face continued to be a blank wall. She kept going. "Each grape farmer in the valley will give up ten cuttings from their vines to replant Nimit's burned fields." She stopped talking and waited for the king to say something. Would he object? The silence seemed to stretch on forever.

The king shifted and leaned back. "My army will collect the cuttings," he said. "And we will bring them to you." Franklin spoke as if this were something they did together every day.

"Next petition!" he shouted.

⚜

News spread that Cerise Aikawa was adjudicating petitions on behalf of the king. Archbishop Mellon heard the news and quickly altered it, propagating a story that Saint Cerise and her disciples were now tending to the needs of the poor and unfortunate in Caleddon. Small groups of pilgrims from all over Weslynde started gathering outside the palace. Some of the novices in the abbey began wearing white makeup, and soon Cerise couldn't leave the palace without being mobbed.

After a brief period of freedom while rebuilding the winemaker's processing house, the crew of the *Flying Fish* grew restless again, and when Janis suggested they might be happier away from the strictures and crowds, Cerise obliged.

"There is a vast lake south of here," Skua said. "Clear Lake. There are many fishing vessels there."

"We thought we might get some work and join a fishing crew," Dee jumped in. "Stay sharp in case you need us."

"Tar and I will stay with you, of course," Janis said. Tar grunted her assent.

"The king has been keeping me busy," Cerise sighed. "Go. Of course you can go. Only..."

"Only?" Mae Linn asked.

"Only I wish you would take me with you. Nothing sounds better to me right now than to be standing on the deck of a ship, far away from here."

The next day, Mae Linn, Dee, and Skua passed through the

palace gates, packs shouldered, laughing and singing, happy to be free of Caleddon. Janis was escorting them but planned to return once they were settled.

"There goes my family," Cerise said with a sigh.

Tar, standing next to her with her arms crossed, grunted in agreement.

⚜

To stave off her own feelings of being trapped, Cerise asked King Franklin for an assistant, someone who could get her up to speed on protocol and help her navigate political landmines, but mostly someone she could talk to. Soon after, there was a knock on her door. Tar opened it, and an elderly man with silver hair and a neatly trimmed beard brushed past her into the room, arms full of books and maps.

"I am Rence," he announced, dumping the books on the table. "The king informed me I am to be your personal assistant. You, of course, are Cerise Aikawa of Cordel. I have seen you parading about the palace followed by those sycophant novices. It is long past time we met." He held out his hand, and she took it.

He turned to Tar, who was glowering at him, arms crossed. "You must be Tar, Cerise's trusted lieutenant. It is an honor to meet a legend such as yourself." He bowed and took her hand as well. "And where is Janis? I understand she completes your triad."

"Janis is with the rest of our crew," Tar replied. "She returns tomorrow. The crew went south to Clear Lake. They miss the water."

"You must miss it as well," Rence said. "This stone sarcophagus feels claustrophobic even on a good day." He unrolled a map and spread it out on the table in front of Cerise. "I will set up a tour of Weslynde for you, Ambassador Aikawa. We should travel for a month at least. You need to see the valley of the geysers for certain, as well as the commerce of the salt sea, and you need to meet the common folk who make this province work. And you absolutely need to get away from all these blasted worshipers. Now, I have arranged lunch on the terrace if we step outside." He opened the double doors to the terrace. "Tar, please join us, won't you?"

Intrigued and amused, Cerise followed Rence onto the terrace. A spread of smoked fish, bread, and fruit was laid out on the terrace, and a canopy had been erected to shade them from the sun's rays.

Nice touch, Cerise thought.

"Now tell me"—Rence smiled, handing Cerise a glass of sparkling wine—"what is on your mind?"

Cerise considered Rence quizzically, sizing up this man, all business and efficiency. "How do I get past the abbey without being seen?" she asked.

"Easy," Rence said. "You hide in plain sight. May I suggest you put on one of those red robes that seem to be hanging in every shop window?"

Cerise smiled at his wit.

"Oh, and I should mention," he went on. "As an alternative, there is a secret tunnel that will take you from the palace to the barracks. May I show you?"

"Lead the way!" She stood up, pocketing some fruit and building a sandwich with the bread and fish. "Why haven't I known about you before this?"

"I don't know. I have known about you for a very long time. This way." He led them back inside. Tar grabbed a stave and threw a knife to Cerise, who thrust it in her belt.

"You're coming with us? To show us around?" Cerise asked.

"I am at your service," he said. He cracked open the door, glanced down the hallway, and motioned for them to follow. "Stay close now; it's not far."

Cerise felt better than she had in weeks.

⚜

Rence proved to be a compendium of information about Weslynde: the economy, the politics, and the king. He seemed to appear out of nowhere whenever Cerise needed him. And now that he had provided her with the ability to enter and leave the palace unobserved, she spent most of her time out in the city. She got better and better at avoiding the attention of the church and used her cover as ambassador of Cordel to meet the people who lived and worked in Caleddon. The city was a melting pot of people. There was even a thriving community of immigrants from Cordel, and all three women were thrilled to find a section of the market square that catered to Cordelian tastes, happily scooping up traditional street food with chopsticks.

There were some Argonnians living in the city, but the few Cerise met were suspicious of her and unwilling to engage in conversation. "Haughty" continued to be the word she used to describe them after several such encounters. Native Weslynders, on the other hand, were more than happy to share rumors they heard about Argonne, tales of skirmishes along the desert border, even outlandish stories of Argonnians taking Weslynde children and forcing them to work in the mines. The more Cerise heard, the more she became certain that Argonnians were behind the murder of her parents.

⚜

Cerise was listening to petitions with the king in the great hall when the massive doors swung open and the king's bastard son Barton, followed by his brother Lowden, tramped loudly into the hall, wearing stained traveling clothes. She had not seen Barton since the first day she'd come to Caleddon. The king dismissed the petitioners and stood to greet them. The two men bowed low.

"Welcome, my sons. What news do you bring me?" Franklin asked.

Barton glared at Cerise, clearly surprised to see her next to his father. Waves of hostility rolled off of him. "You received my courier bird earlier?" he asked.

"I did. You said the prince was seen in Nettle Falls and was bound for Riddien. Is there more?"

Barton appeared uncomfortable. "Perhaps we should speak privately?"

"Cerise Aikawa is one of my advisors. What is your news?"

Barton raised his eyebrows in surprise.

"Speak!" The king commanded.

"Prince Jarin has crossed the desert into Argonne."

"Argonne!" The king knitted his brow. "Are you sure?"

"We met a barge family sailing down the Darno. They gave passage to a young man fitting Jarin's description: brown skin, blue eyes, spoke like a scholar. Lowden and I followed the Darno as far south as Gwindell Station and learned that he met up with a pair of Argonnians and crossed into the desert."

"Was he alone?"

"The barge woman said he traveled with a magician. A male. Most likely a field witch."

"Who is helping him?" the king muttered to himself, drumming his fingers on the table.

"Father...Your Majesty?" Lowden asked with a sideways glance at Cerise. "Why would the prince want to go to Argonne? What happened here that made him leave? Barton and I have spent many weeks looking for him. Any reason would be helpful."

King Franklin's shoulders tensed up.

"It's time you knew," the king grumbled, mouth in a tight

line. "The prince is plotting with the Argonnians to take over the commonwealth."

"What?!" Lowden cried out in disbelief.

Cerise involuntarily gasped. She was just as shocked. Jarin was helping the Argonnians?

"Your news confirms it," the king went on. "False stories about his mother have poisoned Jarin's mind. He intends to try to take the crown to Argonne."

"Jarin wouldn't do that," Lowden cut in. "He's not ambitious that way; he never has been."

"He would do that, and he has, Lowden." Franklin's voice was grave. "It's time his betrayal ended. Go and fetch a scribe. A warrant shall be sent to Argonne for his arrest and return."

Lowden bowed and strode quickly out of the hall.

Barton stayed behind, fists clenching and unclenching.

"Is there more?" the king asked.

"I, uh. It's just...no." Barton locked eyes with Cerise's.

"Then you are dismissed."

"We will speak more on this later," Barton sputtered, red-faced. "Alone." He bowed and marched out of the hall, following his brother. The king sat back in his chair and sighed.

"You never told me what Jarin was doing," Cerise said quietly. "You don't talk about him at all." A suspicion was growing in her mind. What if Jarin, her brother, was behind the murders of her family?

"It was time you knew his intentions so you can be prepared for what comes next," Franklin replied. "It's good you arrived when you did."

What comes next? What did he mean? Was Jarin not only her twin but also her enemy?

CHAPTER 15

Gerard Mort stood in the shadow of one of the many watchtowers dotting the palace ramparts. From there he had a clear view of the main plaza while remaining unobserved. Archbishop Mellon stood next to him, nervously twisting his ring. The annual grape harvest was approaching, and commerce in the plaza was at its peak. Vendors were crowded together, their tables and carts overflowing with textiles and summer produce.

Three figures entered the plaza below them; it was Cerise and her two lieutenants. Cerise was wearing a wide-brimmed hat that covered her red hair and hid most of her face, but Gerard Mort was familiar with her disguise. He could make out the outline of a sword hidden under her brown cape. Her lieutenants carried staves they used as walking sticks. They made their way across the plaza, stopping at booths and chatting with vendors.

The mage had grown increasingly frustrated at King Franklin's reluctance to publicly recognize Cerise as his daughter. The king had clearly bonded with her, and kept her at his side, and had all but disowned Jarin, but Franklin insisted on keeping Cerise's identity a secret, and she was known only as the ambassador from Cordel. Gerard Mort knew Cerise was losing patience with this deceit as well, and her many requests to mount a mission to root out the insurrectionists from Argonne had gone unanswered. It was past time to bring the issue back to the surface.

The archbishop tapped Gerard Mort's arm and pointed to the far end of the square. A pair of clerics, wearing the now ubiquitous red robes of Saint Cerise, was leading a group of children across the plaza, on their way to the library. The children kept breaking out of line, shouting with glee as the clerics tried to corral them. The crowd was enjoying the spectacle, laughing and waving. It was time.

Gerard Mort stepped up to the edge of the rampart and made a subtle hand signal. A shadow waved back from the stables near the main entrance to the plaza, then disappeared. The mage clenched his fist, muttering a command under his breath. A few seconds later, shouts came from the stable, and a large bull ox broke through the gate and charged across the square, toppling booths and scattering people in all directions. The agitated animal stopped in the center of the plaza and shook its head, scraping its enormous silver-tipped horns against the plaza stones, sending up sparks. Two handlers raced toward the bull, waving a cloth to capture its attention. One of them jumped in front of it and tried to grab its snout ring, but before he could reach it, Gerard Mort sent the bull a new command and it charged the handler, impaling him on one of its horns. The bull jerked its head upright and flung the man over its back, sending a spray of blood through the air.

The children bound for the library screamed in terror, and the bull swung its giant head toward the sound. The clerics frantically herded the children toward the library doors, red robes swirling, further inciting the beast. Quickly taking note of

Cerise's position in the square, Gerard Mort sent the bull another command. The bull lowered its head and charged the clerics' swirling red robes, knocking one of the clerics to the ground and goring him. The children screamed and scattered.

As he had anticipated she would, Cerise charged across the square to intercept the bull. Her hat flew off, revealing her white face and shock of red hair. She drew her sword as she ran. Her lieutenant Tar flung a rock from her sling, hitting the ox in the side of its face, momentarily distracting it, which gave Cerise the chance to jump on its back. Cerise raised her sword to stab it, but the beast spun around, attempting to throw her off. She was knocked off the bull's back, but she was able to grab its harness strap, and she hung on to its side, her feet dragging the ground. She was forced to let go of her sword to keep hold, and it spiraled away across the square.

Her lieutenants struck the bull about the head with their staves, distracting it while Cerise clambered back atop the animal. Holding tight to its harness with one hand, she reached down over its head with the other and grabbed its snout ring, yanking it straight up and back, making the bull stagger backward and bellow in pain. This gave the second handler time to move in with a rope. He lassoed its two back legs, tripping it and sending it to the ground. Cerise leapt free and grabbed her sword, poised to finish the animal if it got back up.

Gerard Mort released his control of the bull. The beast instantly went limp, exhausted. The mage watched from his hidden vantage point as the handler grabbed the animal's snout ring and calmed it. Two other handlers who had come to help attached restraints to its harness and led the beast meekly out of the square.

With great interest, the mage focused his attention back on Cerise to see what she would do next. She first ran to the wounded cleric and knelt to assess his injuries, then helped others lift him into a cart that was quickly wheeled away. Then she slowly became aware of the crowd behind her, who was wildly shouting "Saint Cerise! Saint Cerise!" Some were even down on their knees with their hands in the air. Cerise turned to face them, and a cheer went up. The children she had saved ran to her and surrounded her with hugs.

Surveying the scene from above, Gerard Mort gave a satisfied smile and clapped his hand on the archbishop's shoulder.

"I have set the trap for you. All you have to do is pull the lever."

⚜

Cerise slipped through the door and took her seat as King Franklin was bringing his council meeting to order. She was careful not to make eye contact with anyone or draw undue attention to herself. The palace was still buzzing over the day's events in the plaza, and she had been forced to retreat to her room to avoid the unwanted adulation. King Franklin expected her at the council meeting, so she had waited until the last minute to make her way down to the great hall, hoping to avoid having to talk to anyone.

Archbishop Mellon of Riddien was attending, which was unusual. The archbishop rankled the king, but Franklin was very adept at playing the power game, and Cerise knew from her own experience that the church was a potent player with influence. "Keep your friends close and your enemies closer," Franklin had quoted on more than one occasion.

"Your Majesty, may I address the council?" the archbishop asked.

"Proceed," the king replied.

Cerise had to smile at the undercurrent of resentment in the king's voice.

The archbishop stood up and cleared his throat dramatically. Once he had the room's attention, he spread his arms to the sky then gestured toward Cerise. "First, let us offer our undying gratitude to Cerise Aikawa of Cordel. She saved the lives of many precious young Weslynders today." There was a chorus of "Hear, hear!" and the council members pounded the table in support.

Cerise's cheeks flushed. She gave a slight nod, which she hoped seemed gracious.

Emboldened by the response, the archbishop continued, "Council members, in our official capacity as the spiritual head of the Church of the Commonwealth, we are pleased to announce that the seat of the church is moving from Riddien to Weslynde. We will set up residence in the abbey next to the palace."

"The prime minister of Riddien is the governing head of the church," King Franklin snapped, eyes hard. "What does he have to say about the church leaving his province?" He turned to the senator from Riddien. "Lenora Kresh, have you heard about this?"

It was clear to Cerise that he had surprised the senator.

Mellon went on unperturbed, as if schooling a student. "Canon law is clear. The reigning sovereign is the governing head of the church. You are the sovereign, not the prime minister."

"I know what the law says." The king bristled. "But as you well know, the prime minister has effectively remained in charge ever since Riddien joined the commonwealth. That was over two hundred years ago. What has changed?"

"What has changed is who is next in line to the throne." Archbishop Mellon glanced at Gerard Mort and dabbed his brow. "Your firstborn will be the next governing head of our church."

"Jarin?" Franklin asked, confused. "How does that change things?"

The archbishop paused for effect. "Not Jarin. Your firstborn daughter, Sabrin né Franklin. The one we revere as Saint Cerise."

For a moment there was silence, then it was as if someone had set off a bomb. There was an uproar, and several members jumped to their feet. Cerise, who had only been half listening to the archbishop, jerked her head up in alarm. Senator Kresh and Senator Intsimi were looking directly at her, mouths open.

Franklin leapt up, pulled out his sword, and threw it down on the tabletop, where it clanged loudly, startling everyone. It spun to a stop with the tip pointed at the archbishop.

"There will be order here, or you will all spend the night behind bars." The fury in his voice was unmistakable. The room quieted, and the king nodded to the palace guards. "Close the doors. No one leaves." The metal doors shut with a clang.

Cerise sat forward in her chair. All her senses were on alert. She counted eleven in the room. The guards were armed, but others might also have weapons hidden in their clothing. Taking advantage of the momentary silence, she stood up. "May I speak?"

"Sit down. Do not say a word," Franklin snarled.

She sat. *Hear what he says before you act,* she thought.

The king's nostrils flared. "I do not tolerate rumors and disinformation in my court." He glared at the archbishop, who mopped his forehead. "If there is a claim regarding my family, I expect it to be presented to me in private. Is that clear? And no one, *no one* but me decides who does or does not have claim to my crown. Now, everyone sit down."

He paused until everyone was seated, then he leaned forward and put his hands flat on the table. "Nothing that has been said or will be said tonight leaves this room, is that understood?" He made eye contact with each person, and once he was satisfied he had regained control, he sat back down. "What the archbishop has said can't be erased, so we must discuss these matters now, as they affect the security of the commonwealth. Archbishop Mellon, since you touched off this firestorm, would you care to explain yourself?

Archbishop Mellon nodded and pulled at his collar. "As I stated, the center of the Church of the Commonwealth is no longer—"

"Who is Sabrin né Franklin?" Senator Toberon Intsimi, the Argonnian, shouted defiantly. He pointed at Cerise. "Are you telling us that this woman is your child? Have you broken the contract with Argonne? Is Jarin né Franklin the heir or not?"

"Senator Intsimi," the king said, holding his voice steady. "I understand your shock. All will be explained. Please sit—"

The senator from Argonne did not let him finish. "Then you don't deny it? She is your daughter? Show me the proof. Argonne does not take kindly to broken contracts."

"Silence!" Franklin pounded the table, red-faced. "Sit down and listen!"

A guard came up behind Senator Intsimi and pushed him back into his seat. The Argonnian shrugged the guard's hand off of his shoulder, but he remained seated. The king gestured to Gerard Mort, who had remained quiet and calm during the commotion. "Magician. Explain."

"Cerise Aikawa of Cordel is the firstborn child of Lady Tregan Anthelia of Argonne and King Franklin né Rosin of Weslynde. She is Prince Jarin's sister. I have verified this myself. It is indisputable. She bears the royal sigil. She is Sabrin né Franklin, of the royal house of Weslynde."

The room was quiet while this sank in. Senator Intsimi slumped back in his chair and rubbed his eyes. Others glanced back and forth from the king to Cerise with puzzled expressions.

"Thank you, Mort," Franklin said. "The truth is, we were

not aware that my daughter, Sabrin, even existed until three months ago. No one was."

Lenora Kresh suddenly gave a surprised gasp. "By the gods, are Jarin and Sabrin twins? They are a curse!" The room erupted again.

"Where is Jarin?" Senator Intsimi shouted over the fray. "Is he alive?"

Franklin picked up his sword again and pounded it against the table until everyone was silent. "There will be order here." His voice shook. Once he had mastered himself, he nodded to the general. "Where is the prince, General Drissen?"

"Prince Jarin is in Argonne," General Drissen said. "We have intelligence reports suggesting he is leading an insurrection against Weslynde. The king has issued a warrant for his extradition to Caleddon."

Cerise's heart plummeted, her fears confirmed. Her own brother leading those terrorists. Innocent people killed at his command.

Senator Intsimi stood up again. "This is outrageous. I stand here in front of you, your trusted brother, and yet you send your spies into Argonne behind my back?"

"Sit down, Toberon," King Franklin said wearily. "The reports came from your own people."

Before he could say more, Senator Kresh interrupted, hands shaking in agitation. "Is no one going to address the curse of the twins? Both twins cannot be allowed to live. This will affect us all. Remember the salt sea? The great plague? What is the church's position here?" She turned to Archbishop Mellon.

"The church believes Saint Cerise is the true heir to the throne and divine leader of the commonwealth." Archbishop Mellon's eyes brimmed over with religious zeal. "Prince Jarin should be captured and, uh"—he searched for a word—"quarantined to prevent the curse."

Cerise gripped the arms of her chair and looked at Gerard

Mort questioningly. He appeared unruffled by the news. What was he up to?

"This is outrageous!" Senator Intsimi screamed. "Argonne believes that Cerise, or Sabrin or whatever you choose to call her, is an imposter and should be the one quarantined. Put into lockdown immediately. Franklin, do your duty!"

A sudden surge of energy poured through Cerise. She stood tall, shoulders back. "Council members." Her voice rang with authority; it demanded attention. Everyone stared at her, riveted. "You make these claims about me, but all the while no one has bothered to ask me what I think. No one speaks for me. I speak for myself. I came to Weslynde not because of who you claim I am but because I wanted your help. I wanted your help to find out who is killing the people I love and to put a stop to it. Instead, all I see is chaos, and all I hear is crazy talk of twins and contracts and quarantines. I want no part of that. When you are ready to engage with me on things that really matter, let me know."

With that, she walked purposefully to the door. In her heightened state, she was acutely aware of each person's position in the room and if they posed an immediate threat. Anger radiated off of the senator from Argonne. *No surprise there*, she thought. The king's guard stood in her path, brandishing his spear and blocking the door. Cerise shot her arm forward as if it were made of lightning, grabbed the guard's spear, and used the weight of her body to pull the guard forward and down to the floor on his back, relieving him of his weapon as he fell. She spun around and pinned him down, the point of the spear on his chest. The other guard sprang into action and ran toward her.

"Stop or he dies," Cerise said darkly. The guard stopped in his tracks, rebuffed by the threat in her voice.

"Father. Am I your prisoner?" she asked, keeping her eyes on the guard.

Franklin stood up, red in the face, eyes blazing. Gerard Mort stepped behind the king and put a hand on his shoulder as if to calm him. The fire left the king's eyes, and his shoulders slumped.

"No." Franklin cast his eyes down. "You are free to go."

Cerise slipped through the door and closed it behind her. She put her forehead against it and took a deep breath, heart pounding. She figured she had two minutes or less to find Janis and Tar and make it to the secret tunnel before Franklin rallied and sent his guards to capture her. She raced down the hall, heading for the north wing.

⚜

"This is not how this was supposed to go," Cerise said, stuffing her pack.

Janis stood at the door, holding it slightly ajar and peering through the crack. Tar drew the curtains shut.

"Things never happen according to plan," Rence said.

"I'm not sure where I should go."

"May I suggest you go to the abbey?" Rence offered.

"What?" Cerise set down her pack, incredulous. The church was the last place she wanted to be.

"You are exposed in the palace; everyone now knows you are the king's firstborn and Jarin's twin. Some in Franklin's court will try to kill you to ensure that their positions are maintained. Others will try to kill you to prevent the curse. On the other hand, the church stands ready to provide you with a thousand zealots who will leap off the ramparts for you if you but utter a single word. The king will not dare mount an attack against the church. You will be safe there."

"I want nothing to do with the church. They are all snakes. It is unclear to me now how this plays out, Rence. I feel cornered, like I am walking into a trap."

"You have time," Rence said. "Once you are safe in the abbey, I will help you formulate a plan. You have more resources than you know."

"Rence, why are you helping me?"

"I promised your mother I would keep you safe. I intend to keep that promise."

"You promised Maemae?" she asked, confused.

"Your mother. Tregan Anthelia. I swore an oath."

"You knew who I was? All this time?"

"Since the day you were born."

Cerise let this sink in. The story of her life continued to baffle her. "But, Rence, you are the king's man!"

"We have much to discuss, but now is not the time. Now go while you still can." Rence opened the door and pushed her through it. Cerise raced down the hall, flanked by Janis and Tar, heading for the secret door.

King Franklin stood frozen for a moment after Cerise's abrupt departure from the council meeting, his mind in a fog. The haze slowly lifted. Everyone in the room was staring at him. The guard Cerise had bested was returning to his feet.

"Follow her and see where she goes. Bring her back if she tries to leave the palace," he ordered. "Go quickly."

The two guards hurried out the door.

"Listen to me." His voice was stronger now, the momentary weakness gone. "You senators are to remain here with me, as well as General Drissen and my house mage. Everyone else get out." The archbishop opened his mouth to protest, but Franklin stopped him. "The church is dismissed. And, Mellon, keep your mouth shut. You have caused enough trouble today."

Archbishop Mellon looked like he wanted to strangle something but said nothing and stormed out, followed by the others. General Drissen closed the door behind them.

Franklin gathered everyone to the table. "The news of Sabrin will be all over the city by tomorrow morning," he said. "There is no way to contain it. The people will want to know how this changes the monarchy, what has happened to the prince, and if the twins are a danger to Weslynde. I don't believe in the curse, but there are many others," he said, glancing directly at Lenora Kresh, "who do, and they will spread the myth, sowing panic and discord."

His fingers drummed the table as he pondered what to do next. Ever since her arrival, Cerise had captured his imagination and his heart. She was the child he had always wanted. He was already picturing the monarchy under her rule; she would be a worthy queen and would continue his legacy. But what about Jarin, his son...how was he going to deal with Jarin? Was he truly prepared to do what needed to be done? He wouldn't endanger the crown.

He cleared his throat. "The church has made its position clear. They wish Cerise to be declared my successor, my son Jarin found and eliminated to prevent the curse. I do not expect them to behave rationally in this matter."

"What happened to Prince Jarin?" Toberon Intsimi pleaded. "Please tell us. Why do you think Argonne is implicated?"

"Prince Jarin vanished without warning as soon as he found out he has a sister. His disappearance was a shock to all of us." The lies came easily to Franklin. "He had outside help, and he headed straight across the desert to Argonne. He must have been planning this move for quite some time. I am deeply troubled by recent news that someone new is leading the Argonnian separatist movement and their tactics are improving. I believe Jarin is their leader." *It is done,* he thought. *I have given up my son.* He wondered why it didn't hurt the way he'd thought it would.

"That ragtag fringe group is not a movement and never was. Jarin né Franklin is loyal and could not possibly be involved," Toberon said, eyes flashing. "You give them too much credit, Franklin. They don't represent Argonne, which, I feel I must repeat, remains loyal to the commonwealth."

"The separatists have been a thorn in my side for twenty years," the king shot back. "Ever since Tregan died and they made a martyr out of her. Murals of her litter the streets of Isidima. I've seen them."

Toberon stiffened. "Why do you feel the need to blame all your family problems on Argonne?"

"You are walking a thin line tonight, Senator," Franklin hissed. He regretted now having sent the guards after Cerise. He wished they were here to throw the senator in a cell, if only to shut him up.

"You are not helping, Toberon," Senator Wilmount said, breaking in and pressing Senator Intsimi firmly back into his seat by the shoulders. Senator Wilmount stepped in front of him, taking him out of Franklin's line of sight, and asked, "Your Majesty, what is it you need from us?"

"Finally, a voice of reason," the king said. "I need to get in front of this before the church spreads their lies. The people need assurance that the crown is never taken by surprise."

"Can't you deny Cerise's claim and silence the church? Banish Archbishop Mellon to Riddien where he belongs? Just have the girl arrested," Senator Wilmount suggested.

"Cerise has won the hearts of the people," King Franklin said. That much could not be denied, and it was part of the reason he admired her. "The church has waged a very successful propaganda campaign. She's a hero, a living saint. That kind of zeal can't be silenced by an edict. If I come out against Cerise, there will be protests. I fear even riots."

"What are you going to do?"

Franklin had already decided. He was going to declare for

Cerise, and damn the consequences. "I'm going to make an announcement tomorrow morning. I will give a speech from the balcony, declaring that a miracle has occurred and my lost daughter, kidnapped as a baby, has been found, and that Sabrin né Franklin is my firstborn and the rightful heir to the throne." The king surveyed the room. "I need each of you to stand beside me in solidarity. Are you with me? Stand and make your pledge."

One by one, chairs slid back, and the group rose and pledged. Only the senator from Argonne remained seated.

"Senator Intsimi, your pledge," the king said firmly.

"What will become of Jarin, your son?" Toberon said bitterly.

"I love my son," King Franklin said. As soon as he said it out loud, he knew it was true, but it was too late to turn back from this path. "But Jarin made his choice when he chose the Argonnian separatists over Weslynde, and he must be held accountable. A warrant for his arrest has been issued, and if he is still alive, he will be found and brought here."

"And the curse?" asked Senator Kresh.

The damned curse. A myth dreamed up by the church. Franklin wanted to scream at her. He would lose control of Weslynde if he denied there was a curse; it was a belief too strongly held by the people.

"I am the king. I will protect the people of Weslynde above all else. Once Jarin is captured, Gerard Mort will remove the sigil from his body, and he will be banished to the southern islands for the rest of his days. This should forestall any chance of calamity."

"And if that doesn't satisfy the people?" Senator Kresh asked.

Franklin said nothing. He didn't need to say it. Jarin would die if it came to that.

"You don't understand what Prince Jarin means to

Argonne." Senator Toberon clasped his hands together, pleading with all his heart. "He captivates our people. He gives them a reason to remain in the commonwealth. This strange creature who has moved into your house, this so-called Saint Cerise with her white face and painted eyes, is like a cuckoo bird pushing the other eggs out of the nest. Respectfully, my lord, this feels like a false choice. I need more time."

"Time is something that I do not have," Franklin said. The sigil in his back grew hot, and his voice grew dark. "Enough talk. I need you with me, Toberon. I need Argonne's agreement in this matter. For the sake of the commonwealth, what say you?"

The senator made eye contact with each person in the room, one by one. He found no allies among them. He slowly pushed back his chair and stood.

"I pledge," he said, eyes downcast.

"Good," Franklin said. "We have agreement. Tonight, I will draft a decree naming Sabrin my heir. In the morning, you three senators will sign it on behalf of your provinces. Then we will make an announcement together from the great hall's balcony. Gerard Mort, General Drissen. You stay with me. Meeting adjourned."

The king, the general, and the mage worked late into the night drafting the decree naming Sabrin né Franklin heir to the throne. Franklin signed it and stamped it with his ring. As the wax spread underneath his fist, he had doubts. Something wasn't right. The church had forced his hand. If not for that incident with the bull in the plaza and the ensuing fervor over Saint Cerise, would the archbishop have dared to make his claim? And how had Mellon learned that Cerise was his daughter? Had she told him? She must have. Only Gerard Mort knew who she was, and he trusted the mage with his life. Was Cerise playing a double game? She had come to Weslynde to claim her legacy, after all. Should he really be surprised? Yet another child proving to be a disappointment.

"General Drissen," the king said, rolling up the decree and locking it inside his safe. "In the morning, gather the three senators and bring them to the great hall. They are to join me on the balcony."

"Yes, Your Majesty." The general bowed and left.

"Mort, I'm going to sleep in my office tonight. Post guards."

"At once." The mage let himself out and closed the doors behind him.

The king sat quietly for a moment, then re-opened the safe and pulled out the decree. He set it on his desk while he poured himself a glass of wine, then took the decree and placed it in the fire burning in the hearth. *The game is not over yet,* he thought. He sipped his wine as the paper flared up and dissolved into ash.

⚜

Senator Intsimi could not sleep. He stared at the ceiling, trying to think of a way he could stop this madness. Perhaps he could send a courier bird to Isidima, somehow warn Jarin if indeed he was really in Argonne. He lay awake until an hour before dawn, and right when his eyes were growing heavy, there was a knock on his chamber door. He reached for his knife, instantly on alert. The door cracked open, and Teeg, his assistant, entered holding a candle.

"This came for you by page," Teeg said, handing him an envelope. "You are to open it immediately."

Toberon tore open the message. It was stamped with the king's seal.

· · ·

Senator Intsimi, we have much to discuss that could not be said in open forum. Please come to my office immediately. Tell no one.

"I'm tired of all this palace intrigue." Toberon showed the message to his assistant. "This smells suspicious. Teeg, you'd better come with me." He dressed quickly, then stuffed the message in his shirt and strapped his knife to his belt. Teeg grabbed his sword and followed him quietly down the corridor.

They passed through the palace unchallenged, and as they entered the hall outside the king's quarters, they found the door to Franklin's office standing slightly ajar. Light from a fire flickered through the door into the hallway. There were no guards posted outside.

"Something is amiss," whispered Toberon. His heart beat a little faster as he put his hand against the door and started to push, but Teeg stopped him, motioning that he should be the one to enter first. Toberon nodded in agreement.

Teeg knocked on the door. "Your Majesty?"

Hearing no response, Teeg pushed the door wide and gasped. Toberon elbowed past him and saw the king, silhouetted by the fire in the hearth, slumped back in the chair behind his desk, head lolled over to one side.

"By the gods!" Toberon cried. He rushed in and shook the king, trying to rouse him. "He feels cold."

"Is he breathing?"

"I can't tell. Help me loosen his tunic; it's tight on his neck." They lifted the king out of the chair and laid him gently on the floor.

"Teeg, go get help," Toberon ordered. His assistant started to go, but then Toberon heard him gasp.

"What are you doing here?" an accusing voice behind him snarled. Toberon whipped around and saw Gerard Mort standing in the doorway, flanked by two guards brandishing spears. "Step away from the king," the mage ordered.

"Mort!" Toberon cried. "Thank the gods. Help me. We found the king like this. I can't rouse him. I fear he might be dead."

"You killed the king?" Gerard Mort gasped.

"No!" cried Toberon. "We found him this way. Help us!" He was confused by look in the mage's eyes.

"Assassins!" Gerard Mort placed a hand on each guard's neck and pushed them forward. "Kill them!"

"No, wait!"

Teeg tried to draw his sword, but it was too late. The first guard pierced him through the chest with his spear. Toberon cried out and pulled his knife from his belt. He managed to parry the second guard's spear, but he stumbled over Franklin's body. He turned to catch his balance and felt a searing pain. He lowered his eyes to see the point of a spear jutting out of his chest. With a strangled groan, he slumped to the floor and was gone.

⚜

The two guards stood quietly over the bodies of the slain men, saying nothing. Satisfied that they remained under his control, Gerard Mort stepped around them and picked up Toberon's knife. He knelt over the king and stabbed him, thrusting up under his ribs into his heart. The king jerked, then moaned softly as the breath left his body. The mage left the knife in the king's chest and stepped over his body to reach Toberon. He rolled Toberon's body over and searched through his clothing until he retrieved the message that had summoned him to the king. Next he took Toberon's hand and smeared it in the king's blood and on the knife handle.

The mage then turned back to face the guards, who still

remained in place, staring at nothing. He placed a hand behind each of their necks and pulled them in close until their foreheads touched his own. He closed his eyes and muttered under his breath, speaking words in old majik. Then he released the hold on their necks and pushed them backward violently with a shout.

The guards stumbled back to catch themselves from falling and their eyes flew open. The first thing they saw was Gerard Mort standing in the doorway of the king's office, shouting down the corridor, "Help, help, raise the alarm! There has been an attack on the king!"

CHAPTER 16

Cerise ghosted down back alleys and through gardens to reach the abbey unseen. Janis and Tar were her shadows. The archbishop welcomed them inside and said he would send a message back to the king stating that Saint Cerise was now under the full protection of the church.

They were housed in an abbey room that was both cold and cramped. Cerise rubbed her hands together and blew on them. *I'm getting soft,* she thought, already missing the comforts of the palace. Outside the room's narrow window, the moonlight reflected off the palace dome in the distance. *Did I ever really believe I belonged there?*

Janis built a fire in the tiny hearth, hardly big enough to warm the room. Tar opened a bottle of whiskey she had stashed in her pack and passed it around.

Cerise paced back and forth like a fox in a cage while she told the two women what had happened. "The archbishop exposed me at the council meeting. He revealed me as Franklin's firstborn, and he said I was next in line to the throne, not Jarin. It caused quite a stir."

"I imagine it did," said Tar. "What did the king say?"

"Mostly he tried to contain the chaos in the room. He

admitted that I was his daughter but said nothing about me being the heir."

"What else happened?" Janis asked. "Tell us everything,"

"The shouting really started when the archbishop named me the head of the church."

"The head of the church?" asked Janis.

"It surprised me as well. Apparently, there is some law that states the sovereign is the head of the church, and if I am heir, it falls to me once the king passes. Then General Drissen added to the madness and told everyone that Prince Jarin is in Argonne leading a revolt against Weslynde. That really upset everyone, none more than the senator from Argonne. That man is openly hostile toward the king.

"Jarin is leading a revolt?" Tar asked. "Against Weslynde?"

"Apparently. Then someone in the room figured out that Jarin and I are twins." Cerise laughed bitterly. "That led to a debate as to which of us should be killed to avoid the curse. That's when I left."

"They would really kill you?" Janis asked.

"They used the word quarantine," Cerise replied. "It was a euphemism, and the meaning was clear."

"What a mess," Tar said. "You're in danger. We can't stay here."

"Tar's right," Janis added. "We have to get you out of here."

"I don't disagree." Cerise's hopes of having the king's support were fading, and now there was this alarming news about her brother. "I need to get to Jarin. If he is leading the Argonnians, that means he is my—" There was a knock on the door, interrupting her before she could finish her thought.

Janis drew her sword. "Who's there?" she called out.

"Rence," the voice on the other side answered.

"Let him in," Cerise said, pouring some whiskey into a clean glass. Rence entered and quickly closed the door behind him. Cerise caught a brief glimpse of a few novices kneeling in prayer outside the door. She handed him the whiskey and he drained it.

"As a positive, no one can sneak up on you here," he said, nodding toward the door.

"This is a prison," Cerise said. "I should not have come." She grabbed a chair for Rence and placed it by the fire. "What have you got for me?"

"I've come to tell you the story of your mother."

"Now?"

"There may not be another chance."

She had not expected this, but she realized she needed to know. "I'm ready."

They spoke late into the night. Rence told her of Tregan's dreams and hopes for Argonne, her decision to save both babies, and the charge she put on him, Merta, and a boy magician named Dax to protect her twin babies. He filled in the blanks that Merta had left out. A picture of Tregan the person began to stitch itself together, and Cerise found herself wishing she had known her. She was very surprised when Rence said it had been Tregan's intention to seek Cerise out and raise her in exile.

"Her choice was me?" Cerise asked. Rence nodded. Cerise fiddled with her glass, fighting a surge of emotion. She had lost so much. Everyone who cared about her—Maemae, Min, Luce, and now Tregan. It was becoming clear that her father, the king, cared more about power than he did about her, and he was willing to do anything, even kill her if he had to, to retain it. She cursed herself for allowing Franklin to charm her the way he had. And on top of that, somewhere out there she had a brother who, in all likelihood, was also plotting to kill her. She hadn't asked for any of this.

"The senator from Argonne said I should be quarantined. He wants me dead. The Argonnians are planning insurrection … and the king says Jarin is their leader."

Rence rubbed his hands on his thighs and sighed. "I can't be certain about Argonne's intentions, Cerise, but I do know Jarin. I raised him from a boy, and he is not what you are thinking."

"Then why is he in Argonne?" Cerise asked.

There was a loud banging on the door before Rence could reply. Many voices were shouting in the hall. Cerise stood up in alarm.

"This place is a trap," she cursed. "Why did we come here?"

A voice outside the door, louder than the rest, cried out, "Saint Cerise, open the door! I bring dire news. Open the door!"

"Open it," she ordered, putting her hand on the hilt of her knife.

Tar opened the door on a stricken Bishop Rutter surrounded by a throng packed in the corridor. They were wearing red robes and were shouting and wailing.

"What has happened?" Cerise asked.

"The king is dead." Bishop Rutter shook his head and wrung his hands. Then he raised his voice. "Long live the queen!"

The crowd behind him shouted, "Long live the queen!" and fell to their knees.

A shock run through Cerise. "Get up," she ordered. "Stop this nonsense. Tell me what has happened?"

"Treachery and treason, your holiness," Bishop Rutter lamented. "Argonnian spies have murdered your father."

"Murder?" she said. *At the hands of Argonnians?*

"The general awaits you in the palace. You are the next in line to the crown. You must come now."

She turned around to catch Rence's eye, but he wasn't in the room anymore. Where had he gone? The hallway was jammed with people, wailing and chanting. There was no way she could fight her way through them and escape. The jaws of the trap were closing around her.

"Saint Cerise, you must come with us."

She saw no other option. "Very well, I will come." She signaled to Janis and Tar. "We go together." They pushed their way into the crowd, which parted like a school of fish before them.

⚜

Sabrin né Franklin, firstborn child of King Franklin né Rosin and Lady Tregan Anthelia, known to most as the hero Saint Cerise, strode into the great hall. Her cherry-red hair was pulled back in a warrior's knot, and her piercing blue eyes, outlined in black, swept the room. She kept her porcelain face schooled in an expression of grim resolve. Her sword was slung across her back, and when she walked across the polished floor, those in the room parted before her. Janis and Tar flanked her, balancing their staves with practiced ease. Archbishop Mellon and Bishop Rutter followed behind them, heads bowed in reverence. A stream of clerics in red robes tried to enter, but General Drissen ordered the doors to the great hall closed.

The king's body lay on a table directly beneath the dome, covered by a fine gold cloth. His face appeared waxy in the torchlight. Cerise stood silently at his side while Archbishop Mellon placed his hands on the king's forehead. The gathering bowed their heads as he offered a quiet blessing. Someone stifled a sob. Standing behind the king's body on the far side of the table were the members of the council she had met with the night before: General Drissen, looking very stony, and the senators from Weslynde and Riddien. The senator from Argonne was missing. The king's bastard son, Barton, and his brother Lowden stood next to them. Barton openly glowered at her, his face red with rage, while Lowden consoled a grief-stricken woman sitting in a chair next to him. That was where the sobs were coming from. She saw at least a dozen soldiers in place around the room and in front of the doors. Everyone seemed to be holding their collective breath, waiting for her to do something.

She touched the king's hand that lay across his chest outside the gold cloth. It was icy. His death saddened her greatly, and the memory of the day they'd gone hunting together came to her mind. She had felt something that day—something close to kinship, even affection. *Another loss,* she thought. *Another attack on one of my own.* She went down on one knee and bowed her head in respect. The room remained silent except for the quiet weeping coming from the woman sitting next to Lowden.

After a brief moment, she got back to her feet. "What happens now?" she asked the general, who was standing near her.

"Why is this woman here?" Barton called out from the other side of the table. "She is from Cordel, not Weslynde. Why is she the first to speak?"

"Patience, Barton," General Drissen replied quietly, holding his hand up to keep the calm.

Barton's anger was unmistakable. Cerise wondered if he would lay claim to the throne now that his father was dead and Jarin was missing. She guessed that the woman weeping next to Lowden was Clare, Franklin's consort. *These are my relatives,* she thought. *How strange.*

"What happens now?" General Drissen repeated. "It is a fair question. Here is the answer: until Franklin's heir takes the throne, the head of the armed forces assumes command as regent." He raised his voice a notch so all could hear. "That means I am in charge. Does anyone here question this?" He made eye contact with each person, lingering on the faces of Archbishop Mellon and Barton. No one spoke.

"Good," he continued. "Now, regarding the next in line to the throne. If King Franklin had no legitimate heir, or if the named heir was for some reason unable to fulfill the duties of the crown, protocol determines who is next in line. If that were the case, the next person in line would be you, Barton."

Barton shifted on his feet at these words, looking as if he very much wished to speak.

"That, however, is not our problem. In fact, Franklin has two heirs that bear the royal sigil and have claim to the throne."

Barton cursed under his breath.

"One is Prince Jarin né Franklin, whom we believe to be in Argonne fomenting an uprising. The other is the king's daughter, Sabrin né Franklin, whom you know as Cerise Aikawa from Cordel and who stands before you now." The few clerics who had made it inside the room started chanting, "Saint Cerise, Saint Cerise." The room began to buzz.

Barton and Lowden appeared stunned. *They must not have been informed,* Cerise thought.

"Silence, everyone!" shouted the general, motioning to the guards. They struck the shafts of their spears against the ground three times in succession. The room quieted at the sound. "The king is dead. There is a story here to tell, and I will be the one telling it. Hear me well, and let no one doubt my words. The king of Weslynde, sovereign of the Western Commonwealth, has been murdered, and the senator from Argonne, Toberon Intsimi, is responsible for his murder."

The Argonnian! Of course! Cerise thought. He had been hostile to Franklin; he'd even threatened her life. She should have known, and if she had been paying attention, she might have been able to stop it.

Drissen went on, "It appears that Senator Intsimi and his bodyguard were Argonnian terrorists. The senator's bodyguard had a trident tattooed on his palm, which is their symbol."

"Why kill the king?" Cerise asked. "It was me who posed the threat, not King Franklin."

"King Franklin announced his decision to name you, Sabrin

né Franklin, heir to the throne, instead of Jarin. He drafted a decree to that effect that was to be read to the people this morning. Senator Intsimi killed the king to prevent the decree from going into effect."

"Are you certain that he did it?" Cerise asked.

"Gerard Mort caught the senator in the act."

"Bring Senator Intsimi here!" she demanded. "I will know his reason."

"He is dead. Killed by the king's guards. If the house mage had not arrived when he did, we might never have known who was responsible."

Cerise seethed with anger. The Argonnians had to be stopped. She would find Jarin and make him pay.

With both his fists, Barton pounded the table upon which the king's body lay, startling her back to the moment.

"I don't believe any of this," he yelled. "My father would never abandon Jarin, the son he has groomed to be king since the day he was born. He wouldn't name someone else his heir. And even if he did, I am next in line, not this sideshow circus freak."

"I was there, Barton," Lenora Kresh said. "He made us pledge to recognize Sabrin as heir."

"It's true," Senator Wilmount added. "A decree was drafted by the king."

"Where is this decree?" Barton said. "Show it to me."

The general set his jaw. "It is missing."

Barton laughed in disbelief. "Of course it's missing! This is a fairy story you tell, General. There is no decree!" he raged. "Send for Jarin at once. The people of Weslynde recognize Prince Jarin né Franklin as king."

"The church recognizes Sabrin né Franklin as queen," Archbishop Mellon shot back.

They will tear themselves apart over this, Cerise thought. *It's madness.*

The king's consort, Clare, suddenly cried out. "By the gods, they must be twins!" She pressed her hands to her chest and had to be supported by Lowden. "It's the curse, the curse of the twins. The curse is what killed my Franklin. The curse killed their mother Tregan. These twins cannot be alive on this earth at the same time." She stared at Cerise in horror. Barton put his hand on the hilt of his sword. Cerise gave a hand signal to her lieutenants to prepare to fight their way out of the hall.

"Stop this!" yelled General Drissen. "Calm yourselves, or you will be removed."

Two of his guards put their hands on Barton's shoulders. He shook them off but made no further moves. Clare placed her hands over her face. Cerise became aware that Gerard Mort was standing behind her.

When did he get so close? she thought.

"General, if I may," the mage said. "I believe Cerise has information that would be of interest to the group." As he said this, he hovered his hand over her shoulder.

A crackling noise filled the inside of Cerise's head, and a buzzing sensation tickled her shoulder. She whipped around to face him. "What are you doing? Move away."

Janis yanked the mage away by his arm. He wore a surprised expression. Cerise didn't give him another thought as a new idea surfaced in her head. She turned back to face General Drissen and the rest. "General, let me find the insurrectionists behind the death of the king. I will find Jarin, my brother, and bring him to you."

"She needs to be quarantined," Barton fumed. "Don't let her leave."

"The church will not allow you to lay a hand on her," Archbishop Mellon threatened.

"I will have order!" the general shouted.

Cerise noted the smugness in the archbishop's eyes. It was

as Rence had said. General Drissen wouldn't launch his army against the church or lock up their greatest icon, Saint Cerise.

"Cerise"—General Drissen turned to her—"I would welcome your assistance finding those responsible for the king's death, but I ask that you don't leave the city."

The general, too, is trying to find a safe way through this battle-field, she thought.

"But, General," Barton yelled out. "The curse! Don't let her—"

"That is my order," Drissen snapped. "I am regent and leader of the commonwealth. Do you question my authority?"

Barton ground his teeth but shook his head, turning away to hide his fury.

"A warrant will be issued demanding Prince Jarin's extradition from Argonne. Franklin's successor will be named once the prince has been returned to Caleddon. That is my command." Drissen spoke grimly. "Now, you will all join me on the balcony as I announce the death of King Franklin. I need not remind you how important solidarity is at this time."

As the general led the group to the balcony, Cerise drifted toward the back. She quietly signaled Janis and Tar, and the three of them slipped out a side door.

Gerard Mort watched Cerise leave the hall. His mind was in turmoil. Everything was going as planned; the church had effectively boxed Drissen into a corner, making him unable to deny Cerise's right to be queen, but Cerise had somehow resisted his attempt at controlling her, and she had not aligned herself with the church or claimed her birthright. She was proving herself too clever. He doubted the church could control the commonwealth without Cerise as its leader, and if he couldn't control her, then how would he control Weslynde?

And how had the girl had managed to get Drissen to let her investigate the king's murder? If she connected him to the murder, all would be lost.

There was a solution. Cerise would have to be martyred, ideally after she had a child. Then he could make himself regent, and everything he wanted could be done in the name of Saint Cerise. It would take time and planning. In the meantime, he had to ensure that Cerise continued to think of him as an ally. He closed his eyes and sussed the sky metal in her sigil. He located her familiar metallic signature and slipped out of the hall to follow her.

⚜

Cerise dashed across the courtyard and out the palace gates, followed closely by Janis and Tar. She ignored the gateman who hailed them.

"Are we going to Clear Lake? Pick up the rest of the crew?" Janis asked as they ran.

"No," replied Cerise. "We need to talk to the guards."

"What guards?" asked Janis.

"The guards who killed the Argonnian senator. I need to understand what they saw."

"Cerise, stop," cried Tar. She planted herself in front of Cerise. "Those people back there want to kill you. We need to get you out of Caleddon now, before it's too late. The general is probably announcing that you are Jarin's twin from the balcony while we stand here wasting time. Once he does that, a mob will form."

"The curse of the twins isn't real," Cerise said. "And I need to know if the senator acted alone or if the Argonnians are behind the king's murder. The guards may have seen something that helps me."

"Don't risk your life on this," Tar pleaded. "It's not worth it."

"I have to do this. I have to be certain." Cerise had to know if Jarin was behind this. It consumed her. "We'll be gone by tomorrow; I promise." She dashed off toward the barracks. Janis and Tar ran to catch up.

As Cerise approached the entrance to the barracks, she saw Gerard Mort hurrying their direction from a side street, black robes billowing behind him. She cursed silently but continued forward.

"Cerise, there you are. I saw you leave the hall. I assumed you were going to interview the guards."

"You figured that out rather quickly," Cerise said, not pausing her stride.

He matched her pace. "The house mage is responsible for knowing everything that happens in the palace."

Cerise stopped and turned on the mage. "Tell me exactly how the king died. What were you doing there that late at night?"

"I will tell you everything I know. We can go to my quarters after we interview the guards."

Cerise crossed her arms. "I will conduct these interviews without you. You understand why."

"I do," Gerard Mort said, acquiescing. "I only wish to help."

"I will seek you out in your quarters. Go there and stay there."

"Until then," Gerard Mort replied.

⚜

As she entered the barracks, the mage tried again to link his mind to her sigil but was rebuffed by the charm someone had put in the ring. *Who embedded her sigil? Who had that much power?* He muttered a curse and headed to his quarters. He had to regain her trust. A plan began to formulate in his mind.

⚜

Cerise followed a young soldier to the room of one of the guards. He banged on the door two times, waited for a second, then opened it and stepped aside. The guard inside was sitting at a small table, staring at nothing, hands wrapped around an empty bottle.

"Wait in the hall," Cerise said to her crew. She stepped into the small room and took the empty chair. "Sir. I am Ambassador Aikawa. I was asked to talk to you about what happened to the king." Cerise noted his blank expression and spoke a little softer. "What is your name, sir?" He didn't respond. "Your name, sir," she repeated, a little more insistent now.

"Griff," the guard said, continuing to stare down at his hands.

"Griff. You are not in trouble. General Drissen put me in charge of investigating the king's death. I need you to tell me everything you saw—leave nothing out. In this you will honor the king." She paused, but the guard said nothing. Was he even listening? "Start by telling me where you were when Senator Intsimi arrived at the king's office." Cerise noticed his hands were shaking. "Speak," she commanded. Energy flowed out of her chest and into her voice.

Griff looked up at her as if she'd slapped him. "I left my post," he blurted out. "I had to. I had to piss. I told Stevyn."

"Stevyn is the other guard?" Cerise asked.

"Yes. He said go ahead. He stayed in position, guarding the door. He said go ahead."

"You left your post?"

"Around the corner there's a window we do our business out of."

"Where was Stevyn?"

"In front of the door."

"He was still guarding the door when you came back?"

"Yes."

"Alone?"

"He was with the house mage."

"The house mage?"

"The mage came to see the king." Griff's eyes were dilated, and he rubbed his hands like he was washing them. "When I came back...I, we, heard noises. Inside. We opened the door and there was yelling. Inside. The king was on the floor and the Argonnian had his hands on him. I heard someone yell assassins."

"Who yelled assassins?"

"The mage." He grimaced as he spoke. "The mage yelled assassins, and we went in. We killed them with our spears."

"The mage was already in the room with the king when you came in?"

"No. He was out in the hall with us. He was with us. In the hall. He was not in the room." He sighed deeply as if relieved to have finally said it.

"Where was the king?"

"On the floor. With a knife in his chest. The Argonnian was on top of him. We were too late."

"How did the Argonnians get in the room? How did they get past you?"

"The window was open. It was supposed to be locked. We were too late." He pushed his chair back and climbed into his cot and wrapped his arms around his legs.

She tried asking a few more questions, but the guard turned his back to her and would say nothing more.

"I will return after I speak to Stevyn," Cerise said, frustrated. She left Griff curled up in a ball and joined the soldier who had brought them there.

"Take us to Stevyn," she ordered.

The soldier led them to another door not far down the hallway. The door thudded against something when he opened it. He forced the door open, moving a chair that was blocking it, and Cerise saw that the guard named Stevyn was hanging by a noose from the ceiling; a stool lay on its side underneath him. They quickly cut him down.

Cerise loosened the rope from the man's neck, but his face was already blue and cold. "Go and tell General Drissen what has happened. Run." The soldier sped away down the hall. Cerise frowned and turned to Janis and Tar. "This whole thing is not what it seems. We need to find Gerard Mort."

The trio hurried back across the sunlit courtyard and through the palace doors, pounding up the marble steps and down the echoing corridor.

As they approached the mage's room, Cerise heard yelling and the sound of things breaking. Tar threw herself against his door and burst through. Gerard Mort was backed into a corner, facing two hooded figures holding swords. Before Cerise could react, the mage flung his arms wide and shouted a command in old majik, sending the assailants' swords flying across the room. It wasn't enough, however, to stop their advance, and they leapt on him, slamming his head into the wall. One of them drew a knife and raised it.

Cerise sprang into action, grabbing the attacker's knife hand and twisting it. She brought her elbow down hard on the assailant's head, knocking them to the ground. She quickly pinned the attacker with her foot. Then she drew her sword and held the tip against their throat. Satisfied, she quickly noted that Tar had the second assailant face down on the ground and was holding a knife to their ribs. Janis helped Gerard Mort climb back to his feet, and, in a rage, he came over and ripped the hood off the one Tar had pinned, revealing him to be an Argonnian, eyes blazing with hate.

"Who are you?" Gerard Mort demanded. The man bared his teeth and growled, then tore his arm free from Tar's grasp and slammed his fist hard into the side of his own neck. Tar gasped and jumped back as the man's body went into spasms and a green foam began to bubble from his lips. A chemical smell filled the air. Cerise looked down at the man she had pinned and saw that he had punched his own neck as well and was writhing underneath her foot. Both men gurgled and spit froth. They were dead within seconds.

"Don't touch their faces," Gerard Mort warned.

Cerise kicked the Argonnian's hand away from his neck and saw a needle protruding from his ring. She pounded her fist against the wall and swore.

"I've seen this man before," Janis said. "He works in the kitchen. And look at this. He has a trident tattooed on his palm."

"This man as well," Tar said.

"That is the symbol worn by all Argonnian soldiers." Gerard Mort leaned back against the wall and dabbed at a cut on his head. "They must have infiltrated the staff. Tell the general to lock down the palace."

Cerise nodded quickly at Janis, who ran off down the hall.

"Thank you for coming when you did," he said. "A few more moments and..."

"We were coming to question you," Cerise said. "One of the guards we went to interview was dead, a rope around his neck. It looked like suicide, but I don't think it was. Frankly, I suspected you. But now with this attack...I am sorry."

"No need to apologize," Gerard Mort replied. "I would suspect the same. Senator Intsimi must have planned this for quite some time." He sat heavily in a chair and wiped the blood from his forehead. "It's clear now that I was next on the list. The situation is worse than I thought. We need to bring in all the Argonnians working in the palace for questioning. And, Cerise,

I fear you may be next. Please be careful." They were interrupted by the sound of palace guards running to their aid.

"Now can we go?" Tar asked.

"Yes, Tar," Cerise said. "We need distance between ourselves and this cursed palace."

"You are leaving?" the mage looked surprised.

"The news I am Jarin's twin has broken," Cerise replied, "and there are too many people who wish me harm. Not only Argonnians. I can't be looking over my shoulder every second."

"Where will you go?"

"That I shall keep to myself. It seems best, don't you agree?"

The mage frowned. "Let me help you. You are the rightful heir to the throne. Drissen will not dare dispute it. The curse will be dealt with somehow and Argonne brought to justice."

"Time to go!" Tar said through gritted teeth. Cerise nodded, and they headed for the door.

"I suggest you wait until dark before you leave the city," the mage called after them. "Get word back to me as soon as you can."

Cerise turned back and eyed him carefully, searching for any artifice. His expression was sincere. "I will," she said and sped down the hall.

⚜

Cerise tried to avoid being seen, but the abbey courtyard was packed with worshipers and there was no way to get around them. They cheered as she approached the arched gateway. Tar helped her push her way through the throng. They found Janis and Rence waiting for them inside.

"This is madness," Cerise said, leaning against the closed door.

"It's worse than you think," Rence said. "When General Drissen broke the news of who you are, the streets around the palace filled. And in spite of the cheering crowd outside the abbey, not everyone is happy."

"Count me among them," Cerise muttered.

"Beware of Barton and his brother," Rence cautioned. "His soldiers are clustered near the palace. The general sent courier birds to the prime ministers of Riddien and Argonne with the news of the king's death. In those letters he named you Franklin's firstborn. The birds are swift and will reach them in the next day or two. The general has summoned them here to Weslynde."

"Why?"

"They are to determine the next sovereign of the commonwealth."

"The king's heir assumes the throne. That means Jarin."

"Normally, but this situation is unprecedented. Prince Jarin's rumored defection and your sudden appearance out of thin air, not to mention the curse of the twins."

"The curse," Cerise scoffed.

"You will have to deal with it, one way or another." Rence steepled his fingers against his lips. "You are no longer safe in Caleddon. May I ask, what is your next move?"

"Find Jarin," Cerise said. "He is the key to this. He has the answers; I can feel it. In spite of what you told me about him, I fear he is my enemy." Her shoulder buzzed as if confirming this. "We leave after dark. My crew set up a camp at Clear Lake, and we will go there first. Rence, you said the prime minister of Argonne has been summoned to Caleddon. How will she travel to get here?"

"She will follow the Wess River from Argonne, crossing both Endelas Lake and Clear Lake. It will take them some time to make the journey."

"Then we will meet her on her way here," Cerise said. "Perhaps she can lead us to the prince."

"Prime Minister Kokheli is a tough old crow," Rence warned. "Unpredictable."

"As am I. We should get along fine."

Cerise penned a note for Rence to give to General Drissen, stating that she had gone to arrest Prince Jarin and bring him back to Caleddon. Once it was dark, they left the abbey through the scullery entrance, hiding under a tarp on a supply wagon. From there they made their way down to the docks along the Wess River, confiscated a canoe, and paddled down the river toward Clear Lake. They joined the rest of the *Flying Fish*'s crew late the next afternoon.

Her crew had rented an old fishing vessel and had begun selling fish at the local market. Skua told her that the news of the king's death had reached Clear Lake shortly before they'd arrived and that the local pub was already packed with fisherman waiting for more news. Cerise took cover inside the fishing boat's cabin to avoid being seen, and as soon as it was dark they slipped their moorings, letting the current carry the old vessel out into the lake, away from prying eyes.

That night Cerise had a dream. She had drawn her sword and was standing over Jarin, who was lying on the ground in front of her, pleading for his life. She wasn't sure how she would respond.

PART V

THE CURSE OF THE TWINS

CHAPTER 17

J arin opened his eyes. The ceiling above him slowly came into focus. It was carved from raw stone, and for a brief second, he thought he was back in the torture room. His body stiffened in panic. Then he noticed ornately carved molding and elegant tapestries hanging from the walls. The air smelled of astringent. He heard a slight splash and felt a warm and soothing caress on his leg. He became aware that he was lying in a bed, naked, his left arm bound tightly across his chest. An Argonnian man about his age was bathing him with a sponge.

"Where am I?" Jarin croaked.

"Ah, you are finally awake." The man smiled warmly, setting aside the bowl of scented water and feeling Jarin's forehead. "Your head is cool; that is good. Welcome back, my prince— I mean, Tuval. You are in Tregor Anthelia's villa, and you are safe."

"Who are you?"

"My name is Toree. I'm taking care of you." He covered Jarin's body with a soft linen sheet and arranged his pillow. "You have been here for a week now."

"What happened to me?" It hurt when he tried to move.

"You were abducted by ransom seekers. Senator Anthelia and a magician from Weslynde rescued you. It was a near thing; you almost didn't make it back to us."

"Was the magician called Dax?" Jarin asked.

"That is his name," Toree said. "Now stop talking and rest. I must tell the healer you are awake; she will answer all your questions." He took the bowl of water and left the room.

Jarin tried again to move. His pinned arm made it hard to roll over. He was too weak to sit up and could only turn his head from side to side. He gave up trying to sit up and craned his neck, taking stock of his surroundings. Shafts of sunlight from deep inset windows created squares of light on the wall. The furniture in the room was finely made and polished, and thick carpets covered the floors. Cool air circulated gently through the room. The door opened, and Toree entered with Tregor at his side, followed by an Argonnian woman.

"Jarin," Tregor said, grabbing his free hand. "Thank the gods you are awake."

The woman brusquely pushed his grandfather out of the way. "I am Talesa. I am the healing woman, and this is my nurse, Toree." Toree winked at Jarin and flashed a crooked smile. Talesa touched Jarin's neck with dry fingers, feeling his pulse. "How do you feel?"

"Tired ... and hungry."

"That is good. We will bring you food. Now sit up so we can take a look at your shoulder."

Toree lifted Jarin to a sitting position. The nurse was large and well-muscled, but his touch was surprisingly gentle, and he took care not to jostle Jarin's injury. The healing woman carefully unwound the bandages wrapped around his arm and shoulder. Pain jolted down his back when he tried to extend his arm.

"Try not to move your arm," Talesa said.

"Too late," Jarin groaned. "What happened to me?"

"Someone tried to carve this metal ring out of your back," Toree said. "It must have proved harder than they thought, so they gave up. The bone of your shoulder blade is grown half over it."

"Hand me those tweezers," Talesa ordered. She pulled the gauze away from the wound and used the tweezers to pick out maggots, depositing them in a tray by the bed.

"What are those?" Jarin asked, nose wrinkling.

"Worms," Toree said in an eerie voice. "They are eating you from the inside out."

"They are maggots," the healer said. "I put them there to clean out the wound, and they have done their job. The red lines of infection have disappeared, and the skin around the edges is pink and forming a crust." She smiled for the first time. "I am very happy with how this looks. We should proceed with the skin graft before it scabs over."

"Skin graft?" Jarin asked.

"I suggest you talk to Senator Anthelia while we do the graft. Tregor, can you distract him?"

"Distract me?" Jarin asked, anxious now.

"Toree, roll Jarin onto his stomach—be careful of his arm," Talesa ordered.

Toree gently turned Jarin over while Talesa prepared her tools. Tregor pulled up a chair next to Jarin's face as Toree spread numbing oil across the wound and on his buttocks.

"What are you doing down there?" Jarin asked.

"Harvesting skin for the graft," Toree said. "The best place to get it is from your ass. Don't worry; you'll get used to the curly hairs growing out of your shoulder."

"Toree, do your job," Talesa chided.

Tregor filled Jarin in on the events of his rescue while Jarin tried not to picture what was happening behind him. The men who had taken him to the boat had gotten away, but the man Dax had locked in the torture room had confessed they were hoping for a reward from Weslynde. Tregor didn't know how they had come into possession of Jarin's warrant and was worried there was a spy in the prime minister's council.

"All finished," the healer said. "Drink this." She held out a small glass full of green liquid. Toree helped Jarin onto his side and put the glass to his lips. Jarin swallowed the bitter drink and then asked, "Where's Dax?"

"Sleep now," Toree said, gently lowering him back down onto the pillow. The room around him dissolved into oblivion.

Jarin's shoulder healed well, but it looked ugly. The raven's wing tattoo had been marred by the skin graft, and the sigil's scrollwork no longer rested on the surface of his skin; instead, it stuck out a little above the scar, occasionally snagging on his tunic. Toree had Jarin do stretches and lift objects to build back his arm strength. Jarin progressed quickly, but it would take a long time before he would remaster his fighting abilities with his staff.

Tregor visited him daily and brought him news, including news of Dax. The magician had not come to see him, and it vexed Jarin. He asked Tregor to have him come.

"Dax is very busy at the chameli training center," Tregor said. "In fact, he is now in charge; the old magician, Angus, left Isidima."

"But I must see him."

"I have told him your wish and will tell him again." Tregor placed his hand on Jarin's arm. "Do not worry about him."

Jarin's frustration continued to grow, and after two more days without word from his friend, his patience ran out. He would go to Dax if the magician would not come to him. Tregor balked at first, but Jarin wore him down and he finally relented, insisting, however, that Jarin go with an armed house guard. He sent Toree along with him as well.

When Jarin arrived at the training center, he saw Dax standing in the middle of the sandy arena, working with a dozen carrier beasts and their handlers. The chameli were outfitted with troop platforms and battle harnesses.

"Is that him? Toree asked.

"Yes, that's Dax," Jarin said, smiling with excitement.

"He's quite handsome," Toree noted.

"He doesn't bed with men, Toree." Jarin frowned at the nurse. "Don't bother him."

Toree chuckled. "Oh, now I see how things are. You are in love with him, and I have made you jealous."

"No, it's not like that," Jarin protested, embarrassed. "We've been through a lot together, that's all."

"Of course." Toree laughed. "I also see you have not taken your eyes off of him since we arrived."

Dax saw them and motioned the handlers to take a break. He waved them over. Jarin wanted to hug him but held back, aware of Toree's eyes on him. Dax put his hands on Jarin's shoulders and held him at arm's length.

"Tuval! You look well. How are you healing? Let me see." He turned Jarin around and lifted up his tunic and inspected his scar. "Well, you won't win any beauty contests, that's for sure. This may end your reputation among the serving boys."

Jarin's cheeks flushed. He glanced at Toree, who stood with his arms crossed and a big grin on his face.

"Who are your companions?" Dax asked.

"These are my bodyguards I must have with me at all times," Jarin said sarcastically. "This is Toree, my nurse, and this is Tidian, Tregor's house guard."

"Welcome to you both," Dax said.

"I have wondered where you were," Jarin said, unable to keep the hurt out of his voice.

"Tuval has been asking for you every day," Toree interjected. "We can't shut him up."

"Toree!" Jarin elbowed the nurse in the ribs. "Why haven't you come to see me?" he asked the magician.

"I've been busy," Dax said, not meeting his eyes.

Is Dax avoiding me? Is he angry?

The magician brightened, covering the moment. "Let me show you what I have been doing." He led the group over to the carrier beasts. When he got close, the handlers settled their beasts on the ground and stepped politely to the side.

"Watch now," Dax said, and he made a slight hand signal. All twelve beasts rose to their hind legs, heads stretching in the air. Jarin noticed their metal body armor extended across their bellies. Dax signaled again, and they lowered back to the ground. The sand beneath their feet scattered with a low whomp.

"Charge," Dax whispered in a soft monotone, and the twelve animals sprang forward, lumbering straight at Dax and Jarin, heads down so that the armored plates they wore faced the men. They showed no signs of slowing down.

"Dax?" Jarin asked nervously, taking a step back.

"Stop," Dax said, softly again. The carrier beasts skidded to a stop and settled in front of them, their giant heads only a few steps away. A wave of sand kicked up by their sudden halt spread across Jarin's sandals.

Dax went down the line and place a hand on each chameli, and their cheek spots glowed blue in response. "I've been able to modify the charms in their snout rings. I can send one signal to multiple animals at the same time, and I don't have to touch their rings anymore." His excitement grew. "I can talk to them merely by being near them. And they are smart, Jar—uh, Tuval. The Argonnians have them doing complicated tasks in the mineral caves that I didn't think they could handle. There are at least five hundred mature beasts here that are large enough to wear battle armor and carry troops. Do you realize that?"

"Five hundred?" Jarin touched the nose of the nearest beast, caressing the knobby surface of its hide. Its throat rumbled in response. An idea began to form in his head. "They bond with us, don't they?"

"They always pay more attention to the handler who works with them the most."

"We could bond each one to a soldier instead of a handler." Jarin stroked the beast thoughtfully.

"A soldier?"

Jarin studied Dax's quizzical expression. Was Dax making fun of him? He wasn't sure. He shook his head. "It was only a thought."

"Finish your thought."

Jarin pulled Dax away from the others and took a breath. "I've been thinking. If we were to return to Weslynde, if ... I were to reassert my position as my father's heir ... then having the strength of the Argonnian army behind me riding atop bonded carrier beasts would—"

"—strengthen your hand," finished Dax. "So, you've decided what you are going to do."

Jarin said simply, "What I have to do."

A messenger wearing the Argonnian prime minister's crest came running into the arena. He saw Jarin and dashed over to him. Tregor's guard moved in front of Jarin to shield him.

"My lord...Tuval," the messenger said, breathing hard. "I bring bad news."

"Speak," Jarin said, stepping around Tregor's guard.

"My lord, the king of Weslynde is dead."

Jarin's stomach dropped. "What did you say?"

"King Franklin is dead. Please follow me, my lord; the prime minister is waiting for you."

✢

The council room in the ziggurat was packed with grim-faced officials listening to Tregor Anthelia read from a message scroll. The prime minister of Argonne, Tharisa Kokheli, perched next to him in her wheeled chair, greatly resembling an old crow. Jarin found a spot in the back of the room next to Dax. He was struggling to process the news, but mostly he felt numb. He had worked out a plan, a way to return home, to show his father he was strong and to rebuild his trust, but now his world had been upended, again. Overwhelming loss and isolation overtook him.

Tregor read down through the scroll. "The king died four days ago. It's taken that long for the courier bird to reach us. They are calling it an assassination, and they are naming Senator Toberon Intsimi of Argonne the assassin." There were gasps of disbelief around the room.. "This accusation is outrageous."

"Keep reading," Prime Minister Kokheli croaked, her black eyes glittering. Her claw-like hands gripped the arms of her wheeled chair.

"General Drissen, the head of the Weslynde army, has been installed as regent until a successor is named."

Senator Talani stepped forward. "There is no question who the successor is. It's Prince Jarin né Franklin, daughter of Tregan Anthelia." Jarin recognized her as one of the senators he'd met his first day in Isidima. She caught Jarin's eye and quickly looked away.

"Don't interrupt," the prime minister snapped.

Tregor continued, "The prime ministers of Riddien and Argonne are hereby summoned to Caleddon immediately to consider the matter of succession." He turned to the prime minister. "This part pertains to you specifically. Prime Minister Tharisa Kokheli is to demonstrate fealty to the commonwealth and extradite Prince Jarin to Weslynde immediately. The prince shall account for his defection to Argonne and involvement with the Argonnian separatist movement." He looked around the room to gauge reactions to this news, purposely avoiding eye contact with Jarin. "An investigation into the king's assassination at the hands of Argonnian terrorists is now underway. And finally, there's this." He laughed bitterly. "Ambassador Cerise Aikawa of Cordel is formally recognized by Weslynde to be none other than Sabrin né Franklin, King Franklin's firstborn from his union with Tregan Anthelia of Argonne. As such, she has a legitimate claim to the throne."

"Do you mean Saint Cerise, the albine?" someone asked. "She is Jarin's sister?"

"She is the one," Tregor answered and rolled up the message scroll. The room grew noisy as the council members expressed their surprise and shock.

"Where is Tuval?" The prime minister's gravelly voice cut through the noise. She craned her scrawny neck, and the council members stepped aside so she had a clear view of Jarin. The room grew quiet. "Ah, there you are, hiding all the way in the back. Come here." Jarin stepped forward, and Dax came with him. "This young man is Tuval, a caravan boy from Weslynde." A few in the room furrowed their brows and shifted uncomfortably. "Tuval recently arrived in Isidima from the north. Come closer, Tuval," she said, curling her bony fingers. "Since you are from Weslynde, perhaps you can tell us. Are you aware that Prince Jarin has a sister?"

Jarin exchanged glances with Dax and said carefully, "I heard the news the day I left Caleddon."

"And did you know that Jarin and this Sabrin woman are twins?" she queried, raising her eyebrows and gripping her chair. There were some gasps at this news.

"I have been told this."

"Then you must also know that according to Weslynde law,

one of the twins, either Jarin or this Sabrin...this Saint Cerise woman, must die." Her bony hand trembled, and the beads hanging from her wrist clattered. "I would prefer it to be the girl, but..." The room grew very quiet as she stared into Jarin's eyes. Jarin struggled not to look away. She held his gaze for a few seconds, then settled back in her chair and let the moment pass. Jarin swallowed, his heart hammering. Anxious muttering filled the room.

"This is a dark day." The prime minister sighed, and the room quieted again. "The king is murdered and the blame has been left at our doorstep. Our beloved Tregan Anthelia defied the law and gave birth to twins, and those fools in Weslynde allowed them both to live. The prince of Weslynde is now a fugitive, and Argonne is said to harbor him. The most honorable Senator Toberon Intsimi, my cousin and my friend, lies dead in Weslynde and is accused of assassination, which is an insult to Argonne that I will not tolerate. Now I am summoned to Caleddon, like a child to the headmaster's office, to debate who should rule the commonwealth, a commonwealth that appears to be coming apart at the seams."

"Prime Minister, if I may—" began Tregor. Tharisa Kokheli held up her gnarled hand and silenced him.

"It is a good thing that none of us know where Prince Jarin is." Her eyes narrowed, as if daring someone to speak. "Or we would be obligated to take him into custody and escort him back to Caleddon in chains. Whoever started the rumor that the prince is in Argonne is wrong. That rumor has no merit. Prince Jarin is not in Argonne." She looked around the room, then back at Jarin. "Tuval of Weslynde, you and your companion are dismissed. We thank you for attending this council session, but we have private matters that we must now discuss. Good luck to you."

The doors behind Jarin and Dax silently opened, and they were ushered out of the council room. Guards escorted them down the hall and out the main entrance of the ziggurat into the bright desert sun, closing the great iron doors behind them with a loud boom.

⚜

Dax shaded his eyes against the sun. The guards outside the ziggurat ignored their presence. "They are giving us a chance to get away."

Jarin stared at him, his face blank. Dax took him by the arm and led him down the road away from the building.

"We should leave tonight. I will go down to the training center and get us some transportation. I will meet you at Senator Anthelia's villa, and we will leave from there. Jarin, are you listening?"

Jarin nodded weakly.

"We will find a way to fix this. Come on." Dax hustled him through the palm-lined streets to the gate outside Tregor's villa. "I must go to the training center, but I will be back for you. Go inside." Jarin looked at him blankly. Exasperated, Dax pulled Jarin through the gate and banged on the door. After a few moments, Toree opened it in surprise.

"Toree! Good, it's you," Dax said. "Take him inside. He is bereft and not speaking. Don't let him go anywhere, and don't let anyone else in. I will come back for him." He put his hands on the sides of Jarin's head and looked deep into his eyes. "Go with Toree and collect your things. There will be time to grieve your father later. We will mourn him properly, I promise, together." He pushed Jarin through the door and ran down the street toward the market square.

⚜

Toree quietly followed Jarin through the main room of the

villa and down the covered walkway that led to the sleeping wing. Jarin pushed open his door and shuffled over to the window. He took a shuddering breath. Toree put his hand on Jarin's arm and guided him over to the bed. He unlaced Jarin's sandals, then lifted his feet onto the bed. Jarin rolled over onto his side in a ball, and Toree climbed into the bed behind him. He put his arm around Jarin's chest and pulled him tight against his body.

"Rest now," Toree whispered. "I will take care of you." They lay quietly for several minutes while Toree stroked Jarin's hair. Jarin turned around to face Toree, put his arms around Toree's neck, and let his grief spill out. Toree held him and hummed softly, and kissed Jarin's salty tears away. Sometime soon after, once he had calmed, Jarin slowly lifted his head and met Toree's lips with his own.

⚜

Dax picked out a young carrier beast large enough for two riders and instructed Tymm to water it and load it with provisions for the desert, thinking perhaps they might head back to the oasis and hide out there. Once he had everything arranged, he raced back up the steep road to Tregor's villa. Tregor's head of staff met him at the door and directed him down the covered walkway to Jarin's room. Dax knocked softly and put his ear to the door, but everything was quiet. He opened the door and discovered Jarin and Toree tangled up together on the bed, naked. They were asleep. He cursed softly and backed quietly out of the room, angry that Jarin would ignore the danger he was in and cavort with the nurse instead. So much depended on their escape. *The prince will never change,* he thought. As he opened the front door to leave, he met Tregor coming in.

"Dax, you are here. Good, we need to talk at once. Where is Jarin?"

Dax scowled and jerked his head in the direction of Jarin's bedroom.

Tregor read his expression. "I see." He signaled to his head of staff. "Go and fetch Tuval. Tell him to meet us on the terrace. Dax, come with me." He led Dax outside onto a large, covered balcony that overlooked the bay. "Wait here; I will bring food."

The sky was clear and cloudless, the sea a vast expanse of sapphire tipped with dots of cream. Dax leaned over the railing and looked up the coast. He could make out the misty tops of the Serpent's Tail Islands in the far distance. If he left now and sailed up the coast past the islands, he would come to the mouth of the Wess River. From there he could follow the river past the falls to Caleddon, and beyond to Saltbank, his home. What was to stop him? His pledge to Tregan? He had broken that already, having failed to protect Jarin more than once. The prince had almost died because of him, and now it was clear Jarin didn't want his help, preferring the company of his handsome nurse instead. He could leave Jarin with his grandfather and return home. He hadn't seen the Salt Sea since Rence had sent him on this reckless journey, how long ago? Four months? Five? It would be winter in the north, his favorite season. He pictured plumes of steam rising up in the cold air along the waterways, coating the trees in sparkling ice. He imagined the snowcapped mountains rimming the great valley, and great flocks of snowbirds wintering on the smoky lakes and streams.

A small tree-chameli crawled up the balcony railing next to Dax. It looked sideways at him, breaking through his reverie. He laid his palm out flat, and the chameli crawled up onto his hand and wrapped its tail around his wrist, changing color from emerald-green to a contented blue.

Tregor stepped out through the door with a tray of food and a pitcher of wine. "I see you've found a friend."

"The desert creatures respond to me." He stroked the chameli thoughtfully.

Jarin stumbled out onto the balcony a few moments later, wrestling his arm into the sleeve of his tunic. The tree-chameli startled, stretched its rib membranes, and jumped off Dax's hand, gliding through the air to a far-off tree farther down the steep slope.

"There you are," Tregor said as Jarin pulled down his shirt. "Sit and eat. You can't stay here long, and you need energy."

Jarin filled a glass with wine and gulped some down. He wiped his mouth and glanced warily at Dax.

"The prime minister of Argonne leaves for Caleddon in three days," Tregor said. "She believes the summons gives her no choice. I am traveling with her. It will take us some weeks to reach Caleddon traveling up the Wess River. Isidima will be on high alert during her absence, and added troops will be called in from the south to prepare to defend our northern borders."

"Do you really expect an attack from Weslynde?" Jarin asked.

"Jarin, hear this. Senator Intsimi has been framed for the murder of King Franklin. Rumors that Argonne plans to make a move against Weslynde are now rampant. Most Weslynders believe you are leading the insurrectionist movement in Argonne. The Church of the Commonwealth has, for all intents and purposes, taken over Caleddon and is preparing to replace the monarchy with a theocracy led by Saint Cerise."

"You mean Sabrin. My sister. Your granddaughter."

"Don't be assuaged by family ties, Jarin. She is powerful and dangerous, and the church will kill you to ensure she is crowned queen."

"The church? Why would they care?"

"Cerise is their saint. If she is queen, they wield great power. The prime minister believes the church is behind the death of your father, and I agree with her. The archbishop has openly declared fealty to Sabrin."

"We have to stop them," Jarin said. "The church can't rule Weslynde!"

The conversation stopped when Toree came out on the balcony. He was barefoot and was dressed only in a loincloth. "Here is your staff and your pack," he said, holding them out to Jarin. Jarin smiled gratefully.

Dax rounded on Jarin. "How do you expect to stop Weslynde and the church? You don't have a plan. You don't have an army. You seem capable of nothing except bedding your nurse!"

Shock spread across Jarin's face; it was as though Dax had slapped him.

"What are you planning to do?" Dax pressed.

Jarin's expression was a mix of anger and embarrassment. Once he had mastered his emotions, he said calmly, "I don't know, Dax, but there has to be a way. There must be."

"I believe I can help you there," Tregor interrupted. "Follow me." He headed briskly down a flight of stairs that led off the balcony, not waiting to see who followed.

Jarin faced Dax for another moment, then grabbed his pack and staff from Toree and hurried down the steps after Tregor. Dax threw Toree a look that clearly meant "don't follow us" and ran after them.

Tregor led them down a steep path hidden behind a cover of vines until they came to a door that led into the mountain.

"You have a lot of secret doors," Jarin said.

Tregor lit a torch stacked by the entrance and led them inside. After several turns and a flight of stairs, they came to a metal door. Tregor pulled a chain hanging in the shadows and stepped back. A few moments later, a bolt clanged and the door slid quietly inward, revealing a ledge overlooking a large chamber. The space was lit by sunlight streaming from shafts in the ceiling. At least fifty Argonnian men and women were moving about the chamber. Those who saw Tregor held out their arms and extended their palms face up. Tregor saluted them in return, using the same gesture.

"My friends, meet the resistance." Tregor flashed his famous smile.

Jarin's heart beat a little faster. The fog that had been pressing him down began to lift.

The Argonnians below returned to their business, which seemed mostly to be debating. Maps were strewn across tables amidst half-empty plates and mugs. Jarin followed Tregor down the stairs and greeted the people who came up to him, introducing himself as Tuval. As he crossed the room, a familiar voice rang out over the others.

"Tuval! Tuval!" It was Tevin, the caravan driver they had traveled with across the desert. Tevin threw his arms around Jarin, lifting him off the ground and spinning him around.

"My prince! I told you we would meet again!" Tevin grinned.

"You're part of the resistance?" Jarin asked, astonished.

"I lead the resistance!" Tevin laughed. "Now come with me. You as well, sir magician."

Tevin led Jarin, Tregor, and Dax into a small side chamber. Two other Argonnians joined them.

Tregor spoke first. "My friends. This is Prince Jarin né Franklin, my grandson and heir to the throne of Weslynde. Jarin will soon be named the next sovereign of the Western Commonwealth. At his side is Dax of Saltbank, a most extraordinary magician. He is Jarin's confidant and shield."

The two Argonnians who had followed them in introduced themselves. Neither showed the slightest surprise that the prince of Weslynde had suddenly appeared like a ghost in their midst.

"You lead the resistance?" Jarin asked. "What is it you resist?"

"We resist the tyranny of Weslynde," said Tuveh, a fierce-looking woman with flashing eyes. "For too long your province has shut us out. You take all our resources—our precious metals, our carrier beasts, even our magicians—and we receive nothing in return."

Trevon, a powerfully built man with heavily tattooed arms, spoke next. "You treat us like relatives you can't stand and only tolerate on feast days. We say enough of this! We want justice for our people, justice for Senator Toberon Intsimi falsely accused of killing the king, justice for your mother—the great Lady Tregan Anthelia—and justice for you, Prince Jarin né Franklin, whom Weslynde has wrongly forced into exile!"

Jarin turned Trevon's hand palm up and touched his trident tattoo. "You all have this mark on your hand. Are you terrorists?"

Trevon spoke fiercely. "We are not! That slur was coined by the church to stoke fear and division. The church is doing the killing. They kill Weslynders who stand in their way and then blame it on us." He held up his hand, tattooed palm facing up. Tevin and Tuveh followed suit. "This trident represents the three pillars of Argonnian society: freedom, wisdom, and peace. That is what we stand for."

"Do you wish to secede from the commonwealth?"

Tevin spoke again. "There are some in our group who would choose that path. Others still believe in the commonwealth, in Tregan Anthelia's dream."

Tregor put his hand on Jarin's shoulder. "Jarin né Franklin is a fugitive accused of leading an insurrection against Caleddon. His extradition from Argonne has been demanded by the regent of Weslynde. What do you say to that?"

"We'll give them Jarin, but not in the way they expect," Trevon said. "We'll give them King Jarin, the rightful ruler of the commonwealth. We will whip their asses with King Jarin's justice."

Jarin's face flushed. "My mother believed that the power of the commonwealth lay in the combined strengths of each province and that unification meant peace and prosperity for everyone, not just the powerful in Weslynde. She dedicated her life to that dream. She dreamed that someday I would lead the commonwealth and that Argonnians would once again be seated at the table beside their brothers and sisters. I would not crush that dream; instead, I would see it come true."

"We have been waiting a long time for you, my prince." Tevin grinned, bringing out a bottle for a toast.

⚜

Jarin and Dax wandered through the chamber, listening to the voices of a people filled with hope and pride. They shared a meal with the resistance fighters and afterward found a corner to talk privately.

"I have an army that will fight for me," Jarin said. "Not only a nurse in my bed."

"It was wrong of me to say that to you," Dax said. "I was angry."

"Fifty trained fighters, each riding their own carrier beast. Think of it."

"Fifty fighters is not an army."

"But they would make an impact. And I don't have to win a war. I only have to get into Caleddon palace and find my sister. Explain things. Reason with her."

"Reason with Sabrin? Sabrin, who is bent on taking your crown? The famous Saint Cerise, killer of sea serpents, who is leading the church's takeover of Weslynde?"

"I don't believe she is, Dax. I can't tell you why. I feel it; that's all. I think there is a way this could work. We could even join forces, she and I. Fulfill our mother's dream."

"Alright. Let's say that is true. Then what do we do? March up to the front gate of the palace and say, 'Open the doors; I'd like to talk to Sabrin'?"

"No, my magician friend." Jarin smiled. "We magically appear. That's why I have you."

Dax laughed. "Fifty carrier beasts marching up the middle of the boulevard would be hard for me to hide."

"Hard to hide on widely traveled roads, yes, but very hard to see in the high desert. Hard to see winding through the vineyards and orchards of the central valley at night."

"You have been thinking about this. What is your plan?"

"We go in secret. In the middle of the night. All of Weslynde will be focused on the Argonnian prime minister and her entourage traveling up Endelas Lake. We will go a different way, across the desert, and we will walk through Caleddon's back door while no one is looking."

⚜

Tregor Anthelia was ushered into the Argonnian prime minister's private quarters. It was late, and the natural phosphorescence in the walls gave the room a soft yellow glow. Tharisa Kokheli sat hunched in an armchair with a blanket across her lap. Tregor poured two glasses of wine from a pitcher.

"The boy has met with the resistance," he said. "He plans to lead them on a secret mission to Weslynde to overcome the church and his sister, Sabrin, using diplomacy and reason."

"That seems unlikely," Tharisa croaked, accepting a glass from Tregor.

"I don't disagree. I've met his sister. She's a formidable character and isn't likely to back down or disappear."

"Both your grandchildren are unusually resilient. How does Jarin plan to get past General Drissen's army?

"He plans to sneak into the province unseen, using you as a decoy."

"Me? How so?"

"Jarin is hoping that you will travel with a large enough delegation that it will draw Drissen's focus so he can slip in unnoticed behind you."

Tharisa chuckled. "I like it. He sounds like his father. It was never the straightforward path with Franklin." She tapped her glass with her fingernail. "We can use this. Use the chaos Jarin creates to give us time to withdraw our citizens from Weslynde and return to Argonne. While Jarin and Sabrin fight over who gets to rule Weslynde or die from the curse of the twins, we can secure our borders and declare we have officially seceded from the commonwealth."

"And if Jarin succeeds?" Tregor asked. "What's your position then?"

"It depends on what Jarin wants. If he wants to join us, he is welcome here as an ordinary citizen of Argonne, grandson of a revered senator. If he wants to stay in Weslynde and play king and get himself killed while doing it, then let him do that."

Tregor remained silent, contemplating his glass.

"Oh, Tregor, I get that you are fond of the boy. Talk him into it. He's seen Argonne; he knows we are the superior culture. But don't tell him anything except that I depart for Caleddon in three days with a very, very large delegation of courtiers, lawyers, and bureaucrats, all armed to the teeth. Weslynde will not dare take their eyes off me for even a moment."

CHAPTER 18

The prime minister's departure for Weslynde had all the trappings of a parade. Word of her journey had been announced in advance, and a curious crowd had gathered to watch. The day was crisp and clear, and the banners held aloft by her detail snapped in the fresh breeze coming off the ocean. One hundred men and women marched with her, and she scowled imperiously from her palanquin as they traversed the steep boulevard down to the ship waiting in the harbor. A dozen carrier beasts had already been put aboard a cargo ship, and the unusual sight of the huge desert creatures boarding an ocean vessel filled the pub talk that evening. News of King Franklin's death had spread quickly, and the purpose of prime minister's trip became the subject of wild speculation, including her taking the crown and replacing the fallen king as sovereign of the commonwealth. People toasted each other and sang songs of victory. Some said Isidima would now become the center of the commonwealth as had long been their dream.

⚜

Hidden in the desert east of the city, Jarin was planning a

very different journey to Caleddon. As part of that plan, Dax bonded Tevin's resistance fighters to their carrier beasts. Dax had each fighter hold on to their beast's snout ring while he embedded charms that would cause the animal to respond to the sight and smell of its specific rider.

Jarin had insisted Toree join him in the desert to complete his healing. Toree led Jarin through a series of exercises to improve his stamina and arm strength. He brought out staves and sparred with him on the hot sand. At night they shared a tent. During an evening meal, one of the fighters pulled Dax aside and commented on the handsome nurse's involvement with the prince. He then told Dax stories about Toree's reputation as a heartbreaker and skilled seducer of both men and women. The gossip vexed Dax. He didn't like the light it put on Jarin, so he decided to do something about it. He found the nurse alone in Jarin's tent, packing for the journey.

"Toree," Dax said. "I need a word with you."

"I've been expecting you," Toree said, continuing to stuff medicinals into his pack. "You want to talk about Jarin."

"That's right."

"You can rest assured that Jarin is fit to travel. His wound has fully healed and he has regained much of his arm strength. If I keep working with him, he will continue to improve."

"That is good news. You are a good healer, and I thank you, but..." Dax hesitated, then jumped in. "Actually, I've come to tell you that I need to take back your beast. We need it to carry supplies, so you won't be coming with us."

"I see." Toree stopped packing and casually picked up a pipe. He leaned back against a tent pole and lit it with a sigh. "You think I distract him."

"Jarin needs to focus on the mission at hand."

"You mean he needs to focus on you. I see the way you look at each other." Toree took a puff and offered the pipe to Dax, who declined with a slight shake of his head. "Don't worry, magician. I couldn't come between the two of you even if I wanted to."

Dax frowned. "You get the wrong impression. I am Jarin's sworn protector only, his second-in-command."

"You are second to no one according to Jarin." Toree picked up his pack. "Don't worry, magician. I will stay behind in Isidima...for the good of the mission." He stopped at the door to the tent. "I will miss him though. He is very...passionate, and he has a huge heart. Maybe someday you will learn that."

⚜

Jarin planned to travel straight across the high desert and then through the less traveled parts of Weslynde, sticking to the wildlands, crossing fields and vineyards only when necessary. Weslynde's cultivated areas would lie fallow this time of year and would be largely empty of people. It was a tall order to think that fifty great chameli could pass through Weslynde unnoticed, but he planned to travel only at night and take advantage of the beasts' camouflage during the day. Tevin advised him not to bring battle armor, as a beast in full armor would be slower and harder to hide. Supplies were lashed directly onto the backs of the beasts instead of pulled in wagons; this would allow them to travel even faster.

The weather would get colder the farther north they went. The beasts could handle the cold weather for a time, but they would become increasingly sluggish the colder it got. Jarin planned to take them past the Darno geyser basin on the last leg of the journey, knowing the heated water would speed up the beasts' metabolism. Once they arrived in Caleddon, Jarin intended to scale the palace walls at night and seize control while General Drissen was distracted by the arrival of the prime minister of Argonne.

The day of their departure, Jarin met one last time with Tevin and Dax inside Tevin's tent.

"All we have to do," he said, "is subdue palace security, kick the archbishop out of the palace, and force General Drissen and my sister into a parley of some kind."

"That should be no problem at all!" Tevin grinned.

Dax raised an eyebrow. "What about the curse of the twins? Remember the night we fled Caleddon? Hail smashing buildings, lightning crashing all around us."

"Dax, no curse can change the weather. That is a myth." Jarin hoped he was right. He felt good about the plan to get to Caleddon. He was less sure about what would happen once they got there.

⚜

The chameli and their riders set out as soon as the sun set, its rays silhouetting Isidima in the distance behind them and painting the sky above them a brilliant orange. Before them, the moon had risen, and it shimmered in the heat waves coming off the desert. Stars appeared as the sky deepened from orange to indigo.

The dry desert air cooled quickly, and Jarin unwrapped the linen sweatband twisted around his head. Brittle shale crunched beneath his carrier beast's feet, a sound that would vanish once they reached the soft rose-colored sand of the dunes. Thanks to Dax's charms, Jarin could guide his beast by stroking its back; he no longer had to speak a command or touch its ring. He leaned forward and scratched the top of its head; its cheek spots turned iridescent blue in response, making him smile.

Tevin led the resistance up a dry wash carved out by some long-ago flash flood; the chameli fell into a good rhythm, and the miles crunched by. Dax maneuvered his beast next to Jarin.

"Tevin says we continue along this channel and through a canyon until we reach a break in that ridge over there. After that we will be out on the dunes."

"How long will we be on the dunes?

"He says three weeks. Once we get past the sand and into the scrublands, we will have to find water and see to feeding the beasts. There is a desert spring we stop at, but feeding fifty great chameli will be more of a challenge. The Argonnians are hoping we will come across a herd of desert antelope or camel deer."

They rode in silence for a while. A falling star blazed overhead. "Sky stone," Dax said, watching the distinctive yellow-green trail streak across the sky. "Like your sigil."

The meteor vanished behind the ridge. "Sometimes I wish I could get it removed. Sometimes I wish I could disappear into the desert. I could live like this, Dax. Riding at night under the stars."

"What's stopping you?" Dax asked. "It's not the sigil."

They rode quietly for a time, then Jarin spoke. "My father is dead. My mother is dead. It's only me. If Sabrin takes control of Weslynde, everything my mother tried to do will be lost. Argonne will be subjugated. The church will force us all into a rigid set of rules. They worship old gods that aren't even real. They created the 'curse of the twins' nonsense. I don't want to live in that world."

"What about your sister? How will you reason with her?"

"I don't know, but I have to try. I don't know anything about Sabrin. But the thought of Saint Cerise scares the hell out of me."

"Jarin, there's something I never told you." The night sky shimmered overhead. "The sigil Sabrin wears that gives her claim to the throne. I put it there when she was a baby. I embedded it."

"You did what? How?"

"I rescued her. I was the one who took her out of Caleddon the night she was born. I had help from Rence and a woman named Merta. We were all bound to Tregan. We pledged to save her twins."

"You embedded her sigil? But why?"

"I didn't do it on purpose."

"How was that not on purpose?" Jarin's mind reeled. "Is Rence aware that Sabrin is also Saint Cerise?"

"He must be. He knew the baby was an albine. We vowed to protect both of you, Jarin. I am still honoring that vow."

"Both of us? Why didn't Rence go after her then? Why didn't you?"

"Rence thinks you need more protecting than she does," Dax said.

They were interrupted by a series of yips ringing off the canyon walls. A rider ahead of them yelled, "Cave jackals!"

"Don't worry; the jackals won't attack this many beasts. I'll make sure Tevin knows to keep his riders together." Dax urged his beast forward, leaving Jarin to absorb this news.

Once again, he was being handled. Information had been withheld from him. It was clear that neither Rence nor Dax thought he could take care of himself. Jarin knew very well that Dax was the one who had sent Toree away...for 'his own good,' he was sure. It stung a little—no, it stung a lot. He rode apart from the others the rest of the night.

The company traveled up the canyon's dry water course, reaching the top two hours before dawn. Undulating bands of sand dunes, as white as snow in the light of the moon, stretched endlessly into the distance. The night air here was warmer, as the sand released its pent-up heat collected during the day. The carrier beasts lay on their bellies and rooted around in obvious enjoyment. There were no landmarks in any direction, only shifting mountains of sand. Tevin said they would follow the red star in the Sea Dragon constellation that dominated the northern sky. They would need to watch for sand pits and hope no storms came up during the crossing. It was winter, so it wouldn't get unbearably hot, and they had brought plenty of water in barrels lashed to the beasts. During the day, they sheltered under white canvas tarps that reflected the sun, while the beasts buried themselves in the sand, changing to a pale salmon color to match their sandy surroundings.

⚜

For days the resistance marched through the desert, and Dax saw nothing except raptors circling high in the sky above. Two weeks into the crossing, they surprised a wild chameli buried in the sand, waiting for prey. It erupted out of the ground and displayed its luminous throat fan, lighting up the ground around it. It bellowed and kicked up sand with its tail, warning them not to get too close. The carrier beast nearest to it challenged it, rearing up and dislodging its rider in the process. The rider scrambled to her feet and tried to grab the beast's snout ring as the two beasts circled each other, a multitude of warning colors undulating across their bodies. The wild chameli charged forward and headbutted the rider, tossing her through the air. She hit the sand hard and crumpled into a ball.

Dax jumped down and sussed the carrier beast. It settled. The wild chameli charged him, and Dax barely avoided being trampled. He jumped to the side and pushed himself off of the beast's leg. As soon as he touched its hide, he connected with the wild beast's consciousness, sensed its frenzied panic, and was able to calm it. After a few more bellows and sand scrapes, the chameli sank down on its belly and began shoveling sand over itself.

With Jarin's help, Dax lifted the fallen rider off the sand; she had broken her arm. The company's medic set it and wrapped it tight against her body while Jarin praised her bravery. She rallied and soon announced she was ready to move on, summoning her beast to her. Dax helped her remount, and the caravan continued on without further incident.

When they set up camp that morning, Dax went around to all fifty of the beasts, reinforcing their charms. Jarin went with him to assist.

"Did you know you could do that?" Jarin asked. "Control a wild chameli?"

"Not really, no," Dax replied. "It was different. Because it has no ring, there is no command to give. I could sense what it was feeling—anger, fear—so I calmed it."

"Have you ever done that before? Connected to a wild animal, I mean?"

"Once," Dax said with a touch of melancholy. "Many years ago. With a snow cat." He touched the tattoo on his arm, remembering. He said nothing further.

The dunes thinned out and disappeared, replaced by dry scrubland. In the far distance, Jarin could make out the south-ernmost peaks of the Saddle Mountains, lightly tipped with winter snow. It was unseasonably warm and dry, and the brittle switch grass crushed into tinder beneath his feet. The dry conditions proved favorable for the caravan, however. The chameli moved more swiftly in the heat, and the lack of water attracted a potential food source for the beasts; scouts spotted a staggered line of camel deer heading toward the same fresh-water spring they were bound for.

Tevin laid out a plan to catch them. He had the riders arrange most of the chameli in two lines along the game trail, spread apart in the front and close together at the rear, creating a funnel the deer would have to pass through. Once fully camouflaged, the chameli resembled large boulders or thick gray-green bushes. The remaining riders and their beasts hid and waited until the camel deer passed by them, then sprang up and charged them. The deer panicked and stampeded, running straight into the trap waiting for them. Each beast suddenly erupted and snatched a camel deer as it sped past. The riders butchered the remaining meat and packed it on the supply beasts.

When they arrived at the spring, the riders filled the water barrels before releasing the beasts into the spring, where they roiled and churned up sediment before sinking to the bottom of the pool. When the chameli emerged the next morning, they had practically doubled in size and their bellies dragged the ground, like giant slugs. They would not need to eat or drink for the rest of the journey.

The unusual heat continued to hold, and Jarin decided to alter course and travel straight across the central Weslynde valley to Caleddon, since there was no longer any need for a side trip through the geyser basin to warm the animals. They camped at the spring for two more days, estimating that would give the prime minister of Argonne time to reach Clear Lake. Prime Minister Kokheli had planned her arrival to coincide with the spring equinox festival that took place on the lake's north shore, a two days' ride from Caleddon. Jarin wanted to reach the palace shortly after Drissen's army went south to meet the prime minister.

The company spent their time bathing and resting. They made jerky from the camel deer meat. On the morning of the third day, Jarin went down to the water's edge and noticed that the spring was significantly lower than it had been when they'd arrived.

"Do you see the waterline?" he asked Tevin, pointing out the leaves and sticks now stranded in the drying mud. "It's gone down two hands in two days."

"It must be inside the carrier beasts." Tevin chuckled. "The thirsty pigs."

"This spring is too large for that," Jarin replied, not laughing. He stood at the edge of the spring, scratching the scar on his shoulder. It puzzled him. It was a lot of water to go vanishing so quickly. He called Dax over and showed him the water line.

Dax closed his eyes and furrowed his brow. "Water has stopped flowing in," he said, opening his eyes. "In fact, it's draining out. It looks like it's going to be a dry year."

Jarin frowned, unsettled. He shook it off and gave Tevin the command to break camp. They set out under a cloudless sky, sweating under a hot breeze.

CHAPTER 19

Mae Linn was crouched on the deck of the boat, cleaning a fish, when booted footsteps thumped down the pier. A young man was walking her way. He had a Caleddon crest on his jacket, and she nudged Skua, who was rinsing out a bucket next to her. The man bowed when he reached the two of them.

"I have a message for Cerise Aikawa of Cordel," he said, producing an envelope.

"Never heard of him," Mae Linn replied. "Skua, do you know anyone like that?"

"No." Skua shrugged and turned her attention back to her bucket.

The young man was not deterred. "I bring a message from Rence. Perhaps you have heard of him? He told me to go to Clear Lake and find a fishing boat piloted by a crew of clever Cordelian women—a sight not often seen in Weslynde." He held out the envelope. "Will you take this message?"

Skua and Mae Linn glanced sideways at each other.

"I will not tell anyone we have met," the man assured them.

Mae Linn took the envelope, and the young man bowed again and left.

Cerise gathered the crew in the ship's tiny cabin and read the message out loud. "General Drissen has received word that the prime minister of Argonne is crossing Endelas Lake in route to Caleddon. The prime minister is traveling with a large well-armed delegation. She should reach Clear Lake in time for the equinox festival. The general plans to meet her there, then escort her delegation back to Caleddon."

"The festival will set up near where we are camped," Tar said. "That will bring the prime minister to us."

"It will also bring General Drissen and his army," Cerise replied. "I don't want to be here when they arrive." She folded the envelope and put it in her pack. "We sail south today. I want to intercept the prime minister before she gets here and find out what she knows about Jarin's whereabouts. Then we continue south to Isidima."

"Why would she help us?" Janis asked.

"She is under orders to extradite Prince Jarin to Weslynde. I hope to convince her it's in her interest to help me find him first."

The day was unusually warm. The sun beat down on the women as they readied the fishing boat for the trip. Cerise remained covered against the sun's rays and sweated as she pulled ropes and secured cables. She called a break when the heat became unbearable and sought out a nearby tavern. Keeping her face hidden behind a hood and scarf, she found a dark corner and sipped beer with her crew and listened to the local gossip.

"Never seen it so warm," said one fisherman. "There should be snow on the ground."

"My fields are powder dry," complained another. "The ground needs a good soak or it will blow away with the wind."

"The river is high though; it's stretching its banks. There's plenty of water."

"Only because the snow cap is already melting. It'll flood over at this rate. That ain't right."

"I'm thinking to plant now," a round farmer with a red nose said above his mug of beer. "Before it gets any hotter.

"You don't want to be doing that," his neighbor said. "We could still get a frost and you'll lose everything."

Cerise found the conversation strange. Something about the way they spoke seemed ominous. She scratched her shoulder absently.

⚜

They set out early the next morning, letting the lake's current carry them south. They planned to dock at the fishing port of Shandling and from there follow the Wess River on foot as it made its way down to Endelas Lake.

Cerise relaxed for the first time in weeks. She was back on the water, and she was with her beloved crew. Janis stood at the prow, watching for any obstacles under the surface. Tar was busy mending a fishing net that probably didn't need it. Skua and Mae Linn were playing stones in the shade of the sail. Cerise looked up at the helm and pictured Luce piloting the ship, and a sudden pang pierced her gut. Dee was at the wheel, and when she saw Cerise, she let out a joyous whoop. As if in response, one of the many geysers that dotted the lakeshore erupted, sending a large flock of crimson waterbirds aloft. They all cheered. It was good to be on the move.

The air was still for most of the day, and they drifted along slowly, sails limp. Late in the afternoon, however, a dry wind kicked in, stirring up the waves. The sail billowed, and they covered a few extra miles, which lifted their spirits. When evening fell, however, the wind showed no sign of abating, so Cerise had them anchor in a tiny cove off one of the lake's many islands, passing the night out of the choppy waves.

The next morning, the wind remained stiff and waves buffeted the boat incessantly. After a rough day of sailing, they reached the village of Shandling. They moored the old boat and cleaned it thoroughly, then covered it with tarps, knowing that they might not be back for some time. Tar found the port master and paid for storage, and they all headed for an inn he recommended. They ate a simple meal and secured rooms for the night. While they were eating, an old man at the bar recognized Cerise and approached her.

"Begging your pardon." The old man smiled and shuffled his feet, pulling his hat off of his head and clutching it to his chest. "You be that holy woman they been preaching about, ain't you? That Saint Cerise?"

"What can we do for you?" Cerise replied in a firm voice, hoping it would put the man off. The women all exchanged glances, recognizing her mood.

"Oh, I don't need nothing really," the man said. "But the catch has been poor of late, nets empty more often than not, and I thought—"

"I can't help you," Cerise cut him off. "I'm not a magician. I'm only a sailor."

"Maybe a blessing—"

"Here." Cerise pulled out a coin and slapped it on the table. "Have a drink on me." She pulled the hood of her jerkin down over her forehead, ending the conversation. The man took the coin over to the bar, downcast. The women guffawed at how disgruntled she was.

"How do you expect to be queen if you don't like your subjects?" Dee teased her.

"I never said I wanted to be queen." Cerise frowned.

"Then we've traveled a fair distance for nothing," Dee grumbled. The others waited for Cerise's response.

Cerise drained her ale. "I'm going to bed. We leave early." She banged her mug down and left the table.

⚜

"Something's up with her," Tar said in a low voice after Cerise had climbed the stairs to the rooms above them. "She's gotten all fidgety and restless; I've not seen her like this before."

"Let's not leave her by herself," Janis said. "We need to stay ready just in case."

"In case what?" asked Mae Linn.

Janis shrugged. "Just...stay ready." She drained her drink and retired up to their rooms. The dry wind rattled the windows for the rest of the night.

⚜

The women shouldered their packs and set out on foot early, following the Wess River as it tumbled down through wooded hills into Endelas Lake. The water was extremely high and had overflowed its banks in a couple of spots, covering the road. They passed groups of people portaging small boats around rapids that had sprung up. Two hot and windy days later, they arrived at the north shore of Endelas Lake, an angry gray expanse of white-capped water that disappeared over the southern horizon. The hot wind was relentless, and it flung grains of sand into their eyes. White sprays of water pounded against the pilings of the nearby wharf. Cerise rubbed her itching shoulder against a tree and wondered if the wind would ever die down.

They crossed over a large suspension bridge supported by ornately carved posts and entered the small town of Normothe, home to a well-known spa. Normothe boasted a huge field of hot springs and mud pots full of minerals said to slow the effects of aging. The spa itself was a grand building, and Cerise assumed the Argonnian prime minister would lodge there after the long journey across the lake.

A sailor docking his boat told Cerise that the prime minister's barges were moving northward very slowly, hampered by the rough waves. He said it would be at least another day before they arrived at Normothe. Cerise directed her crew to set up camp on the shore to wait, but the winds rattled their tents to the point they threatened to collapse. They broke camp and secured a room at a small rustic inn near the spa.

Cerise was waiting when three massive barges appeared over the horizon the next day. The persistent winds had grown stronger, sending sheets of brown water flecked with foam across the pier and far up the bank. Several locals wrestled their fishing boats across the waves to guide the prime minister's flotilla into port. The barges themselves were in disarray. Shelters that had been erected on their flat surfaces had blown over. A sailor told Cerise that three Argonnians had been swept away and were lost. The barge carrying the giant carrier beasts had capsized, and the chameli now bobbed behind in the water like giant wine barrels, tied to the barge and each other with thick ropes.

Cerise and her crew joined the locals helping the Argonnians disembark. A few were so weakened they needed to be carried ashore. A bevy of Argonnians surrounded the prime minister and lifted her off the barge in her palanquin, much like ants would carry a grasshopper. Cerise pushed forward and raised a welcoming hand but was immediately blocked by the prime minister's guards. Cerise shouted in greeting as her palanquin went by, but the prime minister ignored her. Cerise was sure she had heard her and wondered at the snub. Then she saw

Tregor Anthelia. He recognized her immediately and greeted her warmly. Cerise was greatly surprised, remembering their last heated encounter aboard the *Dreike* so long ago. They had to shout to hear each other over the wind and agreed to talk later.

The prime minister's delegation wound its way up to the main lodge at the spa, and Cerise wondered if she should follow and insist on a meeting. As she was thinking this, an Argonnian woman ran back down the road and handed her a slip of paper. She had been summoned to appear before the prime minister for an interview after sundown.

An interview? Cerise pondered. Who was interviewing whom?

She returned to their inn to escape the wind. The innkeeper was boarding up windows, and the crew hurried to help. Cerise's shoulder was aching, and it hurt to hold slats of wood over her head while Skua pounded nails into place. *It must be a pinched muscle*, she thought. She tried stretching and rotating her arm, but the pain persisted, and so she sought out Janis and asked her to realign it. She lay down on one of the small beds in their room, and Janis pushed down on her shoulder with her palm a couple of times. Cerise felt a slight pop, and the pain eased.

"Your shoulder feels hot," Janis said. "I can feel it through your tunic. Do you want me to take a look?" She started to pull up the fabric.

"Not now," Cerise said. "It feels better." She remembered the last time her shoulder had burned this way; it had been the day she'd descended into Weslynde to meet her father for the first time, the day of the freakish hailstorm. Was the sigil in her back making her bones sensitive to changes in the weather? Min had often complained of that.

⚜

When dusk fell, Cerise headed over to the lodge, taking Tar and Janis with her. The wind had died down somewhat but was still making its presence known. The staff ushered them into the spa's great room, a large round gathering place made of rough-hewn logs stacked three stories high. Huge beams formed a geometric pattern across the ceiling. The staff took their weapons but placed them where they could be easily retrieved.

Several Argonnians were present, but no one greeted them. The spa staff were pouring pitchers of wine into glasses, so Cerise took one and surveyed the room. There was a large stone fire pit in the center of the room, but it was dark, and the chimney hole in the top of the ceiling had been closed against the wind. Chairs had been set up in a circle at the far side of the room, and Cerise had her first good look at Tharisa Kokheli. The prime minister glowered imperiously from her wheeled chair placed on a platform higher than the rest of the room. She was having a discussion with a white-haired man in an embroidered robe. Cerise thought he was a Weslynder but could only see him from behind.

Tregor Anthelia broke away from the group and came over to greet her.

"Cerise Aikawa." He bowed slightly. "Or should I call you Sabrin? It is a pleasure to see the white angel again; I only wish it were under different circumstances. We mourn the loss of your father, the king."

"Hello, Grandfather," Cerise replied, startled by his candid acknowledgment of who she was. *Everyone in the room must know*, she realized.

"Grandfather! I like the sound of that." Tregor flashed his charming smile. "Allow me to make amends for the way I treated you the last time we met. I very much hope to spend more time with you on this journey." He raised his glass in a toast, and Cerise clinked her glass with his.

"Your apology is unnecessary. I have a knack upsetting people. Tell me, Tregor. What news of my brother?"

"Your brother?" Tregor sounded puzzled.

"The prince. Your grandson."

It appeared she'd caught Tregor off guard, but he quickly recovered. "Prince Jarin! Your brother, of course. Sadly, no one has heard anything since he disappeared from Caleddon. I fear he may be dead, which would be a crushing blow for the commonwealth. I wish I had better news. For all of us."

Cerise could tell he knew more than he was saying. "I've heard he is alive and is currently in Argonne. I'm on my way there to find him."

"If Jarin were in Argonne, I'm sure he would have come to me by now for help. We were very close, he and I. I miss him." Tregor paused and tilted his head. "Cerise. If you insist on going to Argonne, then allow me to provide you with any resources you need. My villa is at your disposal, and I have a staff there willing to help."

"Thank you," Cerise replied, softening a little. "I hope to spend more time with you as well."

Any further conversation was interrupted by Tharisa Kokheli rapping her ebony cane sharply on the floor. The room quieted.

"The interview will start now," she croaked, turning her gaze on Cerise. "Young Sabrin né Franklin." She raised a bony hand and waved her over. "Come here and let me look closely at you."

The white-haired man who had been conversing with the prime minister turned around, and Cerise caught her breath. It was Gerard Mort! What in the name of the gods was he doing here, and how had he gotten here so quickly? She masked her surprise and stepped up to the front of the platform.

"Prime Minister." She nodded her head respectfully. "House Mage." She gave him a questioning glance.

"Come closer. Here where I can reach you." The prime minister extended a wrinkled claw and pushed Cerise's chin up with her fingernail. She squinted her eyes to get a better look. "Yes, I see it now. You were right, Tregor—underneath that ghastly makeup, she does look like her mother." She settled back in her chair. "Sit down, everyone. Sabrin, sit there, across from me." She pointed at an empty chair. The room settled, and Cerise took the chair.

"We have much to discuss. First, let me say how much I appreciate General Drissen's thoughtfulness. He has sent his most powerful mage and his mightiest warrior here to escort us to Caleddon." She glared at Gerard Mort and Cerise, then added, "In case we get lost on the way." There were a few sardonic chuckles when she said this. "All we're missing now is Archbishop Mellon to guide us forward with a prayer."

Her sarcasm was unmistakable, and Cerise noticed the tendons on Gerard Mort's neck straining. Clearly the mage was not welcome or expected. Was he here for her or for the prime minister?

There was a sudden burst of wind, and the windows all around the great room rattled in their frames.

The prime minister listened to the wind for a moment and then leaned forward. "Sabrin. What do you think is causing this storm?"

"I'm sorry, I'm not sure what you mean." She was surprised by the question. What did that have to do with anything? She quickly glanced over at the mage, but Gerard Mort's eyes were locked on the prime minister.

"This wind. I've never seen anything like it. I lost three of my people because of it. What do you think is causing it?"

"I have no idea," Cerise said, rotating her shoulder to ease a sudden discomfort. "Why are you asking me—"

"There was another storm," the prime minister interjected.

"Twenty years ago. A sudden unexpected snowstorm in Weslynde. People say buildings collapsed. Animals froze."

"A storm? Twenty years ago?" Cerise tried to understand where this was going.

"It stopped as quickly as it started. It happened the very day your brother was born."

"My brother?"

"Prince Jarin. Your twin."

Cerise went still. The threat now was clear.

Tharisa Kokheli went on, "There was yet a different storm. Do you remember, Sabrin? It was the day you crossed the mountains from Cordel and entered Weslynde for the first time."

"A hailstorm, a bad one. I remember." Her shoulder throbbed.

"A hailstorm. Crops were lost. Homes destroyed. Children died in that storm, Sabrin." Silence filled the room. "That storm, too, ended as quickly as it came. It ended when Jarin disappeared. Some say he died in that storm and that is what ended it." She paused and let her eyes scan everyone in the room, lightly drumming her fingers on the arm of her chair. "Some say because he died that day, the curse of the twins was averted. But he didn't die—in fact, he is nearby. Do you know how I know?"

Cerise puzzled this over for a second, then a horrible realization came over her. "Because of this storm." A huge gust of wind shook the building.

"Yes, Sabrin," the prime minister said. "Because of this storm. This storm, which has been created by you and your brother. And the only way to stop it is for one of you to die."

Cerise instinctively reached back for her sword, which was not there. As she did so, a jolt of pain shot through her back, and she doubled over, holding her arm. Janis reached over to steady her, but Cerise stood up and shook her off, mastering her pain. She pushed her shoulders back and walked up to the prime minister's platform and looked her directly in the eyes. The prime minister sat back in her chair, and her guards moved in to protect her. Tharisa waved them back.

"What do you intend to do with me?" Cerise asked.

"Me?" Tharisa Kokheli raised an eyebrow. "It is not up to me to choose which of you lives or dies. But one of you must. Tell me, young Sabrin, what do *you* intend to do? How are you going to save the people of Weslynde, keep this province from sinking into the ocean or burning up in flames? How are you going to stop this storm? Who lives and who dies, Sabrin? We can end this today."

At those words, the room devolved into chaos. Several Argonnians ran for their weapons and blocked the doors, shouting that Cerise should not be allowed to leave, that the curse of the twins must be ended here and now. Janis and Tar took up fighting stances around Cerise. They were weaponless, and they were only three facing at least twenty Argonnians now armed and closing in.

Cerise picked up her chair and was preparing to use it as a weapon when a loud cracking noise reverberated through the air and the stone hearth burst apart, sending clouds of gray ash throughout the room, obscuring everything. The three women rushed toward the door in the confusion, grabbing their weapons as they went. Tar slammed the man guarding the door to the floor, and they ran out into the night.

"Let her go. Let her go!" Tharisa Kokheli's voice boomed across the room, surprisingly loud and strong for a woman so frail looking. She banged her cane against the floor, and the noise in the room settled along with the clouds of ash.

Gerard Mort sussed Cerise's sky metal, and it flared up like a match in his mind. She was heading for the nearby inn. He was starting to slip out after her when something new entered his consciousness: a wave of energy emanating from her sigil, an angry orange thread he could see in his mind. It spooled out of Cerise and disappeared somewhere over the horizon. He closed his eyes and followed the thread. It stretched for miles and miles until it finally came back to earth, ending in another ring of sky metal. *By the gods*, he thought, *it's Jarin!* The energy beam connecting the two sigils crackled in his mind, sending off shards of dissonance into the atmosphere, stirring up the wind above them. In shock, he realized that the proximity of the twins' sigils to one another was increasing the severity of the storm.

His concentration was broken by Tharisa Kokheli's continued banging of her cane on the floor. She was insisting, using her considerable power over the group, that Sabrin be given time to solve the problem herself. He was the only one who could see, however, that she gave a subtle hand signal to one of the guards near the door, who nodded and slipped outside.

⚜

As soon as they reached the inn, Cerise gathered the women together.

"What happened back there?" Tar asked. "The fire pit exploded. How?"

"The mage saved us, I think," Cerise replied, still a little breathless. "So that we could escape. Now listen. The Argonnians think the curse of the twins has brought about this storm. The people here will kill me now to try to stop it. We can't stay here. The only thing we can do now is find Jarin and resolve this somehow."

"Resolve this how?" Tar asked. "Kill Jarin?"

Cerise frowned, looking out the window to see if they had been followed. "I don't know. I mean, what if the curse is true? Pack your things; we leave now."

"Where are we going?" Dee asked.

"Isidima," Cerise replied.

There was a sudden sharp knock on the door, and everyone pulled out their knives.

"Open it," Cerise ordered. "We stand and fight."

Skua opened the door quickly and stood behind it. Gerard Mort filled the doorframe, robe billowing. Leaves blew past him into the room and the candles sputtered.

"Let me in," the mage demanded.

"Enter," Cerise said. "You saved us." The women sheathed their knives and made space for the mage. "What do you want, Mort? We haven't much time."

"You are in danger. The prime minister intends to kill you to stop the storm."

"In that we agree," Cerise said.

"I know where Jarin is, and there is a way to end this storm."

"How?" Cerise asked in surprise. "Tell us."

"Does your shoulder hurt?" Gerard Mort asked.

Cerise touched her arm, puzzled by the change of subject. "Yes. It burns."

"It burns because your sigil feels your brother's presence. Close your eyes."

Cerise frowned, reluctant to take her eyes off the mage.

"Stop wasting time. Close your eyes. Now!"

Startled into compliance, she closed her eyes.

"Focus on your sigil," Gerard Mort said. "Find the pain. Tell me where the pain is coming from."

Cerise focused on her shoulder. It throbbed with bursts of pain that matched her heartbeat. It was as if she were being poked by something sharp. She opened her eyes and turned around to see who was jabbing her. There was nothing, only the watchful faces of her crew. Now that she had turned, the pain was in front of her.

"It's coming from in there." She pointed to the door of the small back room.

Skua rushed through the door and returned. "There is nothing there," she said.

Cerise entered the room, followed by the mage. The pain was still in front of her. She went to the small window, which was boarded up against the storm. "It's outside. The thing that is driving the pain. What is it? What am I feeling?" she asked the mage.

"You feel your brother," Gerard Mort said. "Your sigils are at war with each other, like two magnets turned the wrong way. The closer together they are, the harder the resistance. It's causing this storm."

"How do we stop it?"

"The only way to stop it is to remove the sigil from your body."

"Remove the sigil?" Cerise asked. "This will stop if I remove the sigil?"

"Removing it will render its power inert," the mage said.

"Then take it out. Now." Cerise started to pull off her jerkin.

"I can't, not without killing you. I didn't embed the sigil in your shoulder, so I don't have the power to remove it. Only the mage who placed it in you can reverse the charm and extract the metal from your bones."

"Try anyway," ordered Cerise. She flung her jerkin on the bed and turned her back to Gerard Mort. The sigil's scrollwork glowed green-gold on her skin, no longer hidden by the fish-shaped tattoo.

"Cerise, I can't."

"Do it!"

Gerard Mort nodded. He closed his eyes and raised his hand, palm forward, over Cerise's back. He began chanting under his breath. His brow furrowed, and beads of sweat sprang up on his forehead. His arm began to shake. The runes on the sigil shone brighter and brighter until a blinding spark burst from Cerise's shoulder and encircled Gerard's hand, causing him to jerk back in pain. Cerise cried out and fell to her knees.

"I can't remove it." Gerard Mort panted. "Only the mage who embedded it can do that."

Cerise pulled herself up and put her jerkin back on. "Who did this to me? Who embedded the sigil?"

"I don't know." Gerard Mort rubbed his hand. "A powerful mage. The magic in the charm is very strong, stronger than any I have encountered."

Cerise slammed her fist against the wall in frustration. Then she had a thought. "You embedded Jarin's sigil when he was born, yes?" she asked. "Can you take his sigil out? Can you remove it?"

"I have that power, yes."

"Then that's our plan. You will come with us to find Jarin, and you will remove his sigil."

"But how are we going to find him?" Dee asked. "He could be anywhere."

"He's out there. That way." Cerise pointed through the back wall. "I can feel him now." She picked up her pack and slung it over her shoulder. "Are you with us?" she asked the mage.

"I am," Gerard Mort replied. "We need to leave now."

Cerise grabbed the door handle, but Gerard Mort put his hand against it.

"Someone is out there!" he hissed. He pressed his forehead against the door and closed his eyes. "In the trees beyond the path, there is a man with a crossbow. Waiting for you."

"We can go out the back window," Cerise said. "Can you stop him?"

"I can disable his weapon," Gerard Mort said.

"Wait till everyone's out, then do it. I will stand with you."

Tar took down the boards covering the back window, and the women climbed out, disappearing into the woodlands behind the inn. Cerise and Gerard Mort climbed out after and crept around the corner of the inn. An Argonnian archer was crouched behind a tree stump with a crossbow cradled on his lap, watching the door of their room. Gerard Mort clenched his fist, depressing the trigger on the archer's crossbow, sending the metal bolt into the stump in front of the man, causing him to jump back in surprise. Like a cat, Cerise sprang forward and kicked his head with her heel. He fell and did not move again.

"More are coming," Gerard Mort whispered. They ghosted into the woods.

CHAPTER 20

J arin huddled in the shadow of an old barn, gazing across
the patchwork of Weslynde valley. The vines in the fields
were withered and limp, baked by the sun. Normally at
this time of year, the dark soil should be blushing green with
new growth. Instead, everything was gray-brown and lifeless.
Dust devils swirled across the stubble of last year's crops. In the
distance, the city of Caleddon still shone bright, its white buildings and terracotta roofs climbing up the gentle slopes around
the palace. The morning sun glinted off its golden dome. A
shimmering mirage of the city hung above it in midair.

The wind had stopped during the night, but its aftereffects
could be seen everywhere. North of the city, a fire was burning,
black smoke mushrooming into the sky. In the near distance,
Jarin made out a roof torn open, a silo flattened. South of the
city, the Wess River had overflowed its banks, and a number of
vineyards were now beneath a muddy lake. In the far distance,
the mountains were capped with gray rock instead of snow.
Jarin was sobered. The Weslynde he knew was a paradise, a
rich valley full of fruit trees and fertile vineyards, crystal lakes
and shooting geysers. This Weslynde was burnt and lifeless.

Jarin licked his chapped lips and rubbed his back against

the side of the barn, scraping the surface of the sigil that protruded from his shoulder. It was tingly and hot. He wiped the dust away from the corners of his mouth and spoke to Dax and Tevin, who stood with him in the shade.

"We can follow that streambed that curves in close to the palace wall and cross there," he said, pointing out their route. "If we move out at dusk, we should make it to the palace walls at least two hours before dawn."

"What's on the other side of that wall?" Tevin asked.

"Training grounds. It's flat inside and big enough to accommodate the carrier beasts. Once we're over the wall, we can position ourselves around the perimeter of the palace and lock the gates from the inside. There are three gates—the east gate you can see. There is one like it on the west side, and the main gate looks south and faces the river."

"Won't the gates be guarded?"

"They will, but they will not be expecting an attack from inside the walls. Drissen's army should have left for Clear Lake by now to meet the Argonnian prime minister. Once we are over the wall and inside, we can send a dozen beasts and riders to each gate. That should easily overwhelm any guards who stayed behind."

"That flood south of the city may have changed their plans to meet the prime minister," Dax pointed out.

"That should work to our advantage as well. Anyone not at Clear Lake will be helping with the disaster. The palace will be empty, and there will never be a better time. We get inside, barricade the gates, and secure the palace. And remember, we don't kill anyone. They are not the enemy. Our goal is to capture General Drissen, Gerard Mort, and my sister, Sabrin."

"A decorated general, a powerful magician, and a legendary hero," Dax said dryly. "That should be easy enough. Those three are dangerous, Jarin."

"We're dangerous too," Jarin replied. He wished he felt as confident as he sounded.

⚜

Dax followed Jarin back down the hill to the riders' encampment at the bottom of a shallow gully. The resistance fighters were huddled in the shade, and the camouflaged beasts resembled boulders scattered along the dry streambed. Jarin suddenly cried out in pain and twisted around, scrabbling at his shoulder.

Dax steadied him. "Jarin, what is it?"

"It's my scar. Where they tried to take the sigil out. It's like someone is stabbing me."

"Let me look."

Jarin pulled off his vest, and Dax examined the scar. The skin was puckered and lumpy but well healed. The sigil, however, was glowing a bright green-gold. Dax touched it, and a bolt of static energy stung his hand.

"What was that?" Jarin asked.

"I don't know." Dax shook his fingers. "Your sigil. It's glowing like it did the day we met. Hold still." He closed his eyes and hovered his palm over Jarin's shoulder. The sigil blazed in his mind, a churning ring of molten metal. It resisted his intrusion, but he continued to suss it, working his way around the sharp edges of its resistance. He sensed a filament of energy pulsing out of Jarin, popping and twisting, rippling in the air. It became a thread of light in his mind, and he was able to follow it as it stretched away across the valley, leading him toward something that became brighter and brighter the closer he got to it. His body tingled with a strong sensory memory. He gasped and opened his eyes in surprise.

"What is it?" Jarin asked. "What did you feel?"

"Sabrin," Dax whispered.

"Sabrin? What do you mean?"

"I can feel her sigil. It's connected to yours. I know where she is."

"The sigils are connected?"

"They don't want to be. They are fighting each other. I can't explain it."

Dax closed his eyes and followed the thread once more. He sensed bolts of discordant energy blasting up into the sky and down into the earth along its path, violent and unstable. "She's on the move. In this direction."

"How far away is she? Can you tell?" Jarin asked.

"Two days, maybe...she is south of Caleddon."

"Then we should be inside the palace before she gets here," Jarin said. "We go tonight. Straight across the valley."

"Are you fit to travel?" Tevin asked. "You are hurt."

"I'm fine. Now that I grasp what it is that I'm feeling."

Jarin hunkered down with the fighters and tried to nap as best as he could through the hottest part of the day, ignoring the ache on his shoulder. At dusk, Tevin had the fighters rouse the beasts, and they headed out in a long line, two beasts wide, straight across the valley, breaking through fences and trampling through the vineyards that lay between them and the palace.

A farmer appeared on his porch as the long line of chameli crashed through his squash field. Jarin signaled to Tevin as the farmer ran from his house to his horse, which was still harnessed to a buggy. The horse was lean and could clearly outrun a chameli.

"No one dies," Jarin shouted as a rider steered his beast out of the line to engage the farmer. The carrier beast intercepted the farmer's buggy before it reached the gate to the road. Jarin cringed as the carrier beast struck suddenly, taking off the horse's head in a single bite. The stunned farmer jumped off the buggy, falling backward on the ground. The Argonnian rider threw a sack of coin down to him.

"That's not how I would have played that," Jarin said to Tevin as the shocked farmer scrambled back inside his house.

"He is still alive." Tevin grinned. "As you commanded."

"And free to run to his neighbors for help. We need to move faster."

They made their way through the rest of the night unchallenged. The moon had set by the time they reached the palace walls, and the beasts shifted their color to a dark gray that matched their surroundings. They stopped at the edge of the tree line, looking for sentries. A broad strip of grassy turf lay between them and the wall. Two torches lit the watchtowers on the palace rampart on an otherwise dark edifice.

"They will have scouts in the woods," Jarin whispered. "I'm surprised we haven't seen any." As if on cue, a man on a scout beast burst from cover near them and went hurtling across the open field toward the palace.

"Dax!" Jarin hissed. "Stop him."

Dax reached out his arm, and the scout beast skidded to a halt halfway across the open space, practically throwing off its rider. Dax pulled his arm back to his chest, and the scout beast darted directly to where Jarin and Dax were hiding. The rider realized his peril and managed to roll off right as the beast stopped in front of Dax. Tevin grabbed the scout beast's rider and pulled him into the trees, clapping his hand over his mouth. Jarin looked up at the wall anxiously, but there was no movement. He realized he had been holding his breath. He exhaled and noticed the scout beast was still focused on Dax, waiting for a new command.

"Dax, do you remember where the general's quarters are?"

"That window up there, near the top." Dax pointed.

"I have an idea."

A few minutes later, Dax darted across the opening atop the scout beast, disappearing up and over the wall.

There was still no movement on the palace rampart. Jarin decided he could wait no longer and gave Tevin the signal. The fifty great chameli burst out of the tree line, snapping branches and scattering dried leaves. They lumbered forward in a wide line across the grassy strip of land toward the wall. They were halfway across when a cry went up from the rampart and two sentries pointed down at them. The beasts reached the wall before the sentries could react and started climbing, footpads adhering to the smooth stone. The sentries managed to push a small section of metal barrier into place before the beasts reached the top, creating an overhang with metal spikes pointing downward. Twenty such barriers would have been needed to cover that portion of the wall, and the beasts easily made it over the top.

More sentries raced in from other sections of the ramparts, and a pair of archers found their mark, piercing the hides of two beasts. One fell from the wall. The other, angered by the pain, began attacking anything that got close to it. Its rider was able to calm it while another pulled the arrow from its flank.

The odds were overwhelmingly in Jarin's favor, and, in a short time, a dozen sentries were corralled in a corner of the training grounds inside the wall. Jarin jumped off his beast to face them.

"Stand down. I am Jarin né Franklin, prince of Weslynde and your lord. Drop your weapons and stand down."

All but one sentry dropped their weapons, and the remaining sentry was quickly subdued. Jarin gave instructions to Tevin, who dispatched his riders to secure the three city gates. He had successfully made it inside the palace walls.

⚜

The scout beast carried Dax straight up the palace wall and over the tile roof that led to the general's quarters. The beast slithered silently onto the balcony outside the general's bedchamber. Dax pulled on his concealment cloak, put his hands against the outside wall, and closed his eyes. He sensed one person inside, lying in the bed. There were several weapons in the room, but none near the bed. The balcony door was propped open. *A security misstep*, he thought. He sussed the interior door that led to the hallway; it was locked, but someone with a key could enter. It did have a crossbar that would prevent entry if lowered. He sensed two people standing outside the door with metal on their bodies: most likely guards with swords. He wrapped his cloak around him and silently slipped through the balcony door.

The commotion on the other side of the palace had not reached the general's ears, and he was snoring softly. Dax crept past the head of the bed and sank into a corner. Then he clenched his fist, and the crossbar on the room's door dropped into place with a metallic clang. The general jumped out of bed and scrambled for his sword. Dax stepped up behind him, put his arm around his neck, and clapped his hand over his mouth.

"I mean you no harm," he whispered. "I bring a message from Prince Jarin."

The guards banged on the door.

"Tell the guards you are fine."

General Drissen tried to jerk free, but Dax held him tight, pressing the point of his knife against the general's back. A key rattled in the lock, and the door banged against the crossbar.

"General!" shouted the guard. "Are you alright?"

"Tell them you are fine," hissed Dax, taking his hand away from the general's mouth.

"I am fine; I just need a moment," shouted the general. "Stand down."

The banging stopped.

"I have done what you asked," the general muttered. "Show yourself."

Dax released his neck hold and stepped back. The general whipped around to face him.

"Who are you?" General Drissen asked, rubbing his neck. "How did you get in here?"

"I am Dax. Prince Jarin has taken control of the palace. You are not his prisoner if you do exactly what I say. You must order palace security to stand down immediately to prevent bloodshed."

"Where is Jarin?" Drissen demanded.

"He is...busy...securing the palace."

The cries and shouting in the courtyard below were now unmistakable. Dax led the general to the window. A dozen carrier beasts had his sentries pinned against the west gate, hands in the air.

"All I see are Argonnian invaders," the general grumbled.

"They are Jarin's fighters. Tell the guards to stand down. Time is of the essence so that no one dies," Dax warned.

General Drissen put his hand on the crossbar. Dax readied himself to fight. He saw the general tense his shoulders then relax.

"You have the upper hand...for now." The general faced the door and shouted, "I am opening the door. Sheathe your weapons and stand back."

He lifted the crossbar and opened the door. His two guards were poised for action, but their swords were sheathed. When they saw Dax standing behind the general, they went for their swords. The general held up his hand and stopped them.

"Hold. Prince Jarin has taken control of the palace. Tell everyone that the prince is in charge. Bloodshed is to be avoided at all costs. I will join you shortly."

"But, General," one guard cried.

"Go now! That is an order."

The guards saluted and ran down the hall.

Dax sheathed his knife. "Get dressed."

General Drissen lit a candle and appraised Dax in its light. "You wear a concealment cloak. Two went missing the day Jarin disappeared; I assume that is one of them." He dressed quickly. "And that trick with the crossbar...you're a magician, aren't you? A powerful one."

Dax said nothing.

The general pulled on his boots. "Take me to Jarin."

"I am here." Jarin stood in the open doorway with an Argonnian fighter, weapons drawn.

General Drissen didn't recognize Jarin at first: the way he was standing, feet apart, tall and proud, his dark skin lean with muscle, his hair tied back and braided with beads in the Argonnian style. The woman next to him was even taller and stronger looking, every inch a warrior. He would have to play this carefully.

"My boy," the general said. "I thought you were dead, despite all the rumors otherwise."

Jarin pushed his way into the room, forcing the general to step back.

"Put down your weapons," the general said. "I won't fight you."

Jarin lowered his staff, and the woman sheathed her sword.

"Where is the house mage?" Jarin demanded. "Where is my sister?

"They are gone from the city." General Drissen replied. "What is it you want?"

"To secure the palace and make sure no one else gets hurt."

"And then what?"

"I intend to make things right," Jarin said simply.

"By leading an Argonnian revolt against Weslynde?"

"No! By preventing one. Argonne is not responsible for my father's—for the king's death...but someone is. Someone is trying to sow dissent and destroy the commonwealth. I won't allow that."

"The king was murdered by an Argonnian, Jarin. There were witnesses."

"That makes no sense," Jarin said. "Argonne has nothing to gain here. Someone else is behind this, and I need to stop it." He paused, then added in a softer voice, "And I need your help to do it."

Drissen was caught off guard by Jarin's openness and sincerity. The passionate man standing in front of him was not the drunken youth who used to terrorize the palace staff. Jarin believed what he was saying. "Your man Dax here claims I am not your prisoner. Is that true?"

"You are not my prisoner," Jarin said. "You are the regent of Weslynde. And as regent, your role is to protect the commonwealth until the sovereign is crowned, a commonwealth that includes the citizens of Argonne. Will you execute that charge?"

Drissen smiled grimly. "Let's start with securing the palace. We need to show ourselves together, quickly."

CHAPTER 21

The midnight moon backlit the chaotic scene in front of Cerise. The wind was howling stronger than before, and the trees above her thrashed furiously. Broken branches littered the ground. The river had spilled out of its banks and churned furiously around the anchor posts supporting the suspension bridge they needed to cross. It wouldn't be long before the flood took the whole thing into Endelas Lake.

She crouched with her crew against a building out of the wind. "We have to cross the bridge now." Cerise had to shout to be heard over the roar of the wind. "Run. Go. In single file."

Skua went first, followed by Dee, Tar, and Mae Linn. They splashed through the water that was already streaming across the road and onto the wooden ramp leading up to the suspension bridge. Mae Linn slipped on the wet wood, but Tar grabbed her and pulled her upright and onto the bridge. The bridge itself dipped down in the middle, and for several heartbeats the women disappeared from view. At last Cerise saw them running back up the slope on the far side of the bridge.

"Alright, they're across. Let's go," Cerise yelled.

Janis went first, followed closely by Cerise, and finally Gerard Mort.

The river was rising fast, and water now poured across the center of the bridge where it dipped down. They grabbed the rope railings and waded into the torrent. Cerise looked behind her and saw that Gerard Mort had turned back the way they had come.

"What are you doing?" Cerise screamed. "We have to cross!"

"Do you intend to walk all the way to Caleddon?" he yelled back, holding on to one of the bridge supports.

Cerise pushed Janis forward and said, "Go! We will meet you on the other side." She started back after him. She needed the mage alive once they found Jarin.

When Gerard Mort reached the high point on the bridge, he raised his hand in the air and shouted some words that were lost in the wind. A few moments later, out of the gloom, one of the prime minister's carrier beasts, still wearing its passenger platform, came lumbering toward them.

Cerise's eyes grew wide in alarm. "It's too big!" she yelled. "The bridge won't hold it." Already one of the huge ropes suspending the bridge over the water was unraveling and the bridge was starting to list.

"Go!" Gerard Mort shouted, running back down the bridge. "It will follow us."

They hung onto the ropes and pulled themselves through the water that had breached the surface of the bridge. When they reached the far side, they scrambled up the bank and joined the other women away from the river. Cerise turned in time to see the carrier beast climb onto the bridge. The weakened ropes strained under its weight, but it looked as if they would hold. They cheered it on. It was almost across when an uprooted tree spinning down the river slammed into the bridge like a battering ram. The suspension ropes holding up the bridge snapped and fell, wrapping themselves around the chameli. Then the entire bridge span twisted upside down and sank, taking the beast with it. The support posts came unmoored and were pulled in after. The remaining bits of wreckage sank into the river and disappeared.

"Let's find a place out of this wind." Cerise cursed bitterly, regretting the unnecessary loss of the huge animal. She abandoned the idea of following the road and set out through the woods, looking for any shelter she could find. The others shouldered their packs and followed.

⚜

The women and the mage spent the rest of the night huddled in a ditch. Shortly before dawn, the wind abated and everything was still. Not a bird chirped; not a leaf rustled. The sun rose on a parched landscape. Gerard Mort put his ear to the ground.

"Is it over?" Cerise asked him.

"No," he muttered. "It's changing into something else." The thread of energy leading them toward Jarin was more intense now, and the dissonant waves spitting from it disappeared into the ground. A slight tremor rumbled in the earth deep, deep below them. "The prince is on the move again. He is heading to Caleddon."

"We are circling around each other."

"If he continues on this path, he will reach Caleddon tomorrow. It will take us at least four days to travel around Clear Lake on foot. Jarin will be safely locked inside the palace when we arrive." What would they find once they got there?

"We have no other options, magician. We have to get to him and stop this madness, no matter how long it takes." She dusted herself off. "We move now."

⚜

Cerise found a trail that took them north through the

woods. They came upon a clearing, and right as they stepped out of the brush and into the sun, they were startled by a great crashing in the woods behind them. Branches cracked and shrubs exploded, and a giant carrier beast burst into the clearing, its passenger platform still lashed to its back, trailing a length of rope with bits of bridge attached.

"It survived!" Cerise shouted, greatly relieved.

Gerard Mort grabbed the beast's snout ring and settled it to the ground, its body sloshing like a water bag. The women swarmed over the chameli and set about performing repairs to the platform, cutting away the bridge remnants and taking inventory of supplies. A sack of potatoes was still lashed to the platform, and, given their limited food supply, this was a welcome find. Skua and Mae Linn took blankets from their packs and rigged up a canopy over the passenger platform for shade. Rejuvenated, they set out again, urging the beast forward at a rapid clip. Cerise felt better about their prospects of reaching Jarin before it was too late.

They reached the southern shore of Clear Lake midday. Cerise had been hoping to cross the lake on the fishing boat they had stored at Shandling, but there was not a breath of wind and sails were useless. They were forced instead to follow the winding supply road that ringed the lake.

The lake was swollen with the unseasonable snowmelt that had poured out of the distant mountains. Its waters now covered parts of the supply road and had swallowed an entire fishing village. They skirted around the inundated spots in the road, navigating toppled trees and even some buildings flattened by the wind. Late in the day, they came upon a group of villagers trying to free a family from a collapsed house. Cerise told the mage to stop the beast.

"We don't have time," Gerard Mort hissed. "The very ground beneath our feet is beginning to break apart. Can't you feel it?"

"We have to do something," Cerise replied, swinging down from the platform and leaping off the still-moving chameli. Her crew jumped down after her and began helping the villagers pull boards off the rubble.

"We will regret this delay," Gerard Mort grumbled as he directed the carrier beast to follow them.

The women tied ropes to the rafters of the collapsed house and tied the other ends to the carrier beast and were able to pull the collapsed roof off the house. They found three people alive underneath. As they remounted, Cerise promised the villagers she would return and help them rebuild.

They camped overnight beside the lake. When they rose the next morning, they discovered the lake's flood waters had rapidly receded, so much so that there was now exposed muddy lake bed. They mounted up and continued on until they came to a small grotto in a grove of trees. It was clearly a hot spring used by the locals and included a rock-rimmed pool and a shelter made of stone. Several wooden benches ringed the pool. However, where steaming hot spring water should have been bubbling out of the grotto's entrance into the pool, there was only a thin column of steam rising from the cave's entrance. The pool itself was bone dry.

Gerard Mort stopped the chameli and slid down off its side. He got down on one knee and put his hand on the ground. Cerise jumped down and joined him.

"What is it?"

"The spring is dry, and that bothers me," Gerard Mort said. "Stay clear of the crusty ground around the pool."

"Why?"

"Be quiet." He closed his eyes and placed his palm against the ground for several minutes. Then he stood and brushed off his hands. "Where is Jarin now?" he asked her. "Can you tell?"

Cerise closed her eyes and focused; needles prickled her

back. "Caleddon," she said, pointing north. "He's inside the palace."

"Cerise, there is a fault line in the earth below us, deep underground, which travels the same direction you are pointing."

"A fault line? What is that?" She rotated her shoulder to ease it.

"A crack in the rock below us," he said. "The rock that protects Weslynde from the magma underneath."

"Magma?"

"Lava, molten rock. Have you learned nothing of this? Don't you wonder why there are geysers everywhere? Weslynde sits on top of a rock that forms a lid that covers a gigantic pot full of molten lava, and the lid has a crack in it. If this crack starts to widen, all that molten lava will spill out of the pot and Weslynde will be consumed by fire."

Cerise was so astonished she almost laughed. "Weslynde sits over a pot of lava? What you say is hard to believe."

"Yet it is true." Gerard Mort grew red in the face. "Every magician's apprentice knows this. Are you through asking questions?"

"Only one more," Cerise said. "What do we do about it?"

"Cerise. You are causing this fault line, this crack, to grow. You and your brother. I can feel it. Just like you caused the flood and the wind. The imbalance I feel emanating off your sigils grows stronger by the minute. We need to break the connection between the two of you. I fear we may not reach Jarin in time, and there is only one other option, as you know."

"Touch her and you die," Tar growled. She had come up behind them as they talked. Her hand gripped her knife.

"You can't take all of us out with your magic," Janis shouted down from above. The crew of the *Flying Fish* stood atop the carrier beast, weapons out, ready to jump.

Gerard Mort held out his hands palms up. "I need Cerise to

live. If I wanted her dead, it would have happened before now. Stop this nonsense and sheathe your swords."

No one moved. Tar tightened her grip on her knife.

Gerard Mort sighed and clenched his fist. The carrier beast came alive and twisted around violently. The women staggered and fell off its back. The beast rounded on them and roared in their faces. They flattened themselves on the ground

"Tell them to stand down," Gerard Mort ordered Cerise calmly.

"Stand down," Cerise shouted. The beast stepped back, and the women picked themselves up and sheathed their swords. The chameli settled on the ground. Cerise realized the mage had the ability to overpower them all with a word. She had no choice but to trust him. "This crack. Can you stop it from breaking open?"

"No, not without breaking the connection. But I can cool it down, buy us some time maybe. But not for long. We must reach Jarin."

Cerise nodded, not really understanding what he meant by cool it down. "We leave now. Everyone aboard." She started to climb up the beast and was suddenly seized by a sharp burst of pain, as if someone had touched her back with a hot coal. She cried out and clapped her hand over her shoulder, trying to reach the painful spot on her back. A surge of energy leaped out of her and radiated northward.

"The prince!" the mage cried. "He's moving. Fast."

"He's coming here!" Cerise gasped. As she spoke, the ground underneath them trembled, and a jet of superheated steam shot out of the grotto's cave entrance and whistled into the sky.

CHAPTER 22

J arin leaned out over the palace rampart. There was not a
breath of wind, and the air smelled like rusty nails. The
river's flood waters had receded during the night, and the
vineyards south of the city were now a sticky soup of mud and
debris. A group of people in the distance were pulling a
trapped oxyn out of the mire. Not a speck of snow remained on
the mountains. Jarin could not remember a time when he
hadn't seen snow there. Everything was parched and dusty.

A crowd of people stood below him in the baking sun,
waiting for the locked gates to open. A cluster of novices
wearing red robes chanted protests. One held a sign that read
'Save Us, Saint Cerise.' Jarin crossed farther along the wall to
check out the other side of the city. The view there was not any
better. The public baths, normally crowded this time of day,
were empty of both people and water. The hot spring that fed
them was dry, its waters replaced by a thin column of steam
that swirled up and dissipated into the sky. Similar steam vents
drifted up along the far side of the river. It made him uneasy.

The palace was bleak and dreary. His father was dead, and
gone with him was his oversized presence that filled the halls
and animated the people around him. His father may have

been moody and unpredictable, but life with him had always been exciting. Rence, too, was missing. Jarin questioned the staff, but no one had any information as to his whereabouts. Had Rence been caught helping him escape?

General Drissen had kept his word, dutifully carrying out Jarin's commands. The palace was secure, and Jarin's Argonnians stood watch at the gates. There was enough foodstuff in the pantries to withstand a siege for several weeks, but the well had gone down three feet since yesterday. To make matters worse, the carrier beasts had broken out of their makeshift pen and had taken over the courtyard's pond. The large beasts had absorbed most of the pond's water into their bodies, and there was little left to sustain the horses and other animals kept inside the palace walls. The chameli would be hungry soon, and the stable master warned Jarin he could either feed the beasts their remaining horses or let them climb over the walls and fend for themselves. Both choices sounded disastrous.

Jarin's shoulder ached more now than it had when the heat wave had begun. He closed his eyes and focused on his sigil. Sabrin was less than two days away. He left the wall and trotted down the stairs into the main hall. General Drissen was there, engaged in a conversation with three men and a woman—geologists from the university; he recognized them by their dress. The geologists started whispering to each other when they saw him. One bowed in respect. Jarin's presence in the palace was supposed to be a secret, but clearly rumors had spread.

General Drissen saw him and frowned. "You will want to hear this." He motioned to the geologist in front of him, a short man with a sweaty brow. "Repeat what you told me."

"We represent the geologist guild of Weslynde, part of the school of magic." The man blotted his brow. "We oversee the thermal heating system that fuels Caleddon."

"I understand what it is you do," Jarin said. "Go on."

"The system is breaking down. We've no idea why. The

water caves beneath Weslynde are disappearing. It is the interaction of that water with the caldera beneath Weslynde Valley that creates our geysers and powers our machines. Without water, nothing works."

"We've had droughts before," Jarin said.

"There is more," the geologist said. "One of our magicians has the skill to see deep in the earth. Tell them, Migda."

Migda, a thin woman with dark eyes, stepped forward. She wore a magician's insignia on her sleeve. "The ground below Weslynde is getting hotter. There is a large underground fissure that runs down the river valley between Caleddon and Clear Lake that seems to be expanding. We...we think it's similar to the one that broke open and created the Salt Sea hundreds of years ago."

"Gods," Jarin swore. "What can be done?"

"Getting water back into the ground might cool it for a time. The high wizard of Riddien could open the ground below the river and let the water pour down. But she is far away. Gerard Mort is likely the only other mage alive capable of opening cracks in the earth, but he is missing."

"Gerard Mort went south to meet the Argonnian prime minister's delegation," General Drissen said. "Send a rider immediately. Bring him here."

The geologists bowed and turned for the door. As they were leaving, Jarin overheard one of them whisper, "It's the curse of the twins."

General Drissen had clearly heard it too and raised an eyebrow. "You've been exposed. When the church finds out you are here, they will blame you for the flooding and the drought."

"I need Dax," Jarin said.

"Jarin, if the people turn on you, I won't be able to stop them."

⚜

Jarin found Dax with the chameli in the training yard. He was charming each beast into a dormant state, slowing their metabolism so they wouldn't be hungry. The ones he had already charmed looked like haystacks scattered around the yard.

"How is the mood inside the palace?" Dax asked, moving to the next chameli. Sweat plastered the hair on his chest—he was tired from expending his magic.

"Surprisingly calm," Jarin replied. "But it won't last. There is a crowd gathering outside the walls, and Drissen's soldiers are returning from the flooded fields. We don't have enough Argonnians to keep them out if they want to come in. And there is this new problem."

"Only one?" Dax pacified another animal.

"Ground tremors. The geologists are expecting an earthquake or something even worse. They say there is a crack opening up in the earth between here and Clear Lake. They think the curse of the twins is causing it."

Dax wiped his hands on his wrap skirt. "There is no curse, remember? I recall you telling me that."

"And I still believe it," Jarin asserted. "Dax. This is urgent. Can you tell what's happening under the ground?"

Dax got down on one knee and put his hand on the ground. He closed his eyes and focused. The pressure of rock pressing against rock was easy to pick up. The fault line below them was building energy on a massive scale. His heart started to beat a little faster. Then he sensed something else. The energy emanating from Jarin's sigil, the thread connecting him to Sabrin, arrowed south along the same path as the fault line, sending erratic waves down into the ground beneath them.

⚜

DAX JERKED HIS HEAD UP. "Jarin, the sigils. The dissonance between them is causing this!"

"Dissonance?" Jarin didn't understand.

"The sigils are fighting each other. They are creating the breaks in the earth." Dax's face showed alarm. "The closer Sabrin gets to you, the worse everything gets." He grabbed Jarin's arm. "Jarin, the sigils are causing this. You and Sabrin are causing this!"

"What do you mean?" Jarin's shoulder started throbbing.

"We have to break the connection between the sigils. The sigil has to come out of you."

"Then do it. Take it out!"

"I can't. I didn't embed it. It fights me when I try to connect with it. Only Gerard Mort could remove it. He put it in you."

"Then how do we stop this?" A new thought struck Jarin. "Does one of us have to die? Do I have to die?"

"That would break the charm. The sigil would go inert. But, Jarin ..."

"What about Sabrin's sigil?" Jarin asked. "Can you take it out? You said you put it in."

"I did," Dax said. "I'm not sure how I did it. Maybe I could remove it if I got close enough."

"Then that is what we have to do. We've got to get to Sabrin and remove her sigil. We should take some riders and go. Now."

They raced up the stairs and ran along the rampart. The throng of people gathered outside the walls had grown, and they were no longer standing quietly; instead, they were chanting and raising their fists. The road in front of the gate was clogged with people, many wearing the red robes Jarin had seen earlier.

"We can't break through that mob," Dax said.

Jarin thought quickly. "What about taking scout beasts? If it's only the two of us, we can outrun them."

"The two of us against Sabrin's warriors?" Dax asked. "From what I've heard, they win every fight."

"Maybe we won't have to fight. We can explain what's happening. Can you think of another way?"

"General Drissen will take back the palace if you leave. He will have his army, and you won't be able to get back in."

"Well, then," Jarin said. "We won't tell him we're leaving."

"Are you leaving?" said a voice behind them. Jarin spun around. General Drissen was standing there.

"General," Jarin said. "We have to get to Sabrin."

Jarin quickly explained their plan to find Sabrin, remove her sigil, and stop the earthquake. He realized as he said it how ridiculous the whole thing sounded. No one spoke for several seconds.

General Drissen cleared his throat. "I was coming to tell you that I can no longer guarantee your safety inside the palace. Rumors have spread that the curse of the twins is causing the drought. From what you told me, I would venture to say the rumors have merit. Sooner or later, someone inside these walls will try to kill you."

Jarin gripped his staff. "Are you going to let us go?"

"I can't stop you, can I? Not with your magician standing beside you and a palace full of Argonnians."

"Then we leave immediately."

"There is more you should know," the general said. "A courier bird from Nettle Falls arrived a short while ago. The prime minister of Riddien has crossed the gap into Weslynde, leading what was described as a great host of holy warriors, bearing both weapons of war and banners of Saint Cerise. Stopping the earth tremor may not stop the approaching storm, Jarin. Your sister may have already won."

Jarin's spirit faltered at this news. Dax's face remained neutral, leaving the decision up to him. "I have to try," Jarin said.

General Drissen nodded gravely. "Then go. But I have one request. Riddien is on its way here, and my force is down at Clear Lake. I could use fifty warriors atop carrier beasts right now. Will Tevin and his riders stay and defend the palace with me?"

Jarin smiled. "Let's ask him."

⚜

The two scout beasts slipped unnoticed over the north wall of the palace and disappeared down a dry culvert that led to the river. Jarin quickly remembered how uncomfortable riding a scout beast was. He kept his head down as the two beasts clawed their way through the dense brush and raced across the muck-filled fields south of the city. After two tortuous hours moving at a precipitous pace, Dax called a halt near the top of a bluff so they could get their bearings. Jarin groaned as he unwound his legs from the stirrups and arched his back to get the kinks out. Mud coated his tunic and leggings. As he stretched to his full height, a searing pain jolted through his body and he doubled over, crying out in pain.

⚜

The dissonant energy pulsing out of Jarin's body assaulted Dax's consciousness. It was a waving curtain that stretched away in front of them and down into the ground below their feet. Great pressure was building in the rock below them.

"It's getting worse," he said, helping Jarin up. "I don't know how much longer before something—" He broke off as the ground shook violently.

They were knocked off their feet, and they tumbled down the incline toward a widening crack that suddenly opened in the ground in front of them. Jarin grabbed the woody branch of a bush and hung on. Dax came sliding down behind and collided with him. Jarin put his arm around him and pulled him in tight. They clung to the bush together as vents of superheated steam whistled out of the ground along the newly opened rift below them. A few seconds later, the ground stopped shaking and they were able to stand, and they scrambled back to the top of the hill. A line of scalding vapor plumes led off southward, marking the path of the fissure.

"That wasn't the end," Dax gasped.

Jarin gritted his teeth. "My shoulder...We've got to keep going; we have to get to Sabrin. Where are the scout beasts? Where did they go?"

Dax sussed them and located them by their snout rings. He sent a command, and the beasts became visible. They had camouflaged against the side of the rocky bluff away from the melee.

"It's not much farther," Jarin yelled. "I can see her in my mind."

Dax nodded and signaled the beasts, who raced forward, following a line of newly born steam vents that stretched away south.

CHAPTER 23

Cerise grabbed Gerard Mort and pulled him back from the scalding steam jetting out of the cave entrance. The air around them shimmered with heat. The ground below them buckled and shuddered, knocking them off their feet as they struggled to gain distance from the maelstrom. The carrier beast bellowed and stampeded out of the grove, spilling the women off its back as it disappeared into the dense woods. The ground tremors subsided, and they all scrambled up the nearby hill, putting distance between themselves and the vortex of steam whistling from the cave.

"Jarin is coming. He is almost on top of us." Gerard Mort panted as Cerise helped him up the slope.

Cerise could sense him too. How was he able to move so quickly? He must possess some kind of power she had not anticipated. Her idea of simply persuading him to submit so Gerard Mort could remove his sigil now seemed implausible. Her shoulder burned.

An explosion erupted behind her, and she was knocked forward onto the ground. She rolled over and looked back. The grotto was gone, and in its place was a widening column of black ash. Chunks of molten rock blasted out of its sides. A pool of lava welled up out the ground, consuming the rock pool and nearby structure as it spread out across the grove. Everyone was scrambling up the slope, trying to get as far from the inferno as possible—everyone except Gerard Mort.

The mage had gone back down toward the ash column. He was on his knees in front of the lava pool, driving his staff into the ground as if he were trying to poke a hole in the earth. He hunched his shoulders and bowed his head and yelled something that was lost in the roar of the eruption. The ground shook again, and Cerise was thrown backward before she could reach him. Gerard Mort threw his arms wide. To her shock and surprise, a huge waterspout appeared above Clear Lake, spiraling up into the air. Almost simultaneously, it fell back in on itself, replaced by a gigantic whirlpool in the lake. She watched in disbelief as an enormous geyser of steaming water erupted out of the ground in front of them, quenching the black smoke and molten rock. Cerise realized the mage must have somehow cracked open the bottom of Clear Lake, sending cold water down into the fissure, cooling the molten rock. The water spattered and hissed as it hit the lava pool, sending clouds of white vapor boiling upward. The ground continued to shake, and Cerise lay pinned, unable to move.

Another strong tremor shook the earth, and Jarin's scout beast stopped, refusing to go any farther. Beside him, Dax's beast had frozen as well. The two beasts began to writhe and claw at their saddles, scraping the men's arms and legs. Jarin rolled off the back of his beast; Dax did the same, and the two scout beasts sped away. As Jarin picked himself up, an enormous column of steam whistled into the sky over the next rise in front of them.

"That's her," Jarin cried. "She's there, by that vent. Let's go."

He grabbed his staff and stumbled forward across the heaving earth. Dax caught him by the arm to support him, and together they raced up the rise. They reached the top and looked down. A chaotic scene was unfolding in front of them. A huge steam vent jetted out of a cave next to Clear Lake, twisting like a tornado high into the sky. Trees and shrubs nearby were snapping into splinters. A carrier beast lumbered off through the trees, dragging pieces of its passenger platform behind it. At least seven people were scrambling up the hill in their direction. Jarin recognized Sabrin immediately, not only from her famous white face and red hair: an angry light radiated from her body, and the sigil in Jarin's shoulder lit up in response. His ribs began vibrating.

There was an explosion, and the grotto below them erupted into a cloud of black ash. Molten rocks rained down on the ground around them, and a pool of orange-white lava began to spread out along the ground. Jarin was knocked backward by a blast of hot air, and as he scrambled to get up, Jarin saw one of the people below them, a white-haired man in a black robe, turn and face the inferno.

"It's Gerard Mort," Dax shouted.

"What's he doing?" Jarin cried.

"He's trying to stop it. That's not possible!"

⚜

Dax pushed his skill toward the mage. Gerard Mort was opening a rift in the ground below the lake; it was unlike anything he had ever imagined could be possible. Then he realized the house mage had detected his presence, and before he could withdraw his magic, Gerard Mort entered his mind and annexed his skill. Dax's body seized up as Gerard Mort sucked the magic from his soul. He gasped and fell forward onto his face, unable to move and unable to stop it. He tried to call out to Jarin, but he could no longer remember how to speak words.

⚜

Jarin gasped as an enormous waterspout spun up out of the lake then crashed back down, replaced by a whirlpool swirling angrily on the water's surface, beginning to take the lake's water down into the earth below. The column of ash and molten rock in front of him changed into a hissing, billowing cloud of steam. A few moments later, the ground stopped shaking. Jarin turned to Dax and saw him lying face down on the ground, not moving. He crawled to him and pushed him over onto his back. The magician's eyes had rolled up in his head. His limbs were stiff.

Jarin slapped his cheeks. "What's wrong. Get up!" As he was crouching over him, trying to rouse him, the crunch of footsteps sounded behind him, and he spun around.

"Brother." It was Cerise. She stood over him, sword drawn. A bright aura surrounded her, shimmering and pulsing. The sigil inside Jarin thrummed and hummed. Did she feel it too?

Her blue eyes narrowed, and she put the tip of her sword against his chest. "I have imagined this moment many times," she said. "But I never pictured you as an Argonnian. Seeing who you really are makes this easier. Come with me. Now."

"Where?"

"To him." She jerked her head at Gerard Mort, who was still on his knees, facing the maelstrom. "We are going to end this catastrophe."

"Sabrin, listen to me." He had to get through to her. "I know how to stop this—"

Not waiting for him to finish, Cerise grabbed him by the arm and yanked him to his feet, then shoved him down the hill in front of her.

"You have to listen," Jarin cried, stumbling forward. "We need Dax; he can stop this." She ignored him and pushed him again. The women who were with her closed in behind them, weapons drawn. They stopped about a dozen feet from Gerard Mort.

The mage pulled himself up using his staff for support and turned to face them. His face was haggard and gray. Blood ran from his nose. He saw Jarin and chuckled under his breath. It quickly changed to a raspy cough.

"Jarin né Franklin," he said, mastering his cough. "You have been a thorn in my side for twenty years. It's time for that to end." He focused his bloodshot eyes on Cerise and hissed, "Kill him. Cut off his head and stop this horror."

"No!" Jarin and Cerise cried out in unison.

Cerise stepped around Jarin. "That was not our agreement. Remove his sigil as you promised." The ground underneath them began to rumble again.

"We are out of time," wheezed Gerard Mort. "Either he dies or we all die."

"Sabrin, listen to me!" Jarin pleaded. He was desperate now. "There is another—"

Cerise grabbed Jarin and yanked him in front of Gerard Mort. "Remove the sigil, Mort. You gave your word."

Gerard Mort looked at her, then smiled grimly. "As you wish."

"Wait, stop. You have to listen, both of you." Jarin tried to twist free, but Cerise tightened her fist around his arm. Her grip was like iron.

One of the women with her grabbed his other arm, and something sharp pressed against his back. "Stop moving or you die," she growled.

Jarin stopped struggling. The mage laid a bony hand on his chest, over his heart. Would it hurt? "Please," he said softly.

Gerard Mort closed his eyes and began muttering in old

majik, quietly at first and then with more intensity. He raised his staff in the air above his head and, with a shout, closed the hand he held over Jarin's heart into a fist and yanked it back quickly like he was pulling a rope. Jarin involuntarily lurched forward, but the two women held him in place.

"It hurts!" He screamed.

The mage pulled again, and Jarin screamed louder. His shoulder popped out of its socket. His ribs felt as if they were being crushed. He couldn't catch a breath.

"What are you doing?" Cerise yelled. "You're hurting him."

"I'm removing his sigil as you asked." Gerard Mort's eyes were black. "Through his heart!" He pulled again, and Jarin cried out in anguish, throwing his head back and arching his back.

"You're killing him!" Cerise let go of Jarin and reached for the mage's arm.

There was a sharp crack, and Gerard Mort's staff, which he still held over his head, disintegrated into dust. The mage staggered backward as if pushed. Jarin gasped in relief and slumped forward onto his knees.

⚜

Cerise looked at the mage in bewilderment, not comprehending what was happening, Someone pushed her aside from behind. It was the man who had appeared with Jarin. He slammed into Gerard Mort, sending him sprawling onto the ground. He put his knee on Gerard Mort's chest and held his sword to his neck.

"Do you yield?" he yelled.

Cerise's crew raced forward to pull the man off the mage, but Cerise put up her arms.

"Wait!" she shouted. They stopped—swords poised.

"Do you stand down?" the man yelled again at the mage, who was twisting on the ground under his knee.

"Dax?" Gerard Mort wheezed. "Tregan's pathetic little field witch Dax? Is that you?" A realization came over his face. "Was that you who helped me send the lake on top of the fire? You have grown, little Dax." The mage reached out an arm and feebly scrabbled on the ground with his fingers. "Can you feel beneath the earth, little Dax? It's coming apart under our feet. Do you feel it? The world is ending, and there's only one way we can stop it."

Gerard Mort moved faster than a snake could strike. He threw gravel into Dax's face with one hand and, with his other, sent Dax's sword flying.

Dax staggered back, hands on his face, giving Gerard Mort time to roll over and stand. Cerise leapt forward, but the mage thrust his arm at her, palm out, barking a command in old majik that sent Cerise and the rest of her crew sprawling backward. With another command, the mage sent their swords vibrating out of their hands.

⚜

Dax rushed back in while Gerard Mort was focused on Cerise. He threw his arms around the mage, pinning his arms to his sides. His momentum sent the two of them tumbling down the hill onto the crusty ground next to the steaming lava pool. A new rumbling struck the ground beneath them; the earth buckled, and they were tossed apart. Gerard Mort gained control first and scrambled to his feet.

"Your foolish prince dies now," he screamed at Dax.

The earth shook again, and the mage took a few steps back to keep his footing. He raised his arms and bellowed a command that made the air around him vibrate. Dax heard Jarin scream in pain behind him.

"NO!" Dax spread his fingers and sent his skill into the crusty ground under Gerard Mort's feet. The ground crackled like breaking ice. Horror dawned on Gerard Mort's face, and he locked eyes with Dax as the crust below him broke open and he fell through into the orange-white lava below. Superheated ash jetted out of the broken ground, and Dax crab-walked backward to keep from sliding into the molten pool after the mage. The ground in front of him continued to crumble, and new gouts of steam and smoke shot upward. He was losing strength, sliding back down toward the abyss when he felt hands pulling him away from the lava pool. Jarin had him by one arm and Cerise had the other.

"What have you done?" Cerise cried. "He could have stopped the earthquake!"

Dax lurched sideways as another earth tremor shook them. He grabbed Cerise by her hand and pulled her close. "Listen to me. I am a magician. I can still stop this. I can't remove Jarin's sigil, but I can remove yours."

"What?" Cerise gasped, clearly in pain.

Arcs of blue lightning spit and hissed between the twins.

"I embedded the sigil in your shoulder the day you were born. I can take it out. It will stop the earthquakes."

"I don't trust you," she yelled, shielding her eyes from the intense glare.

"Sister, please!" Jarin cried, his hands on her shoulders.

The rift in the earth erupted again, sending more black ash into the sky. A shock wave rippled through the ground, and white-hot lava started to well up through different cracks around them. Nearby trees burst into flames and disappeared into the ground. Dax stumbled backwards, and Cerise fell forward on top of him. For a moment they lay still, her eyes locked with his, and her face grew calm.

"Do it," she whispered. "Take it out." She scrambled off him and sat back up. "Do it now." She ripped off her jerkin and turned her back to him.

Dax put an arm around her chest and pulled her back against him. He placed the palm of his free hand down on her glowing shoulder. Sparks shot out between his fingers. The shaking ground made it difficult for him to keep his balance. Arms encircled the two of them; Jarin and the women had closed in around them, forming a protective circle, holding them in place. Blinding sparks of light danced in the air around them. Dax felt the same odd sensation he had experienced twenty years ago—some part of himself poured out of his chest and down through his arm into his hand. He began to mutter words he didn't know. The bones in Cerise's shoulder softened and slowly unknit themselves from the metal ring, and a few moments later, the sigil began to protrude from her shoulder blade and press upward, her skin and bone knitting back together behind it. Cerise moaned and shuddered, and then her head lolled back against him. A lump of hot metal pressed into Dax's hand. It was out.

The world changed. With a deafening boom, the fissure closed in on itself, and the smoke above it drifted off into the air and dissipated. A few remaining rocks fell back to earth, spattering on the ground. The scorched trees nearby crackled and slowly burned out, and the whirlpool in the lake vanished; a final wave washed up on the shore with a sigh. Everything was quiet.

The women and Jarin unlinked arms and stepped back from their huddle. Dax had his arms wrapped tightly around Cerise, holding her up. She slowly stirred and stretched. Dax held up his hand in front of her face and opened his fingers. A misshapen lump of green-gold metal glittered on his palm. She took it and examined it, then closed her hand around it. She was strangely calm and safe with his arms around her and found no need to speak or move. She leaned back into him for a few moments then gradually became aware of the others watching and pushed his arms away. Tar handed her the tossed-off jerkin, and she put it on.

Dax was shattered; his magic clearly depleted. Cerise helped him to his feet. He managed to take three steps before his knees buckled and he slumped back to the ground.

Jarin caught Dax as he fell and lowered himself to his knees, cradling Dax in his arms. The magician's eyes rolled up inside his lids, and his head fell back on Jarin's lap. Jarin gently caressed his head, marveling at the sudden stillness around them. He realized his back no longer hurt. The ache in his chest was receding. A bird chirped, and a soft breeze caressed his face, bringing a hint of moist air behind it.

They spent the next few hours regrouping. The women beat out the remaining small brush fires and gathered up their supplies, which had been strewn across the ground. When Dax finally regained consciousness, he was still disoriented, soaked in sweat and shaking with chills. Dee covered him with a blanket and sat with him.

Cerise handed Jarin a waterskin, which he accepted gratefully. She tilted her head, beckoning him to follow her, away from the others. They climbed up a boulder that overlooked the lake and sat together without speaking, relishing the cool breeze that blew in from the north. A bank of clouds was cresting over the Cordel Mountains, and Cerise thought she could make out white streaks under the clouds—snow was falling.

Cerise finally broke the silence. "What was it like, growing up in the palace?"

"I don't know. Lots of rules. My father wasn't around much, and my brothers bullied me."

"Barton and Lowden?"

"Yes. My half-brothers. They were older. And bigger."

"I've met them. I can see how Barton could be a bully."

Jarin chuckled. "What about you? Tell me of your life in Cordel."

They swapped childhood stories. Cerise told Jarin about growing up the child of seaweed farmers and her love of the sea. Jarin told her about the adventures he had when he snuck out of the palace. They grew comfortable with each other, occasionally breaking into soft laughter. Cerise responded to the earnestness in Jarin; he was so open and trusting.

Cerise finally asked him what was pressing on her mind. "Why did you flee Weslynde?"

"My father—our father—locked me up the day you arrived. I had to escape. He was going to kill me.

"Where did you go?"

"Argonne."

"Why Argonne? Why go there?"

"My mother—our mother—was Argonnian. I wanted to find out about her. No one in the palace would talk about her. I met up with my grandfather in Isidima. He told me things I didn't know. She was fighting for the Argonnian people."

"I met Tregor too. I found him to be...complicated. Why did you come back to Weslynde? Why didn't you stay in Isidima?"

"Weslynde is my home. This is where I belong. And I wanted to..." He broke off.

"Wanted to what?"

"I wanted to avenge my father and stop the church. They killed him, Sabrin; the church killed him."

"He was killed by Argonnians, Jarin."

"I don't believe that. The church was behind it." His eyes went cold.

"Jarin, I was there. The senator…"

"Argonnians don't go around killing people, Sabrin. The senator was framed by the church, and they placed the blame on Argonne. Your church, by the way," he added resentfully.

"It's not my church, and my name is not Sabrin," she protested. "My name is Cerise."

"Saint Cerise." In Jarin's mouth it was a curse.

"Saint Cerise is not real." Her anger flared. "And you think Argonnians don't kill people? Argonnians killed my mother and my father. Argonnians killed my love, my Luce." Her voice broke. "Argonnians murdered the king, Jarin. They murdered your own father. The prime minister of Argonne tried to kill me two nights ago. And you are leading an Argonnian revolt against Weslynde. Argonnians can all go to hell as far as I'm concerned."

"Our father—" Jarin began.

"He was never my father. And your Argonnian mother was never my mother. Her choice was clear. She sent me away to survive on my own and made you, her little Argonnian baby, the prince of Weslynde."

Jarin looked at her, open-mouthed, too shocked to speak, and then Dee yelled.

"Ship! I see a ship!"

They stood up on the boulder. Beyond the now muddy expanse of shoreline where the lake had receded, a steam-powered fishing trawler was heading north across the smooth water. Cerise's crew ran to the shoreline and whistled and waved. The captain of the trawler waved back and turned the wheel. A rowboat was launched, and the captain came ashore.

The trawler had left Shandling when the weather had broken in their favor. The buildings in Shandling had been largely spared from the earthquake. More devastating was the flood that had inundated the town. They were bound for Caleddon to get supplies and timber needed to rebuild the Shandling pier.

"May we come aboard and go with you to Caleddon?" Cerise asked. "My crew can assist you in stocking supplies for the trip back south."

"Aye, that would be a help. Gather your things. We leave as soon as you're ready."

Cerise followed Jarin back to their camp in silence. She passed by Dax, who was crouched next to a small fire, a blanket draped around his shoulders. He glanced at her as she passed, and she found herself drawn into his green eyes. He smiled at her, which made her blush. She stomped away, swearing at herself, fingering the lump of sky metal she had put in her pocket. She shook her head to clear it and called the crew together. They quickly gathered around her.

"What are you planning on doing now?" Jarin asked, joining her after a quick check on Dax.

Cerise picked up her pack and shouldered it. "I have five warriors with me. There are only two of you." She nodded at Dax, who sat slumped over. "And your dangerous friend is weak. That means I am in charge. We are returning to Caleddon, and we are delivering you to General Drissen, alive, per his orders. Get ready. We leave shortly." She strode away to make final preparations with her crew.

⚜

Jarin sat down beside Dax and blew out his breath.

"That went well," Dax observed dryly.

"There's no reasoning with her. She thinks I'm leading an

Argonnian revolt and it's her job to turn me in. We've got to get to Caleddon before she does. Riddien's warriors may already be there, giving her the upper hand. We've got to stop this."

"Our friends, the scout beasts, are waiting for us behind that thicket." Dax glanced at the bushes behind them. "I never released them from their service, and they returned on their own a little while ago."

"That's fantastic! But can you ride?"

"I'm fine. Sometimes it's best to let people see what they think they should see. Are you ready? Where is your pack? Grab your staff and help me up."

Jarin fetched his staff and helped Dax to his feet. The magician made a great show of leaning on Jarin and paused every few steps to catch his breath. Jarin shouldered his pack and helped Dax into his. The women were putting out the fire and taking supplies down to the shore; no one was watching them. When they were a few steps away from the edge of the thicket, Dax lightly touched Jarin on his arm and winked at him. As he did so, a large tree down by the lake suddenly made a great cracking noise and fell, twisting around and smashing into other trees on its way down. The women turned at the noise and watched it fall.

Dax and Jarin slipped into the thicket and onto the waiting scout beasts. Dax signaled the beasts to find home, and they sped away unnoticed, north toward Caleddon.

CHAPTER 24

A light rain blew in just as Jarin and Dax reached Caleddon. They climbed a hill overlooking the city, and Dax boosted Jarin up onto a branch of a tall tree. Jarin pulled Dax up after. From the top branches, they had a good view of the palace and its surroundings. The road below them was crowded with people, and a great many tents had been set up in the plaza in front of the palace's main gate.

"That's Drissen's army," Dax said, pointing to the rows of tents lined up in a field west of the city. "I'm guessing there's a company of at least two hundred."

Several brightly colored pennants floated above a large, tented pavilion set up in the plaza outside the palace gates. "Those are my brothers' colors," Jarin said. "Red on a yellow field is for Barton. Blue on yellow are Lowden's. There are a lot of Weslynders gathered around those flags."

"Do your brothers have claim to the throne?" Dax asked.

"If I'm dead, they do. Barton is next in line. He would have Sabrin to worry about, of course."

"Would they try?"

"I don't know. Barton is the hothead. He threw me down a well once. I probably deserved it."

"It's going to be hard to get through that crowd," Dax mused. "And we don't know what kind of reception awaits us."

"Everyone is still outside the palace waiting to be let in," Jarin noted. "Tevin must still control the gates."

"Most likely the Argonnians are besieged, Jarin."

They talked out various strategies, but most of them ended with the two of them trapped inside the palace with no way out. Jarin gazed off to the east, out of ideas. The late afternoon sun had broken through the rain clouds and lit up the faraway Saddle Mountains. His eyes wandered down the Weslynde Highway as it stretched away toward the distant peaks. A tiny cloud of dust was lifting off the road.

"Dax, look over there," Jarin said. "Riddien is coming. Saint Cerise's army." Even at this distance, he could make out the red banners of the church.

"They will be here in a few hours," Dax said. "And your sister must be past Clear Lake by now, less than a day away. You need to make a move before she meets up with that army."

"We need to get a message to General Drissen," Jarin said.

"I agree, but how?"

"We can send a courier bird."

"We don't have a courier bird, Jarin."

"Yes, we do. Two of them." Jarin grinned. "They are just bigger and have no wings." He cast his eyes down at the two scout beasts below them, wrapped around the trunk of the tree.

He and Dax climbed down from their perch, and Jarin rooted through his pack, looking for something to write on. He found a tattered scroll stuffed in the bottom and unrolled it. It was the summons for his extradition, complete with blood-stains, retrieved from Jarin's kidnappers. Jarin found a graphite stick and scrawled a message on the back. He rolled it up and gave it to Dax, who tied the message to his scout beast's saddle.

"How specific can you be about where to send them?" Jarin asked.

"I can put one in the general's lap. He wouldn't like it."

Jarin laughed. "In the same room would be good enough. How do we make sure Tevin sees it as well?"

"We can't. Our best bet would be to send them where we think the general and others are likely to be gathered."

"Send them both into the great hall. Put them in front of the throne. That's where the general conducts business. Even if he's not there, his staff will be, and the commotion the scout beasts cause should bring them."

Dax nodded and knelt in front of the scout beasts, taking each by its snout ring. The beasts began to agitate excitedly. He lightly brushed the beasts' foreheads.

"Go," he whispered.

The beasts dashed off, heading straight as an arrow for the palace. From his vantage point, Jarin could see people on the road scatter, then a tent collapse in the plaza.

"They made it," Dax said. He pulled their concealment cloaks from his pack, and they vanished down the hill.

The great hall erupted into chaos when two riderless scout beasts came crashing through a window in the dome overhead and landed in the middle of the room, turning in circles, climbing over each other, and lashing their tails. The palace staff jumped back as one of the beasts slammed into their worktable, scattering papers across the floor. The other beast spied a table full of food and climbed on top of it, collapsing it as it devoured chunks of a large smoked fish. Handlers were called, and they soon arrived, followed by Tevin and General Drissen.

The handlers moved in and calmed the beasts. Tevin spied the message Dax had tied to a leg grip. He untied it and gave it to General Drissen. The general scanned the note and rolled it up.

"Find my captain and tell him to station his troops in front of the palace gates," he said. "We are about to have guests."

⚜

The light rain had ended by the time Dax and Jarin reached the main boulevard, and the air smelled fresh. They side-stepped puddles and slipped unnoticed through the crowds. The crush of people got denser as they neared the plaza. Torches were lit and vendors were doing a brisk business. Many Weslynders had lost everything in the flood and needed food and materials for shelter.

There were two groups of protesters bunched up outside the main gate. The church protest was sizeable; their signature red robes filled half the square. Banners that read 'Long Live Queen Sabrin' waved alongside the ones that read 'Saint Cerise.' The other group of protesters was amassing next to the pavilion bearing Barton's colors. They had staked out the grounds in front of the gates and seemed to be blocking the church.

Jarin and Dax stole over to Barton's pavilion. As they got close, a small side door in the palace wall next to the main gate cracked open, and a man in palace garb slipped out. Jarin recognized General Drissen's chief of security and gave Dax a nudge. The security chief said something to the guards stationed in front of the gate, and one of the guards ran out of the plaza. The security chief did not reenter the palace; instead, he made his way inside Barton's pavilion.

"General Drissen must have gotten our message," Jarin said. "We need to get in there."

They pushed inside the pavilion unchallenged. Jarin threaded his way to the front of the crowd. The chief of security was talking to Barton. Barton nodded and put his hands in the air. The noise inside the tent grew quiet.

"We have received word that the prime minister of Riddien is approaching the palace," Barton announced. "He brings with him a sizable contingent of armed followers dressed in red, the color of Saint Cerise. General Drissen has ordered his army to take defensive positions around the palace. He wants the plaza cleared. He's asking us to help."

There was a chorus of complaining. A few shouted that they were not going to move until they knew what was going on inside the palace.

"There's more." Barton's voice rang out. The crowd hushed. "Prince Jarin is here, now, somewhere in the city. He has declared himself the rightful king and he is asking for our allegiance."

This caused great excitement. There were a few cheers of "Long live King Jarin," but one large man bellowed over the top of the others, "Jarin has filled the palace with his Argonnian cave jackals; we see them on the ramparts. He wants Isidima to be the new capital!" There was a chorus of boos.

Barton held up his hands again to quiet the crowd. "The Argonnians inside the palace follow General Drissen's orders," he yelled. "They are protecting Caleddon from Saint Cerise and her false claims."

"The Argonnians killed King Franklin!" shouted another man. Several others voiced their agreement, and those opposing them began to protest angrily. Barton was losing control.

Jarin realized he needed to seize the moment or fade away for good. "It's now or never," he whispered in Dax's ear. He slipped off his cloak and handed it off to the magician, then stepped into the cleared area in front of Barton. The room gasped in surprise as the prince of Weslynde suddenly appeared among them.

"People of Weslynde." A surge of energy poured from his chest through his voice. "Argonne is not responsible for my father's death."

The stunned room fell silent.

"My brothers and sisters. There is a crack in the alliance. Each province is starting to distrust the other two. False claims have been whispered in your ears by those who would break us apart. Followers of the false church march our way as we speak; they are almost on our doorsteps. They are responsible for the death of the king. They seek to step through the crack in our resolve and replace our freedoms with restrictions. They have exploited a hero, a woman they call Saint Cerise, and they plan to use her to grab the seat of power for the church and the church alone. King Franklin loved Weslynde," Jarin continued. "He loved the people of Weslynde. But he understood that the commonwealth flourished because of the gifts all three provinces: Weslynde, Riddien, *and* Argonne. I, Jarin né Franklin, son and heir to Franklin né Rosin, your prince and soon your king, share that belief. I will do everything in my power to ensure that the commonwealth remains united and strong."

"What would you have us do?" asked Barton.

"Stand with me." Jarin's voice carried hope and resolve. "Be an unyielding wall around Caleddon. Be the Weslynders I know you to be." He raised his arm over his head and made a fist. "Will you stand with me?"

"Long live King Jarin," shouted Barton as he thrust his fist high. "Long live the king."

The room erupted into cheers, and fists shot into the sky. "LONG LIVE THE KING."

⚜

Drissen's troops filed into the plaza. They far outnumbered the church protestors, who were quickly ushered away from the palace walls. Jarin, Dax, Barton, and Lowden slipped inside the gate.

Jarin caught up with Barton. "Honestly, I didn't expect you would give me your allegiance like that. I expected resistance."

"I didn't do it for you," Barton said. "You are a drunken sot. I did it for your mother. She treated Lowden and me like we were her own boys. I'm glad to see some of her grace and eloquence has finally rubbed off on you, else I'd have to throw you down the well again."

Jarin absorbed this with some chagrin. His mother was still looking out for him.

General Drissen and Tevin were waiting for them in the great hall. A cask of wine was cracked open and food was brought. They stood around the table, eating with their hands and making plans. Jarin told them of the astonishing events that had occurred at Clear Lake: the end of the earthquakes and the death of Gerard Mort.

"The storm is over," Jarin said. "I think for good."

"Jarin's and Sabrin's sigils were incompatible," Dax said. "They repelled each other and it affected the world around them, creating the curse, if you will. When Sabrin's sigil was removed, everything was restored."

"Sabrin is still dangerous," Jarin said. "If she joins the army from Riddien, they will rally behind her. She is their saint. She believes the Argonnians killed the king, and she thinks I'm responsible for it. I couldn't dissuade her."

"Where is she now?" Barton asked.

"She has to be close. She should be here by morning at the latest."

"The prime minister of Argonne is not far behind her," Dax added.

"Argonne stands with Jarin," Tevin said. "We can count on the prime minister to fight on his behalf when she arrives."

General Drissen looked skeptical. "Your prime minister's

own senator killed the king. That's hard to brush aside, despite what you say about her loyalty to Jarin. Argonnians also attacked Gerard Mort. They had infiltrated the staff and were inside the palace! They wore tattoos with the symbol of the separatists."

Tevin opened his palm, revealing his trident tattoo. "A tattoo like this?"

"Like that," General Drissen admitted. "I've seen your tattoo before. It doesn't alter my concern."

"We all have them. It's the symbol of Argonne. It's on our flag."

"You have shown me honor and respect these past few days, Tevin," General Drissen said. "I am convinced you would support Jarin as king. But I must be honest with you, there are many Weslynders who will not welcome Argonne back into the palace merely because Jarin is on the throne. There will have to be a reckoning at some point."

Jarin frowned. "We need a path forward. A reckoning, as you put it." He thought for a moment, and then it came to him. "Riddien and Argonne are on their way here because you summoned them. You called for a summit to decide who takes the throne, correct?"

"Unprecedented, I know, but the king was dead and your loyalties were in question," the general answered.

"You also ordered me to be arrested and brought here, demanding that I give an accounting of myself. And in that same summons, you recognized Cerise Aikawa as Sabrin né Franklin, King Franklin's daughter. I assume that pronouncement still stands?"

"It does," General Drissen said.

"Then there is nothing to do but see your commands carried out."

"Jarin," Barton cautioned, "don't give your crown away. You are the heir."

"Hear me," Jarin said, certain now. "This is the only way forward without bloodshed. It's the reckoning needed. Yes, we need to defend the palace against the church, but there must be agreement among the three provinces as to who will lead the commonwealth."

"You bear the sigil, Jarin," Barton said. "You are next in line. That is the law."

"I seek consensus," Jarin said. "I don't want to be king if it means fighting off different factions of the family for the rest of my life."

"We won't follow Saint Cerise or her church," Tevin said.

"My sister told me that she isn't Saint Cerise and that Sabrin no longer exists," Jarin replied. "She wants justice like I do, but I don't think she wants to be queen." He glanced at Dax, who had been standing in a shadow off to one side, arms crossed. "Dax. What do you think?" Dax's opinion mattered to him more than anyone else's in the room.

"It's a risk, Jarin," Dax said. "But I think it's a risk worth taking."

⚜

Jarin rose before dawn the next morning and, as was becoming his habit, climbed up to the rampart to see the lay of the land. The prime minister of Riddien, Baldo Koenig, and his host of red warriors had arrived during the night and, finding the palace closed to them, had set up a large pavilion with many tents out in the parkland near the public baths. Jarin had met him once when he was young. He remembered him as a blustery, red-faced man who liked the sound of his own voice. He'd seemed huge back then, with white-blond braids extending down his back and more braids in his beard.

A multitude of banners waved in the breeze above the pavilion. Interspersed among the red flags of Saint Cerise was the banner of Riddien and the Church of the Commonwealth's winged lyon. There was also a new flag he had never seen before, a yellow tower on a field of dark blue. Baldo Koenig's soldiers, along with a great throng of church-faithful dressed in red, were spread throughout the park, setting up tents and tending cooking fires.

A messenger appeared out of the Riddien pavilion and headed for the palace, riding one of the huge steppe-horses so prized by their people, its shaggy coat and long legs adapted for the snows that covered the northern steppes during the long winters. Jarin had only seen a few steppe-horses in Weslynde, and this one was magnificent; its mane and tail were tightly braided, and its glossy silver coat had been sheared down to its fetlocks for the warm weather. The messenger, a young woman with long yellow braids, rode proudly into the plaza, and the palace gates swung open as she approached. She crossed below Jarin's perch on the rampart, and the gates closed behind her with a clang. Jarin trotted down the stairs to meet her.

He joined Barton, Lowden, and General Drissen in the courtyard. Dax and the Argonnians remained out of sight as he had requested. A steward ran out with a step stool to assist the messenger's dismount from the tall horse, but she dismissed him and jumped lightly down on her own. She marched forward and handed General Drissen a sealed scroll.

"I am Reyna, granddaughter of Prime Minister Baldo Koenig. The prime minister asked me to express his condolences to the family of King Franklin né Rosin and is honored to be included in the memorial ceremonies planned." She stood as straight as a poker. "He also looks forward to the summit whereby the matter of royal succession will be decided." Here she paused and scrutinized Jarin skeptically. "The prime minister is, however, dismayed to find armed Argonnians inside of the palace and demands to know why. He insists that he be immediately admitted and provided quarters as is his right as a prime minister of the Western Commonwealth."

Jarin admired her poise. Prime Minister Koenig had made her his representative for a good reason.

"Well met, Reyna, granddaughter of Baldo Koenig," General Drissen said. "Please tell Prime Minister Koenig that he is welcome to join us here in the palace at his convenience. Rooms have been set up for his arrival. We ask, however, that his assembly, including his army and any members of the church, remain in the parklands where they have set up camp. Caleddon palace has implemented additional security measures in the wake of King Franklin's death. Rest assured we intend to ensure the safety of the prime minister during his visit."

"I will convey your explanation and invitation." Reyna crossed her arms and showed no sign of departing. She looked pointedly at the scroll she had handed the general.

General Drissen opened the scroll and read it. He frowned and stepped away from the messenger for some privacy. He handed the scroll to Jarin. Jarin read it, then handed it on to Barton. The three huddled together.

"This states that the high wizard, Samora Fulgor, has traveled here with the Riddiens." General Drissen kept his voice low. "She is here to support Riddien's interests in matters concerning the commonwealth. As far as I remember, she has never left Riddien before. She's the most powerful mage alive and could disrupt things. I find this news a little disturbing."

"Gerard Mort became Weslynde's house mage thanks to her," Jarin said. "I wonder how she will take the news of his death."

"I wonder that too." The general returned to the messenger. "The high wizard is most welcome as a part of Riddien's entourage. Please extend our invitation for her to join us in the palace."

"Expect a reply before the sun passes its zenith." Reyna bowed and left the chamber.

⚜

Baldo Koenig stomped into the great hall as if he were the king. He threw his cloak on the floor and demanded someone bring him a mug of ale, cursing when it did not appear fast enough. A handful of advisors buzzed around him like bees. At his side was the head of the magician's guild, High Wizard Samora Fulgor, a tiny woman of indeterminate age, dressed in a black tunic and leggings under a long cloak edged in fur. Her hair was silver, pulled back into a knot, but her face was smooth. Her skin was pale, marking her as Riddien. She walked unaided but carried a staff topped with an amber gemstone.

Jarin had to bend slightly to take her hand. How could someone so small be so powerful? She grasped his hand and pulled him down close to her face. Her grip was strong and firm. She squinted and peered into his eyes. Jarin felt exposed, like he was undressed.

"Pah! As I expected. Your compassion makes you weak," she hissed.

Jarin's eyes widened as she placed the end of her staff with its polished stone against his chest.

"Your sigil could give you power, but you block it. Your father was the same. He was too soft to rule effectively, too easily manipulated."

Jarin tried to pull away, but her grip was like a vise.

"Your sister has the power," Samora continued. "She used her sigil well."

"How do you know about my—" Jarin hesitated, then realized how she knew. "You made the sigils!"

"And I can unmake yours, young Jarin. Heed my warning: don't be so soft."

She released his hand, dismissing him. Jarin stood upright, looking around to see who had observed their exchange. No one seemed to have noticed. His shoulder tingled, and his heart pounded in his chest.

⚜

Dax was in the stable rubbing oil on a scout beast. Suddenly his mind lit up as if someone had shined a light directly in his eyes. At the edge of his consciousness, he sensed, rather than heard, a voice that whispered, "Come to me." He looked around; no one was there. He shook his head to clear it. It continued to bother him as he worked oil into the chameli's hide.

CHAPTER 25

Hungry and road weary, Cerise entered Caleddon's plaza. The women had marched through the night to get there and had not slept since they'd disembarked at Clear Lake. To her surprise, the palace gates were shut and a line of uniformed soldiers stood in front of them. She started forward to query one of the soldiers, but before she could reach him, a young man in red robes came running up to her from a side street. Tar blocked his way and pushed him back.

"Saint Cerise! Saint Cerise! A word if you please," the novice cried out over Tar's shoulder.

"Don't call me that." Cerise scowled, annoyed by yet another sycophant. She had already attracted a small crowd of them as they made their way through the streets to reach the palace.

"Many pardons," the man apologized. "I was asked to find you. I bring a message."

"Let him pass, Tar."

Tar stepped aside and the young man bowed low before Cerise.

"Who asked you to find me?"

"Archbishop Mellon, your holiness. He has a pavilion set up

east of the palace. He asks that you join him there at once. He has information you need to hear."

"I don't have time for the archbishop," Cerise said. "I need to get inside the palace." She badly wanted to speak with General Drissen before Jarin arrived.

"Please Saint, er, I mean, Cerise. Please come with me, I beg you. It won't take long. The archbishop wants to prepare you for what you will find inside the palace."

"Why? What's inside?" Cerise asked.

Janis stepped up beside her. "Cerise, look up at the rampart."

Twenty Argonnians carrying crossbows had appeared on the rampart over the gate, providing cover for the soldiers lining the plaza. There was no way she would be able to get past them.

"Argonnians," she cursed. "Jarin must already be here." *How does he move so fast?* She swallowed her displeasure at having to deal with the archbishop and nodded to the novice. "Alright, we will go with you; lead us."

They followed him to the parkland where Riddien had set up their pavilion. When the church-faithful saw her, a great cheer went up and they came running from the surrounding tents and cookfires, laughing and weeping and trying to touch her. Her crew made a ring around her, and they pushed their way inside the main pavilion. There they found Archbishop Mellon in discussion with a small group of church leaders, including Bishop Rutter, Caleddon's house chaplain.

When the archbishop saw her, he broke off his discussion and led her to a quiet corner where they could talk. Cerise noted that Bishop Rutter followed them.

"You are wise to have returned," Mellon began. "I need to bring you up to speed quickly if we are to succeed. General Drissen has called for a vote to determine who succeeds King Franklin. Each province gets a vote, and the majority will decide. The prime ministers of Riddien and Argonne represent their provinces, and General Drissen will vote on behalf of Weslynde."

"A vote?" Cerise asked, surprised at this news. "Isn't the line of succession written into law? A contract was signed. The successor is Franklin and Tregan's firstborn. Are they are deciding between Jarin and me?"

"Jarin's alliance with Argonne raised suspicions regarding his loyalty, and your legitimacy is still being questioned, in spite of all the proof that's been presented."

"It's disgraceful." Bishop Rutter wrung a cloth in his hands.

"When is this vote to take place?" Cerise asked.

"They are waiting for the prime minister of Argonne," Mellon said. "The prime minister of Riddien is already inside the palace, as are Jarin and the king's two bastards. There really is no precedent for this. It could break the monarchy."

"That's not the worst part," Bishop Rutter blurted out. "The palace is overrun with Jarin's Argonnians! When they arrived, they kicked us out and have banned the church from entering. It's blasphemy. Whoever they choose will be illegitimate unless they are sanctioned by the church."

"Peace, Rutter." The archbishop laid a hand on the bishop's shoulder.

"Cerise bears the sigil," Bishop Rutter continued. "She is the rightful queen. She is Franklin's firstborn. Her legitimacy cannot be questioned."

"I no longer bear the sigil," Cerise admitted. "It was destroyed to stop the earthquakes. Sabrin is no more."

"You don't have it?" The archbishop's face registered shock. He sputtered for a moment, then recovered. "It doesn't matter. You are still Franklin's legitimate child, his firstborn. Lacking a piece of metal in your arm doesn't keep you from taking your place as queen."

"Queen was never my goal," Cerise said flatly.

"Oh, no!" Bishop Rutter gasped in dismay.

"Cerise, listen to me!" Archbishop Mellon clasped his hands together. "You must do this. You must accept your destiny. Jarin is compromised. He is weak. No one will follow him. You are the leader Weslynde needs."

"And Jarin is a heathen. He disrespects the church and flaunts the gods," Bishop Rutter said.

"If you continue to interrupt, I will have you dismissed," the archbishop said, exasperated. Bishop Rutter bowed his head and took a step back.

"Cerise, without you the commonwealth will be overtaken by Argonne," Mellon continued. "You have the power to save it, and the church will unite behind you. The prime minister of Riddien plans to throw his support to you. We think the prime minister of Argonne will vote for Jarin, but that won't matter if General Drissen votes in your favor. We believe he will. He knows you are the rightful heir; he has seen the proof. We, the church, stand with you, and the general knows very well he needs the church on his side."

Cerise considered his words. She thought about how Jarin had run away at the grotto rather than stand with her. Maybe they could have solved this together if he had stayed instead of running. And now she'd arrived in Caleddon only to find he had packed the palace with Argonnian fighters. He was not to be trusted. She didn't want to be a queen. Her reason for coming to Weslynde in the first place had gotten so twisted up. But as queen, she could stop Argonne.

"Very well, I will fight for my birthright."

"They are waiting for you at the palace. You need to go and fight for what is yours. And you need to get us inside the palace with you. The prime ministers need to see how important their alliance with the church is."

"How can I get you inside? The palace is well guarded and I can't simply countermand the general's orders."

"There are over a hundred seasoned Riddien soldiers outside this tent. They are dressed in red robes and have pledged their allegiance to you. The sight of you leading them will persuade the general to let us in."

Two novices arrived with flatbread and cheese, and the discussion broke up. Cerise was famished; she hadn't eaten anything except a bite of salted fish on her way here. She excused herself and gathered her crew. They took some food and sat in the shade of a tree with spreading branches. Cerise described the situation to them.

"Do you even want to be queen, to be part of all this?" Janis asked her.

"I never wanted that, no. But ... "

"But what?"

"I don't want the Argonnians to get away with this. If Jarin is king, I will never have justice. He won't punish his own people."

They chewed their flatbread thoughtfully.

"I miss the sea," Dee said after a bit. Everyone agreed.

"I do too," Cerise said. She loved these women very much. "Hear me. This is not your battle. You don't have to stay. You are all free to go live your lives."

"We would never leave you," Janis said. "If you need to right this wrong, we will be at your side."

"Queen Cerise!" Tar pulled out her knife and placed it in front of Cerise. "We are at your service."

One by one, they all took out their knives and laid them atop each other on the ground. Cerise hesitated, then slowly put her knife on top of theirs.

"Together we have always been invincible," she said. "We will forever be the crew of the *Flying Fish*, no matter what." She stood up and held out her palm. The others put their hands on hers, then fell into a group embrace. When they separated, Cerise put her hands on Tar's and Janis's shoulders. "I am ready for anything. But I am not above increasing my odds of winning. Let's see if we can get the church inside the palace."

⚜

Shortly after learning that Cerise had arrived in Caleddon and had joined the Riddiens at their pavilion, Jarin received word that Prime Minister Tharisa Kokheli was approaching the gates. Her delegation had set up camp south of the plaza, and their carrier beasts had already been taken to the hot caves to be fed and watered. She entered the great hall in her wheeled chair along with Tregor Anthelia. Jarin went to meet her and got down on one knee.

"Ah, Tuval," she said in mock surprise, taking his hand. "How remarkable that I should find you, of all people, here to greet us in Caleddon. Do tell Prince Jarin how grateful I am that he arranged such nice weather for us. Tell him there must be no further earthquakes if he is to be king."

"I'll make sure he knows." The corner of Jarin's mouth tweaked up in a half-smile.

She dropped her smile and leaned forward. "It was a near thing, you know. You're lucky to be alive." Jarin nodded soberly. She sat back and gazed dismissively at the hall's majestic marble columns rising to the golden dome. "This will be my last trip to this accursed city if I have anything to say about it. I prefer the comforts of Isidima to this rustic hunting lodge."

"I will always remember my time in Isidima fondly," Jarin replied. "The gardens, the ocean, the kidnappers, the torture."

She glared at him. "Have someone show us our rooms." She wheeled away to speak with the prime minister of Riddien, leaving Jarin awkwardly balanced on one knee. Tregor Anthelia held out his hand and helped him back to his feet.

"You did well, Grandson." He flashed his charming smile.

"It's not over yet, Grandfather. I had the opportunity to

meet my sister, your granddaughter, on my travels. She is a force to be reckoned with, one not easily put off her quarry."

"Indeed. She has a fire in her heart," Tregor said. "Like your mother did. But you have it as well. You will make a fine king. Now tell me where I can find Captain Tevin. I wish to speak with him."

"He is on the rampart overlooking the main gate, preparing for Cerise's arrival," Jarin said, motioning toward the door leading from the hall. "Don't get trampled."

Tregor looked at him quizzically, then nodded his head and walked briskly to the door. General Drissen stepped up next to Jarin once Tregor left. He leaned close to his ear.

"Cerise is mustering a force at the Riddien encampment," he said. "I sent the invitation."

"Let's see how she responds," Jarin replied.

A page dispatched from the palace arrived at the Riddien pavilion and handed Cerise a sealed note. She opened it in front of Archbishop Mellon and read it out loud.

"Cerise Aikawa of Cordel. You are required to attend a summit tomorrow morning in the golden hall. The successor to the throne of Weslynde will be determined at that meeting. Rooms are waiting for you and your crew inside the palace. Archbishop Mellon and all clergy are to remain in their encampment until the results of the summit are released."

"They don't even call you Sabrin né Franklin!" Bishop Rutter scoffed. "This is insulting. The church should have a say. The sovereign sits at the head of the church."

"Not since Queen Rosin, I understand," Cerise said dryly.

"That was a mistake that will be rectified once you are crowned queen," the bishop huffed and dabbed his brow.

Cerise didn't like this blowhard, but she needed him and his followers in order to make things happen.

"I will need your soldiers if I am to get you an invitation," she said to the archbishop. "Introduce me to the captain and tell him that we march to the palace in one hour."

"The soldiers of Riddien are yours to command, my queen." The archbishop bowed.

⚜

Shortly after dark, Cerise entered the plaza leading one hundred seasoned Riddien fighters. A host of church-faithful carrying torches followed. Cerise hoped this show of strength would force Jarin to negotiate and allow her to bring the archbishop into the palace. She was also counting on her assumption that General Drissen wouldn't open fire on Saint Cerise.

Ten of Drissen's soldiers stood in front of the gates. They were lightly armed and didn't pose much of a threat. More unsettling were the twenty Argonnian archers on the rampart overhead. For now, they were watching calmly, weapons down, bows unstrung.

"I wish to negotiate terms," she yelled loudly. "The Church of the Commonwealth must be included in these matters."

There was a creaking and a metallic boom as the double doors of the main gate swung outward. *Progress,* Cerise thought. *The plan is working.* She planted her feet and crossed her arms. But instead of a negotiator stepping out to meet her as she expected, a line of massive carrier beasts in full battle armor appeared, each carrying several well-armed soldiers. More and more beasts appeared until they formed an impenetrable wall between her soldiers and the palace.

"By the gods, Cerise," Tar muttered, voicing Cerise's own thoughts. "Where did they come from?"

A uniformed Weslynder slid down from the foremost beast and walked over to Cerise. He was unarmed.

"General Drissen." Cerise recognized him immediately. She nodded out of respect.

"Cerise Aikawa," the general said. "It's good to see you again. You do like to make an entrance."

"I could say the same of you," Cerise said. "I don't remember any carrier beasts inside the palace."

"They were a gift from your brother. He's a resourceful lad. You two should spend more time together."

It was obvious Jarin was giving the orders. Cerise looked up at the rampart, taking a moment to think and saw that Dax was standing there, watching her. Seeing him there brought back an intense memory of the moment he'd taken her sigil from her body. The way he had held her after the sigil was gone. Something had passed between them at that moment. She had seen inside him. They had barely spoken five words to each other, but she knew that during his life he had experienced both great love and great loss, as she herself had. She felt a connection to him she had never experienced with anyone before. His eyes were focused on her, and she looked away, her heart beating a little faster. She put her hand in her pocket and clasped the lump of sky metal.

"Shall we go in?" General Drissen asked, breaking her reverie. "Your soldiers are welcome to return to their pavilion and wait until tomorrow."

Cerise was caught. There was no way to turn this to her advantage. The carrier beasts would easily crush her soldiers, and her arrows could not penetrate the battle armor. Archbishop Mellon would have to wait outside. She wasn't ready to give up, however. She was firstborn and presumptive heir.

"After you," she said calmly, masking her turmoil. The carrier beasts parted and let them pass.

⚜

Dax stepped back from the rampart's edge once Cerise had passed through the gates below. He trotted down the stairs, hoping to pull her aside and talk. The bond he had experienced with her when he'd removed her sigil welled up inside him again at the sight of her. He rounded the corner and almost stumbled into a small woman with silver hair. He mumbled an apology and started to go around her but found his feet unwilling to move. Cerise vanished around a corner with General Drissen. The woman stood quietly, holding a staff topped with an amber stone. She peered up at him, her black eyes two slits.

"You did not come when I called," she said.

"I don't know what you mean."

"Don't try to be clever." She rapped his shoulder with her cane. "We need to talk. Come."

Dax was suddenly free to move. With a shock, he realized the waif-like woman must be Samora Fulgor, the high wizard. She set off at a surprisingly fast clip down the hall, not looking back. Dax hurried to keep up.

She took Dax to the room that had been set aside for her and invited him to sit at one of two chairs placed near the open balcony doors. A gentle night breeze brushed his face. He sat, watching her carefully. She rang a bell, and a steward appeared holding a tray of dried fruit, cheese, and a pitcher of wine. The steward began setting up the food on a side table.

"Look closely at that man." Samora gestured toward the steward. "Tell me what you see."

Dax frowned. He glanced at the steward and then back at her, puzzled. "I see a steward."

"No, you fool. Look at him."

The steward finished setting up the refreshments and started to leave. Dax didn't see anything unusual and shrugged.

"A moment," Samora said to the man. The steward nodded and stood quietly, waiting for instructions. Samora glared at Dax as if he were stupid.

Dax took a breath. The steward stood patiently. There was nothing remarkable about him. Samora rapped Dax's knee with her staff.

"Really look!" she commanded.

Startled, Dax focused again on the steward and, without thinking, sussed him with his skill. The man's bones were in good health. He had an arm fracture that had mended well. Dax focused on his head. There was a metallic object at the base of the skull. A tiny ring of...sky metal! Only a trace amount, embedded inside the man's head where it met the spine. He looked at the high wizard in surprise.

"You may go," Samora said to the steward. The man bowed and left. She poured two mugs of wine and handed one to Dax. "You don't know what to look for because you have not been taught how to see. You have the potential to be a house mage, yet you scratch about like a field witch, playing with your lizards in the sand."

"How did sky metal get in that man's head?" Dax asked. The hair on his arms prickled.

"Now you ask good questions." Samora smiled in satisfaction. "How indeed, and why?"

"Only a high mage could have done that...Mort!"

Samora sipped her wine. "How far can you stretch?" she asked. "Show me." She sat back in her chair and brushed something off her robe, waiting.

Dax quaffed his wine and set the mug down. He settled in his chair and grabbed the armrests. With one last sideways glance at her, he closed his eyes and reached out with his skill, not focusing on any one thing. As always happened, his mind was overwhelmed with impressions. Stone, metal, textiles, water, fire, earth. The world was moving, churning. It was chaos, and it hurt. He pulled back.

"Try again," Samora said. "Don't cast such a wide net this time."

Dax nodded. *This time*, he thought, *focus on sky metal, nothing else*. He reached out, sending his skill across the palace. Bits of sky metal appeared to him like stars in the evening sky. Jarin's sigil appeared first, blazing bright in his mind, a beacon. Next he located Cerise by the lump of sky metal she carried in her pocket. Their combined brightness threatened to crowd out everything else, but after concentrating for a moment, he was able to fence them off in a corner and reach past them. There. He picked out three new pinpoints of sky metal in three different places. The first was in the steward who had left them. He was moving down the hall toward the kitchen. The second was inside a palace guard standing in the great hall, and the third point, very distant, appeared below the ground, in a chamber carved out of stone. There was something wrong with that sky metal's signature. A weird unease hit the pit of his stomach, and he opened his eyes.

"I have to go." He stood up.

Samora leaned forward and pressed the amber stone against his chest. "We are not finished."

"I'm sorry. I have to go, now." He pushed her staff aside and ran out of the room.

Dax followed the old guard to down an underground hall-way. The guard's lantern cast shadows that jumped along the rock walls as they passed. They stopped in front of a rusted metal door with a grated window. It was dark inside.

"Who is in this cell?" Dax asked. "Why is he locked up?"

Whoever was inside had sky metal in his neck, and the wrongness of this metal's signature permeated the small room.

"His name is Griff. He's crazy as a loon. We keep him locked up so he won't hurt no one else."

"He hurt someone?"

"Tried his best to kill 'em. One of his mates called him a coward, and Griff here, without a word, put a knife in his arm."

"He called him a coward?" Dax asked. "Do you know what he meant by that?"

"Everyone here does. Griff was guarding King Franklin the night he was murdered. Griff and his mate killed the cursed Argonnians, but they was too late to save the king. Now, instead of being a hero, Griff here gets called a coward, and I guess he went crazy."

"May I talk to him?"

"It's your time to waste. He don't make no sense. There's a candle on the table." The old guard unlocked the door. "Griff," he called out. "You got a visitor. Be nice."

The door squealed on its hinges. Dax stepped inside, and the guard locked the door behind him. Moonlight shone through a narrow window high up on the wall. His eyes adjusted to the gloom, and he found the candle and lit it. The cell was cramped but clean. Griff lay on his side on a cot, curled up in a ball.

"Griff." Dax touched him lightly on the arm. The man flinched but did not turn or look at him. "My name is Dax. May I talk with you?"

"I won't be home for supper tonight," Griff mumbled and rolled tighter into a ball.

Dax sussed the tiny ring in the man's neck. The charm was ugly and warped. It fought his intrusion, but not with the same level of resistance as Jarin's sigil. He concentrated and found a gap in the spell and was able to probe around inside. The charm sent out little jolts of pain, as if someone were pricking his skin over and over with a pin. He could tell what it was doing to Griff —it kept him from holding on to a chain of coherent thoughts. He placed his hand on the back of Griff's neck.

"Here now, what are you doing?" grumbled the guard, holding up his lantern and peering at him through the grated window.

"Only a little neck massage; it will make him feel better, I promise."

"Don't hurt him none. It ain't his fault he's crazy this way."

"I won't."

Dax sat on the cot and put his other hand on Griff's shoulder. Griff trembled and scrunched up tighter. Dax pressed his index finger against the skin at the base of Griff's skull. The energy in the sky metal buzzed around his finger, stinging him like angry bees. It was almost unbearable. Dax sank into the charm, unthreading it, breaking it apart, and finally feeling it evaporate. He removed his finger and stood up, wiping the sweat off his brow.

Griff reached behind him and rubbed the spot on his neck. Then he unwound slowly, rolling over for the first time.

"Who are you?" he said, sitting up and scratching his head. "Where am I?"

"My name is Dax. You are safe inside the palace."

Griff looked around. "How did I get in here?"

"What do you remember?"

Griff furrowed his brow. "I don't remember ever being here. Last thing I remember was guard duty. Graveyard shift. With the king." He stopped, and a look of horror crossed his face. He grabbed Dax by the hand. "The king! The king is dead! He was stabbed!"

"Who killed the king, Griff?"

"It were that house mage, that Gerard Mort fella; he

stabbed the king with a knife." He jumped to his feet. "We've got to stop him."

"By the gods!" roared the guard standing outside the door. "The magician?"

"Sleep now," Dax said, pulling Griff up to his chest and wrapping his palm around the back of his neck. "You are going to feel better soon." Griff slumped back onto the cot. Dax went to the cell door. "Open the door, quickly!" The guard unlocked the door and let Dax out. "When he wakes up, give him what he wants. I will return for him." Dax flew down the hall and up the stairs.

CHAPTER 26

Cerise held the dress in front of her and frowned at herself in the mirror. One of the palace staff had presented her with a long shift made of gold satin paired with an ornate beaded over-dress in garnet. A pair of embroidered slippers completed the outfit. It was majestic, stately, truly made for a queen. *Tregan would have worn something like this,* she thought. She had come from the bathing room, her hair still wet and loose about her shoulders. She hardly recognized the woman in the glass. Her porcelain face was bare of any makeup; soft arched brows and long auburn lashes framed her bright blue eyes. Without its warpaint, her face was soft, feminine. The woman in the mirror reminded her of the alabaster bust of Tregan Anthelia she had seen in Isidima, forever ago. She smoothed the dress against her body. What would Dax think of her wearing it? She scoffed at the unbidden thought and tossed the dress on the floor. She pulled on her stained travel clothes and tied her red hair up in its warrior's knot. Much better.

Shortly after she'd arrived, she had debriefed General Drissen on the events at Clear Lake and the death of Gerard Mort. He'd said her version of the events more or less confirmed what Jarin had told him. Then she'd gone searching for her brother. She needed to know where his allegiance lay—was it with Weslynde or with Argonne? The sight of all those Argonnians on carrier beasts overrunning Caleddon palace seemed to bear out the latter. But before she'd even made it out of the great hall, the prime minister of Riddien had cornered her. He'd lectured her on the importance of aligning with the church, how having the church as an ally could make or break the monarchy. She'd managed to extricate herself without overtly insulting him and climbed the massive staircase up to Jarin's quarters. His doors had been blocked by two fierce-looking Argonnians. They'd told her he was in a private meeting with Tregor Anthelia.

"Either let me in or bring him to the door," she had insisted. "Tell him it's his sister."

"The prince said no one is to disturb him. Give us a message, and we will tell him you were here."

The two Argonnians had been large and imposing, but she'd been pretty sure she could fight her way into the room without shedding too much blood. She'd pushed between them to rap on Jarin's door, but they'd closed in, putting their hands on their sword hilts. Their defiance had only confirmed where Jarin had placed his loyalty. They weren't worth fighting with, and Jarin wasn't worth reasoning with.

"I have no message for the prince. Don't bother telling him I was here." She'd stormed back down the corridor. A page had gone past, and Cerise had told him to go find Dax, the magician. The page had returned a short time later to tell her that the magician had left the palace and no one knew where he was.

She'd paced around her room and attempted to meditate the way Min had taught her, sitting cross-legged and focusing her thoughts inward. She'd held the lump of sky metal in her hand and rubbed it with her thumb, but none of it had helped.

Had her strength been ripped from her body along with the sigil? Her thoughts had turned again and again to Maemae and Min and her beloved Luce and how she was failing them. What was she even doing here? Sleep had eluded her the rest of the night.

It was clear to her now, as she stood in front of the mirror and lined her eyes with black, that Jarin had thrown in with the Argonnians and it was up to her to stop him. She put aside her unease, fully resolved to secure the crown and avenge her family. When she stepped out of her room, Janis and Tar were there waiting for her. Her strength returned at the sight of them. They entered the great hall side by side.

⚜

Sunlight streamed through the windows encircling the golden dome. In the center of the hall was a long table ringed with chairs. A few knots of people had already gathered. The prime ministers of Riddien and Argonne were having some kind of debate. Tharisa Kokheli leaned forward in her wheeled chair, and Baldo Koenig was waving his hands in the air. General Drissen was speaking with a small woman holding a staff topped with an amber stone. Jarin was on the far side of the room talking with Barton and Lowden. He was wearing a Weslynde uniform and looked very much like a prince, his hair now in loose waves. He noticed Cerise and walked over to greet her with a smile, but she chose to ignore him and went to join the prime ministers.

A door opened on the other side of the hall, and Dax came running in, boots drumming on the marble floor as he sped toward the general. He had news to tell, but the general put up his hand to stop him.

"Now that we are all here," the general said in a loud voice, "let's get started. Prime Ministers, if you will, please sit on this side of the table, and members of King Franklin's family please sit here, opposite them. Samora, you are here, next to me."

Dax stepped closer to him and urgently whispered in his ear.

"Please take your seats," the general said, signaling for Dax to wait. Cerise kept her eyes on Dax as she sat in the seat next to Barton's. The general finally acknowledged the magician and stepped away with him from the table. The general reacted in surprise to something Dax said, then came back and took the chair at the end of the table. Dax followed and stood next to him.

"Most of you know Dax," the general said, his brows furrowed. "He is Jarin né Franklin's magician. He has important news. Dax, repeat what you said to me."

"I have come from speaking with the guard who was with the king the night he was murdered," Dax said. "He says the house mage, Gerard Mort, murdered the king, not the senator from Argonne."

The room was quiet for a moment, then everyone began throwing questions at him as the implications sank in.

Cerise stood up and pushed back her chair. "That isn't true," she shouted over the others. "I interviewed that guard. He confirmed to me that the senator was responsible."

"He was under a charm put there by Gerard Mort," Dax explained.

"Placed under a charm?" Cerise laughed. "A charm is something in a fairy story. Why are you saying this now, to me, here, in this room?"

People began shouting. General Drissen rapped his knuckles on the table. "Quiet," he yelled. "Quiet, everyone. Let Dax explain. Cerise, please sit."

Cerise slowly took her seat, scanning the faces of the others, looking for signs of deceit. She scowled at Dax. What was he doing? The room grew quiet again. Dax was about to speak when the woman named Samora rapped the end of her staff on the floor.

"The magician speaks the truth." The woman's voice was low and resonant. "The king's house mage was responsible."

Cerise realized Samora was the high wizard of Riddien. The archbishop had warned Cerise about her.

"He embedded rings of sky metal in some of the palace staff," Samora continued. "He was controlling them like beasts, bending them to his will. Dax found one in the neck of the guard who was protecting the king that night. It appears that this abominable practice had been going on for some time."

"If this is true," Tregor Anthelia said loudly, "then Argonne is no longer under suspicion, and there is no reason to delay crowning Jarin as king."

"No!" shouted Cerise, rage filling her. She had to take the throne. She pounded her fist on the table. "This magician is Jarin's man and would say anything to protect him. He is not to be believed. This is a last-minute trick designed to put Jarin on the throne."

"Dax has spoken truth." The wizard focused her intense gaze on Cerise. "We can show you the evidence."

"Even if it is true, it doesn't absolve Argonne of anything!" Cerise cried. Her chance for justice was crumbling before her eyes. "Argonnians killed my family." She pointed at Prime Minister Kokheli. "You tried to kill me!" She jumped to her feet and rounded on Jarin. "And you filled the palace with your Argonnian guard dogs."

"Cerise, you misunderstand." Jarin stepped up to her, arms outstretched.

"Stay back!" Cerise drew her knife and brandished it. Janis and Tar flanked her.

"What are you doing?" Jarin pleaded. "I'm not trying to hurt you."

The house guards ran forward. Cerise saw them and

grabbed Jarin by the wrist. She twisted his arm and threw him off-balance. In an instant, she had her arm around his neck and the point of her knife on his back.

"Stay back," she said, breathing hard now. The guards stopped.

"Hear this, all of you." Tears ran unchecked down her eyes. "There must be an accounting. Argonne must pay."

"Cerise, stop," Jarin choked out. "I didn't do anything."

On the other side of the table, Dax raised his hand in the air. He sussed Cerise's knife and clenched his fist, sending a command to knock it from her grasp, but suddenly his focus was obliterated, as if someone had delivered a hard blow to his head with a mace. He staggered sideways and looked over at the high wizard. She was glowering at him.

"Don't interfere." Her voice was inside his head; her lips hadn't moved. She turned her eyes toward Jarin, and Dax followed her gaze. Jarin's body was glowing. His sigil blazed inside his chest like a shining star. Dax knew that he and Samora were the only ones in the room who could see it.

Jarin held himself very still. Cerise's arm was tight around his neck, making it hard for him to breathe. But he felt calm, and he whispered softly, in a voice just for her, "Cerise, my sister. I hear you. We can talk this out."

"No!" Cerise protested. "Talking won't fix things. It won't bring them back. Nothing will bring them back."

He felt her great anguish and wanted to take it from her. "Sister," he said quietly. "I am so sorry. I didn't know. I will help you."

The arm around Jarin's neck loosened, and Cerise's knife clattered on the floor. The guards rushed forward to restrain her.

"Stop," Jarin ordered. "Let her be." He turned to face her and spoke again in that voice just for her, his forehead against hers. "Cerise, I feel the same as you. I do. I too want an accounting. We both have lost. Our father, our mother...and each other. We lost each other."

"Jarin, I'm so angry." Cerise choked back a sob. "I couldn't save them. I couldn't..."

"You're so strong, so brave," Jarin whispered. "A legend. People sing songs about you."

"Only crazy people." She angrily pushed away her tears.

Jarin took her by the hand and let his heart speak. "You should be queen."

Cerise stepped back and gently removed her hand from his. She slowly regained control, and the softness in her face disappeared. "There's too much pain, Jarin." She regarded the Argonnians seated at the table. "And I'll never trust them."

"Trust me, then," Jarin said softly.

Cerise searched his face, locking eyes with him. She held his gaze for a moment, then her expression softened again and her body relaxed a fraction.

She nodded slowly. "I do."

"Good. Shall we let this game play itself out, then?" he asked, indicating the others at the table. "Let the people decide?"

Cerise nodded again and rolled her eyes. "If we must."

"We're ready to continue," Jarin said, taking her hand again. This time she didn't let go. The others sat back down, chairs scraping. No one spoke.

General Drissen cleared his throat. "I trust there will be no more outbursts—"

The door on the side of the hall flew open with a loud

bang. Everyone jumped. An elderly man with white hair and a neatly trimmed beard rushed through the door, followed by a short woman wrapped in a dark cloak and hood. It was Rence.

"Are we too late?" Rence cried. "Tell me we are not too late. We came as fast as we could."

Two guards stepped in front of them.

"For the gods' sake, move aside, move aside. Do I look threatening?" Rence pushed his way through them, leading the small woman by her hand. The guards closed in behind them and followed. They stopped at the table. Both were breathing rapidly as if they had run a long distance.

"Many pardons, General." Rence bowed. "But you will want to hear this." Then he noticed the twins sitting next to each other. "Cerise! Hello again! And, Jarin, my boy! I see you two have met at long last. Good, good." He clapped his hands and rubbed them.

"Rence!" Jarin smiled joyfully.

"What is it you want, Rence?" General Drissen asked, exasperated.

"I'm here to solve your problem, Drissen. Isn't that what I always do?" Rence replied.

"Say what you came to say, then," the general said, red-faced. "And who is that?" he asked, pointing at Rence's companion.

"Oh, yes! Yes. Exactly. Well, I can't think of anything clever to say at the moment," Rence quipped, "so you'd best show yourself, my dear."

⚜

Rence's companion reached up and pulled back the hood of her cloak. It was Merta. Cerise leapt up, wrapped her arms around Merta, and held her tightly, unable to speak. They sank onto a nearby bench, and Cerise buried her head in Merta's chest while Merta stroked her arm.

"Hush, now, everything is going to be fine." Merta kissed her forehead and cradled her.

After a few moments, Cerise sat up and wiped her eyes. "Oh, Mama, I miss Baba so much."

"He lives here now." Merta touched Cerise's chest. They hugged each other again and wept softly.

***

Another chair was brought to the table, and General Drissen called the group back together. Cerise sat Merta by her side, still holding her hand.

"This woman is Merta," General Drissen said. "She was Tregan Anthelia's personal attendant and was present when Tregan gave birth to Jarin and Sabrin. Rence claims that Merta has information that will shed new light on these proceedings. Merta, will you tell us your story?"

"Oh," Merta said softly. "My story is not special. Cerise here is the special one; you should talk to her. She killed a sea dragon with her bare hands."

"Merta, what happened the night your house burned down?" Rence prompted her.

"Oh, that." Merta wiped her palms on her dress. "That was not a good night."

Merta told them how her husband Min had come inside the cottage to tell her that an old man, a Weslynder by the look of him, was coming up the lane. How she recognized that the man was Gerard Mort. He had found her at last. She told them how she and Min grabbed what they could and fled out the back door, but the mage caught them in the garden. Min had been so brave, swinging a rake at Gerard Mort, but he fell and hit his head on a rock. The mage dragged her away and put her inside a crate on a wagon, then laid Min's body on the wagon bed next to her. All she could do was watch as the mage set fire to the house. She remembered being locked in a dark shed all night next to her dead husband. When light showed through the slats the next morning, strange men unlocked the crate and took her away with them.

"These men," Cerise asked. "Were they from Argonne. Did Argonnians kidnap you?"

"Oh, no, no," Merta said. "They were fishermen from Cordel. There were no men from Argonne. Argonne is a very long way from Cordel. I grew up in Argonne, you know."

Merta told them she had been taken to a small island with nothing but the pack she had taken from the cottage. There she was made to work for a cruel man who made boots for rice harvesters. She was his slave.

"How did you escape?" Cerise asked.

"The pack I brought with me. It once belonged to poor Dax. I kept it with me after he died."

"Dax the magician?" General Drissen asked.

"That's right. Do you remember him?"

General Drissen nodded slowly, looking from Dax to Merta as she continued with her story. The bootmaker had searched Merta's pack and taken the coins he found there but left her the other items inside: a change of clothes, a sewing kit, a book, and a seashell necklace that Cerise had made as a child.

"Every day I would open that bag and take out the necklace and hold it in my hand and pray to the gods that you were safe and living a good life. One day I reached into the bag and could not find the necklace. I took everything out and felt around inside, worried that the lining had worn through. There was a flap at the bottom of the bag that I didn't remember, and beneath it was some folded-up fabric. I pulled it out. I remembered seeing it once before, in a cave on my way to Cordel, that horrible day Dax died in the avalanche. It was a cloak, darker than the night sky. It reminded me of him, so I wrapped it around myself. Then there was a knock at the door. I was afraid, so I backed up into the corner of my room. The boot-maker came in and looked around and called out my name. He looked right at me but didn't see me. I knew then that the cloak was special. It was magic. Dax was a magician, you know."

"How did you get away?" Cerise asked her.

"I thought if Dax had left me his magic cloak, I should use it. So I waited for the next supply boat to dock, and when no one was looking, I pulled the cloak tight around me and hid down among the crates and bags. The boat sailed away, and I was free."

"It was always Gerard Mort," Cerise sighed. "How did I not see it?" Jarin put his hand on hers. She shook her head bitterly.

"Merta," General Drissen said. "I would like to ask you another question."

"Go ahead; ask me all your questions."

"Is your daughter Cerise the child of Lady Tregan and King Franklin?"

"Of course," replied Merta. "She is their firstborn. Sabrin né Franklin. She bears the sigil if you don't believe me. It's hidden under a tattoo."

"Firstborn? Are you sure?"

"Yes. I was there when Tregan gave birth to Cerise. I took her and handed her out the window to Dax. He was magic; did I tell you that already? I think he was fourteen. Then I went back to help deliver the second baby, Jarin né Franklin." Merta seemed to notice Jarin for the first time. "Are you Jarin? You were so tiny! You've gotten so tall!" She put her hands to her mouth. "You look just like your mother. Oh, what a day this has turned out to be!"

"You handed Sabrin out the window?" General Drissen prompted.

"I handed her to Dax, yes. He was outside on the wall

waiting for her. We took her to Cordel to raise her, he and I. It is what Lady Tregan asked us to do." A cloud suddenly crossed her face. "Poor Dax died crossing the mountains. He saved us from the storm."

Dax went to her and held out his hand. "Merta, it's me. Dax."

"Dax?" Merta looked up at the magician. Recognition slowly spread across her face. "Dax? You grew up!" She reached out her hand, and he pulled her up. They hugged for a moment, then Merta held him at arm's length so she could see his face.

"I thought you died. In that terrible avalanche." Merta wiped her face with her cloak. "What happened to you?"

"I fell. I hit my head," Dax said softly.

"Why didn't you come back to get me?"

"I lost myself...for a long time. Rence found me and brought me back. I'm sorry." He pulled Merta into another embrace.

⚜

General Drissen tapped his knife handle on the table. "This has been a morning of revelations. Does anyone here believe that the king's murder was committed at the hand of an Argonnian, was the result of an Argonnian plot, or that Argonne, and by association Jarin né Franklin, is responsible in any way?"

There were soft exclamations of "no" around the table.

"So noted," General Drissen said. "Merta's account of Sabrin and Jarin's birth confirms what we had presumed, that Cerise was born first and is the elder twin. Taking that into account, plus earlier confirmations regarding the authenticity of her sigil, does anyone here doubt that Cerise Aikawa is King Franklin and Tregan Anthelia's firstborn child, Sabrin né Franklin?"

Again, the response was no.

"By her rights, and by our laws, Sabrin né Franklin, called Cerise Aikawa, is next in line for the throne of Weslynde."

"The sigil was destroyed," Cerise said. "Sabrin né Franklin no longer exists."

Samora Fulgor steepled her fingers and addressed Cerise. "A new sigil can be forged, and it alone does not determine who you are."

"Today I call upon the leaders of the three provinces to declare their support for the next sovereign of Weslynde, who by our laws will lead the Western Commonwealth." General Drissen stood and addressed the two prime ministers. "Are we agreed that Sabrin né Franklin is to be crowned queen?"

"The province of Riddien does so agree," Prime Minister Koenig said. "Long live Queen Sabrin."

"The province of Argonne does not agree." Prime Minister Kokheli spoke angrily, gripping the arm of her chair. Everyone stared at her. "You called us here to vote, to choose who will rule. Now you want a meaningless endorsement of what you have already decided. Have you changed the rules?

"We didn't have the information we have now," the general replied. "All the questions have been answered. There is no debate here."

"Weslynde continues to dodge and feint to get whatever they want," she sneered.

"Prime Minister—"

"General, wait." Jarin stood. "You did call Argonne and Riddien here today so that their voices could be heard. A successful leader is only successful when they have the support of their people. A vote should be taken." He turned to Cerise. "Sister, do you agree? Will you listen to the voice of the people?"

Cerise saw Jarin clearly for the first time. He genuinely cared about the future of the commonwealth, not only

Weslynde or Argonne. She knew now what he meant when he said he wanted to make things right. "I agree with Jarin. There should be a vote."

General Drissen nodded respectfully. "Very well. A vote, then. Argonne, what say you?"

"Prince Jarin has been schooled in government and commonwealth law since birth," Tharisa Kokheli declared. "Consideration should be based on more than birth order. Argonne chooses Jarin."

"Jarin should be king," Barton said.

"Hear, hear," Lowden added.

"Riddien chooses Sabrin to lead us forward," Baldo Koenig insisted.

"We have set an interesting conundrum before us," General Drissen said. "It appears the vote won't be unanimous. Very well. Commonwealth law states that in matters that impact all three provinces, a majority vote by the leaders of two of the three provinces is needed. So, I ask each of you, are you prepared to follow those rules, even if you cast a losing vote?"

"Aye, we will," said the prime minster of Riddien.

All eyes turned to Tharisa Kokheli. Her black eyes glittered, and she clenched and unclenched her jaw. The silence stretched out for a few moments and then she said, "We will."

"Sabrin and Jarin. Will you abide by this vote?"

Jarin glanced over at Cerise, and she gave an affirmative nod. "We will," they said together.

"Very good," General Drissen said with a deep sigh. "Crisis averted. Since I am acting leader of Weslynde province, mine is the tie-breaking vote. Long live Queen Sabrin."

⚜

Jarin was stunned. Even though he knew Cerise deserved to be queen, he hadn't thought it would actually happen. He slumped back in his chair. What did that mean for his future? What did it mean to be a prince without power? Did he have a place in her court? He caught the grim look on Tharisa Kokheli's face before she masked it. Argonne was not happy, he knew. The prime minister of Riddien, on the other hand, was smiling broadly. Jarin realized having Saint Cerise on the throne meant Riddien and the church were closer than ever to the seat of power in Weslynde. The thought of Archbishop Mellon standing next to the throne, whispering into Sabrin's ear, made him shiver. He had sanctioned the vote, so there was nothing he could do.

***

Cerise sat quietly. She rubbed her hands on her legs and clasped her fingers together. Janice's and Tar's joyous laughter rang out behind her over the noise of the others. General Drissen walked over to her and held out his hand. She let him lead her to the dais at the end of the hall. Everyone followed. He gestured for her to step up onto the dais, in front of the throne. She climbed up, still not believing, and turned to face the gathering.

"Long live the queen," General Drissen said.

"Long live the queen," everyone repeated, bowing low.

Cerise looked down at them. Maemae was weeping with joy. Janis and Tar had broad grins on their faces. Jarin seemed stoic, but he nodded to her respectfully. The prime minister of Riddien was beaming, and the prime minister of Argonne was stone-faced. She was queen! As queen, she could accomplish so much. Good could be done; rights could be wronged. It was crazy. She felt a little giddy at all the possibilities suddenly spread before her. She threw her head back and laughed in surprised delight. Caught up by her mood, the room laughed with her. Blue sky shone through the windows above her, bright and beautiful. It reminded her of the sea. Her beloved sea. White foam running down the waves, crashing against the sides of the *Flying Fish*. Sails snapping, the call of seabirds, her crew shouting to one another across the wind. She brought her eyes back down to the great hall: thick tapestries draped across the stone walls, massive marble columns carrying the weight of the golden dome above, the guards standing stiff in their uniforms, the protocol, the ritual, the faces looking up at her, greedy with desire or churning with discontent. The joy that had filled her vanished.

The room was starting to break up. Jarin had moved away to speak with Dax. The Argonnians were huddled together, having some sort of debate. The prime minister of Riddien was waiting to speak with her. Cerise felt separate and apart from all of them, as if she were standing at the far end of a long hall. Even General Drissen, standing next to her on the dais and waiting for her instructions, seemed distant.

"General Drissen."

"Yes, Sabrin."

The name jolted her. "Walk with me." She led him away from the others. "Jarin is next in line to the throne after me?"

"Until you bear a child and name them your heir, Jarin is next in line."

"Good. That's very good." She took a deep breath and let it out. The general tilted his head quizzically. "I abdicate."

"Sabrin."

"Don't call me that. It's not my name. I abdicate. Is that clear? Jarin will be king. Now make the announcement."

EPILOGUE

Dax tightened the steppe-horse's saddle and gave it a vigorous pat. The horse shook its mane, eager to be on the road. He stepped into the stirrup and hoisted himself onto its back. "Are you ready?"

"I am," Rence replied, shouldering his pack. "You will need to help me up. I'm afraid I don't have your long legs."

With the help of an attentive handler, Dax pulled the old steward onto the horse's back behind him. The silver steppe-horse, a coronation gift from Prime Minister Koenig to King Jarin, hardly felt their combined weight. The stallion proved to be somewhat of a show-off, high-stepping and arching his neck whenever he saw someone new to impress. Dax had to make several stops along the road to accommodate passersby who wanted to admire the beast and get the latest news about King Jarin. Rence took these opportunities to "build deeper relationships with Jarin's subjects," as he put it, so their progress was slow.

King Jarin's coronation was a barely a week behind them, but already Caleddon had returned to normal. The plaza was full of vendors, and attention had turned from palace-watching to repairing buildings and planting fields damaged by the quakes and the floods. The prime ministers of Argonne and Riddien had left for their provinces, and Jarin's Argonnian resistance fighters had returned to Isidima, riding atop their parade of carrier beasts, traveling by road this time, leaving fences and livestock intact.

Dax and Rence were traveling to Clear Lake to say goodbye to Cerise and Merta. Cerise had left the palace the day after the coronation, taking her mother with her and setting up camp with her crew on their fishing boat. She had refused Jarin's multiple pleas to remain with him in Caleddon, telling him her only desire was to return home to Cordel and the sea. They were planning to depart for Cordel the next morning.

The crew of the *Flying Fish* welcomed the men warmly, and they celebrated together with a simple meal of fried lake squid washed down with plenty of wine. After the meal, they lit a fire on the beach and shared stories.

The connection Dax had to Cerise was as strong as ever. Without needing to speak, the two stepped away from the others and walked down to the end of the long pier. The sun had dipped behind the Cordel Mountains, and the lake reflected all the colors of the evening sky. Dax noticed a small group of worshipers dressed in red watching them from a respectful distance along the shore. He knew they would come no closer. They had learned, having faced the wrath of Tar several times before. Cerise appeared to ignore them, but he could tell that their presence, even at that distance, set her on edge.

Dax stood next to her for a long time, not speaking, gazing out at the sparkling water, content to be by her side. She was fingering the lump of sky metal, which hung from her neck next to Luce's seashell fossil. The first star appeared over the lake, and he took her hand and held it.

"Where will you go?" Dax broke the silence. "Back to Sudo Bay?"

"Perhaps, or somewhere no one has heard of Saint Cerise. The southern islands maybe."

"That seems very far away."

"Or not far enough." Cerise paused. "Come with us. You would like life on the sea." She stroked his arm softly.

When she touched him, Dax experienced the pull of the ocean, the thrill of piloting a ship under full sail. "I would like it," he said. "I would like to sail the sea with you." He looked deep into her eyes and threaded his fingers with hers. The world she was offering was nothing he had ever imagined and suddenly everything he wanted. He started to tell her this but stopped himself.

She put her hand on his chest and cocked her head slightly. "You are going to stay. I can feel it inside you."

"Jarin asked me to be his house mage." He tried to make a light moment out of it. "And Rence says Jarin needs more protecting than you do."

"Not anymore."

She was right, of course. Jarin had fully come into his power. His sigil glowed like a beacon in Dax's mind, even all the way down here in Clear Lake. The sigil didn't possess Jarin the way Franklin's sigil had controlled him. Instead, it enhanced what was already inside him: Jarin's compassion and empathy, his curiosity and optimism and desire for fairness.

"You are right about Jarin," he conceded. "He will be a fine king. But there's something else."

"Tell me."

⚜

Before she'd left for Riddien, Samora Fulgor, the high wizard of Riddien, had met privately with Dax. During that meeting, Samora had tried to talk him out of becoming Jarin's house mage.

"You are not ready," she had said. "You have great talent, but it is like a lightning storm; it fires wildly and randomly with no warning. And just like lightning, it burns things."

"My skills are growing; I can tell."

Samora had scoffed. "You are undisciplined and feral, like a wild snow cat. You think you can interfere with the natural order of things without consequence. You want to keep Jarin safe, but in your need to protect him, you hold him back. You need to get out of his way. Let him grow. Stop being his shield and his weapon."

"What do you propose I do?"

"Come away with me to Riddien. In less than five years, I can train you to become the next high wizard. I have lived for many years, Dax, more than you may think, and in all that time I have never met another like you. You are one in a hundred thousand, but if you do not learn to master your magic, it will burn you up and kill you. Without discipline, you will become like Gerard Mort, corrupted by your own power, and it will destroy you. That is the future I see for you."

⚜

More stars now danced on the lake's mirrored surface.

"You want to go with her, don't you?" Cerise said. "You want to be high wizard."

"I've stumbled around in the wild for twenty years, Cerise. I want answers."

"But you love Jarin."

"I do," he acknowledged. "I don't want to leave his side."

He could tell she was waiting for him to say that he loved her more. It was true, he did, but he had made his choice. He squeezed her hands and bowed his head. He wouldn't say the words if he couldn't live up to them.

"Dax. I won't hold you back, and I won't be the third

choice." She reached over and kissed his lips lightly. He gathered her into his arms.

They joined the others back at the campfire, where Rence and Merta were telling stories of their time together in the service of Lady Tregan. Long after the fire died down and the others had gone to bed, Dax put his arms around Cerise one last time and kissed her softly. She took him by the hand and led him into her tent.

She was still asleep when, shortly before dawn, Dax and Rence climbed on the king's steppe-horse and started back to Caleddon.

⚜

The thermal spring that fed Caleddon's public baths returned to life, and when King Jarin got the news, he ended his council meeting early and went to see for himself. When he arrived, he found a group of Weslynders already at work, chinking the mortar between stones and rerouting water flows, preparing the baths to open. The king immediately peeled off his clothes and joined them, and that was where Dax found him—knee-deep in water, wearing nothing but a broad smile on his face as he plastered a crack in the side of the pool, his copper body gleaming in the sun.

"You can't ever seem to keep your clothes on," Dax chided, smiling down at his friend.

"Dax! You're back!" Jarin's face lit up. "You smell like a steppe-horse. Get in at once!"

Dax laughed back at him and began unlacing his boots.

THE END

ACKNOWLEDGMENTS

This novel was the result of a writing exercise. Each week, my writing partners and I would meet, select a writing prompt, write for fifteen minutes, and then read what we had written to each other. This particular week, when the fifteen minutes were up, I kept on writing and continued to write for another two years.

First and foremost, thanks to Bryn Donovan for writing and publishing her book, *5,000 Writing Prompts*, and including the following prompt that became the inspiration for Weslynde:

"The birth of twins was considered bad luck in their country, so his father ordered his twin sister to be killed at birth. Someone disobeyed the order and she's still alive."

I want to thank Britta Jensen, author, editor, and founder of the Writing Consultancy. Britta's encouragement and awesome coaching helped me put on the page what was happening inside my character's heads.

I want to thank my editor, Laura Josephsen, whose professionalism, candor, warmth, depth of writing knowledge, attention to detail, and ability to retain and recall tiny inconsistencies in the narrative and highlight them proved invaluable.

And of course, I want to thank my writing partners, fellow Spark Plugs Tom Semmes and Reed Waller, who held my hand every step of the way, brainstorming with me on plot, characters, magic, world building, editing, proofing, publishing...(I could go on and on.) Without Tom and Reed, there would be no Weslynde.

And finally, I want to thank my husband and biggest supporter, Ray, whose unwavering belief in me gives me courage to get up and keep trying every single day.

A GUIDE TO PEOPLE, PLACES, AND CREATURES OF WESLYNDE

MAJOR CHARACTERS

In Weslynde

Franklin né Rosin: King of Weslynde. Birth father of Jarin and Sabrin.

Tregan Anthelia: Royal Mate (per contract) of King Franklin. Birth mother of Jarin and Sabrin. Daughter of Tregor Anthelia. Argonnian.

Jarin né Franklin: Prince of Weslynde. Son of King Franklin and Tregan Anthelia. Heir to the throne.

Rence: Member of King Franklin's personal staff. Serves as liaison to Tregan, and later as Jarin's butler.

Merta: Tregan's personal attendant. A Cordelian raised in Argonne.

Dax: Apprentice magician in service to Tregan. A Weslynder raised in Argonne.

Gerard Mort: Caleddon's House Mage.

Clare Oedenth: King Franklin's unofficial consort and mother of Barton and Lowden.

Barton: King Franklin's son by Clare Oedenth. First born.
Lowden: King Franklin's son by Clare Oedenth. Second born.
Gwyn: Healing Woman assigned to monitor Tregan's pregnancy.
Amilee: An abbey novice.
Bishop Rutter: Caleddon's House Chaplain.
General Drissen: Head of Weslynde's army and Caleddon's security force.
Toberon Intsimi: Argonnian Senator.
Archbishop Mellon: Leader of the Church of the Commonwealth. From Riddien.
Baldo Koenig: Prime Minster of Riddien.
Samora Fulgor: The High Wizard of Riddien.

In Cordel

Cerise Aikawa: a.k.a. Sabrin né Franklin, Daughter of King Franklin and Tregan Anthelia. Raised from birth in Cordel by Min and Maemae Aikawa. Captain of the Flying Fish.
Tar: Crewmate, Flying Fish.
Janis: Crewmate, Flying Fish. From Weslynde.
Luce: Crewmate, Flying Fish. Cerise's lover. From Riddien.
Dee: Crewmate, Flying Fish.
Mae Linn: Crewmate, Flying Fish.
Skua: Crewmate, Flying Fish.
Maemae Aikawa: Cerise's mother (aka Merta, Tregan's personal attendant).
Min Aikawa: Cerise's stepfather.
Tregor Anthelia: Argonnian Senator. Father of Tregan Anthelia.

In Argonne

Tevin: Argonnian caravan driver.
Timeer: Argonnian caravan driver.
Tharisa Kokheli: Prime Minister of Argonne.
Toree: A nurse.

LOCATIONS

Argonne: Capital is Isidima. A desert province to the south of Weslynde. Economy based on mining and manufacturing. Abundant mineral resources, fishing, ship building, and agriculture, (dates and desert foods, breeding and training of the great chameli).
Riddien: Capital is Riddienstad. A grassland province to the east of Weslynde. Economy based on agriculture; including livestock, grains, and textiles.
Weslynde: Capital is Caleddon. A wide fertile valley between two mountain ranges, the Cordel Mountains and the Saddle Mountains. There is abundant geo-thermal activity present (geysers, hot springs). Economy based on agriculture (grapes, fruit trees, salt shrimp), and advanced education, (Magical arts, Medicine and Science, Geology).
Cordel: Capital is Sudo Bay. A country to east of Weslynde, nestled on a narrow strip of land between the Cordel Mountains and the Circling Sea. Economy based on fishing and agriculture (rice, seaweed used for food, medicine, textiles).
Western Commonwealth: A united coalition of three provinces: Weslynde, Riddien, and Argonne. Led by the reigning monarch of Weslynde. The seat of power is held in Caleddon.

HIERARCHY OF MAGICAL PERSONS

High Wizard: Master of telekinesis and telepathy. Gifted with the Sight. Creates magical instruments of power/talismans (sigils, concealment cloaks etc.).
Mage: Master of telekinesis. Gifted with the Sight. Performs spells and sets charms.
Magician: Gifted with the Sight. Performs spells and sets charms. (skills vary).
Field Witch: Gifted with the Sight. Untrained or feral. (skills vary).

HIERARCHY OF THE CHURCH OF THE COMMONWEALTH

Monarch: Government head of the Western Commonwealth. By agreement among the Western Commonwealth provinces, the King or Queen of Weslynde. Symbolic head of the church.
Archbishop: Spiritual leader of the church. Governs church policy.
Bishop: Head cleric aligned with the government leaders of major centers of population. Reports to the Archbishop.
Cleric: Religious scholar and teacher. Performs rituals and ceremonies. Reports to a Bishop.
Rector: Leader of a rural congregation. Reports to a Bishop.
Novice: Has taken vows to serve the church. In training.

CHAMELI

Chameli: /kə.mel.i/ A four legged reptile-like creature capable of changing its skin color to match its surroundings. Chameli are indigenous to the desert region of Argonne and only reproduce in hot desert climates. Breeds vary greatly, and range in size from 2 feet long to 30 feet in length and can weigh as much as an elephant. Chameli have been domesticated by the Argonnians and perform different services as beasts of burden:

- Carrier Beasts: 25-30 feet long. Used to pull cargo and carry multiple passengers
- Mining Beasts: 15- 25 feet long. Used to dig tunnels and haul rock and ore
- Scout Beasts: 8 – 10 feet long. Can carry one rider. Extremely fast. Used for short scouting trips
- Messenger Beasts: 2 – 3 feet long. Used to carry messages that have been tied to their bodies.

EXCERPT FROM DAX: BOOK 2 OF THE WESLYNDE CHRONICLES

The sound of water trickled somewhere nearby. I blinked my eyes and rubbed them, but I could see nothing, not even the hand in front of my face. I drifted back into darkness.

The smell of rotting meat filled my nose and my stomach did a little flip. I opened my eyes. A dim circle of light filtered down from above me, giving shape to my surroundings, which were...what? Everything looked strange to me. Were those rocks? Wet and black? Was I looking up at the moon? It hurt to think; my head was pounding. I gradually became aware that I was lying on my side, and that my back was resting against something warm and yielding. A soothing vibration rumbled out of the warmth and radiated through my chest. It comforted me, reassuring me with feelings of trust and safety. I reached behind me and my fingers sank into velvety softness. A fur blanket? I tried to make some sense of this but concentrating made my head hurt worse. I touched the top of my head. There was a large bump on my scalp, and when I pressed it, a searing gout of pain flashed through my entire body and I jerked violently in response. Whoever was behind me scrambled up and moved away. I rolled over to see who it was, but my head spun, and the world went dark again.

Someone was rubbing my shoulder. I opened my eyes. There was more light now. I was lying on the ground inside a large hole or cave. The wet rock wall in front of me reflected shiny points of sunlight streaming down from above. Someone nudged my shoulder again and I rolled over, only to find I was staring into the deep green-gold eyes of a snow-cat. Stunned, I froze in fear as it placed a paw on me and rubbed the side of its mouth back and forth across my chest, making wet marks on my tunic. A thrill of terror ran through my body and I looked around for a rock to hit it with.

Having thoroughly slimed me with its drool, the cat put both of its large velvet paws on my chest, pinning me to the ground. I lay very still, suppressing a scream. The snow-cat flopped down on top of me and rolled over, writhing up and down across my body, legs waving in the air, its low pitched purr rumbling through the cave.

It's still a cub, I thought, not yet half grown.

Satisfied that it had sufficiently marked me as its own, the snow-cat turned in a tight circle and sat down next to me, elegantly wrapping its long tufted tail around its feet, and began washing its mottled gray and white fur with its tongue, ignoring me completely.

Heart hammering, I slowly rolled over onto my stomach and began inching towards the source of the light. I only managed to move a short distance when I heard a hiss and a low threatening growl. A shadow filled the cave's entrance above me and a much larger snow cat appeared, holding a white hare in its jaws. This cat's ears were flattened and its lips were curled back in a snarl, exposing long saber like fangs buried deep in the hare. I crab-walked backwards over to the side of the cave and pressed my back up against the wall, whimpering with fear. The big cat leapt down into the cave and faced me, dropping the hare, crouching low and snarling.

The cub, who had watched this exchange from the safety of a corner, suddenly sprang up in play, wrapping its front paws around its mother's neck and biting her as if she was prey. The mother snow cat hissed and cuffed the cub out of her way. The cub scrambled backwards in mock alarm and then bounced sideways, tail arched, ready to continue the game.

The mother snow cat crept towards me cautiously, liquid eyes staring into mine, so close now I could smell her sour breath. I averted my eyes in respect and held myself still, waiting for the pounce. I tried to keep my lip from trembling. The cat hesitated for a moment and smelled me, lips bared in a grimace. She held her breath, then blew it out in a huff and shook her head. Her muscles relaxed and she sat back on her haunches. She had decided I was not a threat. I must smell like the cub, I thought. I am drenched in its drool; the cub was scent-marking me. I had no time to ponder this further as the mother cat turned around and lifted her tail. I recoiled in disgust as she sprayed my chest and face with jets of pungent urine, then proceeded to kick dirt and gravel over me with her hind legs.

Now satisfied, the mother cat settled herself between me and the cave's entrance. The cub gave the dead hare a few shakes, then cuddled up against its mother's belly. She pinned the cub down with a paw and began giving it a bath. I watched them in terrified silence, shivering a little, until, exhausted, I fell asleep once more.